STRANDED
Awakening, book 1

STRANDED
Awakening, book 1
Joshua Wingerd

Wingerd Writings
2017

STRANDED: Awakening, book 1

Copyright © 2017 by Wingerd Writings, Victorville, CA 92394.
ISBN 978-0-9996342-2-6

www.lilwritr.wordpress.com
www.lilfytr.wordpress.com

First Printing: 2017

Scripture quotations found on pages 41 and 98 are taken from The Holy Bible, English Standard Version® (ESV®), Copyright © 2001 by Crossway. Used by permission. All rights reserved. (References on page 39 are from Mark 7:20-23 and Ephesians 2:1-5.)

Scripture quotations found on pages 59, 137, and 241 are taken from the THE HOLY BIBLE, NEW INTERNATIONAL VERSION®, NIV® Copyright © 1984, by Biblica, Inc.® Used by permission. All rights reserved worldwide.

Scripture quotations found on pages 304, and 335-37 are taken from the NEW AMERICAN STANDARD BIBLE®, Copyright © 1995 by The Lockman Foundation. Used by permission.

Ordering Information:
Special discounts are available on quantity purchases by corporations, associations, educators, and others. For details, contact the publisher at the following email address:
lilfytr92@gmail.com

U.S. trade bookstores and wholesalers: Please contact Wingerd Writings at the email address listed above.

DEDICATION

To the real Mr. Uro,
who believed that my "struggle to believe
will soon be resolved, and that it will result
in you having a strong and enduring faith."

and

To my parents,
who lovingly put up with "Jay Liyfer"
for the first 18 years of my life.
I'm sorry for the stress and heartache.

INTRODUCTION

To the reader:

YOU HOLD IN YOUR HANDS a project that has been in process for more than seven years now. In fact, my childhood friend Joey (name altered) and I first came up with the basic idea of this book when we were in seventh grade back in 2004/2005. It had originally been intended simply as an adventure novel about a group of friends living like Robinson Crusoe on a tropical island paradise. I finally wrote the first few sentences of what would become this novel in the spring of 2009—my junior year of high school—"Jay Dregniw had mixed feelings about the week to come. Part of him was excruciatingly excited for his senior trip, but another part was dreading it with all his being." (You will still find these sentences within the story, but they are no longer the opening.)

After I graduated high school in 2010, it quickly began taking the shape of the story you now hold in your hands. Around the same time I started actively writing this book, my life was forever changed, which quickly became a point of concern, especially when I began to nail down the theme and exactly where I wanted to go with this novel.

Total transparency: there are places in this book that make me cringe. There is language that isn't the cleanest. There are statements that are blasphemous on their own. But what is an author to do—even a Christian one—when all of that is part of the point he's trying to get across? I don't want to give more away than

1

necessary, so I will just say, "Yes, this book has a very specific point."

With that said, I will put you at ease, at least a little. This book contains no f-bombs. The five letter b-word does not appear. The Lord's name is not used in vain. However, you will read some softer versions of coarse language throughout. I prayed long and hard about this fact over the past several years of working on the book, and I have been led to keep what is now present as a way of drawing a contrast, especially since I have two sequels planned for this novel.

At the very least, I hope you can forgive my characters for their—at times—dirty mouths, and believe me when I say that just because I have them cursing—at times—does not mean that I condone cursing. If you can forgive them and believe me, then I hope and pray that you enjoy what follows.

In addition, I must offer thanks to those who gave input on the earlier drafts. Whether simply a minor question, or a perusal of the whole draft, your input was incredibly appreciated. Thank you for your time.

Sincerely,

Joshua Wingerd
November 13, 2017

PS. Please don't spend an excessive amount of time trying to figure out who is who in this semi-autobiographical story. Enough of the facts and names have been changed to make nailing anything down with certainty next to impossible. Again, this is primarily a fictional story.

CHAPTER 1

(Day 1, 6:30 p.m.)

I OPENED MY EYES and confusion hit me like a pick-up truck. (I know it's a stereotypical way to begin a story, but it's exactly where this experience began, so it's how I will begin recounting it.)

My nose was buried in dirt. It smelled stale, and it was clear that rain hadn't been around for a long time. While nothing else was clear to me in that moment, for some reason I knew that my hometown rarely got rain. However, the sight that was presented to me when I raised my head was anything but familiar to me. I was laying down in the middle of a burnt-out forest. The trees stood as ghosts of the trees that they had once been. Some were taller than others, but none were green as far as my eyes could see into the distance. *What a place,* I thought to myself. *This is going to be fun.*

It was then that I realized that I was sweating. I looked around to see if I could spot the location of the sun in the sky, and, sure enough, after several seconds, I found it low in the west. However, that did little to assure me that this was going to be a comfortable vacation. The temperature had to be at least 90 degrees, and the humidity was sweltering. I felt like I was sitting in a bowl of honey, except instead of smelling sweet, it smelled like dirt.

I was confused. I couldn't remember anything—even my name—except that I was sure I didn't live here. However, I really didn't remember where I lived, so I decided to stand to my feet and explore the place in which I found myself. As I stood to my feet I saw a lone mountain, which rose conically from its base to a flat peak, in the distance. *Sweet,* I thought to myself. *I can figure out exactly where I am from the top of that mountain.*

I set out west, toward the mountain. *Is there any danger here?* the scared portion of my psyche questioned.

I didn't want to think about that possibility. I remembered always being told by my parents: "Safety first." And sure, this would have been a good time to employ it, but I didn't care about the advice my parents had given me. *It doesn't make life any easier.*

You don't know what—or who—else is here, the scared part reminded me.

It was true, and maybe I was a little worried. *Who isn't a little scared at some point?* I would be fine. I was sure of it. *If there are lions or tigers here, as long as I don't bother them they will leave me alone. Same with snakes.*

I continued walking, working on keeping those thoughts suppressed. *Think positive,* I told myself; that was my life motto, and even if it wasn't before, it certainly would be now. The palm tree cemetery had given way to a stretch of long grass. However, the long grass wasn't standing up; it was dead, scattered across the ground. Rocks of varying sizes dotted the landscape as if hurled by an angry giant in a fairy tale. Some were as large as a person; some were smaller than a quarter. There were no trees, not even burnt-out husks, in my current position, and I was sweating like a dog. The ghostly forest resumed a hundred yards ahead, but I felt as if I'd never reach it, and even if I did reach it, I knew that their dried out trunks and fronds would not provide shade.

Ten minutes later I was in the forest. As I walked, I observed the appearance of the trees more closely. I touched one and soot came off on my fingers. I walked from tree to tree in the sweltering heat, observing their appearance, trying to determine where I was. All of the trees I inspected were burned. Some were worse than others, but they all showed signs of being burned. *It seems to have been a tropical paradise at one point in time,* I reasoned.

My eyes glanced toward the mountain standing in the distance, and I had to look away, because the sun was right next to it—incredibly bright in the evening sky. It reminded me of yet another personal fact: *I prefer overcast days to sunny days.* However, there wasn't a cloud in the sky, and I didn't expect that to change any time soon. I hoped it would rain, and my positive thinking philosophy urged me to keep hoping for that.

Still, as I walked through the palm tree forest, there was an unusual peace in the place. It was silent. No noise. Not even birds were chirping. No people. No technology. Nothing but nature. It was beautiful. It really was. Tall ghosts of palm trees stretched to the cloudless sky. Brown grass surrounded the base of the palm trees. Boulders were scattered around randomly. Despite the absence of life in the place, it was a perfect get-away.

I wonder if I have it to myself.

Don't get your hopes up, I told myself.

Shut up. I don't want any more negativity.

I'm just being realistic.

Well maybe I don't want to be realistic. Anyway, there's no reason to say that is realistic. (I had inner debates with myself all the time. They were normally just as pitiful sounding as this one.)

While I was enjoying the peace—still walking west—I heard running water. I was overjoyed. It was coming from ahead of me, *probably behind those boulders up there.*

I ran to the rocks and to my surprise, I was correct. I walked down the boulder, which was actually just a flat rock that sloped down into the standing pool of water. The pool was fed from the north by a stream, and it left the pool to the south by another stream. *It's the perfect spot. If I had to camp here—wherever "here" is—I'd choose this site.*

I waded into the crystal clear water and it came up to my hips. It felt amazing compared to the heat of the sun. It was refreshing and cool, and for a few minutes I forgot about the lack of shade afforded by the dead palm trees. I waded out and lay down to dry on one of the flat rocks that sloped into the pool. The rock was warm and I immediately understood how snakes feel. *This is the life.*

I lay there for several minutes. I finally sat up and freaked out for the first time in this story. Three duffel bags, towels, and junk food wrappers were scattered around the palm trees ten steps west of my location. *Other people.* I didn't know what to do. *Should I stay; should I run?* I didn't know.

I decided on neither. I stood up, as water dripped off my clothes and splattered into the dust on the ground, and I walked west again, continuing my venture toward the mountain.

As I passed the stuff that was scattered on the ground I found where the unopened junk food was stored. I grabbed a bag of CHEEZ-ITS and a chocolate bar and continued heading toward the mountain.

I ate the chocolate bar as I walked, but stuffed the crackers into my pocket. *I hope they don't get totally crushed in there.* I finished the chocolate and stuffed the empty wrapper in my pocket. *I don't want to give away my presence.*

Just then I heard voices moving toward me. I couldn't make out words, but I knew they were getting closer. A boulder was sitting a few paces away, so I decided to hide behind it. *I'll wait for them to pass, and then I'll continue on my way.* I made it behind the boulder just in time. This rock was not flat, but rather very bulky and covered in little holes like a sponge.

"Dat was craze, homie," said a male voice. "Da fire was huge. I don' know how we made it safely down here. It looked like it was about to explode, but it didn'. Dat was sick, homie. I'm so happy to be alive."

It sounded like the voice's owner had stopped walking. I warily poked my head around the side of the rock, hoping that no one would see me.

The voice's owner was four paces away from me, standing next to another guy who was about the same height. They both looked about eighteen years old, they were both white, and they were both smoking cigarettes. Both had on plain-white, baggy t-shirts. The difference between the two came in clothing and hair styles. One had a blonde buzz cut, and the other wore a grey, flat-brimmed baseball cap straight forward over his shaggy black hair. The black haired one wore green basketball shorts, and the blonde one wore long sagging blue jeans. Both were muscular—not ripped—but they both clearly worked out a little every day or so, or were just gifted with a decent body type.

I ducked back behind the boulder to consider my own appearance. I looked down to see a scrawny guy with no muscle. From wrist to shoulder, my arms were just about the same circumference the whole way. I was wearing a white baseball cap that said ANGELS on it. My jean shorts cut off above my knees at that moment because my knees were bent as I sat behind the boulder. On my torso was a blue polo shirt. *I guess I overdressed*, I joked in my mind.

I poked my head back over the rock, hoping that I would remain invisible.

"I'm happy to be alive too, Joey," the black-haired kid said.

So the blonde kid is Joey. That's cool. Is he friend or foe?

The black-haired kid turned toward my hiding spot, so I ducked back behind the rock again. *Please don't hurt me.*

"Come on, Joey," he said. "Follow me. We've barely explored this island." A pause. "Joey, what ya staring at?"

7

"Dere's, dere's," he began. "Dere's somethin' behind dat rock."

I'm done for. I stayed hidden behind the rock. *Please don't walk over here.*

Joey was still talking. "Kevin, it might jump out and scare me. I hate getting' scared. Ya know how I am when dat happens. Don' ya remember what I told ya 'bout da time we were at Jay's house and his mom scared me?"

So the black-haired kid is Kevin? Is he friendly?

"I remember," Kevin said. "I see nothing though, bro. Ya need to control yo' fears. I've never known an almost nineteen year old to be as big a scaredie cat as ya."

"Shut up, homie. I ain' scared."

"Don't lie, bro." He paused. "Now get moving. We need to get back to Justin before it's dark."

"I ain' lying."

The footsteps started up again, heading east, away from my location.

My mind started spinning. *Who are they? I'm trapped on an island? What was on fire? Who's Justin? Who's Jay? What's going on?* The thoughts crashed through my mind like a pinball in a machine. *I want answers, but I don't want to die.* My heart beat had accelerated like a drag racer during their conversation, and it was just beginning to slow down. Half of me wanted to talk to Joey and Kevin, but another half told me I could survive on my own. I took off my hat and used it to fan my sweating face.

No matter what I chose, I decided I needed to get moving again. *Who are they?*

If I'm truly on an island like they said, I have no need to go to the mountain, I figured. *Follow them,* my mind told me.

Shut up! I shouted at myself. *I am not ready to die and there is no way to know for sure if they are friend or foe.*

Weren't you listening? Joey's scared of getting scared. He won't touch you.

8

I had to admit that that was a good point. *But it can't possibly be that simple. What if it's an act? His speaking habits could be a ploy as well. Maybe they just want me to follow them so they can kill me.*

You're absolutely ridiculous. Don't be scared. Be a man and get answers.

I'm convinced. I was nervous, but I stood up, repositioned my hat backwards on my head, and set out east anyway, forsaking my investigation of the mountain to pursue Joey and Kevin. I started jogging.

*   *   *

IT DIDN'T TAKE LONG for me to catch up to them. They had been slowly ambling away from my hiding spot, smoking and laughing up a storm.

The two minutes it took me to reach them had been filled with questions—ones I wanted answered and ones I didn't. *Can they answer my questions? Are they going to kill me? Who else is here?*

They must have heard me following them because they turned around. When they saw me, their reaction took me completely by surprise.

Joey, the blonde, spoke first. "Jay! How's it goin', homie?"

I'm Jay? I was shocked. *These guys were at my house one time?* I put my hands on my backside to slide my fingers into my back pockets, but the feeling of mud coming off on my fingers surprised and grossed me out at the same time, so I changed my mind about the placement of my hands. *It's from wading in the pool and hiding from these two by sitting in the dirt.*

Before I could respond to Joey, Kevin—the one with the grey cap—greeted me too. "What ya been up to recently, Jay?"

"Who are you two?" I was finally able to spit out. *They act like they know me, but I have no idea why. I've never seen them in my life, have I?*

"It's Joey and Kevin, your friends from church," Kevin said.

Joey continued Kevin's thought. "Yeah, Jay. Are ya losing it? We've hung out almost every day since kindergarten. We spent da night at each other's houses, ding-dong-ditched, went to birthday parties, and have growed up at church together too. Did ya hit yo' head or somethin'?" He lifted his shirt to wipe the sweat off his face.

It sounds familiar, but I don't know. He could be trying to trick me. All I want is answers. Sure, Joey just gave me some, but I'm not positive that it is true. I finally stopped thinking and decided to speak. "You tell me if I hit my head. You said something was on fire. Maybe I hit it then."

"It's possible. Ya clearly ain' feelin' so good after da crash." Joey's face looked concerned as he took a drag on his cigarette.

"Crash!" I yelled. "What crash?"

"We were on an airplane. It crashed just offshore o' dis island. It was da freakiest thing ever—flames all around us. I thought we were going to die." Joey grabbed me by the shoulders and shook me. "Homie, I'm so dang happy to be alive."

"Me too," I replied. I gave Joey a look that told him to get his hands off me. *Other than supposedly being my best friend, who does this guy think he is?*

Joey slid his hands into his pockets—a sheepish grin covering his face.

"Where'd the plane go down?" I asked. *Maybe if I see it, some of my memory will return. So many pieces are flying through my head; all I want is for them to fit together into one complete puzzle.*

"It was over there," said Kevin, pointing east with his right hand. "Why ya ask?"

I explained my hypothesis about my memory returning.

Joey vetoed it. "Ya don' wanna do dat, homie. Some annoying li'l punk named Jared declared himself king o' dis place. Kevin and me got kicked out for disagreein' with him."

"Yeah. He's some rich kid. Thinks life owes him everything he wants." Kevin's facial expression showed disgust.

I need answers. Maybe this Jared guy can help.

Kevin continued, "I can't stand the guy."

Joey interjected. "His girlfrien' hot as hell dough. I'd tap dat."

"You'd—" Kevin started.

I cut him off. "I need answers. Ima go find out some stuff. Don't stop me."

"What ya need answered?" Joey asked.

"For one: what's my name?"

Joey answered very matter of fact. "Jay Matthew Liyfer." He clarified the pronunciation before continuing, "Life with an 'r' on the end: Lifer." Then he continued, "Born February 2, 1992. Age eighteen. You live in Desert Valley, California; right up da street from me." He paused as his slurring, sloppy speech resumed. "Ya need yo' social security number too?" He paused again. "I don' have it." He laughed as he took out a new cigarette and lit it.

So I'm Jay, and I'm eighteen? Good to know. "Do I have a girlfriend?" I asked.

Joey looked at Kevin, shrugged, looked back at me and said, "Yeah. Her name is Cami or somethin'." He pulled up on his pants to keep them from sagging off.

"Oh thanks," I said as I felt a smile spread across my face. I started walking away.

"Good luck with Jared," Kevin called. "If ya need a place, we got a camp set up in the middle of the island."

"Thanks. I'll think about it." I ran off east, leaving them behind. The last thing I overheard was them arguing over the Jared guy's girlfriend.

Those two are hilarious, and they seem real enough. I just hope they are who they say they are, but I really have no clue.

So I have a girlfriend? I thought, as my mind changed topics. *Life isn't so bad after all. I hope she's stuck on this island too. If not, this place will suck.*

I kept walking—wondering about Jared and my girlfriend. *Who are they? What are they like? Did Joey and Kevin blow Jared way out of proportion or is he really like that?* The thought made me nervous. *Cami. What does she look like? Is that actually her name? Joey can be hard to understand,* I reasoned. *Either way, I can't wait to find her and tell her that I'm okay.*

As I kept walking, I noticed that the sun was gone, and the shadows were growing on the ground. I also began to notice how tired I was, and I wondered how long it had been since I slept before ending up unconscious in the middle of the island. *How'd that even happen?* I forced myself onward. *I need answers.*

*　　　*　　　*

AFTER TWENTY MINUTES of stumbling through the dead forest, tripping over burnt out roots and scattered rocks, I realized I would hurt myself if I kept going in the dark. The sun was gone, and shadows covered everything.

Don't stop, a voice in my head said. *Don't you want answers?*

I do, I countered, *but I'm tired and I don't want to hurt myself. Safety first, remember?*

I stopped where I stood at that moment, lay down, and closed my eyes for the night.

CHAPTER 2

I AWOKE. However, when I attempted to open my eyes, nothing happened. In fact, I couldn't hear anything either. I tried to move my head, but it felt as if it was cemented into the ground. *This is weird. What happened to me? All I did was lay down for the night. Now I'm stuck. I can't see. I can't hear. What's going on?*

The last thing I remembered was falling asleep on what was supposedly an island. At least that was what Joey and Kevin—who were supposedly my friends—had told me. They had told me that the airplane we were on had crash landed. They had told me something about a girlfriend that I supposedly had, which was weird. I thought that no girl had ever liked me, but maybe I had been wrong. I had gone to look for the crash sight to see if more memories would return, and I had decided to sleep on the way.

Now I can't move, and I can't see, and I can't hear. *What happened?*

Theories tumbled around in my brain. The last thing I remembered was falling asleep on what was supposedly an island. *There was no sign of any electricity here earlier, so perhaps I woke up in the middle of the night and it is just pitch black dark outside? Perhaps the fact that I can't move is that the humidity glued me to the ground. Perhaps the reason I can't hear is that there is nothing to hear; everything on this island is dead. This is a nightmare.*

(Little did I know how accurate that conclusion would be, as I passed out of consciousness again.)

CHAPTER 3

(November 2001)

MY EYES POPPED OPEN, and I was instantly even more confused. In front of me, on the top bunk of a bunk bed, was lying a young kid, sound asleep. I glanced over my shoulder at the clock on the wall opposite the bed, and it showed that the time was 8 a.m. *Where am I now? Wasn't I just lying in the dark on an island trying to figure out what was going on? Why am I in a house now?* On the wall below the clock was a poster of some CARDINAL baseball player who hit 70 home runs one year. Above my head was a ceiling fan that had one red, one yellow, one green, and one blue blade on it. *Whoever this kid is, he is relatively young and he likes baseball.*

I heard steps in the hallway outside the room and looked that way. The next thing I knew, a man, just shorter than me, with dark brown—essentially black—hair was in the bedroom. He flipped on the light, and said, "Jay, it's time to wake up. We're going hiking today."

Jay? I thought, before I vocally asked, "Who are you?"

The man ignored me and walked over to the kid who was sleeping and shook him awake. He wore long blue jeans just above his waist, into which a teal colored t-shirt was tucked. His hair was cut in a flat top formation and his teeth were perfectly straight. *Who is this guy? He looks familiar. How's he know my name?* I spoke again, "Um sir, who are you. Why'd you call my name? I'm already awake, and dressed."

The man ignored me again.

14

The kid sat up and spoke. "Sounds good, dad. Let me get dressed. I'll be ready in fifteen minutes." He couldn't have been older than ten. He had short—buzz cut—brown hair, and a huge smile.

The man left the room and I watched him as he left. *Who is he?* "Hey, why are you ignoring me?" He kept walking, turned, and left the room.

I turned my attention back to the kid. *Who is this kid? Is his name Jay too? That's weird.* He turned onto his stomach, turned to his left, and maneuvered from his bed onto the floor. When his legs were dangling over the edge, he dropped—with a thud—to his feet. His left arm bent at the elbow and popped up to his shoulder as he straightened up his stance. His fist had his thumb tucked inside the rest of the fingers.

I glanced at my own left hand. My arm was straight, my fist was closed perfectly, but my pointer finger was sticking out straight. *That's peculiar.*

I tried to speak to the kid as he walked over to his dresser. "Hey, who are you?"

He ignored me as well and walked out of the room, clutching some shorts and underwear.

The island people are much nicer to me than these people. At least the islanders talk to me.

The kid came back, wearing blue jean shorts that cut off about an inch above his knees and a red shirt with a baseball on the front. He threw his pajamas back up onto his bed and ran out of the room, ignoring my questions.

*   *   *

THE NEXT THING I KNEW, I was in the backseat of a car, driving somewhere. The man and the kid were in the front seat and were talking back and forth. I was sitting, arms crossed, upset over the fact that they were ignoring me. What I had picked up from their conversation was that they were on their way to go hiking on some big rocks, about fifteen miles from their house. The kid was

15

homeschooled and got good grades. The man was his dad, and he worked a lot; when he was done working for a job he normally did projects around the house, but he had taken time out to hang out with his son. *If only my dad did that. All he does is tell me rules and work, work, work.*

Where'd that come from? I wondered.

In a lull in their conversation I tried to talk again. "Hey guys, where are you taking me? Why am I stuck in here? I didn't ask to be kidnapped."

The dad spoke. "Jay," he began.

He's answering me. I smiled.

He continued. "Which rock do you want to climb first?"

The kid is named Jay for sure.

"Let's climb the tallest one. The higher we get, the better."

Come on, I thought. "How come you guys are ignoring me?"

They can't hear you, my mind told me.

Really? That's weird.

His dad spoke again. "Good idea. Let me know if another one interests you more though, and we'll climb it instead."

"Cool, dad." Jay said.

*   *   *

FINALLY THEY ARRIVED at the place they were going. It was a large area in the desert with sandstone rocks that were significantly bigger than your average house, rising out of the desert floor like prairie dogs. There were at least fifteen distinct rocks and I wondered which one was the tallest. *I'll figure out soon,* I decided. Train tracks wound their way through the rocks. The hum of cars on the Interstate could be heard less than a mile away to the north.

"So," Jay's dad began, as he parked their car under a bridge a good distance from the nearest rock, "which one are we climbing today? The tallest one, still?

"Um, let's see," Jay said. He climbed out of the car and walked out from under the bridge so he could see clearly. "Not the tallest this time. We should climb that one." He pointed ahead at a conical rock, about three hundred feet tall.

"Let's check it out," his dad said cheerfully.

"Cool." Jay was excited.

They started walking—as I kind of floated—and ten minutes later, they reached it. *Why don't I even have to walk anywhere? That's weird.* The boulder was a massive hunk of rock stuck in the ground.

Jay's dad looked at it, frowned slightly, and said, "Follow me."

"Okay," Jay answered. "Where are we going?"

"We're going to see if there's an easier way up this one. It's kind of steep."

Steep was an understatement. It was a practically vertical rock face from where they were standing. Impossible for a fourth grade kid to climb. Despite the steepness of the rock, there were many small caves in its vertical face. I imagined cowboys hiding from Indians in the caves back in the wild west days.

As they began to walk, I tried to move my legs. *I can walk myself; I don't need to float.* It was useless. I extended both of my legs straight out as if I was sitting in a chair. *What is this? A movie? Am I dreaming?* Their walk around the rock took fifteen minutes. From the opposite side, it was a sloping ascent at about a sixty degree angle.

"Let's go up here," Jay said.

"I don't think we can make it," his dad stated.

"I think we can," Jay said.

"How about this?" his dad began. "We climb a different one and sometime when you are older we can climb this one."

"Okay, dad," Jay said, contentedly. "Let's climb the one with the stake in the top."

"Good choice," he replied.

This rock was more of a hike than a climb—for them—as I just floated up the trail. The path wound up the rock, dodging yuccas and Russian thistle. I kept on the lookout for wildlife,

17

wondering if I would see anything. It looked as if Jay was doing the same. The smile on his face told me that he loved every minute of it.

"Hey dad, do you think we will see a rattlesnake while we are here?" he asked.

"I doubt it. They normally aren't out this time of year. Three months ago, in August, they'd probably be everywhere though."

"Oh good." Jay breathed a sigh of relief.

Rattlesnakes scare me to death too.

"You know," his dad said, "rattlesnakes are more scared of you than you are of them."

"They are?" Jay asked, dumbfounded.

"Yeah. If you don't bother them they won't have any reason to get you. However, if you start messing with them, they can kill you. So, if you ever see a rattlesnake, don't be scared. Just leave it alone and you'll be fine."

I just said that on the island, I thought. *This is weird.*

"That's good to know," Jay said. "Thanks for the info."

"Haven't you learned that in school?" his dad inquired.

"Nope." He paused. "Well maybe. I just don't remember. I've been doing algebra lately. If $x+1=3$, then x equals 2."

"Very good," his dad said. "I'm glad you enjoy it."

"Me too." Jay paused before adding, "What I really hate doing is writing."

"Yeah, I'd rather do math than write, any day," his dad agreed.

By now, they had reached the summit of the rock. Definitely one of the smallest ones, but it was by far the most interesting. Just west of the peak, a metal stake had been hammered into the top of the rock. How it had gotten there, no one knew, but the fact was—it was cool. Jay leaned back against the stake to rest.

While they rested on the rock's summit, I looked out over the desert. Rocks, sand, and railroad tracks were all I saw until my eyes reached the Interstate. There, I saw cars speeding along, missing this awesome place. It seemed to me that Jay and his dad were the only people who ever came here. *Despite this being the center of the desert, it is pretty cool.*

HONK!

A train was coming. Jay looked around to see if he could find it, and sure enough, there it was. It was headed toward the bridge where they had parked the car. The tracks went diagonally, twenty feet west of the car, so it was safe.

HONK. HONK. HONK!

It was close now. It passed under the bridge, and I began counting the cars. *One, two, three...*

Several minutes later, as the last car passed Jay said, "That train had one hundred and thirty four cars on it."

I wasn't the only one counting?

"Very good. I counted the same amount." His dad was smiling.

*   *   *

LATER THAT DAY, as his dad drove home, Jay passed out in the front seat. I again wondered who these people were and what in the world I was doing with them—moving along as they moved—but otherwise just watching them.

CHAPTER 4

(Day 2, 6:15 a.m.)

I AWOKE to the feeling of a rock jabbing into my back. I opened my eyes to see dirt surrounding me. *Where am I? What happened to Jay and his dad?* I was confused before, but by this point I was really confused. I did a sit-up movement to get myself from my back to a sitting position, and I rubbed my back to ease the soreness caused by the unevenness of the ground.

The sun had not yet risen, but the light was slowly spreading out across the dark sky. Regardless of the sun's position, it was hot. It wasn't yet as warm as the day before, but it was still uncomfortable. I felt nasty. I had sweat while I was asleep, and dirt was stuck to my body. I tried to brush it off, but all it accomplished was spreading it around even more. *I need a shower.*

Fat chance of finding one of those, my mind told me as I stood to my feet. I observed my location. I had fallen asleep between a cluster of palm trees that were all burnt to a crisp. I noticed that there were no rocks in their midst, but there was a tangle of roots. *That explains it,* I thought as I twisted my midsection to crack my back. There were several large boulders in the area, and on my right and left, a twisted pile of burned-out shrubs forced me to continue my course due east or to revert back to going west. It reminded me of the thorn forest erected by the evil fairy in SLEEPING BEAUTY, but on further inspection I realized that these shrubs had no thorns on them.

That was when my mission came back to mind. *I'm supposed to be heading to a plane crash site. It's supposed to answer questions about how I got here. I should even find a beautiful girl there as well. I hope she's okay.*

I walked east, a tangle of burnt shrubs on each side of me. Occasionally, I would have to duck or dodge to keep from touching one of them, but for the most part, there was a clear path cut through the dead vegetation. *It almost looks like someone came through with a machete.*

As I continued to press forward, I heard a growling sound. It startled me, and I might have jumped a little bit. But then I laughed because I realized that I was growing increasingly hungry. *How long has it been since I ate? My stomach is starting to speak to me.*

Finally, the shrub walls ended, and I was looking up a sandy dune. It wasn't terribly tall, and not steep at all. I started the ascent, and my shoes sank into the sand. It took extra energy, but I was able to lift my feet up and continue climbing up the dune. As I crested over the top, I saw ocean in the distance. The thought entered my mind that there was plenty of water there to survive on, in case I needed to satisfy my thirst, but I quickly put that thought to death.

The plane was also there, well submerged in the water. The cockpit section wasn't even visible. DELTA AIRLINES was clearly visible on the tail, and on the wings. It had crashed facing southwest, at a slight angle—slight enough that I could read the wings, though upside down to my vision, and I hoped all the passengers were safe.

When I made it all the way over the top of the sand dune, that hope was confirmed, and I was slightly surprised at what I saw. About twenty yards from the water was what looked like a small village of palm huts. There were ten of them, and they were all just as burned-up as the rest of the trees on the island.

I walked down the hill into their midst. The huts were designed like LINCOLN LOG houses with every other tree attempting to be perpendicular to those on either side; since all the trees were different sizes, the makeshift houses were nowhere close to square. The roofs were made almost entirely of the trees as well, which made sense to me because there were no palm fronds in existence. It looked like I was wandering through a tropical ghost town. The only thing that proved to me that anyone was here was the fact that there was a large area that betrayed a burnt-out bonfire.

I assumed everyone was asleep, and I hoped that I wouldn't wake anyone as I wandered through their makeshift town. *I wonder what kind of people are here? Are my parents here? I hope not.* I hoped that Cami was in one of the huts, but since I couldn't remember what she looked like, I kept walking and didn't waste time looking for her. My main goal was to discover why I was on the island. The plane was lying out in the ocean, and that was where I needed to be. Finally I was at the water's edge. Small swells came in, lapping at the shore, and then rolled back out toward the plane. Each time the water tried to come farther up the shore, but each time it failed and rolled back out to join the rest of its kind.

I waded out into the water, enjoying the cool feeling that it brought. I looked up to the sky, sighed in appreciation, and realized that there were no clouds in the sky again. I dove forward, and my whole body swooped under the water. When my head broke the surface again, I used my fingers to quickly clean myself off. I could feel my long-ish hair sticking out in random directions, and I realized that my hat was floating away, so I quickly grabbed it, rubbed it mostly clean again, and placed it back on my head. I doggy paddled out to the plane since I wasn't in a hurry at all, and by the time I was there, I could no longer reach the bottom with my feet.

There was a large hole in the side of plane, right where it met the water. *That must be where we forced our way out,* I figured. I maneuvered myself over to it, and I realized that my observation was correct. Jagged metal surrounded the hole, betraying a forced exit. *I need to get inside,* I told myself.

While treading water outside the plane, I removed my water-soaked shirt and covered both of my hands with it. After this, I placed them on the edge of the plane. The pressure I exerted to lift myself up, forcing my palms into the jagged metal, hurt, but it was not nearly as painful as it would have been if I was just bare-handing it. I didn't have much upper body strength, so it was a struggle, but I was able to lift myself up enough to where I could rest my chest against the edge. It hurt, but I kept going; a little farther and my belly was on the edge. There was a seat just inside the hole, and I grabbed it and pulled myself the rest of the way into the plane.

I was in pain. Sure, it wasn't the worst injury I'd experienced in my life (and it certainly wasn't the worst that would happen before getting off the island), but I was still in pain. The jagged metal had cut through my shirt, so I threw it out the hole into the ocean. My hands were scratched, but there was no blood on them. My chest and belly on the other hand, were quite pained. A long, bloody line ran from my left side to my right side at the bottom of my sternum. The same was true just below my belly button. It wasn't bleeding too hard; when I put my finger to the cut, I realized that it had almost clotted already.

I stood to my feet, facing toward the tail of the plane, and observed my surroundings. It was completely devoid of life as far as I could tell from my initial glance. The lower section—behind me, toward where the cockpit used to be—was completely filled with water; after several seats everything blended into the dark shadows of ocean water. *I wonder how many dead bodies are buried down there?*

I started the ascent to the top, trying to find my seat and hoping that this would bring some memories back. I passed twenty empty rows that gave me nothing. *Where is everyone? The people in those huts can't possibly be everyone, can they? These planes hold more people than this, don't they?* That was when I saw her. A girl was crumpled up, face down on the ground in front of one of the seats. I stopped in my tracks. *What is she doing in here when everyone else is out on the beach?*

Her dirty blonde hair, which would have hung just below the top of her shoulders if it had been brushed, was unkempt and tangled all over the back of her head. She was wearing a green t-shirt and a medium length denim skirt. I knelt down next to her and gently rolled her onto her back.

Her sparkling blue eyes stared up at me and I flinched when I saw them. "Are you awake?" I asked.

No response.

Below and between her gorgeous eyes, her straight, cute nose rested. A diamond stud nose ring sat in the left side of it, adding to her attraction factor. Her complexion was perfect. Her lips were full—a deep pink color—and, simply put, she was irresistibly attractive. *I would date her if she'd go for a guy like me.*

Before I do that, though, I have to talk to her. I attempted to shake her awake with my right hand on her torso.

No response.

She's dead, my mind said. *No one sleeps with their eyes open.*

"Shut up!" I said aloud. "This beauty can't be dead." I decided to do CPR—not that I'd ever done it before—but it needed to be done. *I was trained at one point,* I remembered, *but I've never actually needed to do it before. I hope it works.*

Please be alive. My lips met hers and I transferred my breath into her mouth. Then I applied numerous compressions to her chest. I went back to transferring air to her mouth, and repeated that about three times before giving up. *It's pointless. She isn't going to wake up.*

As I removed my lips from hers, a crazy thought struck my mind. *Your lips have met before. You know this girl.* I couldn't remember whether that was true or not. *According to Joey I have a girlfriend. This girl can't be her. My girl is alive; she is dead. It can't be her.*

A purse was on the ground on the other side of her. *Maybe she has some identification.* I reached for it, picked it up, and rifled through it. My hand passed over several photographs. *I need identification. Please don't be named Cami,* I begged silently. Then I found her wallet. I opened it up and the first thing I saw was her driver's license. "Camille Queensley. DOB: 12/3/1992."

My first thought was joy. *Joey didn't say Camille. He said Cami. My girlfriend is still alive, somewhere on the island.* It brought a smile to my face.

That was when doubts entered my mind. *He said it was something like Cami. Camille sounds an awful lot like Cami.*

No! It can't be true, I argued with myself. *My girlfriend isn't dead. It isn't necessarily her. Joey didn't say for sure that her name is Camille. It might be someone else.* I was banking on my stay-positive philosophy.

I put the license back into her purse and reached for the pictures. *Do I really want to see them?* I nervously closed my eyes as I grabbed them. I warily opened my eyes and flipped through the pictures. *Please be wrong,* I begged myself.

The first one put my heart at ease as it was a picture of her next to her dog, or what I assumed was her dog. It was a big black and white husky. *I love huskies,* I remembered.

The next photo looked like a school picture. It was Camille dressed in her volleyball uniform. She was wearing a very tight fitting top with the words 'Desert Valley High' emblazoned on it; under that, the number '6' was clearly written. Her shorts were short and tight fitting as well. She clutched a volleyball under her left arm and smiled brightly at the camera. Her hair was neatly brushed, falling straight down and disappearing behind her shoulders. *She's beautiful.*

I was about to move to the third picture when I heard a rustling sound near me in the plane. I jerked my head up and glanced around, but when I heard nothing else I glanced back to the pictures. *Probably just the wreckage creaking,* I told myself.

25

The third picture took me completely by surprise. It was me. I was in a cross country uniform—red tank top and short red shorts—*how embarrassing.* I was looking straight at the camera and I had a lop-sided smile on my face. *I look stupid.* My hair was slightly longer than it currently was, and I wasn't wearing a hat like I currently was.

I had just slid that picture behind the previous when I heard what I could have sworn was a cough. "Who goes there?" I called out.

I waited several seconds for a response, but none came, so I blamed it on the wreckage again.

The next picture explained why she had a picture of me. The JUICE IT UP logo was on the cups in front of us on our table. We were both smiling—mine lopsided again—and my right arm was around her shoulder. She was smiling at me and I was looking at the camera. It confirmed my fears. *My girlfriend is dead.*

The final picture made it worse. Outside of RED ROBIN—based on the storefront logo—we held each other as our lips pressed together.

I yelled in anger as I threw the pictures across the plane. I wanted to cry. *Why suppress it? No one else—living—is in here.* I let them flow. *My girlfriend is dead and I am trapped on an island with people I don't know.* It deserves a good cry.

A voice across the plane's aisle took me completely by surprise. "Isn't it amazing that the plane crash landed without any serious injuries or deaths occurring?" It was a male. He sounded young, and his voice came out smoothly.

I don't care if he is the president; I don't want to see him. I rubbed the tears from my eyes and shouted, "Shut your mouth!" *He doesn't know what he's talking about. Camille, the most beautiful girl in the world, is dead. Dead. Because of the crash.* I picked up her wallet and tossed it in the direction of the voice.

"Hey there," the voice said, before its owner moved out of the shadows and into my sight. His appearance didn't seem to match his voice at all. His voice was so calm and careful, and his words perfectly formed, but his appearance was that of a total slob. He looked to be about thirty years old. His brown hair was almost as long as Camille's, and I could have made French fries in the grease that was practically raining off it. His green eyes were wild, glancing everywhere all at once, and I instantly felt sorry for my comment. This guy had clearly had it tough. To top it off, his tank top was heavily stained, his long blue jeans looked like Swiss cheese, and as he came toward me, the strong smell of beer invaded my nose. *I want to hate him for his comment, but can I? However, it's pretty obvious why he looks the way he does,* I decided in my barely-adult mind.

His eyes landed on Camille's lifeless body and then my tear-streaked face. "Oh. I'm sorry." His breath smelled stale: tobacco and beer. He sat down next to me and put his arm around my shoulder.

I didn't have the heart to move it. "It's not your fault," I said softly. The smell of substances radiated off his person, and I hoped I would get used to it soon.

He was silent for a few seconds, glancing toward the water at the front of the plane. Then he spoke just one word. "God." After a lengthy pause he added, "What a joke." He paused and turned toward me, and when he resumed his speaking, he spewed beer scent into my face. "Take my story for instance."

I turned away from his gaze and looked toward the front of the plane.

He continued, "When I was eighteen I had my whole life planned out. I loved playing baseball, and I thought that that was my future. In fact, I was banking on it. But then, a week before I started college ball, I broke my pitching arm. Due to the nature of the break, it still hasn't fully healed. I haven't played ball for ten years now. Major league scouts never saw me, and since baseball was my life, I stopped caring about life. I dropped out of college and have lived on the streets ever since because my dad wouldn't let me come home. That's a whole different topic, but let's just say he didn't agree with me dropping out of school. I had finally saved enough cash from begging to buy a plane ticket to visit my mom and then the damn plane crashed here." He looked somber as he continued. "If God was real, and actually cared, I'd be playing ball right now."

I didn't expect that. Who is this guy? I turned to face him as I spoke. "I'm sorry, man. That sounds horrible." I hesitated and then decided to ask, "What's your name?"

"I'm Jacob. You?" His eyes stopped their wild glancing, and he looked at me.

"Jay," I said, answering his question. "Your story is similar to mine actually." *Memories are quickly returning.* My mind was being flooded with memories, and I didn't understand how some homeless stranger could unlock my confusion with one paragraph of his life story. "I've wanted to play for the ANGELS for as long as I can remember. But, I had a stroke when I was two years old, so I can't catch very well. That dream went down the toilet. And now, I was apparently on this plane with my girlfriend when it crashed—killing her—and I'm still alive. I don't get it."

"My situation is not that bad compared to yours." Jacob's reply surprised me. "The love of your life died when God caused your plane to crash on some island, and He ruined your life plans by letting you suffer a stroke. I don't understand why He is so heartless."

"I know." I began talking about God. "I've been told my whole life that God loves me, but in all the eighteen years I've been alive, I've seen zero proof of it. First, He gives me a stroke when I'm two years old, and now, my girlfriend—my beautiful Camille—is dead. I hate Him. Why does He do this? It seems He is either not all-good or not all-powerful; or neither. But I know for a fact that He isn't both." *Where did that come from?*

"I've felt the same way my whole life," Jacob mused, as he looked into the void of the empty plane. Then he changed the subject. "Are you hungry?" I realized that I was finally used to the smell of his breath.

28

I am. But, I don't want to move. I spoke. "Not really. I feel sick right now." The realization that I was newly single, combined with the recollection of much memory, and also with the added thoughts about God had mixed and made me nauseous and lethargic.

Jacob replied with a question. "Are you sure? Thinking will just make you feel worse. Believe me—it's all I've done my whole life." He stood up and began to leave.

"I want to stay right now," I said.

"If you change your mind, meet me down shore." He kept walking downhill toward the nose of the plane. "If you want, come and find me. I have a small camp set up there. It's on the southwestern side of the island." He hopped out of the hole in the side of the plane and disappeared from view.

"Thanks." I said slowly, as I stared blankly in the direction he had disappeared. I didn't want to say anything else. I wanted to curl up and die. It had been ages since I ate or drank anything, and I wondered what there was to live for if the one you loved was dead. It took everything in me to glance back at Camille's lifeless body.

I didn't want to move so I stretched out on the ground next to her. I positioned my right hand under her neck and around her right shoulder; I propped myself up and looked her in the eyes and brushed her hair out of her face. It made her look even more beautiful as she lay motionless. When her hair was fixed, I caressed her face with my left hand. It didn't work how I wanted it to and it gave me two more reasons for tears: a dead angel and a stupid, stroke-struck left hand.

I cried. *Why am I here? Why did she have to die? Why do You hate me so much, God? You love some people so much, but hate others. Why am I the latter? The tears came heavier. I'd be more inclined to think highly of You, God, if You'd just audibly speak to me. Tell me You love me.*

God doesn't speak out loud, I told myself.

29

That's false! I've heard someone recently talking about God speaking to them. Who? I couldn't remember, but I have heard it. *I hate hearing it, because it means that God plays favorites. If the person who said that they hear from God was in front of me right now, I'd punch him square in the face. All I want is to hear from God, but He never talks to me. Why? If God created all men equal, why does He only talk to certain ones?* "It's not fair!" I shouted aloud.

I sat up and brushed the tears out of my eyes. *I need to get out of here. I'm sick of thinking about God, sick of thinking about Camille, sick of thinking about my stroke.*

My eyes glanced back at her prone body and the tears returned. So did the memories. *I used to call her every day after school to tell her I loved her. We used to go to dinner and a movie together, often. I once walked to* JUICE IT UP *in the freezing rain to meet her because I had no driver's license at the time.* The memories kept pouring in and I couldn't take it anymore.

I caressed her face one last time, stood up, and walked back to where I had entered the plane. I kicked every chair on the right side of the aisle as I walked toward the exit.

When I hopped out of the exit into the water, I instantly submerged about a foot under the surface, and, when my head broke the surface again, I yelled in pain from the salt water mixing with the minor cuts on my torso. *That was dumb,* I realized, though it was too late to undo that move. It was a painful swim back to shore, but it didn't take long for me to be walking on the sea floor, and then even my waist soon rose out of the water.

It was then that I first heard laughing. I looked up toward the shore and realized that a group of people had gathered around the bonfire, relit it, and were staring at me—whispering to each other and laughing. I counted about thirty people on the beach, and only half at most were laughing together.

How'd they start the fire with no fuel?

But I didn't have a chance to keep thinking about that anomaly. I tripped and fell at least four times as I trudged the rest of the way toward the beach. Each time I fell, a new howl of laughter erupted from the group. The closer I got I realized that they were all young. No one looked older than twenty, and there were about an equal number of guys and girls. *Who are these people? Why are they all so young? Where are the adults? This can't be all the survivors, can it?*

It was then that I noticed a lone person walking toward me. He looked familiar, but I realized that all my memory hadn't returned, so I couldn't place him. He wasn't short, but everything about him looked compact. He looked buff, especially if he was compared to my body build. His blonde hair was cut short all around, but it came to a point in the front. It looked like it would have stood up in the front if he'd have had gel, but without gel it was flopped down and looked like a widow's peak. I had to suppress a laugh; *a widow's peak on a guy.* He was wearing brown cargo shorts that cut off at his knees. His shirt was blue and striped and said AEROPOSTALE across the front.

I tripped again, and salt water and sand rushed into my mouth. I spat as quickly as possible, though I relished the taste of the salt water before expelling it.

"Ha ha ha." It was an obviously sarcastic laugh coming from the kid who was walking toward me.

"What's so funny?" I asked as I stood up.

"You are, Liyfer," he answered. "What were you doing out there? Writing down thoughts of fantasies that will never come true?"

Who is he?

A short, skinny, brunette girl came up to blondie, put her hands around his chest, looked up at his face, and spoke in a borderline nasally voice. "Jared, why was Jay in the plane? Blake already searched the whole thing."

So this is Jared? Seems like Joey and Kevin nailed the description of him, though his first insult doesn't exactly make sense to me. Who's the girl?

31

"Yeah, dummy," Jared spat at me. "Why were you in the plane?" He then glared at me as he bent down to kiss the girl, whose forehead barely reached his shoulder blades. He muttered her name as their mouths were close: Jaime.

It's the girl that Joey and Kevin were arguing about. I have to agree with Joey about her appearance, as I gazed at her up and down. She was wearing skin-tight black jeans that could easily have been painted on, and her pink shirt exposed her midriff completely. A knot in the bottom of the shirt told me that it wasn't supposed to be that short, but rather that she had adjusted it herself. Her straight, auburn-colored hair was cut off just below her shoulders. *She is pretty hot.* I couldn't help but compare her form to the picture of Camille I had seen earlier. *But she is way too skinny.*

Their kiss influenced my vocal response. "I thought we lived in a free country, sex-addict."

His facial expression turned angry. He hurled a river of expletives at me, ending with, "you weak baby. You couldn't win a fight if you were fighting with an MMA master by your side."

At least he can't hear my thoughts, I decided as I stormed toward him and shouted, "Take that back, 'Mr. I'm-So-Cool'."

"Never!" He yelled. "Acknowledge me as king and we'll all be happy." His girlfriend stepped back, into the crowd that had circled up around us.

"I can't be happy right now, dumb—" I trailed off the last word as I took two more steps toward him; my face inches from his. "You're not worthy of being king." I gave him a shove and shouted, "Don't mess with me after learning my girlfriend just died."

"You mean the girl you never got anything from?" Jared asked. "Don't touch me, loser!" He paused. "If you're so upset that your girlfriend died, why are you checking out my woman so strongly? You're nothing but a pathetic loser."

He swung his fist and hit me squarely in the mouth. I put my hand to the spot and it came away bloody. He grabbed my shoulders to prevent me from falling backwards and thrust his knee into my groin. I yelled in pain. *I just want to curl up and cry—maybe even die.* Jared was still holding me up. He kicked my legs out from under me and let me drop onto my left side with a thud. He stomped on my right thigh, and then his fist struck the back of my head. My vision started to fade.

"Get away from me, loser," Jared shouted.

"I gladly will, you dirty piece of crap." *I don't know if he even heard me.* I didn't try to stand, I was too weak. I closed my eyes.

The last thing I heard before passing out was my name being called by someone in the crowd. "Jay Liyf—"

CHAPTER 5

I TRIED TO OPEN MY EYES, but they wouldn't open. *Not this again! What is happening to me?* I tried again. Nothing. I tried again. Again, nothing.

Why won't my eyes open? I paused my thoughts for a second, and heard mumblings around me. *Cool,* I thought. *I hear voices, which is a good change from the last time, but I have no idea what they are saying.* I wanted to think that they were talking to me, but I had no clue. It felt like they were hovering around me. *Maybe my friends are here—if I actually have any friends.*

As my mind instantly turned to what had just happened, I realized that I felt no pain. It didn't make sense. *Jared just kicked my butt. More than my butt though; he'd pretty much kicked my whole body. Everyone had looked on and laughed.* I reasoned, *I don't have friends.* But then I remembered, *Someone called my name as I passed out. Who was that? Do I maybe have one real friend in that group?* Regardless, I didn't understand the island, or the darkness that followed, or the vision of Jay and his dad, or this new darkness. *I hope it all makes sense soon.*

I tried to open my eyes again, but I couldn't get them open. I decided to give up on that idea. Instead, I continued to think about what I had just found out. *My girlfriend is dead. Apparently it's God's fault, though that whole topic seemed to come out of nowhere.* I remembered Joey and Kevin's summary of Jared the

34

night before. *I guess they were right about him. Maybe they can be trusted. Maybe I have a couple friends here.*

Just lying there, unable to move, and not blacking out again, I tried opening my eyes again. It worked this time. They weren't open all the way—barely squinted—but I could see regardless. My vision wasn't clear, but I could clearly tell several things. First, I was now certain I was lying on my back. Second, there were five people by my feet—dressed in white robes—and a sixth walking toward them away from me. Third, I was dressed in white as well. *Am I in Heaven? Did Jared kill me?*

"He's alive," one of the angels said.

I tried to speak but all that came out was jumbled nothingness. *What is wrong with me?*

"He's out and he's trying to speak," the same angel said. "Go get his parents, Michael." A young blonde angel ran out from wherever I was.

Wait, my parents are dead too? I'm confused. Why are my parents dead too? They haven't been on the island. They weren't murdered by Jared like I was. It's all so weird.

My eyes were closing again. I fought to keep them open, but it wasn't working. They shut. I forced them open again. They shut again. The last thing I heard was an angel shouting, "He's going back."

Back where?

CHAPTER 6

(June 2002)

THWAP. "Steeerike one!" an umpire called out.

I opened my eyes to see a baseball field, with a game going on in front of me. I turned behind me to see a familiar face. The Jay kid's dad was in the stands, cheering for Jay. A woman, who I assumed was his wife, was next to him, along with a little girl. I looked back at the field, and there, on the mound, was Jay. The scoreboard showed that it was the second inning, and there were two outs already.

The reality of the situation struck me as I realized what this was. *I'm dreaming. But, it's not just any dream. It's a flashback to my past.*

What was I just seeing? Who were those white-robed people? Why could they hear me? I decided to try to talk to the Jay kid's dad. "Hello sir, can you hear me?"

He didn't hear me. *The crowd is loud, so he can't hear you. Try again.*

I shouted. "Hey sir, can you hear me? Where am I?" *There's no way he didn't hear me that time.*

Again no response.

I'll figure this out soon, I thought, before my thoughts moved to the kid on the mound. *He looks confident up there.* I'd played ball from age three to five for fun, and then from age seven to age ten on a team. *My dream used to be to one day play for the ANAHEIM ANGELS alongside my favorite player—Tim Salmon.*

36

He wound up for a second pitch, and let it go. Swiftly it sped, spinning toward home plate, unfortunately curving away from the plate and the batter. However, luckily for him, the kid swung anyway. "Steeerike two!" shouted the umpire.

Man, he's good. Was I that good back then?

If it was how I remembered my past experiences, Jay's confidence was growing steadily now. The scoreboard showed that he needed only one more pitch before he could rest to prepare for the next inning. The inning prior he had given up two runs, but by this point that was practically forever ago. And he was about to have pitched a scoreless second inning. *Pitching for a baseball team was my calling. What happened? I used to study pictures online of how to throw different types of pitches. I used to throw a good fastball and a wannabe changeup. I still love the sight of a batter swinging and missing a pitch, even if the batter is on the team I'm rooting for.*

Jay threw the third pitch. It flew toward home plate like a heat seeking missile. The batter swung. Crack. He connected and the ball rocketed toward second base. It was a good hit.

I hope the second baseman will catch it.

He did. After it bounced on the ground, he quickly threw it to the first baseman who caught it and tagged the base, three steps ahead of the runner.

"Two innings down, two to go!" Jay shouted as he headed for the dugout.

While he was in the dugout, all I could think about was baseball. What it consisted of. What it had meant to me. What it must be like to be a professional player. I loved everything about it. *The smell of the field; the crack of the bat; the hotdogs, peanuts, and cracker jacks; the action packed into a game; the chance of maybe catching a foul ball; and even sitting in front of the television watching lots of games with my dad. It meant everything to me. I used to go in my backyard and play ball by myself, going through the lineup of the ANGELS—even batting the way the respective player would bat. Being a pro must be amazing, I thought. Getting paid millions to play a game is too awesome. That's what I always wanted to do.*

Those thoughts kept me occupied through Jay's team's offensive time, but the words from his coach's mouth as he took to the field for the third inning ruined his whole day.

I somehow heard it from the stands. "Reuben, you take the mound. Jay, you play right field."

He stood out in right field, looking angry, confused, and sad. *What did he do wrong in the last inning to prevent him from being able to pitch again?*

Reuben is the coach's son, I realized somehow. *He did nothing wrong. The coach just wants to put his spoiled son in to pitch in his place.*

First pitch: double into center field. Next batter: two strikes, four balls, one walk; men on first and second. Third batter: single past the first baseman. It continued on through the next batter who hit in three runs on a triple. Then one out. And another out. The damage was not done though— not by a long shot. Single past the second baseman, scoring the man on third. Home run, to earn two more runs.

Luckily for Jay's team—the Desert Valley Mets—six runs in an inning was the mercy rule. They took to the dugout, but Jay went farther.

How could his coach just throw away the game like that by putting his stupid son in in his place? It was not fair.

He walked into the bleachers to sit with his mom, dad, and sister.

Why should he stay in the game? I thought. *The coach didn't need him. His stroke is ruining his life. How would the pros feel about a kid getting pulled from a little league game after two almost perfect innings? They would refuse him. How would they feel about a kid who has stroke symptoms playing in the big leagues? They would judge him. They would figure that he sucks too bad to be worth anything. Why bother?* That was when the thought hit me. *Baseball is not what I was made for.* I watched as the tears flowed down Jay's cheeks. *He's thinking the same thing I am. It is so unfair.*

I watched him bow his head and pray in that moment. "Dear God, please heal my arm! I really want to play baseball. That's what You made me for, I know it! Please!"

That's what he prayed. I knew it for a fact for two reasons. First, our minds had strangely connected in that moment. Second, I knew I had prayed it on a billion occasions. "Why waste your time, Jay?" I asked, figuring he couldn't hear me. "Prayers are pointless. God is a jerk."

He watched the rest of the game through tear misted eyes, while sitting in the stands next to his family. His team went down 1-2-3. The next inning began. Julian, the assistant coach's son, took the mound. It was a carbon copy of Reuben's pitching, except the team got zero outs during his time on the hill.

The game ended with six runs scored by Jay's team. That was the limit, and Jay vocalized the unfair aspect of it. He had let it be 2-0. Reuben had made it 8-0. Julian made it 14-0. And finally when the opposing team's pitcher was bad enough for Jay's team to get runs, the mercy rule prevented them from winning.

Jay cried the whole way home. *He hates his coach. He hates his left hand. Why? Why? Why? Why is life so unfair for this kid?*

His parents tried to comfort him, but nothing helped. *Baseball had been my dream too, but just like for Jay, it is now gone.* The thought brought anger to the forefront of my mind.

Scene change, I thought as everything faded to black.

CHAPTER 7

(Day 2, 11:00 a.m.)

THE WONDERFUL SCENT of fried fish greeted my nose as I returned to consciousness. I immediately wondered where I was. *There is no food on the island because everything is dead there*, I reasoned in my subconscious state. *In that white place none of my senses work right. And wherever else I find myself, I never recognize smells.*

Another portion of my psyche spoke. *Don't forget. That white place was Heaven. You're really dead. Jesus ate lots of fish. You could be with Him. Now that you're fully there your senses are working.*

I didn't know what to think, so I opened my eyes. I was surrounded by sand, laying on my right side. *Nope,* I told myself. *I'm just on the island. Where's that smell coming from; and how?* In the distance the ocean lapped lazily up onto the beach, rolled back out, and repeated—over and over and over—and watching it calmed my nerves greatly. The sun was practically overhead, and I noticed that my whole upper body—now unprotected since my shirt was probably halfway across the ocean—was growing red with sunburn.

I turned over and noticed a thin guy with short black hair tending a small campfire with his left hand while he held a black book open in his right. He was wearing a blue graphic t-shirt and grey DICKIE shorts. He was deep into his reading, while fish sizzled in a nice-looking skillet set on a makeshift stovetop. The fire was mostly dead, but the embers on which the pan was resting glowed red. *I wonder if he knows what he's doing.*

I was about to open my mouth when I heard him speaking quietly. *Who's he talking to?* "What comes out of a person is what defiles him. For from within, out of the heart of man, come evil thoughts, sexual immorality, theft, murder, adultery, coveting, wickedness, deceit, sensuality, envy, slander, pride, foolishness. All these evil things come from within, and they defile a person." He paused as he flipped forward a bunch of pages in his book, and it was then that I realized that he was reading aloud from his book. He continued by saying, "And you were dead in the trespasses and sins in which you once walked, following the course of this world, following the prince of the power of the air, the spirit that is now at work in the sons of disobedience—among whom we all once lived in the passions of our flesh, carrying out the desires of the body and the mind, and were by nature children of wrath, like the rest of mankind. But God, being rich in mercy, because of the great love with which he loved us, even when we were dead in our trespasses, made us alive together with Christ—"

He wasn't trying to read to me, and I didn't even have a clue what he was reading, but I assumed he interrupted himself because he realized he was burning the fish. He jumped up and moved the skillet off the embers.

It was too late. He muttered in frustration, "I burned them."

The fact that it was too late reminded me that I had been too late to save Camille, and the thought brought the sadness back. *The most perfect girl in the world is dead. Apparently I'd even kissed her. Crazy. Then some guy named Jacob had talked to me. Then Jared—a self-righteous little jerk—had beat me up. How'd I end up away from him?*

And that dream I just had was ridiculous. I've had two since ending up on the island. The first one didn't faze me. But I now realize it was my dad and I hanging out; how often does that happen these days? Never, probably! Otherwise, big deal. The most recent one bugs me though. I had been talking to Jacob about

41

Joshua Wingerd

baseball and the very next dream I have—immediately afterwards— is about the last game I ever played on a team.

I couldn't control myself. I picked up a handful of dirt and threw it away from me. My teeth were clenched and I could feel anger welling up inside of me. I would have shouted if it wasn't for the stranger right next to me. I muttered under my breath, "I loved baseball. Why'd it get taken away?"

The guy who was reading set down his book and looked at me.

Ugh, I was too loud.

He spoke directly to me. "What's up, Jay?"

He knows my name too? Who is he? All I could say was, "Where am I?"

"You're on an island in the middle of some ocean," the kid answered. "Our plane—"

I interrupted. "I know. Our plane crashed, and we're stranded here. That's what I know. What I don't know is who you are."

"I'm Bryce Beyra, your old friend. You got beat up a couple of hours ago, and I carried you out, as well as getting kicked out of the group myself." His facial expression looked glum, but soon lit up. "I went fishing while you were unconscious and I caught some. You're welcome to one if you want." He held a pan out to me. "Sorry I burned them, bro."

"Thanks," I said, accepting the pan from his hands. I was too hungry to care about the charred status of the fish. "Food is food at this point."

Can I really trust him?

Don't worry about it. He's harmless.

The food could be poisoned.

You're starved. Eat. It smells amazing.

I picked it up with my fingers and raised it to my mouth.

A gunshot sounded in the distance and frightened me enough to drop my food in the sand.

42

"What in the world?" Bryce said apprehensively. Fear crossed his face. "How'd someone get a gun on the plane?"

"It's a security fail," I joked, trying to lighten the mood, despite my own frustrations and confusions. I bent over to pick up my fish, but it was sand-coated so I left it where it fell. *Dang it.*

Bryce stood to his feet. "Let's go see where it came from."

I agreed and stood up as well. I limped a few steps before Bryce noticed.

"You okay, man?"

"I think so," I replied. *It only hurts a little and I can walk fine. It's mostly just stiffness from the pounding I took, combined with the lack of use for a while.* It was all centered in my right thigh. *Jared is brutal. What did I do to deserve that, starting with them laughing at me? It feels familiar, but I can't put my finger on what it is.*

We started walking west, toward the mountain. The peaceful sound of waves quickly disappeared, replaced by footfalls from our brisk walking. The burned-out ghost tree forest gave zero shade that close to noon, and due to our walking, I began sweating heavily.

BOOM!

The gunshot went off right behind my head, so I closed my eyes and dropped to the ground as fast as possible. *I'm dead, I'm dead.* I heard someone in the distance yell in terror.

"What in the world?" shouted Bryce. "Why are you on the ground? Did you get shot?"

I opened my eyes to see Bryce standing over me. "That was crazy, man!" I explained. "That gunshot was like right behind my head that time. I'm so confused."

Bryce stared at me like I was crazy. "What are you talking about? That shot came from the same place as the last one."

I'm not crazy. I know what I heard.

"Who screamed?" Bryce asked. "It sounded like Joey."

"Holy—"

Bryce interrupted. "I hope nothing happened to him. He's been staying out of trouble so well recently."

Trouble? I don't know what he means. I stood to my feet, knowing for a fact that the shot had gone off by my head. *He can call me crazy, but that's what happened.*

"Let's go find Joey," Bryce said. "I'm praying that he's okay."

I agreed. We ran off toward the sound. I jumped over rocks and dodged around stumps and trunks: husks of trees. And then I collided into something and fell backwards onto my rear end. It cursed as I heard it fall to the ground as well.

I was dazed for a few seconds, but when I sat up, I saw Joey in front of me on the ground. Kevin was behind him, and some dude with short, spiky, blue hair; slightly gauged ears; a black tank-top; and sagging, stain-washed, black jeans covering his legs was just behind Kevin.

There were no trees where we stood, and the sun was pouring down on us.

"Joey, bro," Bryce started. He looked confused. "What's going on? Why are you running like a maniac?"

Joey stammered an answer as he stood up. "D, d, didn' ya h, h, hear dat sh, sh, shotgun? It sounded like it went off right next to my ear."

"How could it go off next to your ear?" I asked. "It was definitely next to my head, like a half an inch away. I thought I was going to die."

Kevin spoke. "Ya crazy. It was right next to me. It went off between my ears."

Something isn't adding up here.

"You woking smeed, foo'," spat the spiky haired kid. "It was definitely next to my ear so it couldn't have been in between yours. You were like fifty feet away from me when it went off."

Joey commented. "I wish I was, Justin. Ya know I love da stuff." He reached into his pocket and pulled out a pack of cigarettes. "All I got are dese MARLBOROs." He lit another cigarette and took a drag.

"Yeah, Joey," Bryce said. "You need to get off the stuff before you get caught by the cops—again." His face was serious.

"I ain' gone get caught again, homie," Joey said. "I'll outrun 'em next time." He laughed.

I was observing this conversation, too confused to involve myself in it. *There's no way Joey, Kevin, Justin, and myself all heard the gunshot as if we were standing next to each other. And, how did Bryce hardly hear it all? It makes no sense.*

I vocalized my thoughts as I still sat on the ground. "How did you three all hear it like we were together when Bryce and I were like a mile away?"

"Don' ask me, homie," Joey said. He took a drag on his cigarette. "All I know is I almost was blowed away."

I looked at Bryce. "And how did you not hear it at all? It was crazy loud."

"I did hear it. It sounded like it came from the center of the island. Somewhere around here or something. I believe Joey, Kevin, and Justin. But you—man—are you okay?"

"Maybe my brain is screwed. I had a stroke at age two and got my head bashed this morning. I might be insane." I paused. "I doubt it though."

"Don't pull the stroke-card, Jay," Kevin said, glaring at me. "I'm sick of hearing it." He changed to a lighter tone as he turned to the rest of the group and said, "It doesn't matter where the gunshot came from as long as we all good. Anyone hurt?" He wiped his face with his sleeve.

I shook my head, along with everyone else. I stood up at the same time and positioned myself between Joey and Bryce. A circle had formed as we all talked.

"Good," said Kevin. "Let's continue on with life."

Bryce spoke up next. "Where are you guys camped?" He shuffled his feet in the dirt as he added, "I got kicked out of Jared's group for sticking up for Jay."

"I figured ya wouldn' last," Joey said. "How long will Mike last?"

Mike?

Justin answered Bryce's question, ignoring Joey's. "We're at this dope little lake in the middle of the island. Wanna join us?" He talked exceptionally fast, especially compared to Bryce.

I answered positively. My stomach growled so I asked, "Got any food?" *The last time I ate was the chocolate bar yesterday. I still have CHEEZ-ITS, but at this point I can't let them know that I stole them.*

"Nothing good," Justin answered. "These two fatties," pointing at Joey and Kevin, "ate all the snacks we had while I—"

"Somebody jacked some food," Joey said, rubbing his hand over his almost bald head. "So I didn' eat it all."

"A bag of chips and a chocolate bar," Justin said. "Big deal." He shook his head in disbelief. "If they hadn't been stolen you'd still have eaten them."

Uh-oh. I hope they don't hurt me for taking their food.

Justin turned back to me and said, "I searched the whole island and only found berries. No meat. Just berries and leaves."

Seriously? Berries are good, but I want a T-bone steak. I spoke, "It looked like all the plants here were dead. How'd you find berries?" *It doesn't make sense.*

"They are pretty much all dead," Justin said. "However, if you look real close and search like a dyin' foo' for something edible, a lot of the little shrubs have these tiny berries growing almost out of the ground. It took forever to gather a duffel bag full of them, they're so small." He paused. "I've only eaten a few, but I'm ready to get more."

"Well, let's get back to camp so we can eat some berries," Bryce said, smiling.

I guess that'll be better than nothing, I decided. I followed the group as they walked back to the lake in the island's center.

*   *   *

46

SIX HOURS LATER, we were all full of berries. We were sitting, shirtless in the heat and humidity under the evening sun, next to the pool that I had waded in the day prior, and we had been chatting like old friends the whole time we'd been there. *If they are telling me the truth, then that's exactly what we're doing. I'm still not one hundred percent convinced, though.*

The ghost trees littered the whole area, as well as many small boulders. The babble of the stream filled in any silent points in the conversation that was ensuing.

Joey, leaning against a charred tree, held a pack of MARLBOROs out to me. "Ya wanna smoke, homie?"

Well, I thought, *no one's here to get mad at me for it. Why not?* I spoke. "Sure." I was sitting next to him against an adjacent tree, so I reached into the pack and pulled one out. Joey handed me a lighter. I flicked it on but all I got was a spark. *Stupid thing.* I tried it three more times before it actually gave me a true flame; I finally got the cigarette lit and inhaled slowly. I tossed the lighter back to Joey. As I exhaled, I asked, "Why are we even on this island exactly?"

Joey pocketed the lighter. "From what I remember," he paused to take a long drag on his own cigarette, "I called ya 'bout joining me, Bryce, Kevin, and Mike for a trip to Florida. Justin here," he pointed at Justin, "came instead cuz yo' lame butt had to go on a senior trip or somethin'. Some—"

I interrupted. "Is that where Jared and all them came from?" *I don't know who this Mike guy is, but it's not affecting me, so whatever. Honestly, I know almost nothing right now.*

"Ya really are having amnesia, aren't ya?" Kevin asked. "The past year ya haven't stopped talking about how much ya hate a guy in yo' class named Jared who is always teasing ya."

"Yeah," Joey said. "I still thinks dat da nex' time dat happens ya should beat his ass."

Fat chance of that.

47

Joshua Wingerd

Joey continued his explanation. "Somehow we all got on da same plane and it crash landed just off shore o' dis island. Pretty weird, huh?"

I nodded in agreement. *I'm confused. Camille's pictures proved that we went to two different schools.* "Why was Camille with us?" I asked. "How'd she get involved in my senior trip and your vacation?"

Joey turned to Bryce, then Kevin, then Justin, and back to me. "Honestly, homie, I have no clue." He started to say something else but stopped. Then he said, "Guess who is here dough?" His face lit up like a neon sign as he asked it.

Your girlfriend? The president? I don't know anything. I inhaled on my cigarette.

After a pause he answered his own question. "Nicole." Joey took another drag. "Dat one super cute chick I went to Mexico wit'. Derek's here too."

"Is she your girlfriend?" I asked.

"Joey with a girlfriend?" Kevin spat. "Ya kidding?"

Just then my memory of her returned. *She's beautiful.* "My bad. Remember that I don't remember much." I turned to Joey.

"True, true." I was about to say more, but Joey beat me to it.

"Ima marry her, homie."

"Good luck. You need money for her. And that's something you don't got." I laughed as I said it.

Justin and Kevin laughed as well.

Kevin raised his hand as he spoke, "That was a good one, Jay."

"Thanks." I accepted the high-five he offered me.

"Whatever" Joey said as he puffed away on his cigarette.

I do know these guys. I can trust them. They are cool and easy to talk to and they act like I know them. I must. It's obvious. Joey is 'Mr. Cool' who is really a softie. Kevin is 'Mr. Quiet' but still cool. Justin is 'Mr. Jokester.' Bryce is 'Mr. Serious.' I trust him the most for saving me from Jared.

Jared. I don't even want to think about him.

48

Justin asked Joey for another cigarette. Joey acted like he was mad at him for siding with me on the 'poor' joke, but quickly gave in and gave Justin one. *Point proven,* I thought.

"This island is weird, foo'," Justin said, to no one in particular. "I really want to know where that gun came from."

What gun? Then I remembered. *It went off right behind my head. I could have died.* I nodded my head in agreement with Justin. *Where'd it come from? Someone else is here? But where?*

"Me too," Joey said, lighting up another cigarette for himself. It seemed like he was always holding one. He looked at me and asked, "Homie, is dat still yo' first smoke?"

I glanced at my hand, where I was holding the cigarette, to see it half gone. "Yeah. Why?"

"Ya freakin' slow, homie. Always been." He smirked as he took another hit.

I've smoked before? "Whatever, dude," I said. "I like to enjoy it." I took a drag twice as long as normal and started coughing uncontrollably. *I should have made a joke about him being an addict. Good ideas too late—always.*

Joey laughed at my coughing. "Don' die, homie."

I regained my composure and spoke, wanting to completely change the subject. "I have the strangest feeling—"

Joey cut me off. "Dat ya don' know how to smoke? Dat' clear." He laughed.

"Shut up. I'm being serious." I continued. "I have a feeling we're not alone on this island."

"Well duh," Justin said, rubbing his hand over his spiked-up, blue hair. "That naggot famed Jared is here. And apparently your whole senior class."

"Besides them," I said.

"Why do you think that?" Bryce asked.

"The fact that none of those lame high-schoolers, or us, could possibly have brought guns onto the plane. Could we?"

"Naw, you're right, foo'," Justin said very matter-of-fact. "I tried to sneak my piece onto the plane, but they confiscated it."

"You're kidding," I said. *It would be great if it was true, but it's Justin—a clown—so I doubt it. Even his hairdo proves that a fitting title for him.*

"Yep." He laughed. We all joined him.

I took one last drag on my cigarette—it had burned itself out more than I had smoked it—threw it on the ground, and buried it in the dirt. *I'm hungry again. Berries don't satisfy for long.*

The berries that Justin had picked were in the main compartment of his duffel bag. Packs of cigarettes filled the other pockets. The berry section had been full before we dug in upon reaching camp; now it was down halfway. It was in the center of our circle.

I crawled over and pulled it in between Joey and myself and ate handfuls of the delicious berries. They weren't raspberries. They weren't boysenberries. They weren't huckleberries. They were a type of berry I'd never seen or eaten before that day. *They're the best berries I've ever had. If Heaven has a taste, this is it.*

"Dude, bring the duffel bag over here," Justin pleaded from across the group.

"Grab some yo'self," Joey said.

"Please."

"Don' be lazy, Justin," Joey said.

"You're one to talk."

I laughed.

"I ain' movin'." Joey had a smug look on his face.

"I'll give you a fresh pack of smokes."

Joey's face grew bright. He stood up and pushed the bag to Justin as I attempted to grab one last handful of berries. Justin grabbed a handful when they got to him.

"So when do I get dem?" Joey asked about the cigarettes.

"I'll give them to you later, foo'," said Justin in between chews. "I'm eating right now."

"Dat' fine," Joey said. His face dimmed slightly. "I probably smoked enough for one day—"

"Ya can say that again," Kevin said.

I couldn't help laughing along with the group. Joey stared at us, angrily. *It's a joke. He's not really mad,* I thought to myself.

Joey continued when we quieted down. "As long as I gets it by mornin', I'll be happy."

"Perfect," Justin said, holding his stomach after the laughing fit.

Joey sat down next to Justin with the food in between them. Several seconds of silence followed.

I ate the last few berries in my hand. *These are so good. I'm having such a great time right now; I wish I knew more about these guys I'm hanging with. They're hilarious.*

Joey spoke in a soft voice. "Do ya hear dat?"

Everyone stopped moving, and I could hear faint movement and murmuring in the distance. *Whoever it is, they're getting closer.* "I hear it," I vocalized. "I think they're coming our way."

"I hope it' not da guy wit' da gun," Joey said, rubbing his hand over his head.

"I doubt it is," I assured, though I had zero grounds to make that claim. "But yeah—"

An unexpected voice interrupted me as four figures came into view. "What do we have here?" It was Jared. Based on his appearance, I would guess he'd been wandering for hours. He was sunburned, his cargo shorts were ripped up, and dirt and ash were streaked across his face and shirt.

He must have leaned against a tree to rest, and not realized that the burn marks are transferrable. Serves him right. I switched from thoughts to voice. "What are you doing here?" I spat.

"I want some food," he whined.

"Go find some yourself," Justin ordered. "It took me like eight hours to gather all these berries. I'm sure there are more out there."

"Probably," Jared said. "But seeing as I'm king here, I think you should gather them for me. Kings need servants and that's exactly what you are."

51

"We have nothing to do with you," I said. "You've brutally fired all of us from your," I put up air quotes, "service—"

"I only beat you up, Liyfer. Not these posers."

Joey clenched his fists at that and stood up.

I finished my sentence. "You fired all of us, so technically we don't have to do anything you ask."

Justin chimed in, with his hands stuck in his pockets. "Yeah. You're not king of us."

"Shut up, kid." Jared pointed a stubby finger at Justin. "I could kick your butt right now."

Justin stood and put his arms in front of himself in a boxer's stance. "Let's go!"

Joey stepped in between them, holding one arm on Jared's blue-striped shirt and one arm on Justin's bare shoulder. "Stop! If dis fool fights anyone, it'll be me. We'll see who da real poser is."

Jared's face fell at the last statement, but he agreed. "But, if I win, I get all your food."

"And if I win," Joey started, "den ya never come near here again."

Jared appeared to have liked the idea, because he stuck his hand out as if to say, "deal."

Joey didn't accept the handshake. "Get outta here!" he shouted, lunging at Jared.

The rest of us formed a circle around them. Bryce, Kevin, Justin, and I cheered Joey's name. Jared's three cronies cheered for him.

I glanced over to get a good look at who was with him. Three scrawny figures. One relatively short, one medium, and one about as tall as myself. The taller ones were wearing skinny jeans, and the shorter one was wearing jean shorts. The tallest had a flannel on with the sleeves cut off. *Crackhead,* I thought. *It's way too hot out here to wear something like that.* Mister-flannel was wearing a baseball hat flipped backward, as was Mister-short. The other kid showed signs of pain in his face every time Jared got

52

punched by Joey; when he noticed me looking at him, he smiled and waved.

I waved back, though I had no idea who he was, and then I turned my attention back to the fight. Joey's initial lunge had taken Jared completely by surprise. He fell flat on his back with Joey standing over him. Jared's left hand was at his head.

Oh, you in pain, jerk? Sucks for you.

"Dude, help me up," Jared said. His voice sounded sincere. Joey extended his arm. Jared grabbed it with his right hand. He was in the process of standing when he decided to prove his insincerity. Jared swung his left hand and hit Joey in the chest.

Joey let go of Jared and stumbled back a few steps. When he recovered he leapt headfirst toward Jared; his head connected with Jared's mouth. Jared started swinging fists at Joey like a crazy man, but missed every time. Joey stepped left to avoid a fist, and clocked Jared square in the eye. He fell in a heap and Joey looked happy. He punched him again in the other eye just for good measure.

The circle had broken up and only Mister-pain-feeling of Jared's cronies was next to him. The others were gone.

"Nice job," I said.

"Thanks," Joey beamed.

Jared shakily stood to his feet and pointed a finger straight at me. "Shut up." His eyes were both red: he was sure to have black eyes soon, and his lip was bleeding.

I was about to retort, but Justin beat me to it. "No, you shut up. Joey just whooped yo' sorry ass. No food for you." He made a pouty face and laughed.

"I hope whoever has that gun shoots you," Jared yelled. Blood trickled down his mouth.

"Same to you," Justin spat.

Jared turned to his cronies, discovered that only one was there, and then turned back to no one in particular. "Well, I'll be seeing you suckers later."

Joshua Wingerd

Jared sauntered away, being supported by his friend. Their route led them right past me. As Jared passed, his fist swung at my left eye. I collapsed to the ground. Jared's people ran off.

Kevin yelled, "What the—?"

Unconsciousness overcame me.

CHAPTER 8

(September 2002)

I AWOKE to find myself standing in a field of grass. *I'm dead for sure now,* I thought. *This is just like the field in* GLADIATOR. Actually, that wasn't completely true. The grass here was green and freshly mowed. To my left, a car sped down a street about thirty feet away. To my right, houses were backed up against a wall that separated their property from this field. Behind me, I heard voices.

I turned to see younger-Jay, yet again, wearing blue jean shorts that were obviously pulled up too high, because his knees, and about an inch above his knees, were clearly showing. *I remember when I used to dress like that.* I shivered in remembrance. Jay was playing catch with some other kid. Well, it was actually more like drop than catch, because Jay's friend couldn't hold onto the ball. I watched for a couple minutes as he missed throw after throw.

The other kid was shorter than Jay, with blonde hair and glasses. He was wearing basketball shorts that cut off just below his knees. *Who is that? He looks familiar.*

Finally, he asked Jay if he could hit, and I heard the conversation that followed.

"That'll be great, seeing as how you haven't caught it in like forever." Jay laughed.

His friend laughed too, as he picked up the small, aluminum bat. "Shut up and pitch the ball." He was standing with the bat raised, ready to swing.

Jay made an angry face and shouted, "Fine! If you want it, try to hit it, Joey!" He hurled a two seam fastball toward him. Joey swung hard, spun around, and fell down. "Ha ha ha!" Jay laughed as Joey ran to retrieve the ball.

It's Joey! He was telling me the truth. We've been friends since like the fourth grade. I smiled at this realization. I knew at that point that I wasn't alone on the island.

"Throw something I can hit," Joey whined. It took my thoughts back to the scene in front of me as he tossed the ball back to Jay.

"I just gave you a perfect pitch," Jay protested.

"Then why'd I miss it?" Joey complained.

"Cuz you suck," Jay stated. He laughed and continued, "Should I just let you throw it to yourself?"

"Ha ha ha," Joey spat. "You're funny. Throw it again."

Jay wound up for another pitch. Another fastball. He let go and the ball sailed straight and true. Right at Joey's chest. Joey jumped back as quickly as he could, lowering the bat at the same time. The ball tipped off the end of the bat.

Jay fell down in a fit of uncontrollable laughter.

"What's so funny?" Joey asked, as he ran back to retrieve the ball.

When Jay got control of himself, he answered. "That was strike two."

"What the heck, man!" Joey screamed. "Were you trying to kill me or something? How's that strike two? I had to get out of the way"

Jay just laughed. "I can't believe you swung at that!"

"I didn't."

"Well you fouled it." Jay laughed.

"Wait. What?" Joey was confused.

"The ball touched the bat when you jumped away. Strike two."

"Whatever, dude," Joey decided. "Pitch again."

Jay wound up for a third pitch. What he called a curveball. He threw it straight down the pipe, angled toward the dirt, and it hit the dirt in front of Joey. When it bounced, Joey swung and connected.

The ball flew. Into right field, toward some houses. *Foul territory but at least he hit it.* Down it came— into some thick green bushes.

"Good job," Jay announced. "You lost the ball. Those bushes are horrible, and they smell really bad."

"Ha ha ha," said Joey as he ran from the first base tree to the second base tree.

"Why you running?" Jay asked. "That was a foul. Strike two still."

"No," Joey retorted. "I hit a home run."

"Foul."

"Hit."

"Foul."

"Hit."

"Do you know anything about baseball?" Jay questioned.

"I know that I hit it," Joey replied.

"Yes. You hit it. But that doesn't mean it's a home run." Jay paused. "It went foul."

"Whatever, dude." Joey looked dejected.

"Help me look for the ball."

As Joey walked over to help, he said, "If we were playing football, I'd win."

"Yes. You would. I'm too skinny for that."

"Are you calling me fat?"

"No," Jay said as Joey reached him. "Why would I say that?"

"Cuz you're trying to be funny," Joey answered.

"Well, I don't think so. You're bigger than me. Nowhere close to taller than me, but not fat."

"You calling me short?" Joey asked.

"Yes," Jay replied bluntly.

57

Joey playfully punched Jay in the arm.

"Ouch," Jay said. "Why you so mean?"

"Why you teasing me?"

"Cuz that's what friends do."

Joey nodded in agreement. "You know, dude," he began, changing the subject, "I think in nine years, we'll be college roommates. I think we'll be friends forever."

"I agree."

I believe it. Memories are returning about us, and I'm pretty sure I've felt that we'd be friends forever since I met Joey and know I will until I die.

Fifteen minutes later, they hadn't found the lost baseball. They gave up and decided to give up and go home—to Joey's house. I magically floated behind them as they walked, just like the last time I had one of these weird flashbacks. *It's kind of cool,* I decided.

When they got there, dinner was ready. Jay dove right into the meal that was served when everyone sat down at the table. *He really likes this food.* It was some special type of food that Jay had never heard of before but proved delicious regardless.

*   *   *

DINNER WAS DONE, and a herd of people piled into Joey's family's big-white-van that transported their family around the desert. I found out that they were heading to AWANA's. After five minutes of driving they came to a large church whose sign in front read: "Desert Valley Church." *That's my church,* I realized, as we drove right past it. *Huh? Isn't that where we are going?* (I had given up trying to talk to people in these flashbacks. It was pointless.)

The answer was apparently "no," because thirty minutes later we pulled into a parking lot labeled "Desert Bible Church."

*   *   *

AT SEVEN PM the thing started, and games came first. I watched as Jay failed at the running-around-a-circle games. After games, we all listened to a chapel message about being kind to your neighbor. After this, it was memory verse time. I soon realized this was Jay's favorite part.

Jay's leader asked his group, "How many of you guys did your memory verses for today?"

Jay was one of three to raise his hand.

"Okay, Jay," the leader began. "What's First Corinthians 6:19?"

"Do you not know that your body is a temple of the Holy Spirit, who is in you, whom you have received from God? You are not your own," Jay rattled off without missing a beat.

"Very good. What about 1 John 4:15?"

"If anyone acknowledges that Jesus is the Son of God, God lives in him and he in God." Jay was beaming. It was excessively easy.

"Excellent. Last one for this week. What is Matthew 7:8?"

Jay instantly began, "For everyone who asks receives; he who seeks finds; and to him who knocks, the door will be opened."

"Perfect job." The leader then went on to the next kid.

"Hey dude," Joey whispered to Jay, "Are you gonna be a pastor or something?"

"No."

The question was a big surprise to me.

Jay continued, "Why you ask?"

"Because you're good at memorizing verses."

"That's cuz if you try, it's easy. But I wanna be a baseball player. It makes a lot more money than being a pastor."

"Oh, okay," Joey said.

I thought about his words. *A pastor?* It reminded me of what was going on on the island. *A pastor? That was the biggest joke ever, especially since nowadays God hates me. I would never, ever, ever become a pastor.*

Everything went black.

CHAPTER 9

(Day 2, 8:00 p.m.)

I SAT UP with a start. *Joey told me I should be a pastor? That's not the Joey I know. Ha. Plus, why would I want to serve Someone I hate? Besides, He hated me first.*

My thoughts paused before I reminded myself, *It was just a dream. Don't take it too seriously.* My head started pounding and I remembered being knocked out prior to the dream. I lay back down. *I wish I had* ADVIL. (In retrospect, I really didn't need any ADVIL at that point compared to how I would feel by the end of my time on the island.)

Why is my life being replayed in my sleep? I asked myself, changing the topic back.

I couldn't think of anything, so I sat back up, put my hand on my head, and looked at my surroundings. I was alone. No one else was around. My thoughts would keep me company. *I hate the conversations my mind has with itself when I'm alone. They just bring back tons of memories—many of which I don't want—and make me wonder if I have multiple personality disorder. My imagination runs rampant when I'm alone, but I never have time to use it to my benefit. Seventeen stories sit started on my computer, but none have actually been finished. One is 'done,' but it needs lots of work still. So I've completed nothing.*

Why am I alone right now? I want company. Where'd my friends go? Did the guy with the gun kill them? Did a previously unseen wild animal eat them? Did Jared kidnap them?

I looked out across the pool to see the moon perfectly reflected in it. It was beautiful.

The beauty was interrupted by rustling in a plant across the pool. *Someone is playing a joke on me.* "Joey, is that you?" I stood up, put my hands in my back pockets, and stared in the direction of the sound.

No response.

"Bryce?"

No response.

"Kevin?" I was worried now. I balled my hands into fists in my pockets.

Again, no response.

I shrieked, "Who is that over there?" I put my right hand on my head because the shriek made my head throb again.

"Don't be scared," a familiar voice assured. "It's Jacob."

That's a relief. "Why didn't you just come over here? It would have been easier than slinking around over there." *He's quite a character.* I still didn't know exactly what to think of him, but he seemed friendly enough. *And we've both had our share of troubles, so we have stuff in common.*

"I don't know," came his response. Bushes rattled as he walked over to me. "I guess I didn't want to frighten you." His greasy brown hair swung as he walked.

"Next time just show your face," I said. "You had me freaking out just now." I paused before asking, "How long have you been around here?" I sat back down, knowing I had no need to run in the foreseeable future.

"Long enough to see a beaten coward grab a victory. When Jared punched you I was ready to kill him for you. Your friend is quite the fighter though." He sat down next to me and the potent smell of beer and tobacco returned.

"You saw all that?" I was surprised. *It's good to know he has my back as far as Jared goes though.*

"Yeah. You were out for like two hours."

61

"Where'd my friends go?" *That's all I want to know, though Jacob isn't a horrible replacement.*

"They ran off yelling, 'they jacked our food! They jacked our food.' I'm really sorry about that." His expression—in the moonlight—looked caring.

"How are you coping with the island?" I asked.

"I'm okay. I haven't eaten yet, but I'll be fine." He then asked me the same question.

"I don't know," I said. "I've had food, but I keep on having weird dreams about my childhood. It's strange, because I've always tried to find meanings in dreams, but these are true stories so I can't figure it out."

"If I can give you any advice," he began, "don't worry about dreams. They are just the product of an overactive mind. They never mean anything. Don't let them get to you."

That makes sense. "Okay then," I said. "I won't worry about them."

"Good," Jacob said. He looked me in the eyes and asked, "How are you dealing with the death of your girlfriend?"

Ouch. That struck a minor chord in my mind, and combining it with the scent of his breath made me want to retch. *It's so direct.* I felt myself swallowing whatever was in my throat as I answered. "I'm trying not to think about it. As long as I'm occupied mentally with other things, it's not so bad." *It's why I didn't bring her up a few seconds ago. Obviously.* "When I think of her the tears come back."

"That's understandable," Jacob agreed. "I'm really sorry."

"It's not your fault," I stated bluntly. "It's God's." *Whoa, did I just say that?*

Jacob spoke, "You'd think He could have stopped it if He wanted to."

It was exactly what I was thinking. *True. I guess I shouldn't be surprised. The fact that God, Who is all-powerful, couldn't prevent Camille from dying, is enough to make it His fault.* Tears rolled down my face.

Jacob said nothing. He just smiled a toothy grin that was almost creepy in the moonlight.

I changed the subject as I wiped my eyes. "What have you been doing during your time here?"

"Not much," he said. "Just waiting, really."

"For what?"

He shifted his position in the dirt as he answered. "Food. A rescue plane. Something."

"Oh, okay," I said. "I haven't seen or heard a single plane or boat since I've been here though." I put my hands into the dirt behind me and leaned back to stretch my stomach.

"Me neither," Jacob said. "That's why I'm waiting."

"Good luck," I offered, smiling, as I brought my hands back and folded them on my chest. *It's best to be optimistic, but I doubt anyone will rescue us.*

I heard voices in the distance. *Cool, my friends are coming back. At least, I hope it's them.*

"Well, I'll see you later," said Jacob. "I gotta go."

I said, "bye," and he ran off south, in the direction of my classmates, taking his scent with him.

Curses sounded in the distance, signaling Joey's approach.

"How did they just disappear like that, foo'?" Justin's voice asked.

Joey came into view at that point. He spoke a sentence that was originally uncensored, "I got no clue. I can't believe they jacked our food."

Everyone else came into view as I mentally registered what had happened. *Jared's cronies stole our food.*

"I believe it," I said in contrast to Joey's statement.

"Look who's recovered," Justin said, placing his hands in his pockets.

"No thanks to any of you guys," I said. "I woke up and thought you guys had been killed or something."

"Someone's gone be—" Joey interrupted himself. "Are ya feelin' okay at least, homie?"

"I'm good, besides a splitting headache. Do you have any more cigarettes?"

Joey reached into his pocket and pulled out his pack. He threw it to me. I caught it, opened it, pulled out the last cigarette, pulled out the lighter, lit the cigarette, and threw the empty pack on the ground. I tossed the lighter back to Joey. "Thanks, bro."

"No biggie, homie," he said. He turned to Justin and asked, "Now, where' my pack?"

"It's in my bag. I'll get it for you later."

Kevin spoke. "Ya mean: it *was* in yo' bag, right? Yo' bag got jacked. Remember?"

Joey broke into a cursing machine at that realization. *I don't remember this side of Joey; it's a little scary. Don't hurt me!* (If someone was to ask what his favorite word was, this would be more proof that it was probably one with four letters, or at least one with a four letter root). I was scared for Jared's sake by what Joey said, but at the same time I didn't like him either. I told myself I would never go as far as Joey did. To summarize his speech, he said he was going to kill Jared.

Justin grabbed Joey by the shoulders. "Jared dumped out my bag on the ground first, remember? Maybe the packs are mixed with my clothes."

It somewhat calmed Joey down. He walked over to Justin's pile of stuff and began shuffling through it and cussing every few seconds. "Dere ain' a trace of tobacco in here," he announced. "I' gone kill—"

Bryce spoke for the first time in a while, interrupting Joey's rant. "Let's just go to sleep and see how we feel in the morning." His voice was slow and methodical as usual, and it was a pleasant relief after Joey's and Justin's tirades. In fact, Bryce was already stretched out on the ground.

"Good idea," I said. I took a final hit on my cigarette and threw it aside.

Joey noticed and picked it up. It was only two-thirds smoked, so he decided to finish it. "It'll help my stress," he said. He took a long drag on the cigarette.

Wow, you are desperate, was all I could think as I lay down on the ground.

"I'll kill him tomorrow den," Joey announced, referencing Bryce's request, as he exhaled the smoke.

"I'll help you, foo'," Justin said. "That pittle lansy stole my smokes. I had like eight packs left."

"Calm down," said Bryce. "I'm going to sleep."

"Fine," said Joey. "I'll talk to ya homies in da mornin'." It was the last sentence spoken that night.

CHAPTER 10

(October 2002)

I OPENED MY EYES to see younger-Jay sitting on a wrought-iron bench on the front porch of his house. He was crying. Through the tears I could make out only a few of his words. Something about Sandy, and a broken jaw, and a friend, and put to sleep, and a cat. *Oh, this was when Sandy, the cat we adopted from my cousins, had to be put to sleep because of a broken jaw.* From what I could vaguely remember, she was a long haired, brown and yellow streaked cat that had enjoyed sleeping on the back of our couches.

I heard a woman's voice from inside the house. It was probably his mom, and it sounded as if she was looking for Jay. She opened the front door, looked left, looked right, and saw him on the bench. "What's wrong?"

"I'm so lonely, mommy. Ever since Sandy died I have had no one to talk to."

"She was just a cat. How did you talk to her?" his mother asked kindly.

"I, I, I don't know," stammered Jay. "It's just—she listened to everything I said and it was so nice. She never got mad at me either."

His mother acknowledged his words compassionately, and then said, "Why don't you just talk to your brother or sister?"

"They are always busy having fun together, and they never include me."

"I see," she answered. "Why don't you pray for God to give you a new friend?"

"You know," began Jay, who smiled as he continued, "that is a good idea."

It would be, if He answered prayer, I thought to myself. *I'm proof positive that He doesn't.*

"Well you do that, and when you are ready, come back inside for dinner."

"Okay."

"I love you," she said with a smile.

"I love you too."

She stood up and went back inside, and Jay started to pray. "Dear Jesus, thank you for this day," *that's how I always started my prayers.* "Thank you for my mom, dad, brother, and sister. Thank you for dying on the cross for me.

"I really really miss Sandy, my kitty. Please let me get a new kitty soon. Cats are my favorite type of pets. Dogs are slobbery and smelly and loud, but cats are quiet, clean, and collected. Dogs may be man's best friend, but cats are my best friends. I want one.

"Also, please help my left hand to get better. I want to be able to play baseball for a living, but I can't if I can't catch, and I can't catch unless it gets better. In Jesus' name, Amen."

* * *

NEXT THING I KNEW, it must have been a different day, because Jay was wearing different clothes. And I was in his kitchen watching them eat a meal. There were five people seated around the table: Jay, his dad, his mom, another boy younger than Jay—*my brother Zeke*—and a little girl—*my sister Noel.*

There was consistent chatter from the three kids throughout the meal, but it all got silent when his dad said, "Guess what, Jay?"

"What?" he asked in response.

"We're going to a DODGERS game tonight."

Ewww. I hate the DODGERS. The ANGELS are so much better.

67

"We are?" Jay asked excitedly.

"Yes, we are," his dad answered. "And your mother invited Kevin to come along too."

"Yay!" shouted Jay. "Can he come?"

Kevin? The guy on the island with me? So, according to the last few of these dreams, Joey and Kevin are legit, but what about Bryce and Justin?

Jay's mom answered his question. "Kevin's mother said he could, so when your father gets home from work around four thirty, we will go straight over to pick him up and then go to the game."

"I can't wait!" he exclaimed.

"Me neither," his dad said, "but right now I've got to get to work, so have a good day. I love you, Jay."

"I love you too." He hugged his dad.

Jay's father kissed his wife, hugged Zeke and Noel goodbye, and then left the house for the day.

*　　*　　*

THE NEXT THING I KNEW, it was four thirty. Jay threw open the door to check to see if his dad had pulled up yet.

MEOW.

The noise stopped him in his tracks. He had barely passed the edge of the porch and he turned back to look for the source.

MEOW, came the cry again.

I floated over to the porch, just like I always moved in these things, and turned to watch Jay as he crawled under the porch bench, looking for the source of the sound. I could hear him muttering something to something under the bench. *I know what he found. I remember this now.*

A green HONDA ACCORD pulled up, and Jay's dad got out of it. Several minutes later he was on the porch. "What are you doing?" he asked.

Jay backed out from underneath the bench, and answered his dad by showing him the little grey and white kitten in his arms. He said, "Look who decided to hide out on our porch today."

"He's cute," his dad acknowledged.

"Yeah he is," Jay agreed. "He has a really small tail too. I think—"

MEOW, came the kitten's cry again.

Jay resumed. "I think he's hungry."

Jay's dad walked inside and called out, "Elizabeth, do we have any cat food? Jay found a kitten."

"I don't know," came the reply. "Check the garage."

It's Chester. He had a stub tail, and he always freaked out around lawn mowers. *We always wondered if they were connected. I would give anything to have that cat on the island with me.*

Jay's dad walked farther inside the house as Jay set the new kitten down on the porch bench. He sat next to it and let it crawl around on him. The cat was mostly grey, but had a white snout, and white forepaws. The front of his shoulders and his chest and his belly were also white. Everything else was grey, including his two inch tail that ended abruptly—in a nub.

Jay's father came back outside. "Jay, we have no cat food."

Jay ignored him. "Can we keep him?"

"No, because someone is probably looking for him."

Jay's face fell.

"If he's still here when we get home from the game we can put up signs advertising a lost cat. If no one claims him after a week, we will keep him." His dad smiled. "Would you like that?"

"Yes," replied Jay, as his dad re-entered the house to call everyone out to leave for the game. Jay smiled and looked down at the cat curled up on his lap. "Please let me keep him, God," he prayed aloud. He stood up, set the cat down, and walked to the car.

My eyes went shut, and all the chatter of Jay and his family faded away. *Scene change,* I thought.

69

CHAPTER 11

(Day 3, 6:45 a.m.)

I WOKE UP EARLY. It was one of those nights. I tossed and turned all night and woke up every twenty minutes or so wondering how much time had passed since the last time I had awakened. I wondered if it might have something to do with actually sleeping, and not being forced unconscious for the first time in recent memory.

By the time the sun started to peak over the horizon, I decided it would be best to get moving—not mope around doing nothing all day—and enjoy the day to the fullest. Though it was debatable whether there was anything to do besides mope around all day.

Do I still have that cat at home? Chester's awesome. With a stub tail, I felt a connection to him—my messed up hand—and he had been, and maybe still is, my best little buddy.

I sat up, rubbed my eyes, and looked around. My friends were still snoring on the ground. *It brings back the awkward feeling of being the first one awake at a sleepover, but, since this is no sleepover, I'm going for a walk.*

It will make me alert anyways, I decided, rationalizing my reason to go walking. *The dream is why I couldn't sleep,* I reasoned, deciding it wasn't because of injury-free sleep. *It was weird—almost annoying, but not quite. I hate not getting good sleep; it makes me cranky.*

I walked south, toward Jared's camp. *Why that way?* I asked myself. *You don't want to see Jared.* It didn't stop me. *You're going to get another beating. Walk the other way.*

I ignored it and kept walking. *Maybe I will run into one of the girls from my class,* I hoped. I was starting to remember several girls I had had secret crushes on for the past few years. *Maybe in this new environment I'll be brave enough to talk to one of them. Maybe they will pity me because of how Jared treats me.* I doubted it, but it was a possibility regardless.

What about Camille? My psyche questioned. *Don't you need to grieve over her, and not run after another girl?*

I could see three potential girls in my mind. Julia. Kimberly. Nicole. *All three are perfect.* I didn't care about the accusation my brain had just made. *There's no better way to get over someone than to meet someone else. Besides,* I reasoned, *it's not every day you find yourself on an island. Normally "island" means bikini-clad women.* My thoughts disintegrated from there.

Don't forget that this isn't your typical island. Everything is dead except for you and your friends and classmates. It's not exactly the appropriate place for bikinis lounging on a beach. There's no palm tree shade. Anyone smart would realize that people stuck on an island with no shade shouldn't lounge any more than necessary. Sunburns are bad.

That was when I felt the sting of my sunburn. I glanced over at my right arm to see darkness on one side, and, as I rotated it over rotisserie style, I saw lightness on the other side. I poked at it with my left hand and a small circle turned light in the sea of obviously burned skin. *My mom's gonna kill me.* I heard her saying, "You're going to get skin cancer," in my mind. *It's not my fault though,* I reasoned, *since I didn't know my plane would crash on this stupid island.*

I turned my mind back to the girls. They were the only reason I was risking walking to Jared's camp. *I just want someone to care about me. And there's no hope for me if I never talk to them.* I decided to focus on what I could remember about each of the girls.

Julia was first. The class clown. She was shorter than me—not unusual—and the top of her head only barely reached my shoulders when her hair was bumped-up. She was very talkative, often being moved around the class for it. I couldn't remember if we'd ever talked at all though. What her personality lacked, her looks made up for. Her straight brown hair was cut off an inch above her shoulders and it matched her eyes perfectly. She always smiled, showing off perfect teeth, and she had a slender frame. I had dreamt of dating her since first meeting her at the beginning of freshman year.

Next was Kimberly. The class flirt. She was taller than Julia, but still significantly shorter than me. All I really knew about her was that she'd dated every guy in my class—except me—and she was always flirting with somebody. Given her beauty, her antics weren't surprising. Her beautiful brown hair spiraled down to her chest. It was always curled from ear level down, and her eyes were light brown. Her smile and teeth were also perfect, and she was slender too.

Finally was Nicole. Joey's girl—in his dreams. Ever since I had started at the school in ninth grade, Joey had talked about how hot she was. He was stoked that she was in classes with me. He always wanted me to put in a good word for him. She was a good choice too. She was quiet, reserved, and calm. She only got antsy when homework assignments were coming up due. She was very selective with guys. I honestly didn't think she'd ever had a legitimate boyfriend, and I was one-hundred-percent-positive that Joey had no chance with her.

I don't know how long I had been wandering toward the camp, but by the time anything interesting happened, the sun was up in the eastern sky. I would have guessed it was about nine. My arms were clearly sunburned, and I didn't even want to think about my face or neck.

"Jay," came a female voice from my left. The voice was whiny, yet sweet. I recognized it, but couldn't put sound to face until I turned to my left. *The sexy girl who was with Jared when I got onto shore.*

Why is she calling me? It made me nervous; Jared hated it when his girls talked to other guys. *He's probably hiding somewhere near here waiting for me to talk to her so he can kick my butt for a real reason.*

I stared at her again as she walked toward me. *I hope she doesn't realize it.* She was thin, to the point that she almost looked unhealthy. From a distance she could have been mistaken for a child due to her height. She was still wearing her pink shirt, now untied and covering most of her midriff, but it was clear that her arms, neck and face were fried from the sun. Her black jeans left nothing to the imagination, and hugged her legs all the way down to her pink flip flops. She wore large sunglasses that almost covered her whole face. *I want her.*

Why'd she call my name? What am I going to do?

"Jay," she called again. She was traipsing right toward me. Her long, auburn hair swung with each step. I felt her concealed eyes bore into mine, searching for answers. When she finally reached my position, she put her hands on her super-thin hips in a posture that came across as if she was my mother and I was in trouble.

Scary. I was on the horns of a dilemma. *If I ignore her and walk away, she will hate me. If I acknowledge her and talk, Jared will hate me.*

It's better for her to hate you, my mind told me. *Run.*

I should have run sooner, because just as I had turned one-hundred-eighty degrees, she called out, "Jay, have you seen Jared recently? I haven't seen him since mid-day yesterday."

"Why should I care where he is?" I shot back.

I'm so stupid. I shouldn't have just responded to her.

I turned back toward her and continued. "Every time I see that piece of dirt, I get punched somewhere. Do you see my eye?" I paused. "That's only part of my problem."

73

"I'm worried about him," she said, ignoring my question. Her lips were pursed in a concerned look. "He hates the outdoors. He's probably laying on the ground somewhere, injured beyond all recognition."

If that's true, my life will be great. I would have given anything to have Jared dead at that very moment. *That preppy kid is the most annoying person I've ever met. And his hairdo is the dumbest thing I've ever seen. How did I deal with it for four years throughout high school?*

She hadn't stopped talking. "I hope he's okay. He's my best friend."

She might have had more to say, but I cut her off. "He's a pretty pathetic best friend. What do you see in him anyways?" *Girls are confusing. Especially the ones that fall for total jerks.*

"Why do you hate him so much?" she asked. She was indignant. "He rescued me from Johnny, by showing me how bad he was for me. Jared is thoughtful and always does the sweetest things for me. As soon as we both finish college we are going to get married. I love him."

I would never have said the following out loud, but I definitely thought it. *He's sweet because he just wants sex from you. The nicer he is, the more likely you'll be to do it.* All I said, though, was, "Wow." I paused before adding, "I hate him. All he ever does is beat me up and use me as a punching bag. He beats me up. He throws me around. He calls me names." I was mad. "He should die." I shouted the next sentence. "It would rid the world of a huge problem!"

She slapped me across the face to shut me up.

It angered me more, so I spouted off, "He made up those lies about Johnny because he wanted to get in your pants. You're such—"

She slapped me again.

I let a stream of profanities flow, aimed at both her and Jared.

She slapped me again and marched away. "Jared's twenty times the guy you are," she shouted over her shoulder.

I trudged back toward my camp. My mouth tasted bloody. I had talked to a girl; it had gone south. I had no desire to talk to another one again for a while. I'd rather go back and vent my frustrations to the guys. They would help me snap out of it. *Or they'll make fun of me.* That was true. I really didn't want to deal with that, but I figured it would be better than dealing with females or Jared, so I kept going toward camp.

My pace was slow because I was not in a hurry at all. As I sauntered back toward camp, the craziest thought struck me, as my eyes fixated on yet another dead, rotting, burned-out tree. *Jared's heart is just as black and useless as this tree. And his girlfriends' isn't far behind it.* I laughed. *There's no possible way that Jared is twenty times the guy I am, let alone two times the guy I am.*

As my thoughts slowed, the quiet in the air became creepy. When I was at home in Desert Valley there were usually vehicles driving, or people yelling, or at least wind blowing to distract one's thoughts. Not here.

And then my vision brought three people into view. They were all dudes, but I could tell clearly that they didn't belong to my group. They were chatting about school, about the senior trip they were supposed to have been on, and about the boringness of the island. The tallest one—a thin black kid—made a comment about how much worse it was now having Jaime in charge than it was having Jared in charge.

Oh yeah, Jared's girlfriend is named Jaime.

The second tallest of the new group—a thin, pale-white guy with an almost emo-looking haircut—said, "Remember that book we read at the beginning of the semester? LORD OF THE FLIES? Everything about this place is just like that book. The kids in the book almost burned the island completely down right after getting there, and what do we see here? Jared and Jaime both want to play "chief of the island," and we have huts on the beach—even

Joshua Wingerd

though we didn't have to make them. The only question now would be: when does everyone lose their minds and start killing each other?"

The words were hardly off his tongue when all three let out a shout. From where I was walking, I could see the third boy—a sturdy fellow who belonged on a football field—clutch his chest and fall backwards to the ground. The exclamations from the other two made it clear to me what had happened, even though I stopped moving at this point, squatting as low to the ground as I could.

"Where the hell did that knife come from?"

"Your guess is as good as mine, Peter," the black kid explained. "Why'd you have to go and make a comment about people killing each other? Obviously, someone's already started."

Peter ignored him. "David, you can pull through, bro." He paused to collect his thoughts. "Don't die. How the hell am I supposed to explain your death to Jaime? She'll kill me."

The black kid bent down and was silent for a second or two before he spoke. "He's gone, Peter." He paused, as I watched him bow his head for a few seconds. Then he spoke again, "You stay here and watch his body, and I'll go pass the news on to Jaime. I don't think she'll kill me."

"Okay, Derek," Peter said, confusion and concern heavy in his voice.

With that Derek ran off, back toward the beach.

I stood up as Derek started running, wanting answers, but more than anything wanting to be somewhere else. If people were going to die, I wanted to be home. *I miss my house and my bed and my food so much. I hope I'm off this stupid island soon.*

When I started moving, I must have made noise because Peter's voice rang out, "Hey, who goes there? Why'd you kill our friend? Wait, Jay, is that you? Why are you running?"

How's he know my name? But I ignored him, and I sped up faster until I couldn't hear his cries anymore. I decided to keep this news to myself. *No need to frighten the others, especially Joey.*

*　　*　　*

TWENTY MINUTES LATER I crossed back into camp. Bryce walked past me as I took a seat by the pool. He was clutching the black book in his hands again. "I'll be back in a little," he said. "I'm going into the forest to read."

"Have fun," was all I said, though I could have, and maybe should have, said a lot more. Bryce walked away and disappeared behind a clump of ashen trees.

Bryce reads regularly? I had had no clue. This was now the second time in as many days I'd seen him with that book. We had all read the HARDY BOYS when we were younger, but I had convinced myself that I was the only one who thoroughly enjoyed them, or who read them like he was on his deathbed and might not finish before his time. *I know all Joey liked were the occasional pictures. He hates reading—even if the font is as big as his hand. What is Bryce reading now?* I decided I'd ask him when he returned.

You brought a book too, my mind claimed.

I didn't believe it. *I haven't even seen my duffel bag since figuring out where I am.*

Your bag is where you first woke up, my mind explained. *You woke up there; it's perfectly logical.*

Maybe so, I thought.

I wish these internal conversations would stop. They are super annoying.

Joey, Kevin, and Justin were still asleep. *How long does a guy need to sleep?* I wondered. I felt as if the island was bringing out the worst in people. *For those three—laziness; for me—anger. I never would have cussed Jaime out like that at school.* I had a good-kid rep to maintain. *If Jared finds out what I did, I'm dead for sure.* I cursed at the realization.

A screaming person and heavy footfalls interrupted my thoughts. The screamer was getting closer. *Who died this time?*

I got my answer twenty seconds later when Jared came into the clearing from the north. He was screaming like a maniac.

Crap, I thought. *He's mad at me and that's why he's yelling. I'm doomed.*

His noise woke Joey. "What is goin' on?" he asked as he rubbed the sleep out of his eyes and moved slowly to his feet.

Jared was running straight toward me and was about to go past me when I grabbed him by the shirt and brought him to a stop. I pushed him over against a tree, looked him in the eyes and ordered him to be quiet. Surprisingly, he complied.

Joey spoke lethargically. "Homie, why ya—" he cut himself off. He continued when he recognized Jared. He referred to him profanely, and asked, "Why' ya take my cigs?"

Kevin and Justin were waking up now.

Jared ignored Joey's question and simply spat, "There's skeletons in the water."

Crackhead much?

"Wha' da hell ya talkin' about?" Joey asked slowly.

Jared was talking fast. "North of here, in the water, there's skeletons. I picked up a skull with my bare hands. It was trippy."

My hand was still on Jared's blue shirt, pushing him against the tree, potentially adding to his nervousness.

"How much did you smoke last night, fool?" Justin asked, standing up to join in the festivities. "That shinda kit don't normally happen off cigarettes."

"I can prove it to you guys," he said, clenching his fists. "But, I really don't want to go back. It was scary."

"Justin," Kevin began, putting on his hat as he stood up as well, "did ya lace those cigarettes with acid? This kid's on a bad trip."

I had Jared pinned against the tree by his collar, and my three best friends were behind me backing me up, in case he tried anything.

Jared tried to protest, but Justin cut him off. "No, I didn't, but the foo' who sold 'em to me did look a li'l shady so," he shrugged, "I don't know." Then he busted up laughing.

Jared tried again, over Justin's mocking laugh. "I ain't high. Never have been. Ever. Even if I was, I'm definitely not now." He spat on the ground.

"Prove it," I threatened. I was still holding him by the shirt collar. He was trying to wriggle free but it wasn't working.

"I don't wanna go back—" he started.

"And I don't wanna get beat up every day." I looked him in the eyes and shook him back and forth with both hands. His head bumped the tree a couple of times as I yelled, "But it's not like that's ever going to happen."

Joey took my thunder, and added to it. "Good point, homie." He glared at Jared. "An' if I ever see ya touch him again, I'll whoop yo' ass so bad you'll wish ya'd never been born." I could tell Joey was finally alert.

Kevin nodded his agreement at Joey's threat.

My friends are the best. I was glad that at least a couple people had my back in this world.

"Fine," said Jared. "Please don't make me show you what I'm talking about."

"How will we know you're not high if you don't?" Justin asked.

Jared cussed to get across the fact that he was innocent as regarded the cigarettes. He paused to clarify. "Well maybe I tried one. But, it made me sick so that was it. Last night."

"Ya can't be high off one cigarette," Kevin pointed out. "Especially one from the night prior."

"I think he's full of shull bit," Justin said. "I want my smokes back. Damn, I wanna kick his athetic pass so badly."

"So do I," Joey said, pulling up his pants that had started sagging too low. He paused for half a second before adding, "If ya show us da skeletons in yo' ocean, I'll take back what I vowed last night for ya stealing my cigs."

Justin took over. "Actually, my cigarettes. If you don't show us, we'll kill you. It's your choice, hit-shed."

Jared squirmed again, so I exerted more pressure on his collar. His face looked thoughtful. But he remained silent, preferring to run his hand through his blonde hair than reply.

Joey elaborated on the details on Jared's potentially near execution. "Jay will get da first punch while we hold ya down. Den—"

"Fine," Jared said. "I'll show you." He spat in my face before adding, "A punch from him," motioning at me with a nod, "wouldn't even hurt though."

You've had a bad morning, Jay. Teach him a lesson. I acquiesced. I kicked him square between the legs. "How's that feel?"

He dropped out of my hands, gasping for breath. "I'll kill you for that," was all he could get out.

"I'll kill ya if you touch him," Joey reminded. "Stand up. Take us to yo' friends."

"He won't hurt me," I said boldly. "He hasn't gotten anything from his girl yet."

"After that kick though, he won't care about sex," Justin laughed.

"And hotty will be all mine," Joey declared.

Jared cursed at Joey for that comment, and Joey retuned it verbatim as he hoisted Jared to his feet. I backed away. Joey was in control of him now. Part of me was glad that Joey had him, but another part still wanted to take care of him myself. *I would give anything to kill this pathetic loser myself.*

What happened to not wanting to be the one responsible for Jared's death? My psyche asked. *How many people have to die today?*

Shut up. I want to forget about the episode in the forest.

Jared fell down again. "I can't walk," he whined.

"You're going to," I retorted. "Show us these dead guys."

Justin elaborated. "If you don't, we're going to make fun of you forever."

"I don't care. I ain't gonna show you, because I can't walk."

STRANDED

"Ima kill ya if ya don'," Joey said. "Are ya lookin' to die today?" With the hand that hadn't been holding Jared, he broke off a charred piece of tree.

"Why?" Jared asked.

The pain must have made him forgetful. Good job, Jay.

"Remember my cigs," Joey reminded, holding up the tree-piece threateningly.

"Oh, okay," Jared remembered. After a split second of silence he asked, "What if I can get them back to you?"

That's really the best he can come up with? Wow.

Justin replied first. "We'll be cool. But I'll still call you a crackhead."

"I can live with that," Jared admitted.

Joey held out his hand, letting the stick fall. "Hand 'em over."

"What?" Jared was stuttering. "I-I-I don't have them o-o-on me."

"Where dey at?"

"With Ryan, Zac, and Johnny."

"And where dey?"

"Not far from here."

"Take us to dem." Joey again hoisted Jared to his feet, as he picked up the stick again.

"Fine." He didn't fall that time. "Follow me."

Joey held onto his shoulder and followed Jared closely, with the stick raised threateningly. The rest of us lagged about fifteen paces behind. *I hope I can watch Jared get beat with that stick.*

*   *   *

FORTY MINUTES LATER we entered a small clearing in the densest section of the forest I'd yet seen on the island. The dead trees were almost impossible to navigate through, since they were basically growing one-out-of-another throughout the whole area. It had been very slow work even making our way to the clearing,

81

which honestly was only clear of trees. Roots of bushes and giant boulders lay everywhere. If I tried to run quickly through the area I would have hurt myself.

Jared was on his hands and knees looking into a hole in the ground. "Ryan, Zac, Johnny!" he yelled. "Are you in here?"

A muffled reply came several seconds later. "Yeah. Where'd you disappear to?"

"I got out, Johnny," he replied before adding, "and ditched you guys."

"You a-hole!" yelled another voice. "My leg is killing me."

"Zac still hasn't shut up about it," Johnny's voice said to Jared.

I don't know what they're talking about.

Jared got back to the point.

"Zac, it's not going to be the only thing killing you if you don't give me those cigarettes back."

Joey barged in. "He won' be dead, Jared. Ya will."

He turned to Joey. "Why?"

"Cuz I want dem back." Joey looked dead serious, and proved it by showing Jared a rock the size of his head that he had picked up during the walk across the island to replace the crumbly, sooty, tree-piece.

"I didn't even take them. It was their idea." Jared pointed down into the hole.

"Ya expect me—"

Zac's voice interrupted Joey. "Jared, they're all gone. I smoked 'em all last night."

Joey's face twisted in agony. It was clear he was ticked.

I wonder what he's going to do. Wring his neck? Kick him in the nads?

The obvious answer, which I had not thought of, was the one he chose. He threw the rock at Jared's backside, as Jared peered into the hole. Jared let out a yelp and tumbled out of sight. A soft *thud* was heard.

Joey peered into the hole. "Next time I see any of ya," Joey began, "you'll wish ya'd never been born."

A huge explosion rocked the ground all around us, distracting us one-hundred-percent from Jared. I looked around to find the source and it was coming from the direction of main camp.

I shouted in confusion, along with several others, including some from the hole—who we totally ignored.

"The plane exploded," said Justin, very matter of factly.

The four of us turned to go back to camp. My mind went to Camille.

I'd left her body in the plane. Her beautiful body. The one that needed burying was now destroyed. It was blown into bits. She deserved a proper burial.

Get a hold of yourself, Jay.

I hated that voice. *Camille's dead. I can act like this all I want.* I felt like crying.

You can, but your friends will laugh at you. Besides, weren't you going to meet someone new this morning anyways?

I ignored that thought because something else hit me. *This is Jared's fault. He's distracted me from Camille ever since I got back on shore.*

I kicked myself as I walked. I looked up into the sky and wondered, "Why are You so cruel?"

"Who ya talkin' to, homie?" Joey asked.

It startled me. *I said that aloud?* I moved my gaze from the sky to Joey. "I uh, I was talking to, uh, I was talking to no one."

"Okay, homie," he said. "It was kinda weird. Y'alright?"

"No—"

Kevin interrupted. "Of course he's not. None of us are. We're trapped on some stupid island with no food, no cigarettes, and no toilet paper." His face looked angrier at the mention of the last item as opposed to the first few.

I don't blame him. I knew exactly how he felt; in fact, everyone was nodding their agreement. *I miss Camille more than toilet paper though.* I continued to walk with the rest of them, slowly stepping around boulders, climbing through breaks in trees, and melting under the hot, humid sun. My hat stayed in my hands as we walked, fanning my face. It was close to noon.

"Yeah, Kevin," Joey said. "I wanna kill all dose losers. How could dey jus' steal our food and smokes like dat? It's so wrong!"

He clearly misses smoking more than toilet paper. I laughed a little.

Kevin changed the subject. "Do ya think Jared was telling the truth about the water north of here?" He paused before explaining. "He's got quite an imagination—like the fact that he's king of the island—but he seemed really scared about the whole thing. What ya think?"

"If I was making up a story like that, I would have remained completely calm," Justin said. "Actually," he continued, "I would have been completely calm even if I wasn't making up that story." He laughed.

"Me too," Joey said.

Inside my mind returned to David's death. *Are the skulls and skeletons and my classmate's death connected somehow?* However, I didn't want to think about that, so I looked straight at Joey and said, "Bull! You know for a fact that you would be crying to your mama if you'd picked up a skull."

"I would not be cryin' to her," Joey said.

"No ya wouldn't," Kevin said. He laughed. "Ya never talk to yo' mom anymore, Joey."

Joey laughed.

I'm confused. I spoke, "Maybe not, but you'd still be crying."

"I'm not dat big of a baby."

I looked him in the eyes as I called him a liar again. "I heard what you two were talking about the first day here. Something about how you're scared of getting scared. Wow."

"Whatever, homie," Joey said. Then he laughed at Kevin. "I told ya someone was hidin' dat day. It was Jay."

"Duh," I said. Then I changed the subject. "Later today I'm going to go see if Jared was telling the truth. Anyone want to go with me?" No one volunteered, so I continued. "Okay, I'll go alone. Or maybe Bryce will join me."

By that point we had just stepped back into camp. The sound of running water was soothing to my ears. It reminded me of the time when Camille and I had journeyed to the river together. It was such a fun, relaxing time, with my favorite person in the world. *Now she's dead. Unburied. Exploded into bits.* My eyes grew misty. I sat down with my back against a tree and closed my eyes.

Thoughts of Camille's beautiful body being broken into a million tiny pieces, all burning in the flames of an explosion rocked me to sleep. *How can a good God,* I was asleep before the thought was completed.

CHAPTER 12

(August 2003)

I WAS IN A CAR, being driven somewhere. Sitting around me was younger-Jay, younger-Joey, younger-Kevin, and who I assumed was younger-Bryce. I recognized Joey and Kevin from the earlier flashbacks, except that Joey's glasses were missing. Three other kids were in the car as well, and, I recognized the car from my earlier flashback when I was playing baseball with Joey. It was his family's big-white-van. *Where are we going?*

It was at that moment that the audio around me faded in. The seven kids—including Jay—were chattering about how they were all headed to an awesome amusement park for Joey's and Danny's birthdays. Danny was Joey's little brother, and he had short blonde hair in sharp contrast to Joey's mop. They had decided on a water park to celebrate their big day; Joey was turning twelve and his brother was turning ten. The waterpark was called Atlantis Kingdom and it was the first time Joey and Jay and Kevin and Bryce had been able to hang out together in a very long time.

I remember this vaguely: girls, girls, girls. Let's see what I come to remember that I had forgotten.

*　　　*　　　*

THEY FINALLY ENTERED THE PARK, and I watched as the wheels spun in everyone's head to the effect of: "This place is awesome! Let's go!"

Before anyone could actually verbalize anything, Joey's mother, the chauffer of the occasion, spoke up. "Joey, don't do anything until you get properly sun screened."

"I won't," he replied as he set his stuff down by a vacant set of five pool chairs. He immediately grabbed the sunscreen out of his bag and began generously applying it.

"You missed a spot," Kevin pointed out.

"Where?"

"It's about this big." He spread his hand open, and smacked it against Joey's back. "Right there."

"Ouch! dude," Joey exclaimed.

"I'm kidding. I'm kidding."

"But seriously, Joey," his mom said, "make sure you get it covered well. I'll be watching our things while you guys have fun. Make sure you don't let Danny out of your sight."

"Okay, mom," said Joey who quickly finished his haphazard sunscreen job. He threw the sunscreen bottle down and ran off with his friends. Danny and his buddies were close behind.

"What are we gonna do first?" Jay asked.

"Yeah, what are we gonna do?" Bryce echoed.

"Let's check out that waterslide," Joey replied. He pointed ahead at a large, enclosed, twisting and turning slide painted jet-black.

I watched as Jay's jaw dropped when he saw it. He quickly closed his mouth so his friends wouldn't see. The slide looked extremely scary, even to me. *I hate enclosed slides. I like to know where I'm going and enclosed slides are pitch-black dark inside. I'm not scared of the dark. Just rides that are in the dark. It's so freaky.*

Jay decided to be brave, and said nothing about being scared to ride it. *I know he wants them to think he is cool. And what's worse than not being man enough to go down a waterslide? Nothing.*

Finally they reached the slide, and they all stopped. I looked up to see what they were staring at. It was a two hundred foot tall, winding staircase to the top that was completely packed full of people.

"Let's not do this right now," Joey said. "The line's too long."

"But I wanna do it," Danny protested. His little group nodded their approval.

"Then go for it," Joey said. "But we aren't going with you."

"But mom said to stay with me," Danny reminded him.

"Mom won't know," Joey retorted. "Meet us in the lazy river."

Rebelliousness set in early for this kid, I thought. *This explains the crazy kid on the island who smokes, cusses like a sailor, and acts like he's the boss but doesn't lord it over people like Jared does. It all makes sense.*

"Fine." Danny conceded. He and his three friends walked over to the back of the super long line.

Joey then decided on going to the wave pool for a little while. Jay, Bryce, and Kevin eagerly followed as he led the way. I floated along behind them, almost as if I wasn't even there at all.

"That line was ridiculous wasn't it," Jay said, overstating the obvious.

"Yeah," said Kevin. "I think we all saw it."

"I know, it's just that—"

"Just what?" Kevin asked. "Were you scared?"

Well, there goes my—I mean his—cover.

"No," Jay lied.

"You were scared," Kevin replied, almost omnisciently.

"No I wasn't." Jay was lying. Inside, I knew that his only thought was that now the teasing would not stop all day.

"Jay was scared of a waterslide?" Joey asked tauntingly.

Apparently he overheard them and had to join in.

"I thought you weren't scared of anything," Joey queried.

"I'm—" Jay interrupted himself and exclaimed, "Look at that!" He motioned his head over toward a tall blonde in a red bikini, standing by a drink shack, sipping a cola. He had said it too loud though, because she looked at him and his face immediately formed a sheepish grin.

Retard, I thought. *He always scare girls away, even as an eleven year old.*

"Go talk to her," Joey whispered to him.

"Yeah," Kevin agreed. "If you do, we'll stop teasing you."

"Okay," Jay said. "I'll do it." He started to walk over to where she was standing.

I watched him as he walked, staying by the other three. I could clearly see him checking her out, and it made me uncomfortable, especially since he was so obvious about it. *You can't be obvious when you check out a girl, idiot,* I would have said if it would have helped anything at all. I decided to observe her appearance in detail as well. *Why not? She can't see or hear me. Apparently I've already checked her out anyways.* Her skin was beautifully tan. Her hair was clearly bleached blonde—it almost looked white. Her legs looked perfect. She glanced over her shoulder to notice Jay checking her out, and I got a moderate look at her face. Her eyes were green. Her lips full. Her nose was straight and perfectly sized. *Wow,* I thought, *I'm looking at an angel. She's probably my age too; my current age, not Jay's age.* I smiled. *I'd talk to her now if I could.*

I watched as Jay glanced back over his shoulders to see his friends mouthing, "Go on, dude," to him. So he continued. He turned back around, and she was gone.

Where'd she go? I watched as he turned around and sauntered back to his group.

The teasing will surely start back up, I thought.

When he reached the guys they all laughed. "She saw you coming and she booked it. Hahaha."

I watched as his head dropped and I knew that Jay felt bad. Then his head jerked up and he said, "I'd like to see you guys do any better."

Smart kid.

"Challenge accepted," Joey and Kevin replied.

"Bryce?" Jay asked.

"We'll see," he said timidly. "I like someone right now."

"Oh you do?" Joey asked. "Who is it?"

Bryce gave a name that meant absolutely nothing to me. "Katrina Callaway."

"Oh. I got you," Kevin said. "She know you like her?"

"No, but—"

Joey interrupted. "Then she won't care if you flirt. C'mon, dude."

"Okay," Bryce finally agreed. He looked at Jay, "Challenge accepted."

Now I knew that Jay felt alone. Bryce had been on his team for a minute there and now he was on Joey's team. Jay muttered under his breath as they continued toward the wave pool, "I don't really care. It's kind of fun getting teased because it makes me the center of attention. They don't mean it anyways; we're close friends." I could hear it clearly, almost as if our minds were melded together, though he didn't say it loud enough for Bryce or Kevin to hear, both of whom were walking right next to him toward the wave pool.

*　　　*　　　*

WHEN THEY ARRIVED, Joey was the first to speak. "Dude," he exclaimed, "it's bikini heaven!"

I had to agree. *There are tons of them. All of them are beautiful and all might as well be available for Jay to talk to. I just hope he'd be able to get up the courage to say "hi." That would make his day, make me proud, and make his friends respect him.* My eyes scanned the area again. *Dang, they're beautiful.* I glanced around to realize that Jay was standing by himself. Joey was walking toward a brunette in white. And Kevin and Bryce were walking toward twins in purple and blue, respectively. *Well, this sucks,* I thought to myself. *Why is it so hard for me, regardless of my age, to talk to girls? Even on the island, I couldn't bring myself to talk to Julia, Kimberly, or Nicole. And then, when Jaime wanted to talk, I acted like a scared little boy toward her. Why? Not to mention: how did Camille ever fall for me?* That thought hurt.

Jay muttered something else to himself. "I'm scared. Girls make me really nervous. It's probably because they are so much better looking than me. I hate my hair-cut! My face looks weird; my smile is all lopsided. I'm not strong, especially compared to Joey. And I'm so white that Joey has joked that I probably glow in the dark without a shirt on."

He must have forgotten the script for his inner monologues, I decided. *How'd he forget his stroke in the midst of that?*

And, for another thing, Joey has no business making fun of anyone for being white. He's the definition of sour cream.

I glanced back at Jay's friends to see Joey fall over, splashing the girl in white. It freaked her out so she ran away. Bryce and Kevin were doing a little better. At least Kevin was. He was talking to 'purple suit' as I had dubbed her, while 'blue suit' was standing next to her, awkwardly glancing from Bryce to Kevin to her friend.

Joey walked up to Jay, soaking wet. "I was so close, dude."

"I noticed." Jay laughed. Then Jay continued. "Look at Kevin," as he pointed to him.

"Lucky dog," Joey said.

*   *   *

LESS THAN TWO MINUTES LATER, Kevin and Bryce had returned.

"I did it," Kevin announced.

"I saw," Jay replied. "Good job, I guess."

"What were their names?" Joey questioned.

"The one in purple was Cathy. And the one in blue was Sam—short for Samantha."

"Where are they from?" Jay inquired.

"Riverside," Bryce replied, obviously stealing thunder from Kevin.

"How old are they?" Joey asked. *He would,* I mused.

"Cathy is fourteen. Sam is thirteen," Kevin said proudly.

91

"They're not twins?" Jay questioned, sounding surprised.

"Nope," Bryce answered.

"Why'd they leave?" Jay asked.

"They had to get back to their boyfriends." Kevin looked upset.

Jay laughed. "Well that's too bad."

Don't act like you aren't upset. I was disappointed in Jay all of a sudden. *He obviously wanted Bryce and Kevin to do all the work so he could reap the benefits.*

"Let's get to the lazy river," Joey began, "so Danny and them can find us."

"Good idea," said Jay as they set off.

They reached the lazy river, and Joey randomly proposed a new challenge. "The goal is to swim up to a girl, rub her leg, and swim away."

"Sounds fun," Kevin answered.

Sounds dumb, I thought. *I can think of a better, crazier challenge any day.*

"Let's see it," Jay said, challenging Joey.

"Okay. Give me a target."

Just then, the brunette in white floated past and Joey said, "Excuse me, boys." He slowly swam up to her and when he reached her, he went under, grabbed her leg, and swam away.

Actually, Jay had no idea if he actually touched her until she jumped to her feet and looked around—freaked out. "Stupid little boys," she shrieked, shaking her arms as she splashed away from Joey.

A minute later, Joey returned and said, "Beat that."

Thus it had started. Kevin had the next tag, and then Joey and Kevin decided to get as many as possible.

When Danny returned, I instantly remembered exactly what Jay was thinking. *He's nervous. One of Danny's friends is his brother Zeke. Jay can't afford to let Zeke find out that they were flirting with tons of girls. He'd go home and tell their mom instantly. Then Jay would be grounded for life.* I watched as Jay tried to get

Danny's group to go away and do their own thing as quickly as possible. After what seemed like an eternity, they finally left.

I could see that Jay was perfectly content watching Joey and Kevin make fools of themselves. It was hilarious, even for me, to watch them swim up, grab someone's leg, and swim away.

Joey must have decided that it was time for Bryce to join the game. He swam up to Bryce and said, "Hey dude, you see those girls over there?"

Bryce affirmed the question.

"Go grab one of their feet. Don't forget to be sneaky."

"No problem."

He swam over, splashing like crazy, right up to a red-headed girl—fifteen years old tops—swimming with her friends. She saw him before he got there and didn't even flinch when Bryce grabbed her leg.

Jay, Joey, and Kevin all laughed hysterically as Bryce swam back. I shouted, "Get it, bro!" even though no one could hear me. *I remember this so clearly. They do this for the rest of the day.*

"Dude, that was awesome!" Joey exclaimed.

"She totally let you get her though," Kevin added.

"No," Bryce protested. "It was a surprise."

"Not at all," Kevin said. "I was watching the whole thing." He imitated Bryce's swimming style—flailing his arms up and down in the water—and said, "She likes you. There's no other explanation."

"Whatever," said Bryce.

"Your turn, Jay," Kevin challenged.

He's going to fail, I thought. *You got this, Jay, I believe in you. Don't let your older self down.*

"Okay." Jay seemed primed and ready. "Pick the girl."

"Go for her," Kevin replied, as he proceeded to describe a black-haired girl in the red-head's group.

"Okay," Jay said. I watched him swim off. He was halfway there when I saw him come up for air, and I realized that they were all staring at him. I didn't think twice, thinking, *They'll let him pull a Bryce for sure.* But I was wrong. They swam away. As fast as possible, but Jay didn't know. He kept swimming toward them, trying not to come up for air. Right about when he must have had no air left, I saw him stand up, holding his head. He was shaking it back and forth. *Did he swim into the wall? Typical me, I guess,* I decided.

I turned to see Joey, Bryce, and Kevin howling with laughter. Jay's fail was funnier to them than when Bryce had been allowed victory. *The teasing will continue for sure,* I thought.

I turned my attention back to Jay. He was trying to swim upstream in a lazy river. It took a couple minutes, but he finally returned.

When he did, Joey said, "Dude that was the highlight of my day. I'll remember that forever."

The laughing continued, and I watched as Jay joined in. *If you can laugh at yourself, you'll make it in life.*

CHAPTER 13

(Day 3, 2:00 p.m.)

BRYCE WOKE ME from the dream. "Hey Jay, what's up?"

I looked up, wiping dirt and sweat from my own eyes, to see him seated next to me. He was holding his black book in his right hand and a blue duffel bag in his left. *That's my bag*, I thought, though how I knew it I didn't know. I sat up and scooted back against the palm tree I was next to. "I just woke up, so I guess I am," I said, doing my best to answer his question in my pre-alert state. "What about you?"

"Not much. I just finished reading, and I found your duffel bag on my way back, and I figured you might want it. I don't know what's in it, so maybe you won't. I don't know though. It's here if you want it."

I couldn't help noticing that he seemed to be stumbling over his words as I took the duffel bag out of his hands. "Thanks." I briefly wondered why he wasn't talking straight, but then decided it didn't matter. I unzipped the main compartment and transferred my CHEEZ-ITS from my pocket to the bag. *They're crushed beyond all reason, but they're still edible.* I zipped the bag back up.

My mind went back to the dream. I remembered that like it was yesterday. *Joey, Kevin, Bryce, and I being twelve-year-old girl-chasers. Fun times. If I remember correctly, that was when I first became fascinated with the female gender. Prior—girls were gross; after—girls are intriguing.*

Bryce cut my thoughts short. "How was your nap?"

"Good," I said. Then I got curious, "Do you remember that time when we went to Atlantis Kingdom for Joey's birthday?"

He nodded his head to say yes.

"I dreamed about it during my nap."

"Really?" Bryce said. "That was a funny day." He laughed. "Have you had any other dreams like that?" He shifted nervously, flipping around pages in his book—opening and shutting it.

I watched Bryce suspiciously. *He's up to something. Is he really my childhood best friend that he claims to be?* I put that thought out of my mind quickly, given that I had just had a dream about him.

But how trustworthy are dreams? my mind asked.

"I've had a dream of something from my past every time I've fallen asleep or gone unconscious."

"Seriously?" Bryce stopped flipping around in his book and looked at me. "Me too." He paused. "Like last night I dreamed about the time we went trick-or-treating together and played blackjack and bet candy when we returned."

I didn't remember that experience so I couldn't comment. All I said was, "So I'm not the only one?" *That's a relief. I thought I was going crazy.*

"Nope," Bryce said. He started moving to his feet as if he wanted to leave, but he kept tripping on shrubs and was unable to get his balance. His book fell to the ground and flopped open to reveal four columns of text so small I could not make it out from where I was sitting.

I couldn't deal with it any longer. He was acting plain weird. "Are you okay, bro? You're acting awfully strange. It's like you want to go somewhere else, but you don't. Don't get me wrong; if you want to stay, I'd be glad to talk, but if you want to leave, I've got tons of stuff to work through in my mind that will keep me occupied. Just let me know."

"I'm fine, dude." He said. "Seriously, I am. But I'd be totally down with staying and chatting for a while." He stopped trying to stand, and reverted to flipping his book open and closed.

My curiosity got the better of me. "What were you reading all morning?" I asked.

He became instantly still. It was almost as if he hadn't wanted me to ask that question. Then he spoke. "I was reading my Bible. To be specific, the book of First—"

It took me a few seconds for it to register, but when it did I was on full defense. I interrupted and asked, "Since when do you read your Bible?"

His response was immediate. "Since God snatched me out of death."

I was dumbfounded. *That phrase makes zero sense to me.* "Huh?"

"Since I became a Christian." He laughed. "Sorry for the theological wording."

I ignored his last sentence. As I responded, I rubbed my hand through my hair in a frustrated, fatigued fashion. "I'm a Christian too, but I don't read it. It doesn't help at all." I was still rubbing my hand through my hair

"Are you sure?" Bryce asked pointedly. All of a sudden he wasn't the nervous, fidgeting wreck I'd just been observing.

I wondered where nervous Bryce had disappeared to. I answered his question anyway. "Yeah. Every time I read it, nothing happens." *Camille. Jared. Stroke. Reasons could be stacked up higher than the Eiffel Tower; there's no way that the Bible is useful to me.*

"That's not what I meant," Bryce said. He looked serious. Serious like death was in the air, as he looked me straight in the eyes and flipped open what I now knew was his Bible. Then he dropped the bomb on me: "Are you sure you're really a Christian?"

Seriously? Bryce, the kid who rescued me from Jared, is now trying to get me to question my salvation? I'm the Christian. I know all the verses. I just had a dream in the past few days to prove that one. I have all the answers. I've never had sex. I've never gotten drunk. I've never gotten high. Bryce, Joey, and Kevin are the opposite of me, and I'm not a Christian? Really? It was ludicrous. I spoke, "I prayed the prayer at age seven and age ten and age twelve. Maybe even more. So yes, I'm a Christian." *Besides, he knows this. We grew up at church together. He's seen me. He should know.* I wondered how evident my frustration was.

"That prayer really doesn't mean anything, Jay," Bryce said, wiping sweat away again. "Matthew 7:23 makes it clear; First John 2:19 also. Check it out for yourself."

He was still holding what he claimed was his Bible, so I told him to prove it. "Show me yourself."

Bryce flipped the book open, flipped over some more pages, scanned his finger down a column, and started reading. "Matthew 7:23. 'And then will I declare to them, "I never knew you; depart from me, you workers of lawlessness".' "

"Once saved, always saved though," I reminded him. I'd heard it my whole life. Now he was trying to lie to me and say I could lose it. *Are you an idiot, Bryce? I don't even do bad stuff. I smoke, occasionally, and try to get girls—which fails—but otherwise I'm a good guy.* I was totally annoyed with him. *Honestly, if anyone is in the wrong here—it's not me. He's the one shoving his legalism down my throat. He's the one telling me I'm going to Hell. Aren't Christians supposed to be loving?*

"That is true," said Bryce, as he swallowed nervously. "If you are saved, you can never lose it." He emphasized 'never'. "The only question is: are you truly saved?"

I'm alive. I'm saved from a plane wreck. Camille is dead. It brought the memory back. "Shut your damn mouth, Bryce! My girlfriend is dead. Stop criticizing my Christianity. I believe that Jesus died for my sins so leave me the hell alone. I'll be in Heaven when I die. I swear."

"Okay, man," Bryce said calmly, despite my tirade, as he stood to his feet. "I'm glad you believe that. Here's a final challenge. Read the book of First John. Then come talk to me again." He walked away.

Déjà vu, I thought. *First John. Someone told me to read that recently. But who?*

I looked around and it was then that I realized that Joey, Kevin, and Justin were gone. Bryce sat down next to the pool and dipped his feet in. *I don't want to see Bryce. He makes no sense. How can he call himself my friend and say I'm not a Christian?*

Camille. *I miss her so much.* I wished she was still alive. *I could use a big hug and kiss right now. Why was she the only one to die?* It wasn't fair. *Couldn't it have been Jaime? She hates me. She should have died; not Camille. It's not fair!* That's when the tears flowed. *I need to get my mind off her.*

My mind spoke up at that very moment in an attempt to curb my thoughts. *Camille wasn't the only one to die. What about that one kid this morning?*

I pushed that thought away, as I unzipped my duffel bag to see what I had brought along. The CHEEZ-ITS came out first, then a couple random t-shirts, then a pair of jeans, then some shorts, then a button-up t-shirt, and then a notebook. Buried at the bottom of the bag was a little blue book whose spine read: "Holy Bible (NIV)".

I threw it against the nearest palm tree and it fell open, cover up, in the dirt. I threw everything else back in my duffel bag in the order that it came out, except for a grey t-shirt that I put on to give my reddened torso relief from the sun, and I walked out of camp past my Bible. Before I passed it though, I gave it a good kick, and it landed next to the pool, next to Bryce. He looked at me as I ignored the book and kept walking.

His eyes were moist. His lips were moving, but no words were coming out. *He's completely lost it!* I reasoned to myself. I felt his gaze follow me as I sauntered off into the forest of dead palm trees. They would be my friends for the next few hours; *at least they don't lie to me and tell me my beliefs are a sham. They simply shut up and stand there. I wonder if Bryce has pulled the same self-righteous baloney on Joey and Kevin? If anyone needs a sermon it is them; not me.*

I needed to get my mind off Camille, Bryce, Christianity, and God. I remembered then what Jared had said about the skeletons at the north end of the island. I waited until I could no longer see Bryce behind me, and then I turned north and decided to check it out.

*   *   *

I SAUNTERED AWAY from camp, kicking at every dead plant that I could find without deviating too far from my course. *Really? I'm not a Christian?* I vaguely remembered the fact that all my friends had gone crazy during high-school, but I had assumed that was just partying and stuff. *I didn't know Bryce became a holy-roller. He chases girls. He smokes. He drinks. I only do one of those things.* My mind went back to an earlier dream. *If people think I'm supposed to be a pastor, doesn't that mean I'm saved?* It made sense to me. *Bryce is a jerk. There's no way I'm not a Christian.*

Are you sure? another voice in my head asked.

"Shut the hell up!" I yelled audibly at myself. Often the voices in my head were at odds with one another, and I highly disliked the mental disagreements that ensued.

I tripped on a rock and hurled a river of expletives as I went down, scraping my knees. *People really make me mad*, I decided, blaming my mouth on Bryce's forced conversation.

As I stood to my feet, I realized why I tripped. The terrain had completely changed. I had left the shade of the forest and had entered an almost treeless wilderness with the sun beating down on me. I had left the soft sand and was now about to start walking on dark red rock, full of tiny holes. The dead trees that were standing in this portion of the island were few and far between. Most were mangled, splintered, and fallen over, with a few cases where part would be protruding out of the rock. The whole landscape emanated eeriness. I was happy I was wearing shoes to cross this new terrain.

The heat was getting to me. I had spent too long without a shirt—which had not cooled me off, only gotten me burned—but now I felt constricted in the t-shirt I was wearing. I decided to take it off, and I tucked it in my waistband. Wind was nonexistent, but

100

the increased freedom of my upper body greatly added to my comfort level, though it did nothing to free me from the strong hand of humidity pressing down on me.

Camille is dead and it's God's fault.

And Camille took me back to Bryce. *Dang it. I should have brought that up to Bryce. Maybe 'Mr. Christian' can explain how an all-powerful God can't keep my girlfriend from dying. Or how an all-good God won't heal my left hand.* I figured I'd ask the next time I saw him, even though I really had no desire to ever see him again. *Self-righteous people drive me insane.* According to the poster-boy of self-righteous idiots, I wasn't even a Christian. It was preposterous. *I prayed the magic prayer. I admitted I'm a sinner. I believed Jesus died for me. I chose to follow Him. I'm a Christian. Duh.* Just then another thought popped into my head. *Bryce saying I'm not saved is like me saying Camille isn't dead. That's crazy. I saw her with my own eyes. She was dead. Therefore, I'm a Christian. I was there when I prayed. I know it. Bryce is confused.*

I tripped over a rock and cursed as I fell. I stood up and continued on my way. I could see the ocean in the distance. *Almost there. I wonder if Jared was telling the truth?*

Jared. *What did I ever do to deserve the teasing he gave me? Will I ever know? All I know is that if I am ever given the chance, I'll give him a taste of his own medicine. I'll pin him to the ground and wale on his ass until he's a bloody mess. If only—*

The porous rock gave way to sand as I stepped onto the beach. Water stretched away from the island as far as the eye could see. There was nothing special about that since I had grown up with Southern California beaches and was now trapped on an island, but something about the area definitely took my breath away.

Two, tree-lined sandbars stretched out from the main island and formed a sort of bay in between them. The first thing that stood out to me was that these trees were actually alive. The greenery on these palm trees stood in stark contrast to what was in the bottom of the shallow bay—currently devoid of water. It was full of bones.

I rubbed my eyes to double check, and sure enough, I was looking at a bone pile. Skulls, femurs, humeri, sternums, phalanges, and every other type of human bone were laying, as if disposed of, in the little bay. I cursed in confusion. *Where'd they come from? Whose bones are these? Jared told the truth? What a concept!*

I stood there, looking back and forth from the ocean to the bones, laughing that Jared had told the truth. *Joey's gonna wet his pants when he finds out.* I wanted to go back to camp and report back to them about my findings, but I really didn't want to see Bryce. *I want to rip off his head and add it to the collection out there. That's the fate all self-righteous jerks deserve.* I stayed where I was for several more minutes.

The last thing I remembered was something hard striking the back of my head. I collapsed to the ground after a few moments of trying to keep my balance, but everything went spotty and then I was unconscious.

CHAPTER 14

I AWOKE before I opened my eyes. I was getting really tired of repeatedly falling asleep, waking up, falling asleep again, and waking up again; and I was thoroughly sick of it being that I was somewhere new every time it happened. *Why can't I just live life the way normal people do? Wake up in the morning; go to bed at night; wake up the next morning in the same bed. Is that too much to ask?* I opened my eyes.

The whiteness surrounding me took me by surprise. I tried to sit up, but I couldn't move. My mind quickly raced back to the last thing I remembered doing. *I was standing at the beach, wondering why the palm trees on the sand bar were the only living palm trees on the island when something struck me in the back of the head.* My mind froze for a second. *Maybe I got paralyzed.* My mind cursed and railed at the thought. *I don't want to be paralyzed.*

Another voice spoke up in my head. *There's no way you're paralyzed. You're in Heaven. You've been here before. Remember?*

It made sense. *But why can't I move? Where else would I be?*

That was when I recognized the figures in white, hovering around the room like a group of angels, going back and forth from me to other parts of the room. As they moved, I could clearly see their mouths moving, but I could hear nothing. *Last time I could hear. Why can't I now?*

I lay still as confusion enveloped my soul. *If I'm in Heaven then Bryce is an idiot. He told me I was going to Hell. Won't he be surprised to learn that his self-righteous butt was wrong?* I laughed to myself. *What kind of a friend would even say something like that—judging me on my beliefs—let alone think it?* I tried to force my mind to think of something more positive. For some reason my mind always goes back to the most negative thing it can find. *Cami—*

I decided that was out of the question. *I can't think about the most beautiful girl in the world right now, especially when she's not with me.* Nothing else came to mind.

As my eyes darted around the white room, looking for anything else to think about, they stumbled across a picture of a skeleton on the wall across from me. *Bones. What in the world was up with that empty tide pool filled with bones?* It wasn't a very comforting thought. *The reason I ever even went looking for them was because Jared pointed them out. After I found them I got hit in the back of the head by something and woke up here. Weird.*

My eyes continued observing my surroundings. Everything was white. There was nothing that was not white anywhere I looked. My robe was white—*when will I get my harp?*—the angels were white, and then I barely noticed two people who were not dressed in white. *That's odd.*

The man was dressed in a green and black striped shirt. He had short black hair that was turning grey. He was right next to my head on the right side, mouthing something I couldn't hear. The woman was mouthing something as well. I noticed that her hand was on my chest, but if I hadn't moved my eyes that direction I wouldn't have known. I couldn't feel it at all. She was dressed in a blue top and had wavy brown hair. *I wish I knew what they were saying. Who are they anyways?*

I fought to keep my eyes open, but before I knew it, I was staring at the back of my eyelids.

CHAPTER 15

(February 2004)

I OPENED MY EYES, and I was in Jay's living room. It looked to be a different house from the last time I had been in his house. The walls were painted a dark tan color, instead of the plain white they had been at the previous house. *Oh yeah, we moved a couple months before going to Atlantis Kingdom for Joey's twelfth birthday. Actually, the move was right down the street from Joey's house. How much later is this?*

That's when I noticed what was going on. Younger-Jay was seated on the couch with family and friends at his side. To be specific, the friends were Joey and Bryce and Kevin. *Figures,* I thought to myself. Jay was dressed in a long-sleeve, green and white striped t-shirt, and it looked as if he was the center of attention. Envelopes and bags surrounded me. *What is it, his birthday?* I laughed to myself.

By this point in our lives, apparently, everyone was beginning to look the way they looked on the island. Kevin was getting muscular, and his hair was the shaggy-ish black hair that I had grown accustomed to on the island when his baseball cap was gone. Bryce was as thin as a rail, as he always was—apparently—and his hair was cropped short in a sort of flat-top cut. *He'll keep it shorter in the future,* I realized. Joey, on the other hand, was already dressing in baggy blue jeans, sagged half-way down his butt, and he was getting decently muscular as well. His face was suffering from a slight acne problem, and his glasses were still missing. His hair looked like someone had stuck a blonde mop on top of his head; it was cropped perfectly above his eyes, but his ears disappeared under it and it hung down to his shoulders. *That explains the acne,* I thought. *That'll all be buzzed by the time he gets to the island.*

Then I saw Bryce hand Jay a gift. It was the size of a CD and I wondered what it could be. Jay ripped it open and revealed a video game: SPIDER-MAN. *That game was awesome. I wonder what happened to it.*

Joey was next. His gift was "wrapped" in an envelope. Jay slit it open to reveal some money. Fifteen bucks. *Must be before Joey used all his money on smoking,* I thought. *Money is awesome. What a great friend.*

Kevin handed Jay a gift as well. It turned out to be a giftcard to TARGET. *I wonder what I bought with that.*

*   *   *

NEXT THING I KNEW, younger-Jay and his friends were walking around outside. *I'm starting to get sick of these flashbacks where people move around, and I'm forced to float around behind them.* It looked like they were walking down toward Joey's house. I recognized it as the place my last flashback originated at. *It is night though, so I could be wrong.*

"What are we going to do?" Kevin asked no one in particular.

"We gotta go to my crib," Joey began, "so we can get some stuff. I forgot my pillow and blankets."

His vocabulary is turning 'street' slowly but surely, and I was right about his house. I smiled on the inside.

"Lucky duck," Bryce said. "Why do you get to live so close? I forgot my AXE, but there's no possible way for me to retrieve that."

"Sucks for ya, I guess," Joey said.

Jay spoke up. "Why do you need AXE for a birthday party sleepover with all dudes? Isn't that stuff for magnetizing girls to yourself?"

"You don't know what could happen," Bryce answered. "It's best to be ready for anything."

By this time they were in front of Joey's house. He ran inside, leaving Jay, Bryce, and Kevin outside. Less than two minutes later he returned, carrying a pillow and a blanket. He handed the pillow to Bryce, reached into the blanket, and pulled out the biggest yellow flashlight I've ever seen.

"Dang dude," Bryce said. "That thing is huge!"

"I know, right? Ima blind people tonight." Joey laughed.

"I bet you will," Jay said. "Just keep it out of my dad's eyes. He'll be mad. We can get Zeke all we want though." His facial expression spelled trouble.

They walked back up toward Jay's house but got stopped before crossing the cul-de-sac that was in between Jay's cul-de-sac and Joey's house. Girls, at whom the guys caught a peek in the window of a house, stopped them.

"Guys, what're you doing?" Jay asked. *He must not have seen them.*

"There's some hot chicks living here," Joey said. "I think ima sleep outside tonight."

"Well ima sleep naked outside tonight," Bryce spit out.

Joey shouted, "Yeah, homie!" and gave him a high five.

Bryce? Bible reader? The one who claims I'm not a believer? Really? It could have upset me, but I chose to keep paying attention and think about that later.

Jay stuttered, "Let's go," as if that conversation made him uncomfortable.

"I want to knock on their door," Joey said, ignoring Jay.

"Do it," Bryce challenged.

"What should I say when they answer?" he asked.

Bryce thought for a few seconds. "Don't even let them answer. Run away first."

"Ding-dong-ditch?" Joey asked. "Sounds awesome!"

Jay wasn't so sure. Then he spoke, "Let's practice on my house first."

"Good idea," Kevin said. "We don't want to look like fools in front of the ladies. We need to be pros before we get them."

They all walked up to Jay's house. *Jay doesn't want to do it at all. He just wanted to distract them from the girls. Was I really that much of a goody-goody? I'm disappointed.*

They stopped at the edge of Jay's driveway and decided that Joey would be the first to ring the doorbell. He set his stuff down in a pile, walked away, and twenty seconds later was running back mouthing, "I did it!"

I heard the front door open, and watched, and followed, as the four of them booked it around the street corner. *Idiots,* I thought. *Joey left all of his stuff right there. They'll be caught for sure.*

"Who's next?" Joey asked as they walked back toward the driveway. The coast was clear.

"I'll go," Jay volunteered.

Really? I was surprised. Then it hit me. *He knows his family, and knows that he won't get in trouble from them. Others could claim disturbance of the peace and get him arrested—he thinks. He wants to fit in; apparently I've always wanted that.*

I floated behind as Jay walked up to his porch and silently pressed his doorbell. *DING DONG,* was all I heard. He ran as fast as he could back to the corner of the street, and I followed.

"I did it guys," he exclaimed.

Yeah you did, you little rebel. Where is this going? I wondered.

"Let's get those girls' house now," Joey said as he picked his blanket and pillow off the ground.

Bryce and Kevin agreed with a nod of the head, but Jay did not look pleased. However, Jay's opinion didn't matter as they started to walk down the street to the girl's house. *See, that's why Bryce didn't care what I had to say in our earlier conversation. He's never cared.* I noticed that Joey was clutching his pillow and flashlight tight, while his blanket was draped over his shoulder, and it caused me to laugh to myself and forget my animosity toward Bryce.

Joey stopped, set his flashlight down, and reached into his pillow. He pulled out a small cylindrical container. *AXE*, I realized. Joey spoke, "Give me a second, Bryce." I saw Bryce stop walking and turn around. "Let me spray this on myself so the girls can't resist me." *This kid is desperate,* I laughed.

"Give me some," Bryce said.

"Nope," Joey said.

Bryce tried several more times, but Joey was resolute. *He got softer as time went on,* I decided.

Joey turned back toward Jay's house carrying all of his stuff. "I'm going to drop this off," he said.

* * *

FIVE MINUTES LATER he came back, carrying only his flashlight.

"What took so long?" Jay asked.

"Yo' family wouldn't open the door."

"No duh," Kevin said. "They thought you were ding-dong ditching again.

They started walking back toward the girls' house. They were chattering the whole way about how awesome this was going to be; everyone, that is, except Jay. *What a goody-goody.* The house came into view. A guy was now sitting in a lawn chair in the driveway.

"It's their dad," Kevin said. "Let's get out of here."

The other three agreed.

"Looks like you wasted your AXE," Bryce said.

Gotta take a stab when you can, I said to myself.

As they turned around, they noticed a guy watching television through the window of the house opposite the girl's house. Trees attempted to cover the view through the window from the sidewalk, but they didn't stop Joey's vision.

"He's watching porn," Joey exclaimed in a whisper to the others.

"No," said Jay. He was obviously stunned, as he didn't even attempt to look through the trees.

Haha. He hasn't started yet, I joked. *He's missing out.*

"Yep," said Joey. "Let's see how this goes," as he quickly pointed his flashlight at the window and flashed it on and off.

They watched as the guy freaked out, jumped up, and turned off his television. Then they ran as well.

"He was guilty," said Joey, laughing.

Bryce and Kevin agreed and laughed too. *Come on, Jay,* I urged. *Why are you so stiff? Was I really like that?*

They went the rest of the way to Jay's house. Bryce walked up the porch first with Kevin and Jay following close behind. Joey was twenty feet behind them, still laughing and commenting to no one in particular about his flashlight antics. As Bryce walked through the front door he motioned to Jay and Kevin to look to their right behind the pillar next to his front door. Jay's mom was standing there motioning for Jay to be quiet. He kept walking and saw his sister, Noel, crouching behind Chester's cat house. Jay followed Kevin and Bryce through the door and left it open for Joey.

I remember this now. This is what Joey and Kevin were talking about the first day on the island.

When Joey reached the door he had no idea what was waiting for him. Jay's mom and sister jumped out yelling and Joey fell to the ground. Jay, Kevin, and Bryce laughed loudly, falling to the ground in the entryway. It looked like Joey was crying.

"That's what you get for ding dong ditching us," Noel said in the bossy voice only a seven-year-old girl is capable of.

"I'm sorry," Joey blubbered.

"Are you crying?" Jay asked as his mom and sister walked inside.

"No." Joey was insistent. "Why'd they have to scare me though? Why couldn't it have been you?"

Jay answered him, trying to cheer him up, "Because the funny stuff always happens to you at my birthday parties," Jay said. "Remember two years ago when that one kid spilled soda in your lap and my dad said you wet your pants?" Jay was laughing. "You're just prone to bad luck."

I hope Joey grows a brain soon, or the island situation isn't going to work out for him.

Bryce laughed too. "I wanna see that again."

"Shut up dude," Joey pleaded. "I don't feel good."

Jay laughed. "This is one thing I'm never gonna ever forget."

I blinked, and when I opened my eyes, everything was black.

CHAPTER 16

(Day 3, 8:00 p.m.)

I AWOKE AGAIN to see darkening skies overhead. However, I quickly put that out of my mind because something else hit me. *That dream was exactly what Joey and Kevin had been talking about when I first ran into them.* The assurance that I could totally trust them was helpful.

I glanced around my surroundings and realized I didn't know where I was. The wide open space with no trees, the sand beneath me, and the crashing of waves somewhere nearby told me that I wasn't in my camp. The sound the stream and pool made was a soft gurgle; this was the sound of a beach. Then I remembered my first thought on awakening: *the sky is getting dark, and it's not from clouds.* The sun was slowly falling below the western horizon, and the sky was a deep orange-pink hue. The moon was full and reflecting off the ocean in front of me. I still had not seen a single cloud in my whole time here, however long that might have been by this point. It seemed like an eternity.

I gulped out of worry that it was getting dark and I didn't know where I was. I immediately gagged when something gravelly hit my throat, and I began coughing up sand. This lasted a good three minutes before I was content with the taste and feeling in my mouth.

Another wave crashed in front of me. *Water,* I thought, as I stood to my feet. *I can rinse my mouth out.* I ran ten paces out into the surf, dunked my head under, and took a mouthful of water. I

112

swished it and spat it out. I repeated two more times before taking a fourth mouthful and swallowing it. *Salt water tastes so good.* I remembered that I always took at least one drink of the water every time I went to the beach as a child.

As I walked back up to the beach, the surf tried to keep me in its clutches. I tripped and fell three different times on my way back. As I stood up the fourth time, I felt a throbbing sensation in my head. It made me wince. *What caused that?* I thought, but then I remembered getting thumped in the head by something before going unconscious. I reached for the sore spot and felt around. Nothing seemed out of the ordinary, except that the whole area throbbed every time I applied pressure to it. *Weird.* The pain was sharpest where my hair ended and my neck skin began. I felt under my hair at the top of my neck and felt a raised bump. It was a jagged line going diagonal with my hair line.

My curiosity was peaked, so I decided to see if I could figure out what had knocked me out. There weren't very many sets of tracks in the sand. In fact, there were only two that I could see that were anywhere near the water's edge. *Probably Jared's from the day he discovered the skeletons and mine from today.* I followed the path I thought I had taken to the water back to where I had been unconscious, and there it was, next to a depression in the sand.

A chunk of white was all I could see in the fading light. I bent down, picked it up, and felt something crinkle. It was a piece of paper attached to a large knife blade that had a chunk of sharpened bone for its handle. A shoestring was keeping the piece of paper attached.

The fact that it was a bone handle completely escaped my notice at the moment. *I have mail,* I thought happily, but then realized someone had knocked me out with it. *I wonder what it says.* The light was too low from the sunset to try reading it at that time, but I decided that I would read it from the light of one of Joey's lighters as soon as I reached camp again. I put the whole set of treasures into my pocket.

113

I saw three sets of footprints from where I now stood. One came from the southwest and ended where I now stood. *The deliverer's footprints,* I surmised. Another set was obviously mine, coming from the southeast, and continuing all the way into the water. The third was Jared's—staying far from mine, but crossing the deliverer's halfway across the sand. *Well,* I decided, *if I'm to find my way back quickly in the fading light, I might as well follow my footprints back.*

My wet shoes squished in the sand as I set off southeast, taking my shirt out of my waistband and putting it back on. I was walking in the path I had created in my flight from Bryce's preaching. Three hundred yards into my journey, I came back upon the rocky terrain, and the footprints stopped. *Well there goes that idea.*

I turned north and walked back to the shore. One thing I clearly remembered from my first day on the island, and from every minute I spent at main camp, was that the pool in the center was fed by a stream coming from the north. *Where else would that come from if not the ocean?* I decided to walk the shoreline until I found the stream, and then follow the stream until I got to camp again. *I hope this works.*

*   *   *

MY WALK BACK to camp as the last of the daylight faded was much of the same thing I had dealt with since landing on the island. Walking. Brooding. Stumbling. The terrain was uneven as I walked the new section of the island, switching repeatedly between sand and shrubbery, and this was where the stumbling occurred. Tree roots and rocks and small bushes constantly threw off the familiar feel of sandy terrain, so I tried to stay as close as possible to the water throughout my walk, but I naturally veered back to the unclear path.

By the time I reached the stream that led to camp, the sky was completely dark. However, despite the total lack of clouds, no stars shone out through the darkness. The moon however, was brightly shimmering over the ocean to the north. At the stream I turned away from it, walking south toward my people. The darkness was eerie. I hadn't been alone in the dark yet on the island, and the feeling was very disturbing. *The night that Jacob met me by the pool was the closest I've come to being alone here,* I had remembered, which then led me to other thoughts.

I thought of the nature of the island: dead, dry, and deserted. No foliage of any worth—except those delicious berries—grew here. All the trees made the place look like a graveyard. The various-sized rocks strewn about randomly, filled with little holes, reminded me of the mountain rising out of the western half of the island. *Could it be a volcano? That would explain the death to most large foliage. How long since it was last active?* The fact that I'd seen no rain, or even a cloud, since ending up here helped me understand why nothing was green here, but those berries posed a problem for me. *Where do they get nutrients from?* I wondered. And then there was the lack of life on the island. Sure, people were here, but we had all been on the plane when it crashed. No one was native here, and no animals wandered around either, which reminded me of the book we had read that year at school. *In* LORD OF THE FLIES, *they chased pigs around the island they crashed on. Why can't there be bacon here?*

That took my mind to thoughts of God and goodness. *If God was here, and real, He'd not only keep my loved ones alive and help my body heal from the stroke, but He would provide us with decent sustenance.* Having all the walking time back to camp allowed me to dwell for a long time on my understanding of God: His supposed goodness, love, and power, and His perceived wickedness, hatred, and judgment. In addition, Bryce's claims were present on the forefront of my mind. *I'm not a Christian? That's the craziest thing I've ever heard.*

I missed Camille so much. In all honesty, I couldn't remember much about our relationship. *I know we kissed at least once, because of the picture she had, but was it a common occurrence? Was she a good girl, or was she the kind my parents said, "Stay away from"?* I wondered which I would have preferred, but then remembered that she was dead and it didn't matter. *Jared claimed I never got anything from her, but how would he know that?* The loneliness of the walk back to camp compounded all of these thoughts.

And then there was Jared. I hated him. I hated everything about him. I hated that he had a girlfriend on the island. I hated that he was running the place. *He can't tell me what to do.* I hated the fact that every time we ran into each other, I ended up getting injured. It was his fault that I had walked halfway across the island, looking for skeletons, which I found. *What was up with that? Where'd those people come from and how'd they die?* I decided not to think about it.

And then there was the knife and the paper in my pocket. *Jared made me search for skeletons. I found them. The handle on the knife was bone.* I let out a scream as the thoughts registered. I didn't want to think about what it could mean. And then there was David. He had been murdered earlier today. *Are the skeletons connected? Is this island really uninhabited? Is a psycho-killer here?*

My mind cut me off there. *That's ridiculous. There's no food here. How would a psycho-killer survive?* I let it go.

It seemed like it took me three hours from the time I started following the stream until the time I arrived back in camp. The going was difficult. There was no clear path throughout this portion, and the shrubs, dead trees, and rocks constantly had me stumbling and then yelping in pain. This perpetuated my negative thoughts. All I could think about besides the competing thoughts about Bryce, God, Jared, Camille, food, and skeletons was the piece of paper in my pocket. *Does it have writing on it? What does it say?* Finally I saw shimmers of light in the distance, and knew I was close.

"Joey," I called out. "Are you there?"

The shimmer stopped. A voice called out in response, "Jay, is that you?" It sounded like Bryce.

I cursed. *Exactly the person I don't want to see.* I responded that I was Jay, as I stumbled the rest of the way into camp. The shimmer came back as I walked the last fifty yards, and when I came to the end of the stream, and found the pool, the sight took me by total surprise.

Bryce was in the midst of Joey, Kevin, and Justin, and he was holding a piece of paper under the lighter Joey was holding. All three of them were looking at Bryce as he read, though I was too far away, and the words too hushed to be able to make them out. Kevin held a huge knife behind his back. In the shimmer of the lighter, I could see a strange look in Bryce's eyes. Whether it was a threatening look or a being-threatened look, I could not tell. There was a threat in the air, and I did not know why.

"What's going on?" I asked innocently enough. I was not prepared for what followed.

They all turned to face me. Joey spoke next, pulling up his pants to keep them from falling off. "Where ya been all evenin', Jay?"

"Knocked out on a beach," I said. Referring to me as 'Jay' instead of 'homie' put me on edge. I held up the knife and paper combination and said, "I got knocked out by this, though I haven't had a chance to open it up yet." I paused before adding, "Jared was right about the skeletons in the water by the way."

"We got one of those too," Bryce announced, completely ignoring my comment about how Jared had been telling the truth. "We were trying to read it when you arrived." He walked over to me, and extended his hand.

You want me to shake it?

"Hand over the knife and note," he said.

I listened without question.

Bryce took the note off the knife, pocketing the knife and dropping the shoestring on the ground, and muttered something about the poor soul to whom it had belonged. I was getting more and more confused. No one was acting the way they normally did. Joey wasn't his happy, joking, jovial self; Justin and Kevin hadn't

117

said a word; Bryce was acting like he owned the place. He began reading my note aloud while Joey held the lighter for him.

"It's written in blood; just like ours was. And it's directly addressed to Jay this time. It reads: 'Hey Jay. I hope you have been enjoying the island. Wasn't all that sand just delicious? Isn't it nice to finally be away from your parents for a while? I hope you make the most of it. We're gonna get to know each other much better really soon. I can't wait. What about you? Oh, and by the way, I apologize for the primitive nature of this note, but you gotta do what you gotta do. Know what I mean? Don't worry, your blood won't be used—yet. But watch your back regardless. Oh, and one last thing. Jaime, Jared's girl, is with me now. So don't worry about her slapping you anymore. Have a good life, or whatever's left of it. Red Savage, A-O-L'." I realized Bryce stopped reading when he said, "That's all."

I screamed as I forgot all my other problems and questions. *Who wrote that? Whoever it was was right next to me; he filled my mouth with all that sand. How's this psycho—whoever he is—know my name? How's he know I hate being around my parents? What's he mean by 'getting to know me better'? My blood? Is he going to kill me? She won't slap me, true, but Jared will think I stole her and he will kill me.*

My mind was racing a mile a minute. *I have no clue who this "Red" character is.* Before hearing the note, I'd thought the island was weird. I was now convinced it was dangerous. *A killer is after me, and I have nowhere to hide.* It was a terrifying thought that began another internal conversation.

Maybe I can swim to the mainland. The ocean is right there.
You're gonna be trapped here for the rest of your life.
Don't say that. Red is lying. I'll get away.
Don't count on it.

Who in the world is Red? What does A-O-L mean? What kind of sick freak kills people, writes with their blood, and threatens others? I wanted off the island. *Why haven't I seen a single boat or plane around here?*

Maybe Jared has gone on a murderous power trip. It made sense. It would explain why I was next.

It was then that I realized that Bryce was speaking to me. "Bro, you're in a heap of trouble."

"Tell me about it. Do you have any idea what's going on? Who is Red? Why does he know about me? How's he know I hate my parents? What the hell does A-O-L mean?"

"We know as much as you, bro," Kevin spoke. "We were actually looking forward to seeing you so we could get your input on our note."

"What did yours say?" I asked.

"Read it for yourself," Bryce answered. He pulled a folded piece of paper out of his back pocket and gave it to me. I unfolded it and, under Joey's lighter, read the blood-written message slowly.

HEY GUYS,

I HOPE YOU'VE BEEN ENJOYING THE ISLAND. IT'S NICE, ISN'T IT? WELL I MEAN, SURE, IT COULD USE MORE FOOD, BUT BESIDES THAT--IT'S GREAT. OUT HERE, IN THE MIDDLE OF NOWHERE, WITH NO ONE TO HEAR YOU SCREAM. PLENTY OF CUTE GIRLS. YOU ALL LIKE GIRLS RIGHT? NONE OF THAT OTHER WEIRD STUFF? WELL ANYWAYS, ENJOY YOUR STAY--UNTIL IT ENDS. COULD BE SOONER FOR SOME THAN FOR OTHERS. IN FACT, ONE OF YOU WILL BE GONE BY TOMORROW MORNING. GOOD LUCK. HAVE GOOD LIVES-- WHATEVER'S LEFT OF 'EM.

--RED SAVAGE, A.O.L.

My mind went into overdrive as I let the note drop into the sand. *The note he left with me said that not much of my life was left and my blood would be used soon. He's gonna kill me in my sleep tonight! I'm still a virgin; I don't want to be when I die.* I vocalized some thoughts in screams. "I don't want to die! I'm not ready yet, but he said I will. I wanna live. I wanna get married. I wanna have kids." I paused before screaming out in utter desperation, "Don't let him kill me!"

"Don't worry, Jay," Bryce reassured, "I've already decided that Joey, Kevin, Justin, and I are going to keep watch all night. No one can harm you."

That comforted me. *I have true friends. Friends who will keep stuff from happening to me. How'd I get so lucky?* But it still didn't ease the fact that I was scared out of my mind. (My anxiety problems that would resurface later in life were perpetuated by this event—the whole island experience.) Thankfully, my worries were distracted by a new conversation that began between my friends.

"When did ya decide that?" Kevin asked, referring to Bryce's decision.

"After reading Jay's note," he answered. "It was much creepier than ours, though nowhere near as straight-forward. This Red Savage character, whoever he is, is out for Jay. It's obvious." He folded his arms across his chest.

"I want first watch, then," Kevin decided.

"Okay," said Bryce. "Who wants second?"

Joey took it.

"I'll take third," Justin said dejectedly, "since that's all that's even left."

"And I'll take four," Bryce said. "Jay, you just get some rest."

"Sounds good," I said. "Thanks for doing this. Do we have any food yet?"

"Actually, yes we do," Justin announced proudly, rubbing his hand through his blue hair that was no longer spiked. "I got them all by myself."

"What did you get?" I asked excitedly. "Some animals? What kinds?" *It's been way too long since I've had real food. The berries were tasty, but they were no tri-tip or prime rib or bacon. I want meat.*

"No animals," Justin answered. "Berries!" A smile covered his face from ear to ear.

A frown formed on mine. *How can you be happy about berries? I need nourishment. Full course meal. Mainly meat. Retard.*

"Want some?" Justin asked me.

"Are you stupid?" I snapped. "I want real food. There's no worth in those stupid berries. Don't offer them to me again. I'd rather starve than eat anything less than meat the rest of the time I'm on this dang island."

Justin's smile was gone. He walked away slowly.

There was a lot that was driving me insane. *Who is Red? That alone is freaky. The continuous theme of my early life in the dreams is weird. Jared wants to kill me too. No good food is starving me to death. I am not a vegetarian; I'm a carnivore. I need sustenance. Camille is dead. I want the touch of a woman before I am murdered, but my one chance is dead, exploded into a million pieces at the bottom of the ocean. I'm allowed to be angry.*

Bryce called my name, and continued to speak, "You shouldn't—"

I cut him off loudly. "I don't want to hear it, Mr. I'm-better-than-you-cuz-I-actually-read-my-Bible. Don't tell me I shouldn't be angry. If what you told me this morning is true then your God is responsible for all this crap that's going on in my life. He's responsible for a killer wanting to kill me; He's responsible for Camille's death; He's responsible for my stroke. I could go on—"

Heavy and repeated footfalls interrupted my thoughts. *Thank God I'm not gonna get a sermon on that tirade.* I forced a smile.

"Who's there?" I shouted.

"It's Red," Bryce whispered to me. "You could use this more than me," he said as he handed me back the knife that my note had been delivered with, along with the note itself. "What am I going to do with two, especially since you're the one being pursued?"

"Thanks," I said in a hushed tone as I took it from his hand. Then I spoke about the current situation, trying to be positive, "Red wouldn't be that loud and obvious though, would he?"

The sound was still moving closer.

"That's what he wants you to think," Bryce began. "He's not dumb. If he was, he wouldn't have told you that you would die tonight."

It made sense. And it freaked me out. *I'm not ready to die. I hope it's not Red.*

The sound stopped, followed by a crashing sound, and an "ouch!" It couldn't have been more than twenty paces away.

"Who goes there?" shouted Bryce.

"It's Mike Anders," the stranger called back. "I fell and I can't move. Can you help me up, Bryce?"

*   *   *

JOEY, BRYCE, AND KEVIN helped Mike into camp. He was scratched up from plants smacking into his arms, legs, and face. He was dressed in long, straight—now ripped up—blue jeans and a striped t-shirt. On his head was a green baseball cap. Sticking out below his cap, his ears sampled a pair of diamond stud earrings. He was panting for breath—hands on his knees—and when the rush of questions hit him, he held up a hand saying he'd answer as soon as possible.

Kevin shot the first question. "Why'd ya sneak up on us, bro?" He wiped his face on his sleeve.

"I wasn't sneaking," he answered.

Duh. That much noise doesn't constitute sneaking.

"Then what were ya doing?" Kevin asked.

"It went like this," Mike began. "Ever since the crash, I've been chilling in that hell hole known as Jared Seydu's camp. It was all going great—more or less—until the day those gunshots went off. Great, because I was able to hide reasonably well. Not great, because," he paused, shrugged, and continued, "well you know why. It's Jared we're talking about.

122

"Nicole and I would hide out and chat, since we've practically known each other our whole lives. We've both gone to Desert Valley Church as long as I can remember. We're just friends, but I've had my eye on this one girl for a while who is friends with Nicole. So, I decided to use the extra time to get Nicole's opinion on whether or not it would be worth it to pursue a relationship with this girl. The talks went great. But then Jared disappeared after those shots went off.

"Our plane exploded this morning, and that's when things got retarded. Until that moment, life had been even better than it had been when Jared was around. Jaime, his girlfriend, was enjoying the power and not caring about a thing. That is, until the plane exploded. Then she became a control freak and had to know where everyone was at all times, because she let four kids get killed—"

I couldn't stop myself from interrupting. I'd been silent until then, but now I was worried. *I know about David, but the other three? Really?* "Four people—" I started. "Who died?"

"Four kids. Peter, David, Lola, and Jack."

Two of the names meant nothing to me. I couldn't remember for my life who they were.

"Now, if you'll let me finish," Mike continued, "where was I?

"Oh yeah. Four kids were killed so Jaime had to do an extra good job protecting the rest. It turned the whole place into a Nazi Boot Camp. Everyone had different jobs. Blake, Max, and I were made her personal body guards. Everyone else was on shelter duty or food searching.

"The shelters were pretty much built before we got here. Weird, right? But after Jaime got put in charge she wanted them taken from Robinson Crusoe status to HILTON status. Holes patched, roofs fixed; it took about ten hours. However, the food searchers came back empty handed.

"But being her personal bodyguard is probably the dumbest thing I've ever had to do. She—"

Joey interrupted. "She so hot dough."

Mike ignored him. "Blake, Max, and I had gotten sick of it. They told me that they had hidden some booze from the plane in the forest. We decided we would ditch our post and have a good time instead. We decided to leave at six this evening, but when I reached the rendezvous point, I was alone; Blake and Max had pulled a fast one on me. The next thing I heard was Jaime screaming about something, so I booked it out of the area and ran as fast as I could before she found me.

"I'm so happy I found you guys."

"What's so bad about Jaime?" Joey asked.

He only has one thing on his mind. "Dude," I began, "don't even think that. You don't want her." A disgusted look crossed my face. "She's not your type. Stick to Nicole."

Mike laughed. "That's funny. Nicole was asking about you, Joey."

"She was?" Joey was happy. "What' she say?"

"She asked, 'Whatever happened to that crazy Joey kid? Is he still locked up or what's new?' I told her you were here and she was hoping to meet up and catch up a little bit, but now that Jaime's in charge, it's probably not a good idea."

Joey was beaming. "She wants me. It's obvious."

I couldn't control myself. To Joey, "That doesn't mean anything." To Mike, "So you didn't get a letter from the psycho who owns this island? Jaime's not in charge anymore."

Mike's mouth dropped. "What are you talking about?"

I pulled out the note and showed it to him. "It's right here."

Joey tossed Mike his lighter, and Mike read the note quickly, folded it up, and handed it back. "Serves her right." He tossed the lighter back to Joey.

"You're telling me," I said. "That little—whatever you want to call her—drives me insane. I can't stand her." I yawned.

"Ya look tired," Joey told me as he yawned too.

"I think we all are," Mike said. "Let's go to sleep and talk again in the morning."

I'm not ready to die. I can't sleep yet.

"You get first watch, Kevin," Bryce reminded.

"Wait, what?" Mike asked. "Why are we watching?"

"You're not," Kevin answered. "According to another note we got, someone is going to die tonight, so me, Joey, Justin, and Bryce are keeping watch."

Mike nodded to say he understood.

"Toss me the knife, Bryce," Kevin said.

Bryce handed it over, carefully. "Hand it over to Joey in about four hours and then get some rest. Stay safe."

"Will do, bro. See ya in the morning."

Everyone said their goodnights, and within twenty minutes, everyone was asleep. Everyone but me.

I was worried. *The only thing I'm scared of is death. It's how I answer that question whenever I'm asked. Tonight it seems closer than ever before. I don't want to die. I've contemplated suicide before, but then I made a bucket list to complete first. Get drunk. Get high. Get laid. I've done none yet. I can't die.*

After two hours of similar thoughts, I finally fell asleep.

CHAPTER 17

(October 2004)

I OPENED MY EYES to see young Jay sitting at the computer in the upstairs hallway of his house. He had a blank MICROSOFT WORD document open on the desktop and he was staring off into space. I noticed the book that was open on the desk had a writing assignment for him to work on. It read, "Write a story where you meet an old friend after not seeing him/her for twenty years."

That can't be hard. How many friends does he have to choose from? Joey. Bryce. Kevin. Justin. It's obvious. I could type that bad boy up in less than twenty minutes.

I do know who I wouldn't pick if I was him. Bryce and I will not still be talking in fourteen years. He's gone off the deep-end religiously. And I mean, if I'm even alive to know or do anything in a week it'll be a miracle. But if that miracle occurs, Bryce and I will not be friends.

Jay minimized the WORD document, and opened up INTERNET EXPLORER, distracting me from my thoughts.

*   *   *

WHY'D I HAVE TO WATCH HIM on there? Did I really start that at that age? He can't be older than seventh grade. As I heard footsteps come upstairs, the red-headed, freckled face of the woman Jay had been watching on the screen was stuck in my mind.

Just then Jay's mom crested the top step to check on him and his homework. He minimized the internet and quickly pulled his document back up.

"How's it going?" she asked.

"Not well," he answered. "I don't know where to start."

You weren't even trying, you little pervert. Looking at girls in bikinis on the internet is not at all trying to write an essay about seeing a friend after twenty years.

"Start with your name," she told him.

He obeyed. He typed, "Jay Liyfer." He hit 'enter.' He typed "Creative Writing." He hit 'enter.' He typed "10/7/2004." He spoke, "Now what?"

"Give it a title," she offered kindly.

She's going to do the whole thing for him, I thought to myself. *Is this really my mom?*

"Like what?" Jay asked.

"It's based on a story called, 'After Twenty Years,' so you figure something out."

Okay. That's what I thought. I was gonna say, if she gives him the whole thing, that's totally not cool.

Jay spoke again. "What about this?" He typed "Twenty Years Later."

Her face showed disappointment. The title wasn't original, just slightly tweaked from the original. Her words confirmed him though. "Yeah. That'll work."

"Now what?" he asked.

"Write the story," she encouraged.

"About what?"

She was about to answer when the phone rang. She walked next door into her bedroom and answered it as Jay put his mouse pointer on the start menu, right clicked on the internet tab and closed it.

Yeah, you'd better hide that, dummy.

"Hello," came his mother's voice from her room. A pause. "Oh hi." A pause. "No, he's still doing homework. I can have him call you back when he's done though." A pause. "Okay, will do. Bye." She came back out to Jay.

"Who was that?" Jay asked.

"It was Joey. He wanted you to come down and hang out with him, but I told him that you would call him back when your homework was done. Write this story and you'll be free to go."

"I don't know what to do," he whined.

"Pick a friend who you get to catch up with twenty years from now after not seeing them. You could pick Joey, Bryce, or Kevin."

"Okay. I hang out with Joey every day, so I don't think we'd ever not see each other for more than a week at a time." He paused. "Kevin and I have never been that close, because he prefers to hang out with Bryce and Joey away from me." He paused again. "Bryce it is."

Stupid choice.

"There you go, Jay. Write your story. It only needs to be a page. The sooner you do, the sooner you can go play with Joey."

"Sweet. I'll print it off and give it to you before I call him."

"Okay," his mom said as she walked away.

I watched as Jay typed up the following story:

One day Jay Liyfer was walking around in an airport. Right before he got to the gate to board the plane, he saw his long lost friend Bryce Beyra, with his family.

"What's up?" Jay asked.

"Who was that?" Bryce replied.

"It's me, Jay Liyfer, your old friend," he replied.

"Hello Jay!" Bryce said, "Haven't seen you in twenty years."

"It's been that long?" Jay asked, "And who are these people?"

"This is my wife, Faith, and two year old daughter Chelsea. I also have a six-month-old son Bryce, Jr. We are going to Chicago to visit my wife's grandparents," he said, "And where are you going?"

"I'm going on business to Florida," Jay answered.

"Where is the rest of your family?" Bryce asked.

"At home," Jay replied. "My wife, Ashley is at home with our three year old son Tommy and six month old son Michael."

"Please get to gate fifteen for the flight to Chicago," the overhead receptionist said. Both Bryce and Jay went to the same area.

"It looks as if we are on the same plane," Bryce said.

"I guess you are right," Jay said. When they got to the plane they were seated across from each other.

"Hello again," said Jay.

"Where do you work?" Bryce asked.

Jay replied, 'At the NASA laboratory in Denver. What about you?'

"I am a test pilot for the Navy," he answered.

In a few minutes, Jay had fallen asleep. When he woke up the plane was landing.

"What are your brother and sister doing?" asked Bryce.

"Zeke plays for the NFL. He is on the Miami Dolphins. Noel is in college, and is a waitress at Outback. What about your family?" Jay said.

"My brother is in the Air Force, he flies F-22s. My sisters are both married and are stay at home moms." Bryce replied.

"Hope to see you in less than twenty years!" Bryce said.

"Same here, and have a good trip," Jay said.

"Thanks, you too," said Bryce.

And that was the end. *Interesting stuff,* I remarked to myself. *My writing has definitely improved since then.*

I yelled. "Jay, just so you know, in a couple years you're going to be trapped on a deadly island, so you'll probably never have to meet Bryce, the religioso, twenty years later. You'll probably both die on the island." He didn't hear, but I didn't care because I needed to get it off my chest.

Joshua Wingerd

The next thing I knew, my vision was fading to black. *Here I go again.*

CHAPTER 18

(Day 4, 3:00 a.m.)

I WOKE UP to pitch black darkness with a desperate urge to use the restroom. I didn't stand up right away though, because the dream was too fresh in my mind. *Why would I choose Bryce over Joey? There's no way that would work in reality. Me and Bryce never even hung out that much apart from Joey and Kevin.*

My thoughts took a different turn. *I have to go to the bathroom, but I'm too tired.* I tried to ignore the urge, but after several minutes it just made me miserable. I couldn't fall back asleep, and I also couldn't get comfortable, so I finally decided to stand.

When I stood to my feet I noticed Joey, eyes drooping and shoulders slumping, flicking his lighter on and off, attempting to sit on watch. "Ima take a leak," I announced. "Don't worry about me." *He's gonna be out any second, and then I'm a goner.*

Joey answered slowly, "Okay, homie. Don' be gone long."

I continued on my way. *At least he is awake,* I thought. I stumbled away into the darkness, ignoring all the thoughts of terror that flew through my mind, stood behind a large rock, and took care of business.

The dream was all I could think about as I walked back, choosing to focus on it instead of my perfectly reasonable fears of being snatched from behind and strangled to death by Red Savage. *What in the world is going on? Every time I get knocked out or fall asleep, I drift back into my childhood. Why? Is it supposed to teach me something? All it is doing is making me miss the old days.*

I walked back toward Joey, and he spoke. "I'm so tired, homie."

"That sucks, bro. I'm right there with you."

"Wanna chat? It'll keep me awake." Joey's eyes were clearly glazing over, as he flicked his lighter on and off again.

"I can do that," I answered. "How long do you got left?" In reality, all I wanted to do was sleep, but at the same time, I wanted to live more. Ultimately, helping him stay awake would help me stay alive. Also, I wasn't likely to fall asleep quickly on the rock hard ground I was forced to sleep on, especially in the sweltering heat that was killer even in the middle of the night. *It reminds me of vacations in the Midwest during the summer; I'd never be able to live there.* Finally, *As soon as I fall asleep, it'll just lead to another random dream from my childhood—yet again—so why sleep?*

"I'm done in 'bout an hour." Joey yawned.

"Thanks for doing this for me," I said. "I really don't wanna die." I was truly as happy as I'd been throughout this whole experience, and I was smiling, even though he couldn't tell in the pitch darkness.

"It's what homies do," Joey stated. "I've had yo' back as long as I've known ya."

"That's pretty much true," I acknowledged.

It would have been nice for there to be a fire or something—if only for the light, certainly not the warmth—but the repetitive flash of Joey's lighter was the sole source of nearby light. I looked up to see a starless sky—pitch black except for the full moon to the north.

"I worried about ya da whole time I was in Michigan," Joey said. "Not to mention, missed ya."

I didn't quite understand what he was talking about. *Michigan? Why was he in Michigan? Don't we hang out all the time?* I decided to answer appropriately despite my confusion, figuring he'd fill me in in the next few minutes. "Me too," I said. "How was Michigan?"

"It was coo', but dumb at the same time. All we did dere was get high. Drugs, alcohol, and sex were da main things we did. I got kicked outta my aunt's house, where I'd been staying, after da firs' two months. Da homies took me in. We had great times. Dere were some fine babes back there, homie."

"How fine?"

"Fine enough for me to not wanna leave."

"I bet you think any female is cute." I was more prone to tease when I was tired.

"Perhaps," Joey said. "Did I tell ya I almost got arrested back dere?"

"Seriously?" I was shocked. "What happened?" *Apparently, Joey's a cop magnet or something.*

"Well it went like this," Joey started. "I was chillin' outside and dis random guy came up to me, so we decided to chill together. Den he decided to go somewhere, and he asked me to tag along. I said, 'sure,' and followed him. All of a sudden he decided to rob dis old lady. I tried to get him to change his mind, but it didn' work. He robbed her, and I was with him—guilt by association or whatever—when he got caught. I went to jail for da night, which was better den da park where I woulda been, but still—I hate jail! I convinced da judge I was innocent and got freed. I went back to da homies and did drugs non-stop until I came back to Cali."

"Sounds like a waste of a year," I said. *How can anyone like drugs so much?*

"Kinda," Joey admitted, "but at least I got my GED."

"That's good dude. Now you need a job. As do I."

"After we get offa dis island, homie. No jobs here."

"True," I agreed. *If we get off.*

"But I definitely missed ya dis year," Joey admitted.

"Me too. Our old times were so much fun. Remember Atlantis Kingdom when we chased girls the whole time?"

"Oh yeah." Joey laughed. "Dey ran from you but let Bryce get 'em." He paused. "Good times."

"I know, right?" I was happy. *Reminiscing on old times is always fun.* The note from earlier had evaporated from my mind. "Remember when we ding-dong-ditched my house?"

"Yo' mom is evil," Joey said.

I laughed. "You were scared to death. You didn't eat all weekend. Not even cake."

"Ha ha," Joey laughed sarcastically. "Ya calling me fat?"

"You'd better believe it."

Joey punched me in the arm.

A loud snore from somewhere in our camp brought laughs from both of us.

"Remember those girls that threw Starbursts at you?"

"Yeah. Remember da girls dat drove up to my house and drove away after dey saw ya?"

"Yep." I laughed. "Good times. Though they were definitely scared of you—not me."

"No way," Joey said before explaining. "Dey said, 'Dis house?' 'Yeah.' 'Wait, dere's some ugly, skinny, white guy here. He wasn't here da last time. Wrong house.' Den dey drove away."

"You callin' me ugly?"

"You called me fat."

*   *   *

AFTER AN HOUR of more reminiscing, Joey decided it was time to wake up Justin. He walked over to where he was snoring away and shook him awake.

"What's going on?" he asked—half asleep.

"It's yo' turn to watch," Joey said.

"Already?" Justin rubbed his eyes.

"Yeah. Ya got it for da next four hours. When you're done, wake up Bryce." Joey handed him the knife. "Have fun, homie."

"I'll try," he said—yawning.

Joey lay down as Justin walked around camp, trying to wake up.

I lay down too. *Joey is awesome. Of the whole group, he is my favorite. The good times between us are awesome. I wish life could go back to how it was then. I wish I'd written that story about him. There's no way I'd ever not hang out with him at least once a week.*

I fell asleep with those thoughts in mind.

CHAPTER 19

(October 2005)

I FOUND MYSELF in a large gymnasium surrounded by what appeared to be a whole herd of junior highers. I saw a screen in the front of the room with a sign telling me where I was. It read, "Welcome to 'Clans' at DVC," and Easter island heads decorated the background. *Why am I here? The last couple of these flashbacks have been weird. If I could, I would skip them. Why am I even having flashbacks. Am I okay? What's wrong with me? That island is being stupid.*

A guy stood up on stage, and I watched him as he spoke into a hand-held microphone, reading off a piece of paper that he had pulled from his back pocket. "Welcome to Clans: Desert Valley Church's junior high youth program." He paused, cleared his throat, and continued. "I'm Ted Sweet, the youth pastor."

Down in front, a kid interrupted, "You mean minister." Next to him one of the guys held out his hand for a hi-five which he accepted.

"Don't interrupt me," Ted Sweet, said, coolly. He continued. "I'm the youth pastor—"

"Minister," the kid said again. "You haven't finished your pastor's degree. My dad told me. He's one of the actual pastors here."

"Dang. You'd better get some ice for that burn," someone else said. It sounded like Kevin.

An adult—who I assumed to be a leader—came up and called the three disruptive boys out of the large group. One of them was Kevin, and the other one looked like it could have been Mike. They walked back toward where I was standing, and I floated away, without my permission, over to where Jay was sitting. So that's why I'm here. *Jay is here.*

"Apart from that interruption," Ted continued, "let's get on with our night. First we have music, and then afterwards it's time to split off into your respective small groups, or clans. Have a great night."

*   *   *

NEXT THING I KNEW, I was in a smaller room with five kids besides Jay, and an adult leader. Joey was one of the kids. I didn't recognize the rest.

Apparently one of the kids was new, so they went around the circle and gave names. Besides Joey and Jay, there were four kids whose names I didn't catch. The leader introduced himself as Ray, and told the group that he worked for a sewage company. He connected that to the discussion by saying that if anyone was going through any junk in their life, he worked with it every day and they didn't need to be afraid. God would get them through, just like God got him through every day. It earned a giggle from the group, and an eye-roll from me.

Then Ray got more serious. He opened up his Bible to Matthew 11:28, and read through verse thirty. "Come to me, all you who are weary and burdened, and I will give you rest. Take my yoke upon you and learn from me, for I am gentle and humble in heart, and you will find rest for your souls. For my yoke is easy and my burden is light."

He continued speaking. "God wants to help you. Life is tough, but, if you put your faith in Jesus, He will help you. Do you have problems?" Everyone's hand went up. "We all do. What are some of yours?"

They went around the circle explaining what it was. Some said parents' divorce, others said school, and still others said girls. Jay said it was his left hand from his stroke.

Yep. That's the exact right answer. Or the fact that my girlfriend is dead. Or the fact that some psycho wants to kill me. I'm freaking out. God isn't helping.

"It can make you depressed. Maybe for some of you, you already are super depressed. Well this verse is saying it doesn't have to make you depressed. Give it to God and He will take care of it." Ray closed his Bible.

Wow. I started mocking what I was hearing. *"Give it to God; give it to God." What a bunch of garbage.*

Jay raised his hand and Ray called on him. "So, if I just pray, God will solve my stroke problem?"

"Yes," said Ray. He said something else, but neither I nor Jay could make it out.

Jay's going to pray more and more until his hand is healed. Well, he's in for a surprise when it doesn't happen.

Ray talked for another ten minutes and then closed in prayer. When he was done, all six kids ran out of the room with me floating behind them. It turned out that there was a giant game of dodge ball going on in the gymnasium, so they all joined in.

The game was chaos. No one was on a specific team. Everyone was throwing balls at everyone else. I watched as Jay grabbed a ball, snuck up behind Joey, and threw it as hard as he could at the back of his head. It bounced off his head and rolled away. Jay laughed. Joey turned quickly and jumped at him. They both fell to the floor. Wrestling match.

It isn't anger. It's just messing around. Knowing Joey, he was probably looking for a chance to start something anyways.

"This is the best part about Tuesday nights," Jay said as Joey pinned him to the ground.

"Ya enjoy getting beat up?" Joey asked.

"Well, no, but it's awesome to hang out with you. You're just messing around, right?"

The next thing I knew, Ted Sweet was pulling them apart. "This is church. No wrestling."

"But—" Jay started.

"No buts," Ted Sweet said as he walked away. "If I catch you two doing that again, I will call your parents.

Joey made a face at his back and let Jay go. They both laughed.

"Why can't he understand that it was just fun?" Jay asked.

And with that, everything went black.

CHAPTER 20

(Day 4, 11:00 a.m.)

I AWOKE to the heat of the sun bearing down on me from directly above. I heard voices. I stayed still—laying down, listening to what was going on—and tried to gather information before making my alertness known. The voices were tense, spoken in hushed tones, coming from behind me as I was lying curled up on my side on the ground.

"Where' dey go?" I recognized it as Joey's voice.

They? Who's missing? Jared and Jaime? I grew happy at the thought, but then remembered, *There's no possible way I got that lucky.*

Bryce's voice replied to Joey's. "I don't know."

"Ya were supposed to be watching," Joey accused.

"I never got woken up," Bryce countered back, wiping his arm across his face.

So people are missing from our group? Not other groups, but ours. Who's gone? Joey and Bryce are talking. I'm here. That leaves Kevin and Justin. My most recent dream was completely forgotten.

I decided to make my alertness and presence known, cutting Bryce off in the middle of a sentence I wasn't even paying attention to. "Who's gone?" I sat up, rubbing the sleep out of my eyes as I spoke, and taking off my shirt to help ease the sweating I had awoken to. I used it to wipe myself dry before I tucked it in my back pocket.

Joey answered my question somberly. "Justin and Mike are gone."

"What are you talking about?" I exclaimed angrily, as I stood to my feet to observe the surroundings post-kidnapping/potential double homicide. "I'm the one Red is after. It was clear from the notes that he didn't care about Justin and Mike." *Why take them?*

"They disappeared last night," Bryce explained.

"No, duh, Sherlock!" I yelled. "I have eyes. I can see that." I still had no desire to see or hear from Bryce.

At that point I noticed Kevin turn over where he was sleeping. He muttered, "Ya can't catch me, Mr. PoPo," in his near waking moment.

"Watch it, Jay," Bryce said. "He doesn't know yet."

"We don' want him to wake yet," Joey elaborated. "What are we suppose' to tell him?"

I don't know. Do you really expect me to know? I remained silent on that point, and instead I asked in a hushed whisper, "How did they get taken if you guys were awake? I stayed up with you," pointing at Joey, "until you woke Justin up. If you," pointing at Bryce, "never got woken up, that means that Justin was taken while on his watch. This Red character doesn't care if people watch him kidnap and murder; nothing's going to stop him. We're not safe even with someone on watch." I stopped talking because I didn't know what to do. No part of me wanted to stick around here. "There isn't anywhere safe on this island."

"I realize that, Jay," Bryce said, speaking way more calmly than any sane human should, given the circumstance. "But the Lord says that if we trust in Him nothing can harm us eternally from being with Him. You need to be sure you trust Him."

Idiot. "Really, you're gonna pull that crap on me again?" I laughed. "I'm going to wake Kevin up and tell him that God wasn't powerful enough to protect his cousin."

"That's not at all what I'm trying to say, Jay," Bryce said. "But maybe now isn't the right time for this discussion."

"Never is the right time for it," I muttered. *The arrogance of this poser.* "But I *am* going to wake Kevin up."

"You sure? He's going to freak out."

"What do you mean by freak out?" I asked.

"I don't know," Bryce replied. "The possibilities are endless. His cousin and best friend are dead. Why not freak out?"

It was a good point, I acknowledged, but someone had to tell him eventually, so I moved over to where Kevin was lying, asleep. I was not worrying about making too much noise, since I knew he'd be awake soon anyway.

I was about to kick him awake when—WHOOSH, SMACK—a knife struck a tree near my left shoulder. The shock of my life shimmering before my eyes in the blade of the knife knocked me onto the seat of my pants. "What the—" I shouted.

"Where's my girlfriend, Jay?" Jared's voice thundered through the forest.

"I ha—"

Joey interrupted me. "You're really comin' back here?" He added a pile of descriptive expletives to describe his opinion of Jared.

"I ain't scared of you!" Jared shouted. "You're just an overgrown Chihuahua. Mean for no reason; stupid as stupid gets." Jared shouted expletives as he stepped into our clearing. His eyes were pure hate as they shifted from Joey to me after that sentence. His shirt was no longer striped blue, but splotched red.

I didn't want to think about what it meant. Before I had a chance to say anything, Jared shouted again, "Where's my girlfriend?"

"I have no clue. Why would I take her?"

"Unless you have a death wish, I don't know why you would. But I guess you do, because you did. Now, where the hell is she?" By now he was standing over me, and the smell of blood was emanating from his shirt. He pulled the knife out of the tree.

Joey and Bryce rushed to my side, as I stood to my feet, trying to keep myself from gagging at the scent coming off his clothes.

When I had stood to my feet and gotten my gag reflex under control, I spoke. "I have no idea where she is—or—what the hell you're even talking about."

"Yeah." Joey had to throw his two cents in. "Jay just told me yesterday dat she ain't even hot."

You're an idiot, Joey. There wasn't a blunter way he could have said it.

Joey was still talking. "Why would he steal her?" He walked away, leaving Bryce at my side.

Jared's face turned to pure rage. He put the knife to my neck and threatened, "Where the hell are you keeping my girl?"

Inside I was freaking out. I didn't know what to say because I honestly had no clue where she was, and, there was a knife against my neck. One cut there and I was done. *What am I supposed to do?* I glanced to my left to see Bryce, and realized, *At least he has my back when it matters; maybe I'll just ignore his holier-than-thou talk.* I turned away from Bryce to see Joey now behind Jared, picking up a rock. He threw it.

The rock struck Jared in the back and caused him to jerk the knife against my neck. It broke the skin. I yelled. *Sometimes it'd be better if Joey didn't have my back.*

Kevin was still sleeping below where all this was happening.

Bryce threw a punch at Jared. It caught him in the shoulder. The knife dropped from his hand. It fell. The blade impaled itself in Kevin's left shoulder.

"Yeeow!" he shouted, waking up.

"Shut up," Jared said emotionlessly.

Kevin pulled the knife out—now blood coated—and held it in his right hand—pointed at Jared—while he put his left hand over the wound. "Don't tell me to shut up, a-hole. I was sleeping great. Now I'm angry. Shut yo' mouth." He positioned his hat on his head.

I was no longer under pressure and remembered my knife. I reached into my pocket and pulled it out and thrust it toward Jared. "You ready to listen?"

He muttered something unintelligible, and held his hands up in a pose of surrender, but his eyes still betrayed murderous rage.

I'd bet anything that this is Red—perhaps another personality of Jared's.

A few seconds of silence followed, at which point, Kevin spoke. "What is going on?" There was obvious discomfort in his voice as he kept the knife angled toward Jared.

"I'll tell you later," Bryce said.

"Where is Jaime?" Jared questioned.

So he's still on that? Does he not have ears? I hate annoying people. I spoke. "Specifically, I have no clue. Generally, with that Red creep, whoever he is." I decided not to vocalize my concern that Jared was Red. "Look at this note." I unfolded the note from my pocket and read, "Jared's girl, Jaime, is with me now." I started to refold it.

"Wait. Let me see that."

I nervously handed it over. *He'll wonder why Jaime slapped me. What will I tell him?* The truth was too hard. *"I cussed her out, called her obscene things, and she slapped me," will get me killed.* The look in his eyes proved that without a doubt.

Jared scanned the note, with his free hand tucked in the back pocket of his cargo shorts, and threw it back. "How do I know you're not Red? I mean, I got a note from Red saying you had her. Which should I believe?"

"You're stupid," I said, as I picked the note out of the sand.

"That's mature." Jared continued, "But I swear, if you have her—if you even lay one pinky on her—I'll make your life a living hell."

"Yes ma'am," I said. *Technically speaking, my life is already a living hell.* It was nice being able to say whatever I wanted to Jared. I enjoyed having the upper hand.

144

Jared's focused eyes widened and his lip began to quiver as his composure switched from vengeful to vexed. I'd never seen this before. "You have no idea what I'm going through right now," he whined.

"Try me," I challenged. Kevin handed me Jared's knife, and he ambled away with Bryce and Joey. *I don't need them right now anyways.*

Jared's thoughts poured out like a waterfall. "My girlfriend got kidnapped. I don't have anywhere to live. My friends are dead. Your friends want to kill me. What am I supposed to do?"

"I don't know. My situation is worse so I have no idea how to help." I elaborated. "My girl is dead. My friend, Kevin, lost his cousin, Justin, last night. You hate me. God hates me. This island is stupid and scary. And that Red guy wants to kill me. I'm in hell right now."

"My girl will be dead too if I don't save her!" He was angry again.

Why does he only think about himself? I spoke, "I don't have a clue where she is."

"I don't believe you."

"You're perfectly entitled to your opinion, but final answer: I don't have her." I said the last four words slowly so he could not misunderstand me. Then I added, "And besides, even if I did have her, why would I tell you? All you want to do is beat me up. You're probably just waiting for an opportunity to do that right now. Your tears right now are probably fake." I was egging him on. I knew it. *I have my friends; I don't need anyone else, especially a backstabbing, bullying, prideful, girl-crazy jerk.*

Jared wiped his eyes, and as he did, they narrowed down in rage again. "You totally have Jaime. I've seen the way you look at her in the quad at school. You're not telling me where she is because you want her for yourself. I promise you that she'll never touch you though!" He paused before adding, "I'm a wreck right now. Everyone's dying. The note that I got telling me you had Jaime was attached to a knife embedded in Zac's throat. Then, on

145

my way over here, I stumbled upon Johnny's body—riddled with knife wounds in his stomach. I buried it before continuing on my way over here. So really, I'm not in the mood to be messed with right now. All my friends are dead, and my girlfriend is missing." He stopped talking, and rubbed his hands through his hair.

"At least she's alive, a-hole!" I said.

That was the last straw for Jared. He swung at me, but I held up Kevin's knife and he caught his knuckles on it, losing two fingers in the process. "Dammit!" He pulled his arm back and wrapped his hand in his shirt, adding his own blood to Johnny's.

"Had enough?"

"For now." He turned to leave. His face was twisted in agony.

I'm still conscious after an encounter with Jared? That's different.

I watched him saunter off, holding his hand in his shirt at waist level. *He's ashamed,* I thought as I smiled. He kept walking, past Joey, Kevin, and Bryce, and had questions fired at him rapidly. "Where's my cousin?" "Is Jay alive?" "Who'd ya kill to get dat stain on yo' shirt?" "Why do ya like fighting so much?" "Are ya deaf?" "Answer me when I'm talking to ya!"

Jared responded by yelling, "Go to hell!" Then he ran off into the palm tree forest.

When he was out of view I again wondered how I was still conscious. Thus far, every time I'd encountered Jared, I'd ended up unconscious. *I wonder if things are changing for the better; I wonder if it's the calm before the storm.* I hoped for the previous.

Jared had picked on me for two years now. I couldn't remember how it had started, but what did that matter? *Did I look at Jaime wrong or something?* Once, I had yelled at him to stop, but all it had done was cause him to claim that he was just trying to man me up. I didn't know if that was true or not, but I hated being teased, beat up, and tortured. I'd never done anything to deserve it. *Rich kids think they own the world.*

146

STRANDED

Kevin walked over and asked me if I had a moment. His expression was distant. I could only imagine what was going through his head at that moment.

I tried joking with him, but it made him frown. In the end he asked to walk and talk. We set off east, into the forest of sweltering hot and humid palm tree shells that towered into the sky.

I wasn't sure what Kevin wanted to talk about. In fact, I wasn't sure if we'd ever even hung out before—just the two of us. He mostly hung with Bryce while I spent most of my time with Joey.

"What happened to Justin?" Kevin finally asked, wiping his face free of sweat with the sleeve of his non-injured arm.

Seriously? I didn't know. *Red was after me last I checked. I didn't realize he was going to go after Justin too. What should I say? "Your cousin's dead; sorry"? "I wish he'd taken me instead; honest"? which is actually a lie. "I don't know; God's just dumb and does stupid stuff that makes no sense and ruins our lives"? What should I say? None of those are viable options.*

Kevin was still talking. "Bryce has been talking to me lately about God and how I need Him more than anything else, but I don't know. I want to believe it, but when crap like this happens, it doesn't give me any incentive to believe it."

That explains why he wanted to walk and talk. He didn't want Bryce to hear. I answered with a question. "Why come to me?"

"All my life, ya've been the Christian. Ya've known all the verses. Known all the answers. Stayed out of trouble." Kevin's face looked desperate. "I've always looked up to ya. I figured ya'd have the answer to this as well."

He had me cornered. *What should I say?* I figured it out and asked another question. "Why not ask Bryce though?"

"He's gone weird lately. He used to do all the stuff Joey and I do, and he used to get in trouble with us. Now he doesn't do it,

147

and he can only talk about getting us to change. Ya never did any of that stuff."

"Oh," I realized. *I wish I'd done it all though.*

"I mean, look. Here's one key example. You're still a virgin, right?"

"Yeah," I said hesitantly. *I wish I wasn't. It's not by choice. Things just haven't worked out for me.*

Kevin continued. "That's what I thought. Bryce isn't. I'm not. I don't plan to stop getting girls. Bryce wants me to. But, he did the same back in the day. Ya never did. I trust what ya say more."

I was trapped now. *Should I admit that I don't believe Christianity? It contradicts itself everywhere. Sure, I'm a Christian— I prayed the prayer—but no, I don't believe any of it.*

I needed words.

Kevin asked again, "So why is Justin gone?"

I didn't know what to say so I started rambling. "Justin, he's well see, Kevin, God, I, Bible, Camille, Red, murderer—"

Kevin interrupted my babble. "What's going on, man? I just asked a very important question. Please answer it!"

I got a grip and quickly slurred, "God hates Justin more than me. Clearly."

Kevin balled his fist; his face was full of rage; he started to swing his fist. He screamed in pain, and let his arm fall to his side.

Knife wound. I smiled as I breathed a sigh of relief.

"What kind of retarded answer is that, Jay?" He was angry. "I want truth. Not crap!"

"I told you." I repeated, "God hates me, but seeing how Justin is gone, He hates him more."

"Shut yo' lying mouth. I thought ya were a friend. What kind of friend gives a crap-filled answer like that?"

I was happy Kevin was injured. *I'd be dead by now if he wasn't.* "You wanted the truth."

Kevin grabbed me by the shoulders and looked straight into my eyes. "Jay," he grimaced in pain, "is this about yo' stroke again?"

"I don't understand," I lied. *I know exactly what he's getting at.*

"God hating ya. Why would ya say that?"

"Because He does. He took my strength—"

"I told ya. Ya really—"

"He took my girlfriend. God hates me. He wants Red to kill me. I'm still alive though, so clearly He wanted Justin dead more." I had no idea why I was being so open with my thoughts, but it was too late. *What's said is said, as dumb or stupid as it is.*

The last thing I remembered was getting punched in the forehead.

CHAPTER 21

(August 2006)

I WAS SITTING in the back of a car. It was driving relatively fast down a long, straight road. A bridge was coming up that the road went under. The car kept driving, straight through, under the bridge, and out the other side. It made a right turn, around an air conditioning facility, and another right turn, and then another right turn. It drove straight, directly over the bridge it had just gone under.

It was then that I realized what was going on. I was in a car with Jay and his mom. Jay was dressed in a black polo shirt that had the words "Oasis Christian School" stitched in place of the left breast pocket. His mom was driving, and it looked like she was crying.

What did you do this time, stupid? I wondered. *If his mom is crying and Jay has anything to do with it, he will surely hear about it again from his dad when he gets home from school.*

"I can't believe you're going to high school," she said. "It seems like just yesterday was your first day of homeschooling as a kindergartener. Where has the time gone?" She lifted her right hand to wipe her eyes dry.

Okay, so maybe I jumped to conclusions. But what will Jay say to that? If he's not careful, I might not have jumped to conclusions.

He said nothing for several seconds, but then he finally spoke. "I'm excited to go to school. It gives me a little more

150

freedom, and a chance to make lots of friends. I already know a couple people here: Jared, Scott, Max, and Blake. I'm sure I'll meet a bunch more as well."

Jared? The other three names mean nothing to me.

"Remember that the best way to make a friend is to be one. I'm sure you'll be fine." She pulled the car into the school parking lot. "It's just that you're my baby. I'm going to miss your smile around the house."

Jared is one of Jay's friends?

Jay said nothing for a few seconds. Then the thought hit him, "At least we won't yell at each other about schoolwork anymore."

She was silent, and it looked like she might be hurt. Then she spoke, "I guess that it is a good thing."

She probably thinks it will improve their relationship. My thoughts instantly returned to Jared. *Was I really friends with him in real life? Why is he my enemy now? What is wrong? Is it even the same Jared?*

Jay got out of the car; told his mom that he loved her after she initiated it; shut the door; opened the back door, pulled his red backpack with black straps out, and shut the door again; and walked toward the line of lockers in front of the closest building on the quad. Before he even reached the lockers, a group of kids cornered him.

My first thought was that he was getting jumped; he was just a little, awkward looking guy. I laughed at the thought, considering that the only difference between him and I was that I was slightly taller, though still just as awkward. *That's probably the cause of my girl problems.*

Camille. I cursed under my breath, upset at the remembrance. However, I couldn't dwell on it, because the gang of kids had reached Jay.

The leader of the group held out his hand. "Hey Jay, what's up?"

"Not much, Max," Jay replied. "Just psyching myself up for the first day of school."

Oh, it's Max. That's a relief.

"I know what you mean. It's hard, ain't it?"

"Definitely."

"This is Jay," Max began, introducing the new guy to everyone. "We go to Desert Valley Church together. Last spring we were at an event called Milestones together. Good times. He's new to school, so we've gotta make him feel welcome."

What's Milestones? I changed my thoughts, unconcerned. *That was a sweet introduction.*

"Jay, this is Johnny," Max said, pointing to a short kid whose hair reminded him of a hobbit. "This is Zac," a taller kid who was wearing an ATLANTA BRAVES baseball cap. "This is Shelly," a girl with a huge smile and freckled face. "You know Nicole from church, right?" Max pointed to a girl who had dark red hair that stopped at her shoulders, and a friendly smile. "This is Julia," a short, spectacled girl whose brown hair was pulled back in a ponytail. "These are only a few of the people from our class."

"Nice to meet you all," said Jay, whose gaze was stuck on the girl named Julia. Her eyes were the same color as her hair and she was smiling at Jay, showing off perfect teeth.

This year won't be bad at all for him. Sure, he'll be away from Joey and Bryce all the time, but he'll be around Nicole—every single day—which will make for good chats with Joey. I laughed inside thinking, *Good times. And besides, there's always Julia if no one else.*

How many of these people are still alive? I wondered, letting the names disappear from memory.

Jay spoke again, "Where's Jared and Scott?"

Which Jared?

"They'll probably be here right before the bell rings. That's how they roll," Max explained.

"Oh, okay. So what's it like here?"

Johnny—hobbit hair—spoke up, "It's okay. It's stricter than public school, but you'd be surprised at how much you can still get away with." A sly smile spread across his face.

"That's not what I meant," Jay said. "I meant, what are the classes like?"

"If you do the work, they're easy." Johnny frowned jokingly. "If you're like most of us, though, they are hard."

Laziness is awesome. Jay will fit right in.

"If you do the work and don't mess around in class, you'll be painted as a good student, and you'll have respect from all the teachers." Johnny smiled. "Kids like this," pointing at Zac, "are the ones teachers don't get along with."

"That's not true," Zac said. "You're the one who gets the most yellow slips every year."

"Whatever," Johnny said.

BRIIING went the bell for first period.

Jay followed Johnny and Zac and Nicole through the quad to their first class. Spanish One. They all walked in the door of the class, and were greeted by a slender, short blonde woman, whose name was written on the board: "Mrs. Edge." Beneath her name was written, "BIENVENIDO, CLASE."

"This is going to be interesting," Jay muttered to no one in particular.

Spanish. I hate foreign languages. They make no sense to me. Why can't the whole world just speak English. At least English makes sense.

The bell rang again, and Mrs. Edge began to speak. "Bienvenido, clase. Este es nuestro primer día de clase y estoy muy emocionado de tener la oportunidad de enseñar a todos el maravilloso lenguaje del español." She paused as the whole class stared at her dumbly.

There's no way Jay passes this class.

Mrs. Edge continued. "I said, 'Welcome, class. This is our first day of class and I am very excited to have the opportunity to teach you all the wonderful language of Spanish.'" She paused. "By the time the year is done, you too should be able to speak at least that much Spanish. Who's ready to begin?"

Fat chance of that, I thought. *All I know is that she's hot.*

Max leaned over to Jay and whispered, "She's hot."

Jay didn't say anything, but nodded his head as if to agree.

He doesn't want to talk in class on his first day. What a guy! I laughed.

*   *   *

SCHOOL WAS OUT, and Jay was waiting out front for his mom. While he waited, Johnny came over and asked him how he felt about his first day.

"It was great. Spanish is going to be hard though."

"I agree with you there," Johnny agreed. "Well, I'll see you tomorrow," he said as he ran off to his car.

Just then Jay's mom pulled up. He walked over to her, opened the door of the car, and climbed in.

"How was day one?" his mom asked.

"It was great. The teachers were all really nice. The kids took me in right away. Like, right when I got to school, Max Scrawls called me over and introduced me to everyone. It's going to be a great year. No offense, but I think I'm gonna like it more than homeschooling."

"None taken, I guess," she replied. "Sounds like you're going to have a successful high school career, complete with Bible teaching which is not available at public schools. You're very blessed."

"You're right." He thought for a second and continued, "The thing I like the most though is all the people—all the new friends I can make over the next four years."

"That's very true," she said. "You need more good friends. Good, well-behaved, Christian friends. Better than Joey."

Did she really just say that?

Jay replied, "Joey will always be my friend."

"And that's not a bad thing," his mom said, "but what you really need is a best friend."

"Joey," Jay said.

"Okay," his mom said. "I'm glad you had a good day. I'll be praying the rest of the year is just as good." She paused before asking, "Were any of your friends in your classes?"

"Max and Blake were, but Jared and Scott weren't. They're on a different schedule. Blake and Max were in almost all of my classes actually."

Jared again? Count it as a blessing that you don't have class with him.

"That's awesome," his mom said.

"Yes it is," Jay agreed.

You just wait 'til junior and senior year. It won't be so awesome then.

CHAPTER 22

(Day 4, 3:45 p.m.)

I SLOWLY CAME BACK to consciousness. The realization of that dream hit me slowly; what hit me quickly was confusion. I was lying on my back in the middle of a forest of palm trees. The shadows were beginning to lengthen as the sun was slowly falling in the west.

What happened? Where am I? Where is everyone? I sat up, and a throbbing sensation shot through my whole head, and when it did, everything shot back with it. *I was punched in the forehead by Kevin. He is mad at me cuz my deductive reasoning didn't make him happy. Justin is dead. Contrary to the dream I just had, I really don't have any friends at school. It looked so good when it all started, but it quickly became exactly the opposite. This island is all the proof I need.*

You know this island is turning people evil, right? the other part of my psyche said. *How do you know it isn't perfect back home? If you weren't such a pessimist, you'd know these things.*

It probably is. It's obviously turned Kevin evil. In real life he's not.

For once, my brain isn't speaking nonsense. I tried to stand, and pain shot through my head, so I cursed aloud. *I just wish everyone who's turning evil here wasn't against me. I'm the only innocent one right now.* I stood, took two steps, and had to lean against a tree to keep myself from falling.

"Jay," came a voice from somewhere in the trees.

156

"Who is it?" I asked cautiously.

Jacob came into scent before he came into view. Stale cigarettes and cheap beer. I wondered where he'd found it all. *I could totally go for drowning my problems in some liquid mood-changers.* When he came into view, I noticed that he was wearing a backpack that appeared to be stuffed full of something.

He spoke. "It's been a long time and I was just out walking. What's new with you?"

"Just lost and confused and hurt." I rubbed my forehead as my back slid against the tree while I moved to a seated position

"Girlfriend's death still causing pain?" His attempt at an understanding smile showed his rotting mouth. He sat down next to me against a neighboring palm tree skeleton.

The area here was full of them. It was exactly the opposite of our camp. Here the trees bunched up to where walking was almost impossible. Running would be totally impossible. The trees lightened up just northwest of my current location, but here it was a mass grave of palm trees. As we sat together against the dead palms, our knees were bent—pressed against our chests—because there were too many stumps around to allow for stretching out our legs. *How did I not land on any of them when Kevin knocked me out earlier?*

"Yes," I said, answering his question about Camille, and before I let the thought take me back to tears, I added, "but that's not what I meant. I meant physically. I keep getting beat up." I kicked at a plant on the ground.

"Who's beating you up? And why?"

"Originally, this retard named Jared. Now, one of my childhood best friends—Kevin."

"Why would your," he put up air quotes, "best friend," he put them down, "beat you up?"

"Kevin asked me why his cousin, Justin, was gone, and I told him it was because God hated his cousin. I didn't know what else to say to him." Jacob looked interested, so I elaborated. "I got this note from some psychopath that said he wanted to kill me. My

157

friends got a note that said someone from their group would be dead by this morning. By cross-referencing the notes, I figured it'd be me since I'm in their group. However, when morning came, Justin was gone—not me."

"Oh. Okay," Jacob acknowledged, speaking slowly. "What's that have to do with God hating you?"

"You know," I answered. "God stole my strength. God killed my girlfriend. He hates me. All that's left for Him to steal is my life. So, if He took Justin's instead, He clearly hates him more than me."

Jacob spoke the following sentence much more quickly: "I totally understand your logic. It's totally true. None of this would have happened if God loved you, right?" He bent down and picked up a rock.

Jacob speaks my language. I appreciate it a lot. I replied, "Exactly. It makes no sense. Why does the Bible say, 'God is love' or 'For God so loved the world,' when He clearly hates me? It's so contradictory."

"The Bible is a bunch of junk. How can it be true? Eighty different people wrote it over thousands of years. Why'd some stuff get in and some didn't? It's propaganda for the lie called Christianity." Jacob threw his rock at a nearby palm tree stump, splintering it into soot as the rock connected.

"Thank you," I said. I loved these conversations as long as Camille wasn't brought up. "I've been waiting forever for someone to say that. It's exactly the same thing I've been thinking for a while. Except—I am a Christian—I just don't believe the Bible. Christianity is whatever."

Jacob agreed. "Believe whatever you want Jay. It doesn't matter anyway you go. I mean, seriously, how can a loving God send anyone to Hell? Everyone will be in Heaven one day."

"Good point," I agreed. "But seriously, I am sick of getting beat up multiple times every day."

"Why are you getting beat?"

"I have no clue," I said. I really didn't. The only one that made any sense at all was Kevin's punch, but even that was debatable. "Since I've been on this stupid island, I've been knocked out at least five times."

"That's no fun." Jacob wrinkled his face in disgust.

"Any advice?" I asked. *I need help from someone I can trust, and, at the moment, this homeless, smelly stranger is the only one who fits that bill.*

"Take the initiative. Punch them before they can punch you. Next time Jared or Kevin comes up to you, knock 'em out so they can't do it to you."

"Seriously?" I was wary of taking the advice. "I don't think I'm strong enough to do any significant damage." I thought back to the last 'fight' I'd been in and wasn't sure Jacob's advice would work. The only thought that gave me any hope was the memory of two of his fingers getting cut in half like a hot dog when I had held up the knife to block his punch.

"Think positive and you'll be surprised what you can accomplish." He paused, as he took off his backpack, pulled it in front of himself, and unzipped it. "The only other advice I can give you is this: take some of these off my hands and enjoy the distraction from your problems." He held up several packs of MARLBOROS, several magazines, and several bottles.

That explains the smell always being fresh, I reasoned. When the magazine covers were made obvious I instantly grabbed them, folded them, and tucked them in my back pocket for later. I also grabbed a pack of cigarettes, opened it, and with a lighter from Jacob, lit one and gave him one. I passed on the bottles. "You sure I can have these?" I asked, referencing the pack of cigarettes and the magazines in my pocket.

"Yeah," Jacob smiled. "I've got tons more where they came from. Take another pack of smokes."

As I went ahead and took another pack from him, it didn't occur to me to ask where he got them from. Instead, I remembered what happened before Kevin knocked me out, and I was excited to share. "Guess what happened earlier?" I took a hit of my cigarette and waited until he told me to go on. "Jared tried punching me, but I held up a knife that I had been given by the psychopath who wants to kill me, and two of Jared's fingers got sliced off." I laughed. "Serves that jerk right."

Jacob shared a laugh with me, again displaying only one or two teeth in an otherwise hollow mouth. Then he changed the subject. "How are you dealing with the death of your girlfriend?" He fingered one of the many holes in his jeans.

Why does he always revert to that question? I spoke, "I'm okay. I mean, there's too much going on to dwell on it too long. I do wish she'd gotten a proper burial though."

"What happened?" He took a drag on his cigarette.

"Her body was in the plane and the plane exploded." I felt tears moisten my eyes. "She was perfect," I paused to wipe my eyes, "and she didn't get the honor of being buried. It's so stupid." The tears were falling. I inhaled my cigarette to distract myself, and ended up coughing uncontrollably.

Jacob put his arm on my shoulder. "It's okay. You'll be fine."

"Are you sure? I've never known a girl as great as her, and now she's exploded into bits!" I was getting louder.

"Calm down, Jay," Jacob said softly, rubbing my shoulder soothingly.

"It's hard," I said, bawling. "My whole class hates me. My friends are turning on me. The girl of my dreams is dead. And a psycho wants to kill me! I can't be calm!"

"You need something to eat," Jacob offered.

"There's nothing to eat but those stupid little berries," I screamed. "I hate those things!"

"I have real food at my camp," Jacob explained. "We should go get some."

"How far is it?"

"Due west of here." He paused. "Listen."

I wiped my eyes and listened. Voices were headed our way, from the northwest. I looked in that direction. It sounded like Joey, Bryce, and Kevin.

I looked back to Jacob, but he was gone. *Whatever. I'll survive just fine on my own.* I didn't move.

Kevin's voice said, "We were over here when I hit him."

Joey's voice said, "I still can't believe ya did dat."

"He deserved it," Kevin's voice said.

I didn't deserve anything. I was telling the truth, just like he wanted. Why do people get so mad at the truth? It made no sense. *If he's going to claim that he didn't do anything wrong then I have every right to knock him out.* I was not in the mood for peoples' attitudes. Everything was against me. Everything.

Kevin, Bryce, and Joey came into the clearing. Bryce whispered something into Kevin's ear.

Kevin walked toward me. "I'm sorry I punched ya, Jay," he said, holding out his hand.

Shake his hand to show forgiveness or something? I'm not sure.

Kevin continued, "Though I'm pretty sure ya deserved it. What kinda friend says—"

My fist in his mouth cut him off. "You asked for the truth. I gave it. Shut your trap."

He recovered and thrust his fist at my temple. I fell down in a heap.

CHAPTER 23

(September 2006)

I OPENED MY EYES, again, to see my freshman self on the basketball court at school. He was one handed dribbling down the court, with his left hand sticking up in the air. *What a retard*, I thought, losing my island troubles to the comedy of me trying to play basketball. *Does he have any idea how dumb he looks?* I kept watching. Jay stopped dribbling, and held the ball. He faked a pass to a teammate and passed it to the other side of the court. It got stolen by the other team. *Basketball never was your sport. Baseball was.* The other team cleared the ball behind the three-point line, passed it once, passed it back, passed it again, and shot. Two points. Jay brought the ball back in, checking it to the other team.

He was being guarded by a tall kid, dressed in a black uniform shirt, and khaki shorts. His hair was spiked and he looked like he was upset.

Jay shot the ball from the three point line, over the hand of the guard, and it bounced off the rim, onto the backboard, back to the rim, and fell into the basket. A cheer went up from his team.

Jay's guard checked the ball in to Jay who passed it back. Then he went into defense mode. He was squatting down, running back and forth, trying to grab the ball. *That's decent defense. Was I really that good?* The kid stopped dribbling and held the ball. Jay put a hand in his face.

The guard insulted Jay with a stream of profanity.

Great Christian school, I thought.

He was still going, "That's a foul." And then basically repeated his first profane sentence and concluded by ordering that Jay be ejected.

You going to take that, Jay?

Jay gave him a shove. "Stop cussing me out, Darien."

Darien's fist flew, straight into Jay's eye. He went down in a heap.

So the island isn't the first time I've been beat up and abused by my peers?

The game had come to a stop, and the players were crowded around Jay. "Are you okay?" "I can't believe he hit you." "What was even going on?" "Darien, you had no right to do that."

"He shoved me first," he said.

Jay was standing up. His right eye was bruised underneath, and the crowd was commenting on it.

The bell rang, and it was time to go to class. Jay wandered back to his locker, grabbed his books, put them in his backpack, and headed to class. He went into the bathroom on his way. Apparently he wanted to see his eye. *It was getting darker as time went by.* "My mom's gonna kill me," he said.

Yep. I was worried for him.

He walked the rest of the way to class, and when he sat down everyone was commenting on his eye. It took forever for the teacher to get class in order. When she finally saw Jay, she told him to go get some ice for it, which he left to do. On his way out, a girl offered him some IBUPROFEN. *These people are so nice to him. What goes wrong in the future?*

*   *   *

JAY RECEIVED A YELLOW SLIP in his next class. He asked to be excused, and went to the principal's office to find out what was going on. "I didn't do anything," he muttered under his breath.

When Jay entered his office, a name plate read: "Principal Fielding." He welcomed Jay, shook his hand, and told Jay to have a seat. The principal then asked him what had happened at lunch.

Jay explained about the basketball game, the supposed foul, the cussing, the shove, and the reaction. Jay also explained that the only reason he shoved Darien was because he was cussing up a storm which wasn't appropriate.

"Would you shove someone on the street who was cussing?" Principal Fielding asked.

"No, because they're not supposedly a Christian. We're at a Christian school; no one should be swearing."

"That's true," Fielding said, "but the truth is that you took justice into your own hands. The student manual says that fighting is off limits."

He didn't fight. He shoved the dummy, and the dummy started a one-punch fight. This is dumb.

"What's going to happen?" Jay asked.

"I have to discipline you somehow. Normally fighting gets a detention, which is a full discipline point against you. However, seeing as how I understand your side, and you are brand new to the whole school thing, I'm going to give you a lunch detention, which is only half of a point against you."

"Thank you," Jay said. He paused before asking, "What's going to happen to Darien?"

"Seeing as how he's been skating on thin ice as it is, I don't know—maybe suspension." Fielding paused. "Why?"

"I don't know, I just hate to see him get in trouble too. It's my fault for shoving him."

"I understand," Fielding said. He then showed him out of his office, and Jay went back to his classmates. Sixth period was over, and everyone was transitioning to their seventh period classes.

Zac came up to him and asked, "What happened?"

"I got a lunch detention for starting the fight," Jay said.

"Seriously? That's so dumb."

"It's not that big of a deal. I'll live." Jay was happy.

I think it's stupid, but at least Jay is being positive.

Just then Darien walked up to him. I noticed Jay get tense. *What does he want?*

"Jay," Darien began, "I just wanted to say I'm sorry for punching you. Please forgive me. I was wrong."

"I forgive you."

"Thanks, bro. Stay cool." With that he walked away.

That was weird.

The late bell rang, and Jay ran to his last class, trying not to be too late. As I followed him—floating against my will—my vision faded to black.

CHAPTER 24

(Day 4, 7:30 p.m.)

I OPENED MY EYES to find myself back in camp. The gurgling of the stream was the first thing I heard. The sky was darkening. I sat up, and I realized Bryce, Joey, and Kevin were surrounding me. *Don't hurt me. Why do you guys have to gang up on me right now? I don't wanna get beat again.* As the thought ran through my head, so did a sharp, stabbing pain. *Television is so stupid. How can a guy get beat up, but then keep going as if nothing is wrong? There's definitely something wrong with me.*

Joey held out his hand.

Does he want me to shake it? I'm sick of being treated like a little kid. Used as a rag doll and then treated like a three year old. Shake my hand, moron.

"Welcome back, homie," Joey said. "You've been out for a minute."

Joey is a good friend. He didn't deserve the rude comment I just thought about him. I took his hand, and he hoisted me to my feet. "Thanks, bro."

I felt my back pocket, hoping that they hadn't found the magazines that Jacob had left for me, but then I figured that there was no possible way that they had not found them, considering that they had carried me back to our camp from the forest. Much to my surprise, I felt them, still rolled up and sticking out of my pocket behind the t-shirt still tucked there as well.

Kevin was glaring at me. His shoulder was bloody; his white shirt was sweat-stained; and his facial expression screamed, "Why can't ya just kill him?"

He deserves the thought I aimed at Joey.

Bryce whispered something in Kevin's ear. Kevin's face shifted to happiness for a split second, but then it quickly reverted. "I don't wanna see that loser around here."

I hated that kind of talk. "Maybe I hate you just as much," I said. "Ever think of that?" My fist was clenched.

Kevin lunged toward me, but Bryce held him back. "I wanna kill him."

"That's why I'm holding you back," Bryce said.

"Let go."

"No, Kevin," Bryce said. He turned to me and said, "Let's settle this."

"The only way to settle this," Kevin began, "is to get rid of Jay." His face was bloodshot with anger. "Killing him would be the best, but if we kick him outta the crew, I'll make do with that."

"Jay's like my little brother," Joey said, deciding to join the conversation. "We're not kickin' him out or killin' him."

"Well, I can tell who ya like more," Kevin accused. "Take yo' baby brother and get out of my life."

"I ain' leavin'," Joey said staunchly. "Neither is he." He paused. "Oh, and he ain' a baby. He's older and mo' mature than ya."

I was getting worried. *My friends are about to get in a fight over me. This has never happened before. We've always had each other's backs, but now this island is messing everything up. Why is this happening?* I decided to speak my mind. "I can see that you loved your cousin more than your homeboy."

"Damn right, a-hole! And ya should be freaking happy Bryce and Joey are between us. I'd kill yo' sorry little ass right now if I could reach ya."

I got brave and challenged, "Give me your best."

167

Kevin shoved Bryce to the ground and stomped over to me—enraged—but took a fist to the stomach before reaching me.

Joey shook his fist as he spoke. "Leave Jay alone."

"Make me, traitor." Kevin punched Joey in the mouth, drawing blood.

Joey's hand shot to his mouth, and when he saw the blood on it, it was all he needed to excuse a full-fledged fight. He swung at Kevin's nose, drawing blood. Kevin swung at Joey, but Joey blocked it with his left hand. They parried back and forth as they stepped toward the pool. Joey swung again, but Kevin ducked and punched Joey in the knee. Joey staggered back and fell into a crouch. He dove at Kevin, whose back was to the pool, tackling him to the ground; Joey straddled him and laid into him; he socked him in the face three times, and slammed the back of Kevin's head against the rock that bordered the pool before he stood up again.

Kevin's nose was bleeding. Both of his eyes were black. His mouth was streaming blood.

Joey was limping and his cheeks were bruised. "Learned yo' lesson yet?" he asked. He rubbed his mouth with his right hand.

Kevin's response was weak. "That you're a horrible friend?" He paused. "Yeah, I learned that." He passed out.

I was speechless. Joey had just beat up his best friend to keep me safe. *I always thought he'd pick Kevin over me. Wrong.* I clapped him on the back to show my appreciation.

Bryce spoke. "This is tough for me, Jay, but clearly we're having problems. I think you need to leave before it gets any worse."

"I understand," I said. "Kevin hates me, but since you like him more, you're kicking me out." *Some people are unbelievable.*

"That's not it at all. I'm worried for your life. You need to leave, or you'll be killed. I can't hold Kevin back forever. You just saw the truth of that."

It's true. Kevin shoved Bryce down like a mannequin.

He wants a vacation, not a babysitting job. That's why he wants you gone.

I'd be dead if it wasn't for Joey.

Joey's the one who cares. Not Bryce.

I finally interrupted the internal argument by saying, "Why don't we just leave Kevin here to his wounds. The three of us can go off together."

"I can't," Bryce protested. "I need to stay with Kevin."

"You like him more," I said. "I understand."

Joey spoke. "Come on, Jay. We don' need dem. We'll start a new crew—one with lots of ladies. Nicole and me—life will be good. Let's go. Leave da fruits alone." Joey started walking south, toward the beach.

I followed. Joey was closer than a brother, and I had no one else at the moment. The crew had split. I'd never imagined that. Not in my wildest dreams. Kevin hated me. Bryce and Kevin were inseparable. I only had Joey. *I hope he's here 'til I'm rescued.* Finally, I spoke, "I thought you liked Kevin more than me."

Joey answered. "I liked ya two equally, but when he started bein' a jerk, I started being nicer to ya. We have to stick together to survive." He pulled up on his jeans to keep from tripping on them as he walked.

Ain't that right? It's amazing what happens to close friendships when a family member dies, gets kidnapped, or the like.

*   *   *

JOEY AND I ARRIVED at the beach camp just as the sun was crossing the horizon. We passed a guy lighting the camp torches as we entered. He said nothing, and we returned the favor.

During the walk across the island, everything had slowed down for me. Joey and I had talked about the "good times," and we had mused about many more opportunities for such times after getting off the island. The psycho-killer and Jared had all but disappeared from my mind. I was now wearing a green and black button down t-shirt, and I had replaced my bag of CHEEZ-ITS in my duffel bag with the magazines that Jacob had given to me. Joey and I had eaten the crumbs of the CHEEZ-ITS on our walk, and we had also smoked a few cigarettes.

After passing the torch-guy, we were in the crash-site-camp. Despite my reception the last time I had set foot within the camp, there was now no opposition to us being there. With Jared gone and Jaime kidnapped, most of the remaining people were friendly. In fact, one girl's greeting took me completely by surprise.

She had been sitting on the beach, running her fingers through the sand and watching the waves crash on the shore, when she turned to see us crest the hill into camp. She had jumped up, rushed toward us, and stopped several paces ahead of us. "Jay, is that you?" She didn't let me answer before adding, "I've heard some crazy things recently that I really hope are not true."

It's me," I replied, answering her initial question. "Who are you? What kind of crazy things have you heard?"

She ignored my question and hugged me tight. "It's Laura, Jay. I'm so happy you're okay. We've lost too many to divide now. It's been quite a day, and I'm ready to go to bed and start fresh tomorrow." She let go of me, and as she did my curiosity about the crazy things she'd heard fell out of my mind. *I don't have a clue who this is, but she sure hugs good.*

She stepped back and looked at my face. The shadows of torches flickered on her face revealing long, dark hair tied into a ponytail falling in front of her left shoulder. "What happened to you?" she asked. "Your head is all bruised and bashed."

Joey spoke up, preventing my answer at that moment. "Where's Nicole?"

"Who are you?" Laura asked, turning to him.

"This is Joey Birjal," I answered. "Me and him go to church with Nicole. He's safe."

Laura took my words for it. "Probably in her hut," she said, answering Joey's question. "Let me take you to her."

"Sweet." He turned to me. "Did ya hear dat? I'm goin' to visit Nicole."

"I heard," I said slowly. *I don't want him to hit it off with her. I want her.* I needed a girl now, and she was my favorite. *I miss Camille so much.*

A new relationship will help you get over her, my mind told me.

Nicole was the one I wanted. Julia was a close second, but I preferred Nicole. Nicole was calmer; hyper girls drove me crazy.

Laura led us away from the water, toward a circle of huts. We walked past several huts before Laura knocked on the doorpost of one of them. "Who is it?" came Nicole's voice from inside.

I miss that voice.

"It's Laura. I have a surprise for you."

I glanced at Joey, whose face was ecstatic. It was weird that he was silent. He loved to talk, especially when he was happy.

"I'll be right there." Thirty seconds later, Nicole came out of her hut with the torchlight revealing that her amber-colored hair was damp. Her mouth dropped in disbelief. "Joey!" she shrieked. "I haven't seen you in forever. How's life treating you?" She paused. "What happened to your mouth?"

"I got in a fight." He was beaming. "You should see da other guy dough if ya think dis looks bad." He laughed.

Nicole was speechless.

So I helped. "Seriously, the other guy is jacked up."

Joey continued. "Yeah. But otherwise, life is whatever. I haven't smoked in forever..."

Laura motioned to me for us to leave, so I followed, leaving Joey and Nicole to their conversation.

"So how's the trip been for you?" Laura asked, as we started walking toward her hut.

I doubted that she truly cared. *Truthfully, it's hell, but I can lie and say it's all good in the hood.* I decided to ask for clarification. "Truthfully?"

A couple seconds of awkward silence followed, but Laura finally answered in the affirmative.

Joshua Wingerd

I let the waterfall of words flow. "It's hell. My girlfriend is dead. My best friends hate me. The serial killer freak wants to kill me. Jared thinks I kidnapped Jaime, and he wants to kill me. God hates me. No one cares about me. I—"

Laura interrupted me. "Sorry, but I have to interrupt. People are dying all around you. Peter, David, Lola, Jack, Chris, and Jeremy have all been killed. You're still alive. Not to belittle your feelings, but I think you're worrying too much about yourself and not at all about anyone else."

That made me angry, but I didn't want to show it. "What would you suggest?" I asked through clenched teeth.

"For one, open your eyes. Think about someone besides yourself. Do what you can to help someone else. You'll be surprised how much better it makes you feel."

"I'm sure," I spat sarcastically. *I don't care what you say. My life sucks, and I don't care at all what anyone else is going through.*

"Amy is a prime example," Laura said. "Chris died less than two hours ago. She's going through a lot. She needs comforting. Chris was everything to her. She—"

I interrupted. "I lost my other half too. How come no one gives a damn about that?" I continued my rant. "For a Christian school, everyone sure is two-faced. Everyone's emotions matter except Jay's. If Jay is going through hell, no one bats an eye. I'm really freaking tired of this. I just want to go home." I wanted to cry; *not in front of Laura*, I told myself. I spoke again, "Seriously, as much as I hate my home, I just want to go back."

We stopped walking as Laura pulled me close and whispered in my ear, "I know how you feel. I wanna be home too. This island is scary. People are dying. Jared has gone on a power trip. This senior trip was supposed to be fun. It's not that at all." Her voice cracked, and I felt moisture on my neck. "But, we really need to stick together. Until we are rescued, the only way to survive is to stick together." She let go, and she wiped her face with her hands. "Are you with me?"

172

I watched as she backed up and looked me in the eyes. *Don't stop hugging me,* my mind said. *Maybe* she's *my next girlfriend.* I shoved that thought out of my mind as quickly as it came in. *She's a good girl. There's no way that would ever work out.*

What does she mean by 'are you with me?'? Does she want me? I don't want her. A hug, yes; her, no.

She repeated her question. "Are you with me?"

I had no clue what she was asking. *Why'd the question even come up?* "With you for what?" I asked.

"The only way to survive is to stick together. Are you with me?"

I felt stupid. "Oh yeah, definitely."

We walked another minute or two until we were outside Laura's hut. She said goodnight and walked inside. I stood awkwardly outside for several minutes contemplating my next move. *What did she mean by 'Jared has gone on a power trip'? Is he back?* It worried me.

I wondered what Joey and Nicole were up to. Then I decided it'd be better not to think about it. I remembered that Nicole was smart and had her head on straight—nothing was happening.

I walked down to where the water met the sand, and I stared out into the darkness, listening to the crash of waves. The air had an unfamiliar chill in it. It was creepy. *I want a hug to keep warm.* It made me shiver and remember my loneliness even more.

Camille. I miss her so much. I missed our long walks under the moonlight. I missed our hugs, kisses, and mischief. I would give anything to hold her in my arms again.

Would you sell your soul?

Yes! I shouted. *I'd sell my soul to have her back,* and then I started crying.

I sat down in the damp sand and bawled my eyes out. She had been my everything. *Life made sense when she was around. Now she is gone, and I am lost and confused. Why'd she have to die? Her dirty blonde hair I'd been enamored with. Her perfect teeth. Dead.*

I cried and cried until sleep overtook me.

CHAPTER 25

(October 2007)

I SAW JAY again when I opened my eyes. He was walking with Joey and Kevin. It was dark outside. *I wonder what's going on. I don't remember this.* They came to a street, looked both ways, and crossed it. They kept walking until they found themselves in a park. They walked past the playground, and kept going. A long, winding sidewalk-path went around the exterior of the park's property, and they continued down it until it came to a split.

Then they went left, away from the park, down a sort-of-alley that was nicely landscaped on both sides of the sidewalk. Houses stood on either side of the path, just beyond the landscaping

Kevin broke the constant chatter with the first phrase I picked up on. "Hey, Joey, can I get a cigarette?"

"Yeah, homie." Joey reached into his pocket, pulled out a pack, and handed one to Kevin. A lighter followed.

Knowing Jay from these other memories, I would think that he's extremely uncomfortable around this right now. Goody-goody can't stand bad people. He wants to tell them it's bad, but he won't. It will be one against two if he tells them that it is bad for them. He won't bring himself to do it.

By now Kevin had his cigarette lit, and Joey also had one.

Joey spoke, "Hey Jay, ya want to try one?" He held out the cigarette to him.

Oh boy, this just got real. I watched as Jay's face changed over and over again.

"No, dude. I can't. We're going to Bible study and they'll smell it. Plus, it's not Christian. There's a verse that says the body is a temple. I don't want to pollute it."

"Oh, please." Joey took a hit on his cigarette. "I have AXE. It'll cover all the smell. We'll be fine. Plus, that verse isn't talking about that."

"What is it talking about then?" Jay asked.

Joey answered him. "I don't know. But I promise it's not that."

Jay shot back, "You just don't want the truth. I've heard my whole life that that's what that verse is about."

"Whatever," Joey said. He continued, "I still want to know if ya want to try this."

Jay looked back and forth between Joey and Kevin, and then he looked over his shoulder.

Yeah, make sure God isn't watching you. I laughed to myself.

Then he muttered, "Maybe it'll make me cool to them, and it'll give me ammunition at school against Jared." Joey and Kevin couldn't hear him.

Jared? He's started being a jerk now? Figures.

Jay finally answered Joey. "Sure, I'll take one."

"He wants a whole one?" Kevin exclaimed.

Joey whispered something to him, and then he handed Jay a cigarette. Jay took a puff. He instantly started coughing. *He must think that it's one-hundred percent disgusting.*

"Ya okay, dude?" Joey asked.

"Yeah," he got out amid more coughs.

He wonders how anyone can enjoy smoking.

"You sure?" Kevin asked. "You're turning green."

"Seriously?"

"Pretty much."

"I'm fine. By the time we get to the house I'll feel great."

"Okay, homie." Joey paused. "Before we go anywhere though," he pulled out the AXE bottle, "we've got to get rid of the smell."

Jay took the bottle and sprayed a small amount on himself. Joey and Kevin smoked their cigarettes down to the filters, Joey smoked the remainder of the one he gave Jay, and then they sprayed themselves down significantly.

The AXE is because they don't want to be known as druggies. Jay really doesn't—his parents would kill him.

*　　　*　　　*

JAY'S DAD PICKED HIM UP after study. Several seconds after Jay got in the car, his dad spoke. "Were you smoking? I smell cigarette smoke."

"No, dad. It's," he thought for a few seconds. "It's the new cologne smell."

It isn't a complete lie. The smell is cologne mixed with cigarettes.

"Okay." He paused. "As long as you're not smoking, it's okay. I better not ever catch you smoking."

"Yes sir," Jay said.

He doesn't plan on ever doing it again. It is gross to him.

CHAPTER 26

(Day 5, 7 a.m.)

I AWOKE to the sound of waves crashing on a beach. I opened my eyes and saw the same, and I tried to remember why I was there. *Oh yeah. Kevin and Bryce hate me and want me to die alone. Joey cares enough to stay; though where is he? Laura was talking to me last night, and she made me think of Camille. I miss her so much.*

I just lay there on my back, looking up into the abnormally clear sky. *Doesn't it ever rain around here? I've been here for like two weeks and I still haven't seen a single cloud. This is so stupid.* In all honesty, though, I had no clue how long I'd actually been on the island. *I haven't even seen a single boat or plane.*

I rolled onto my side and felt something crinkle under me. Thoughts ran through my mind like a marathon runner. *It's a food package. It's paper. It's sand. It's a book. It's a letter. It's my cigarettes.* I sat up and felt around where the crinkling sound had come from. My worst fears were confirmed. *It's paper; and a letter; and a knife.*

Déjà vu. A note, next to me, connected to a knife, by a beach. The only difference is that this is the opposite side of the island from the last time.

I untied the blood-spattered shoe-string—*Who did this belong to? Justin?*—and unfolded the note. The script was again written in blood, but one section was clearly written by a different person.

178

STRANDED

HEY JAY,
    SO, YOU FEELING SAFE YET? I HOPE NOT. THE TRUTH
IS, YOU'RE IN OVER YOUR HEAD. "IN WHAT?" YOU ASK?
DANGER. DISCOMFORT. DEATH. IN FACT, YOU'RE ALREADY
DEAD--YOU JUST DON'T KNOW IT. MY FRIEND HAS
SOMETHING TO SAY AS WELL. YOU'RE DEAD, JAY. THANKS FOR
SELLING MY GIRLFRIEND TO A PSYCHOPATH. HEAR THAT? KNOW
WHO THAT IS? LET'S JUST SAY HE'S PRETTY PISSED. HE'S
GONNA KILL YOU. I HOPE YOU'RE PREPARED. KEEP YOUR EYES
PEELED. THIS IS ALL JUST STARTING.
    --RED SAVAGE, AOL

I shouted aloud, to no one in particular. "I'm not dead! I'm trapped on this ugly, god-forsaken island. I want to go home. Why is nothing fair? I didn't sell anyone's girlfriend to anyone!" I probably would have continued, but Ryan approached.

The first thing I noticed about him was the fact that he was wearing skinny jeans—*they've been getting skinnier over the past year*, my mind reminded—and it took all I had to not say something rude about it. *Why are you wearing your girlfriend's pants?*

Ryan slurred slightly as he spoke. "What's wrong, Jay?"

He must have heard me yelling. I answered him, "Why do you care?"

"Maybe because I conthider you my friend. I want to help." He paused. "What's wrong?"

Everything is freaking wrong. I didn't say that though. "Read this and find out," I said as I handed him the folded up note.

Ryan unfolded it and read it over quickly. "Why is Jared writing death threats to you?" He handed it back.

"That was Jared?" *It makes sense. He thinks I took his girlfriend. Jared needs help; he's working with a psychopath. Or better yet, the psychopath is Jared, just another of his personalities.*

"Yeah, Jay, this right here is his writing." He pointed at the line that read: 'You're dead, Jay. Thanks for selling my girlfriend to

179

a psychopath.' He spoke again. "It doesn't make thense. Why does he want to kill you?"

Is Ryan really this clueless? I spoke. "Look, dude, I don't know where you've been the past lifetime—maybe pretending to be sick to get out of class—but Jared hates me. He beats me up constantly. I hate it. Now he's pretending I stole his girlfriend so he has a," I put up air quotes, "legitimate," I put them down, "excuse to kill me. He's a murderer. If he kills me, arrest him. Call the cops. Call the FBI. Seriously, my life is in jeopardy!" By this point I was on my feet, kicking sand left and right.

"Calm down, Jay. We're all in jeopardy. People have been dying every day. Who knows who's next." He paused—too long.

"I don't care if he's killed half our class. I heard all about that last night. I'm next. Didn't you read the note? Red said I'm so close to being dead it's like I already am—"

Ryan interrupted. "Actually—"

"I'm talking dude. Don't interrupt me! He's gonna kill me next. Then he's gonna kill you and Derek and Laura and everybody else. Don't think I'm lying. These notes tell the truth. I got one like two days ago. It said someone would be dead by morning, and—whaddaya know—someone was dead by morning. That dead person destroyed my group of friends. I'm not happy. Don't freaking bug me, loser!" Ryan's face showed signs of hurt. *Good,* I thought, *serves him right.*

Ryan turned to leave—*and probably cry*—but then turned back to me. "Before I leave, I just want to say that some kid with black hair gave me a Bible to give to you, but while Kyle and me were walking back last night, thomeone shot it out of my hand. I'm really thorry."

If only he could have shot you too; your grammar is atrocious—I, not me—idiot. I said, "It's not a big deal. I wouldn't have touched it anyways. If the book was worth reading, I wouldn't even be here."

Ryan was speechless. He waved and walked away, leaving me to my thoughts.

I hate people right now. They don't care about me at all. I'm not ready to die. Everyone clearly wants me to die though.

You might not be next. You thought you would be last time, but you weren't. It might happen again and cause more drama.

I doubt it. Red said I was practically dead already. I don't want more people to hate me either. What did he mean by, "it's all just starting," anyways? I've been here forever, and nothing just started.

I picked the knife off the ground and sauntered into camp, hoping to see no one, except maybe Joey.

*   *   *

I GREW ANGRY as I walked through camp and saw smiling faces. Sure, a few of them looked scared, and several were crying, but overall, they were at least forcing smiles. *How can anyone be happy at a time like this? I wish everyone could feel the way I feel. I can fake happiness, but right now I don't give a damn. I'm lonely, scared, and angry.*

Just then Joey walked out of a hut, stretched—exposing five inches of tie-dye boxers—and yawned. When he put his arms back down his baggy white shirt again covered his boxers.

"Joey," I called, "what are you doing in a hut?"

He turned his head left and right, looking for the source of my voice. He looked straight ahead and saw me. He threw his right hand into the air as if to say, "Hey," and then he walked over to me. When he was eight steps from me, he spoke. "Dose palm tree beds are super comfy, homie. Where were ya last night? Dere was an empty bunk in my room for ya."

"I was out on the beach. Thanks for looking for me." In all honesty, I didn't really care though—minus finding the note.

"I'm sorry, homie. Why were you on the beach?"

I cried myself to sleep. Yeah right I was going to say that. "I fell asleep there after talking to Laura."

I got a fist to my shoulder. "So it's you and Laura now?"

181

"No," I spat, with some extra words sprinkled with it. "She's a good girl. I don't go for those. You know that."

"Oh yeah. Ya like dem dirty girls. Da ones yo' parents hate."

"They have no right to tell me who I can and can't like. I'm eighteen."

Joey laughed. "Ain' dat da truth, homie? Dang, I've missed ya da past year."

"I've missed you too." I paused, contemplated a question, and then asked it anyway. "You and Nicole get freaky last night?" I doubted it—*she's got her head on straight*—but it was a fun question regardless.

"If only…" Joey trailed off, shuffled his feet in the sand, and stuffed his hands in his pockets. "We just chatted it up. She told me all about how ridiculous yo' school's gotten, how happy she is to be graduating—drawin' pictures in English class and everythin'. Dat's stupid, homie. I bet ya wish ya was still homeschooled." He paused before adding, "Drawin' pictures would be perfect for me. If I could get graded on my taggin' notebook, dat'd be straight legit."

I laughed at his comment. I loved how Joey's humor could turn my mood one hundred and eighty degrees. I was so enveloped in my conversation with Joey, directly outside his hut, that my classmates' background chatter faded into nothingness.

Joey continued. "She also told me how da best teacher at school is getting fired. Mr. Uro or something, just for slightly different beliefs. Ain' it a shame Christians can't get along?"

I can't agree more. Memories flooded back into my mind. *Mr. Uro is my favorite teacher; the reason I look forward to school each day. He is the only one left who actually cares about his job. The new English teacher is so confused; English isn't art, art isn't English. She thinks they are the same. I have no clue how she got them confused.*

Joey was still talking. "She also said she doesn't understand where all da chaperones went for dis trip. Dey'd been on the plane but disappeared right before da wreck."

"Good point." *Did I miss the rapture? Impossible. I'm saved. I prayed the prayer multiple times.*

Maybe the chaperones are teaching an object lesson? One of them is Red—pretending to kill people to teach something.

That's crazy!

"Part of me wishes they were here," I said.

"Why?" Joey asked. "Ya hate adults."

"True," I admitted. "But—"

"No buts," Joey said. "Ya can't hate and like adults."

"Whatever. I'd feel safer if they were here."

"I wouldn'. Dere'd be mo' rules."

I thought about that for a moment. *Rule—a four letter word that makes me sick. I hate them.*

I decided to change the subject. I spoke slowly, emphasizing every word. "Guess what I got this morning."

He made a stupid joke, to which I told him he was stupid, before I answered my own question. "I got another death threat."

"Seriously?" his smile fell into a frown. "What'd dis one say?"

I pulled it out of my back pocket and handed it to Joey. He read it, handed it back, and said, "Who's his friend?"

"That's Jared."

"I should have killed dat creep when I had da chance."

"We all should have," I spat. "I hate that guy. He deserves to die!"

"Yeah he does." Joey threw his middle finger up in the direction of the mountain.

"Guess what else," I offered.

"What?"

"Bryce tried to give me my Bible last night, but it got destroyed while it was on its way." I laughed as I said it.

Joey laughed too. "Dat sucks."

"Not really. It just goes to show that it's not as powerful as everyone thinks if a simple sniper rifle can kill it. I wasn't planning on reading it anyways."

Joey laughed again. "Good point."

"Yep. If the thing was true, I wouldn't be here. Camille would be alive. Kevin wouldn't hate my guts. Mr. Uro wouldn't be getting fired. I would never have had a stroke. I could go on."

"I feel ya, homie." Joey paused. Then he drastically changed the subject, "Nicole wanted me to go swimming with her dis morning. Wanna come along?"

"Sure," I said. "It beats sitting around bored and worried all day. Besides, Nicole's gotta look fine in a bathing suit."

"Shut up. She's mine."

"Oh really? I didn't see your name on her."

"It'll be dere. Just wait."

"How long?" I laughed. "Five or six more years?"

"Maybe." Joey laughed before saying, "Give it a week."

"Yeah right." *Jokes with Joey are the greatest.*

*   *   *

THE WATER FELT AWESOME, even though I was dressed in jean shorts. I had left my shirt, shoes, hat, and pack of cigarettes in a pile on the sand. *At least I'll feel cool for a while when I get out. Ima stay here as long as possible.* Joey and Nicole had swam some distance away to be with Mike, who was apparently still alive. *Too bad Justin's not around.*

Whatever, I thought in regards to them ditching me. *I can take care of myself.*

Something brushed against my leg, sending chills down my spine. *Oh no, a shark. This is why I haven't watched JAWS yet.*

I reached into my pocket where I felt soggy paper and my knife, and pulled the knife out. I freaked out and started thrashing around, swinging the knife like crazy. I looked down, but the water was too bubbly to see clearly. *I don't wanna be an animal's lunch.*

It brushed against my other leg, by my ankle, swimming the opposite direction. I screamed, as I realized it was too low to reach with my knife. I knew if I pulled my legs up, it wouldn't change the shark's position.

I saw Joey turn toward me. Then I went under. I kicked and thrashed and tried to get away, but there was a strong, poky grip on my left ankle. I couldn't reach it with the knife, and kicking at it didn't help to loosen its grip.

My air was running out. I couldn't inhale through my mouth; I couldn't inhale through my nose. I was going to drown.

What has me? It's not a shark. The grip isn't strong enough. I tried to get my head above the surface so I could open my eyes. *I hate opening my eyes in the ocean.* I couldn't get up; I was sinking lower. I kicked again. Nothing changed.

God, don't let me drown. I don't want to die.

That was the last thing I remembered as my whole body went limp.

CHAPTER 27

I AWOKE to voices. I opened my eyes to find myself back in the white room. Being able to hear was a pleasant surprise, but the light was blinding, so I decided to close my eyes again. *Did I drown? Why is everything so bright?* With my eyes closed I could discern three distinct voices.

One, a male, was talking about vitals. He was saying something about coming to and falling out.

Out of what? I wondered. My eyes were still closed.

A familiar sounding female voice spoke next. "Is he going to make it? I don't know what I'd do if he died." Sorrow was clearly evident in her voice. I knew the voice. It was soft and caring, yet demanding—for answers—at the same time.

Who is it? Camille? No, that was crazy. Camille was dead. I'd seen it with my own eyes.

The first voice spoke again. "I can't promise anything. It really just depends on how much he wants to be here."

That comment took me completely by surprise. *Where is here?* I opened my eyes and was temporarily blinded by the brightness. *Am I dead? Every time I wake up here, I am more convinced that I am dead, but the fact that I always return to the stupid island afterwards makes me question that possibility.*

The voice I hadn't isolated yet spoke. "He's awake." A brief pause. "Jay, can you hear me? It's your dad."

I still couldn't move my head, but as my eyes adjusted to the light, I recognized the man. He was the one in the green and black striped shirt the last time I was here. *So this is my dad? Why is he here?*

The woman came over too, and I recognized her as the woman in the blue top with the curly hair. "And your mom. How are you doing?" she asked.

Both of my parents are here too? How strange. Where am I? I finally saw the source of the first voice, and I realized that he was an angel dressed in pure white. *Heaven? But how can I be in Heaven? Last time I'd checked, I was stuck on an island. Plus, if this is Heaven, why aren't my parents dressed in white?*

I blinked again as I moved my eyes down. *What is this—a bed?* I was in a bed with white sheets. *Why am I in bed? This makes no sense.*

I opened my mouth to speak, but no words came out. *Why can't I talk?*

My mother spoke, "Why can't he say anything?"

The angel answered the question we both shared. "I think he's too surprised to speak."

I doubt that. Something is clearly wrong with me.

"So he's not mute?" my mother asked.

"No. That's not possible." He paused before clarifying, "Actually, it is possible, but no, his tests came back normal."

Tests? Deaf? In Heaven? This is all so crazy. Why am I trapped in a bed? I wanted answers, but none were being given to me.

The next thing I knew, I was passing out again. My eyes were getting heavy. My brain was getting cloudy. And my feet were asleep. The last thing I remembered was my parents telling me to pull through and that they loved me.

187

CHAPTER 28

(January 2008)

I OPENED MY EYES, as I had done numerous times since ending up stranded on the stupid island, and it was starting to feel cliché, but that's not the point. When I observed my surroundings this time, I was in the back of a car; *one of the most common settings for these stupid dreams.* Jay's mom was driving, and he was in the front seat. It couldn't have been much later than the last dream, because young-Jay looked almost no different. His hair might have been slightly longer, but he was still baby-faced—no facial hair—and still talked the same.

"School was great today, except that Ryan was out sick, supposedly," he said. "I have no homework for once, so I can't wait to go see if Joey can hang out."

"Don't you have cleaning chores to do?"

Jay's face instantly changed. "Do I have to do those today?"

"When was the last time you did them?"

He thought for a few seconds, before muttering, "I don't know."

"What?" she asked.

"I don't remember." He looked out the window at the passing businesses that lined the street. WENDY'S. IHOP. CHEVRON. MCDONALDS. "I haven't hung out with Joey in like three days. I chose video games over him 2 days ago, and yesterday I had too much homework. Can I please clean tomorrow?"

"No. You need to clean today. Once cleaning is done, hang out with Joey all you want."

*   *   *

JAY THREW HIS RED BACKPACK on his desk chair in his room. It was unzipped, and a stack of papers came out. I noticed one that read, "To-do: Algebra II, pg. 185 #1-60, odd; Spanish II: conjugate ten verbs in preterit; English 10: translate Shakespeare; etc." *What a liar. No homework, my butt.*

Jay instantly started to clean his room after he put headphones in and cranked up something under the Rap & Hip/hop genre on his mp3 player. *That's my dude,* I said to myself.

He partially rapped some of the lyrics he was listening to, and paying attention to him in cleaning mode helped me settle down mentally. "Allows no swearing . . . headphones blaring . . . Problem child, what bothers him all comes out."

I smiled. *I relate so well to this song.*

Jay kept talking. "He's talkin' back . . . brainwashed from rock and rap." I enjoyed jamming to Jay's music as I was forced to watch what ensued.

He began cleaning his room by going through all the loose papers scattered around his room: whether it was on his desk, his dresser, or anywhere; he threw them all onto the floor. Then he sat down on the floor and organized it: one pile for trash, and one pile for keeping. Most of the trash pile had to do with school; it entered the trash can. The rest was piled on his desk.

This is really boring. The only cool thing about this is his dedication to getting stuff clean.

He then got a dust rag and dusted off every surface in his room. Next, he vacuumed his floor. And finally—after spending about thirty minutes in his room—he climbed the ladder up to his loft bed, and ripped all the sheets off it, and he threw them onto the floor. *So much for dusting your room.* He climbed back down, picked up the sheets, and walked downstairs into the laundry room. He started the laundry and walked out to the kitchen where he found his mom with the house-phone in her hand.

Her face was one that he couldn't describe. It was confused, scared, and distant.

Jay pulled the headphone out of his left ear, paused his music, and sat down at the island in the middle of the kitchen. *Who died?* Jay spoke, "I'm done cleaning. I'm going down to Joey's." He paused. "Are you okay?"

"Jay," his mom began, "Joey's not home."

Joey isn't home? Where is he? "As a homeschooler, he should always be home." Jay and I were speaking in harmony. "Did he die?"

"No," Jay's mother began, "but if he doesn't start to get his life in order, he will die long before his time." She paused. "The phone just rang a few minutes ago, but you probably didn't hear it through your headphones. It was Joey's mom. She..." she trailed off.

"What did she say?" Jay asked, getting louder.

The suspense is killing me.

"Joey," his mom said slowly, "is in juvenile hall." She walked closer to Jay, who stood still as a board.

That's what Bryce was talking about; by senior year Joey isn't getting in trouble with the law anymore.

"What? When? Why?" Jay blurted, and I noticed his eyes misting up.

"His mom told me it happened two nights ago," she answered. "He refused to do his chores and stole a car instead. He's been charged with grand theft auto." She reached Jay and tried to hug him.

"Please don't touch me," Jay said. His eyes were on the verge of tears.

He ran out of the kitchen, rushed up to his room, and climbed up the ladder to his sheet-less bed. And he cried. He screamed, "God, WHY?? My best friend my whole life is now gone.

What am I going to do??? I have no one now! Not Joey, not Jared; Ryan's always 'sick.' Why, God? Why do You do this?"

God didn't do this, I wanted to tell Jay. *It was Jay's own fault. He had just explained that two nights earlier he decided to play video games instead of hanging out with Joey. If he'd gone there instead of playing dumb video games and probably spending time on the internet, Joey would still be there.*

It makes sense. Joey would have done the dishes so that he could chill with Jay. If only Jay had gone over there. Joey would be completely different if it wasn't for that dumb choice. This was all Jay's fault and now, *he can't forgive himself.*

Jay was talking, matching my thoughts exactly. *Weird.* "It also explains the night before, when Joey's sister said he wasn't home. Duh, because he was locked up. Why did this have to happen, God? I thought You protected Christians."

The thoughts made him cry for an hour.

As my vision faded, I had to shout, "God is a lie; this is yet another story that proves it. Don't buy the lie, Jay." I knew he couldn't hear me. It was just something I had to say.

CHAPTER 29

(Day 5, 9:30 a.m.)

I AWOKE to feel someone's lips pressed against mine. I lay still so I could take it all in. *Now I'm starting to remember what a kiss feels like; it's been so long.* I started coughing uncontrollably, and then realized I wasn't being kissed; I was being given CPR. I shifted my gaze to my right where I saw Nicole's bikini-clad body move away from me. *The lips are hers. Joey would kill me if he knew. What's going on?* Part of me wanted to freak out. Another part wanted to take it all in. I sat up wondering, *What happened?* A crowd of my peers surrounded me. Joey, Nicole, Mike, Derek, and Laura were the closest—proximity wise.

I could tell it was Laura because her hairdo matched what I had seen the night before in the torchlight. Her long, red hair was in a ponytail, falling in front of her left shoulder.

"You practically drowned," Nicole announced. Joey, next to her, shook his head affirmatively.

I reached my arm around to my back and attempted to brush the sand off. *That would explain all the sand. I hate this stuff. It gets everywhere.*

Joey added to Nicole's statement. "Yeah, homie. We were all swimmin' when all of a sudden ya screamed and went under. Ya were thrashin' around like crazy, and den ya completely disappeared. I don' know wha' happened, but by da time I reached ya, ya were passed out, sinkin' to da bottom of da ocean. I pulled ya up and swam ya to shore. Nicole applied CPR and den ya woke up. I'm so glad you're alive."

"Me too, Joey." The memory of the incident flooded back. "I thought it was a shark at first, but after it grabbed my leg I realized it was more like someone's hand."

"Who would try to kill you?" Laura asked.

"Jared. Red. Kevin." I paused. "The list grows every day."

"Who's Red?" Laura asked. Her face didn't look caring like it had in the torchlight the previous night. It looked concerned.

"The killer." *I can't believe she hasn't heard the name yet.*

"You know his name? How?" she asked. Her eyes bore into me.

"He left me a note. He signed it himself."

"Do you still have it?" she asked. She held out her hand.

"Yeah. Right here." I put my hands in my pockets and brought them out empty. *My notes and my knife are gone. I had them when I went swimming. This isn't good. How will I protect myself?* I felt my pockets again, pulled them inside out, and realized, *When I passed out I must have dropped the knife onto the ocean floor.*

Joey, who'd been stuck on the non-shark comment, spoke again. "It would explain dese marks in yo' leg." He slid his fingers over my left leg, just above my ankle.

I looked where he pointed and saw four imprints, moving up my leg in a row. Fingernail marks. *Who would want to drown me? Does Red have long fingernails? Who knows? The list of questions in my mind is getting longer, and answers are getting sparser. I'm sick of this.*

Laura asked again. "Where's the note?" Her hand was still extended, and her eyes were still boring into me.

"Uh, I don't know. I must have lost it in the ocean."

Laura shook her head. "Uh huh," she said doubtfully. A look of fear crossed her face.

193

Why does my stupidity, or more likely, my pain, cause her to be disappointed? Also, why did her acknowledgment sound like she doesn't believe me.

Derek, the black kid who'd been there the day David was killed, spoke up, cutting my thought line short. "Well, seeing as how Jay was almost killed, I think it's safe to say he's not our guy."

Huh? My thoughts instantly resumed, ten times faster than before. *Who is their guy? They certainly don't think I'm the killer, do they? That is preposterous if they do. The killer is on a murderous rampage and almost drowned me not an hour earlier. How do they possibly think I'm the killer? What else would they mean by 'our guy' though?* I stayed silent.

Laura shook her head. "I'm not convinced. Remember what I said earlier? That plan is still on."

I'm lost. What had she said earlier? Are they the killers? Is Laura Red? Am I her guy—as in her next target? That's what the note had said, so if she is Red, then she is going to get me. That's the plan she had said—or written—earlier.

Laura spoke up. "Do you want to go for a walk, Jay? Just you and me?"

What a stupid question. Of course I don't. If you're Red, there's no way in hell I'm going to go off alone with you. Then I spoke. "No. You might kill me!" I jumped to my feet and backed away quickly, tripping over my own feet in the process and falling backwards on my butt, which caused a snicker to erupt from the onlookers.

Laura stepped toward me, and extended her hand to help me up. Her face didn't look as accusatory anymore. Her eyes were still piercing, but they had dulled a bit in the past few minutes. "Why would you think that? All I want to do is help you. If anything, I'm worried that you will kill me."

Now she's blame shifting. She is Red. She says I'm Red. I want truth. I am so sick of lies. All I wanted to know was why I was on the island. Why no one liked me. And why someone was trying to kill me. *None of those questions have been answered. And now there're more. Who is trying to kill me? A classmate?*

"Tell me the truth," I finally said, not accepting the helping hand she had offered. "What's your plan that's still on? Are you going to take me off all alone and get rid of me?" I was still sitting in the sand.

"No," Laura said.

Derek elaborated. "We want to be on the same page about who the killer is. About what you know and what we know. Laura offered to walk with you to talk and find stuff out. That's the plan she was talking about."

"Thanks, Derek," she said.

I spoke. "So we just want to share stories? No one is going to get killed?" I felt a smile forming on my face. "I'm down." *I wasn't going to die at her hands. Anything is better than sitting around on the beach alone all day. Even talking one-on-one with a good girl sounds good. Why not? I don't want to be left alone with my thoughts like I was last night.* "When do we leave?"

*   *   *

THE WALK HAD TAKEN US NORTH of their camp, up to a nice spot next to the stream that ran through the island. Sure, "nice" is a very loose word when your entire surroundings look like the Southern California countryside during fire season, but what made this place nicer than another was the nearby trickle of running water. Bunches of rocks lay scattered about no more than thirty paces north, on our side of the stream.

They looked like fun rocks to climb on, but we both stopped walking thirty paces away when she turned and looked straight at me. "So your experience has been just as nightmarish as mine, then," she said. It was more of a statement than a question. I had been describing my adventure so far, after I had heard her explain hers. *Mine has definitely been crazier.*

For her, the stress of being in charge and trying to keep order, while people dropped like flies, was the second worst part.

195

Losing close friends was the worst. She also explained that Jared had come back the day before and had tried to claim the island for himself again. He had been acting weird. The first example of weirdness was how he acted about questions relating to Johnny and Zac. She told me that Jared had beat up Ryan for asking about them, and earlier had snapped at her, "Am I my friends' keeper?" The second example of weirdness she shared about Jared was how he was convinced that I was the killer who had kidnapped Jaime.

In telling my story, I explained the notes about Jaime—in mine, Red had her; in Jared's, I had her—and also pointed out that we had seen Jared earlier, and that he had told us, without being asked, that he had found Johnny and Zac murdered. I then continued by talking about how I was repeatedly going unconscious and having annoying flashbacks about my life. I asked her if Jared was still at her camp, and she said that she didn't know for sure; she hadn't seen him after he beat up Ryan and ran away. From there I explained how I had repeatedly received beatings from him since ending up on the island, and I told her that I didn't want to be at her camp if there was any chance Jared was still there.

She assured me that she was pretty sure that he was not there any longer, and then summed up our conversation to that point by saying, "So your experience has been just as nightmarish as mine, then."

"Yeah, it's been terrible. I never thought I'd say it, but I want to go back to the desert." I paused before adding, "Though it has had its high points: hanging out with friends, being away from rules, being away from God. *Life* is great." I felt a sly smile cross my face as I emphasized the word 'life'. "Constant fear of death though is a different story." *There is nothing truly great about the past few days, but I've got to force myself to think positive anyways.*

"Away from God?" she asked. "What's great about that?"

196

"Everything. I mean look: at school all we ever hear is God, God, God. Look at reality though: a plane crash, no rescuers, a psychotic killer. What more proof do you need? God isn't real."

Laura pointed at a palm tree and asked, "How do you explain this then?"

"What do you want me to explain?" I asked. "It's totally dead."

She ignored my statement, focusing on the question, and asked, "How'd it get here? How'd you and I get here? How'd anything get here? And by 'here', I mean on Earth. You need to have an answer to that question."

"I admit God made it. There's no other explanation. Evolution is retarded—that's not the answer. God made everything and then He ran away from it."

"I can't believe you would say that." Laura seemed surprised.

"Find a verse for me that says otherwise." *Why am I being so honest about this stuff again? My classmates and friends don't need to know these thoughts.*

She was silent for several seconds. She looked left, right, up, and down, and then at me.

I didn't let her think any longer. "It's not like it would matter anyways. The Bible is a bunch of junk. 'Ask and you will receive'? Yeah right. What a stupid lie. I've proved that verse false my entire life. Nothing I've ever prayed for has ever come true."

She didn't speak; she stared at me. The stream trickled on in the silence.

"You're speechless. I'm right." I smiled wryly.

"That doesn't mean anything," Laura said.

I changed the subject. "So what's the real reason you wanted to talk to me alone? I don't believe the whole 'same page' speech that Derek gave."

"That's the only reason. Here's some specifics though. We have no clue who the killer is. You've been acting strange ever since we were stranded here. Logically, we think it might be you,

197

especially after Jared explained to me yesterday that he was told that you had taken Jaime. Before that, Derek told us that Peter yelled your name the day David was killed, and then, when we went back to retrieve his body, both his body and Peter were gone. There was a blood pool where David had fallen and a separate blood trail leading away from the area. No one's seen Peter since."

She was still talking. "I wanted to pick your brain and see what I could find out. So far, lots of anger, and no reason to believe you're innocent. I mean look—you're the first person to give our killer a name—and not a name like 'the Friday Night Killer' or something similar—but rather a proper name. You were seen at the scene of the crime once. And you were named as guilty by Jared. Your proof of someone else having Jaime conveniently floated out of your pocket when you almost drowned. You could have staged that to throw us off."

I turned and started to stomp away.

What were we supposed to think!" She yelled, so I'd be sure to hear as I walked away.

"I am not the freaking killer! I can't freaking believe anyone would accuse me! What kind of a Christian are you, judging me like that?" I didn't even turn around as I said it.

"Come back, Jay!"

"No!" I continued. "In case you don't remember, my girlfriend, Camille, died in the plane crash. She was everything to me. I can't believe you would think I could have killed her. Also, my best friend's cousin was killed, and it destroyed our friendship. Do you honestly think I would want that to happen? That I would kill him and wreck a lifelong friendship?" I finally stopped walking, a good distance away, and turned around to look at Laura. My eyes were on the verge of tears.

Laura started walking over to me. "I'm sorry."

"Leave me alone. I don't want to see you ever again."

Laura stopped walking toward me, turned around, and walked away without another word.

Good riddance.

*　　*　　*

I SAT by the stream on one of the rocks that I had noticed earlier when Laura and I had stopped walking. I had put my shirt and hat back on before going on my walk with Laura, leaving my shoes on the beach since my feet were covered in wet sand. Now that I was alone, I took out a cigarette and lit it. *I'm sick of people assuming stuff about me. They assume I'm weird because my parents are so strict. They assume I love Bible verses because it is easy to memorize them. They assume I'm the killer because I know his name. So stupid, because they'd know the killer's name too if they'd received the creepy notes from him like I had. It is so dumb.* I kicked myself for not putting my notes and knife with my shirt before swimming. *It would have prevented everything.*

Kevin hates me. I've known Kevin since at least first grade, though probably even kindergarten. Friendships rooted that far back don't easily break up. We've gotten in tons of trouble over the years. Not as much as Joey and I, but still lots of trouble. And, in the space of twenty-four hours, it has all fallen apart. Why? If God was real, none of this would have happened. If only He truly existed...

Camille is dead. More proof that God is too. I still remember her beautiful brown hair and gorgeous blue eyes. Everything about her was perfect. Her lips that meshed perfectly with mine—brought the tears to my eyes. *I want a kiss. How long has it been since I kissed Camille—even I can't remember. Why is she dead? I want her back, but I know she isn't coming back.*

God, I shouted in my mind, *if you're real, I hate you!*

My eyes had focused on the trees around me, during those thoughts. Even though they were ashen and splintered and dead, it was clear to my eyes that little green shoots were growing out of them. *That's peculiar.*

Crashing in the trees interrupted my thoughts. "Who goes there?" I called.

"It's Jacob," the voice called back. Then he appeared from behind the trees. "How are you? I haven't seen you in a while." He sat on a rock next to mine, and lit a cigarette as well.

"I've been better," I said, puffing on my cigarette. "My best friends, except for Joey, hate me, and my classmates all think that I'm the killer. You don't think that, do you?" I asked.

Jacob was quiet for several awkward seconds, as he played with the holes in his jeans with his fingers. The stream trickled in the background. He took a drag on his cigarette, and spoke as he exhaled. "Killer? What killer? Am I going to die?"

I was taken aback by his questions. *How does anyone not realize there's a killer on the loose?* "His name is Red. He's been killing lots of people. My friend's cousin. Lots of my classmates. My girlfriend. The list goes on, and it grows every day. Even Jaime, that Jared retard's girlfriend, got kidnapped. I don't know if she is still alive, though it would serve her right if she was dead. She's so annoying." I shivered and pulled my legs up under my chin and wrapped my arms around them.

Jacob looked down, still playing with the holes in his jeans with the hand that was not holding a cigarette. "Wow. That is bad." He rubbed his foot in the dirt. "I hope he doesn't find me. I'm not ready to die."

"You think I am?" I asked. "Seriously, the psycho is going to get me. He said it himself in the notes he sent." I paused before saying, "Oh, and Jared is working for the killer. He wrote part of my last note."

"Wow, that's no fun. You should find Jared and kill him before he gets you."

"I wish it was that easy. He's way bigger than me." I flicked the cherry off the end of my cigarette.

"Size doesn't matter when you have a weapon," He left the last word hanging as if he was going to say more, but he never did. He took a drag on his cigarette instead.

"I lost my knife when I was almost drowned this morning," I said. "How am I supposed to get a weapon?"

200

"You were almost drowned? What happened?"

I explained about being invited to go swimming, and how my friends had swam away from me. I explained the brushing against my leg and being dragged under. I ended with, "But where am I supposed to find a weapon?"

"That sucks. Who did it?"

I was getting annoyed that Jacob wasn't answering my question, but I didn't want to appear rude, so I answered his question. "I don't know. I wish I did, cuz I'd kill them. It was probably Red or Jared. Who else would have it in for me?"

"Kevin?" Jacob asked.

"No," I said emphatically. "He hates me, but he wouldn't try to kill me. I've known him since kindergarten."

"You'd be surprised," Jacob said. "When I was a junior in high school, one of my friends I'd known since second grade brought a gun to school and killed like six people—two of the victims had been his friends." He took a final drag on his cigarette and threw the butt into the stream.

"Maybe he was mentally deranged," I offered. "Kevin isn't. I promise he didn't try to drown me. I swear it on the Bible." I took another hit of my cigarette.

"That swear wouldn't mean anything if you don't believe the Bible, though," Jacob stated, lighting another cigarette. "So I don't really believe you."

That's interesting to think about. If the Bible is fake, swears on it are fake too. "Okay," I said. "I swear on my life that he isn't mentally deranged."

"That's more like it." A smirk crossed his face. "So how's Camille doing?"

Wow, I thought. *The worst possible time to bring her up. And the worst way to word the question.* Tears instantly struck my eyes. "She's dead. Why do you have to word it like she is still alive? I wish she was alive. I want her comfort back. Her hugs. Her kisses. Her laughs. Everything. I miss her so much. Stop bringing her up. Please!"

"I'm sorry," Jacob said, smiling as if he didn't mean it. "I'll stop." He took a drag on his cigarette.

"What is your problem?" I whined. "Do you even care about me at all?" I threw the rest of my cigarette into the stream, too angry to keep smoking it.

"Yes I do," Jacob said soothingly, exhaling smoke.

I was hunched over, crying into my hands.

"I won't bring her up again. I swear on my eternal resting place."

"You do?" I looked up and smiled. *If he swears on Heaven then there is no way he can change his mind or else he will end up in Hell. It is genius.* "Thank you."

"You're very welcome, Jay." Jacob paused. "Hey, I gotta run, but if you want a weapon, meet me at the base of the volcano at noon. That's two hours from now. See you then."

So it is a volcano? I reasoned. *I guess Jacob has been able to explore the island more than me. Red is obviously not after him, which would also explain why he didn't know about the killer.* "Thanks," I said. I wiped the tears from my eyes and smiled excitedly. *In two hours I will have a weapon. Things can start improving.* "See you then," I said as Jacob ran off.

As I listened to the trickle of the stream—alone once more with my thoughts—another sound came to my ears.

It was a distant, solitary voice that was getting closer. "What a load of crap. You're not saved. Seriously? Who says that to their best friend?" It was Kevin. I was worried, but I kept listening. "I've known Bryce for practically my whole life, but I can't stand being around him right now."

Kevin was drawing nearer to me. "So, maybe I'll go back to his little good boy camp after I let out some steam. I hate this freaking island. All my friends have turned into jerks. Jay telling me that God hates my cousin. Joey siding with Jay. Bryce telling me I'm going to Hell if I get killed by the Red guy. What next? This is all so freaking stupid. Bullcrap, I like to call it."

I wanted to run. Kevin was going crazy.

"What are ya doing here?" Kevin yelled.

My mind spun faster than ever, and cursed at the realization, *He saw me.*

Kevin came within five paces of me and repeated his question.

"I was just thinking. What about you?"

"The same. Bryce pissed me off. He said I wasn't a Christian."

"Seriously?" *Maybe we can get on the same side again,* I thought hopefully, before speaking again. "He said the same to me the other day. What's gotten into him? He never cared about church or anything before."

"I don't know," Kevin said. "But whatever it is, I can't stand it. I want the old Bryce to come back. Drinking, smoking, girl-chasing Bryce. Where'd he go?"

"I don't know, man." I thought for a second before continuing. "I never really knew that Bryce. I knew the church going Bryce who didn't push stuff onto others."

"Yeah? You mean the same way ya are? The type that thinks the whole world is out to get him? The type that hates God? The type that tells me that my cousin is in Hell? Dammit, Jay, I want to kill ya so badly."

"Wait," I pleaded. "I'm sorry about that comment. It didn't come out right. I meant to say—"

Kevin grabbed me by the neck, cutting me off midsentence. "I don't care what ya meant to say. All I know is what ya said, and it was some of the stupidest crap I've ever heard. What happened to good-boy Jay? Maybe I can knock some sense back into ya."

I was having trouble breathing. A knock to the top of my head made my world go black.

CHAPTER 30

(February 2008)

I WAS IN A CAR. It was not one I could remember being in before. When I glanced out the windows I recognized it as a white car: hatchback and long hood, kind of like a baseball cap. I laughed at the thought. Young-Jay was sitting in the front passenger seat, and a familiar-looking man was driving, though it was impossible to place him. *Did I get arrested in a highly undercover cop car? Kidnapped? Who is this guy?* We drove past Desert Valley Church, and we kept going a little farther until we stopped at a red light by a CARL'S JR. When the light turned green we kept going straight. We turned into a STARBUCKS parking lot thirty seconds later. *Looks like I'm fine,* I realized. *Who is this guy though?*

Jay spoke as they climbed out of the car. "Thanks, Ted."

"You're welcome. Order whatever you want when we go inside. This is time for a focused talk with you."

"Okay, cool." Jay smiled.

Is this the youth minister from that earlier flashback? I don't know what's going on. Why are they talking?

When inside, Jay ordered a FRAPPUCCINO and Ted ordered a cappuccino. They sat down at a table, while waiting for their drinks, and they partook of small talk, until the barista called their names. They hopped up to get their drinks, and when they sat back down, Ted posed the first question.

"Your mom's been telling me that you aren't doing so well. Why are you so down in the dumps the past few weeks, Jay?"

"For one, Joey's in jail and it's all my fault."

Yeah it is. You shouldn't be such a selfish jerk.

Ted cut him off there. "Why is that your fault?"

"Cuz I could have kept him from going."

"How?"

Jay unloaded the story. "Joey was at home supposed to be doing chores when he decided to leave. I was playing video games when he left. I had thought about playing with him instead of doing video games, but video games won. If I'd just have gone and knocked on his door, he would have had a reason to get his chores done and come outside with me."

"Are you sure?"

"Yes."

Ted's face grew serious. "You have no way to prove that he would have done that."

"You have no proof he wouldn't have," Jay said. "You all are so annoying: you, my mom, my dad. Everyone says Joey wouldn't have wanted to hang out, but—pardon my language—you don't have a dang clue. I've known Joey since kindergarten. He's always gotten chores done in order to chill with me. Don't say that he wouldn't have this time." His voice had risen, and people were glancing over at them from other tables. He continued, "I've known Joey for eleven years. You've known him for like four—if that. I know that he would finish chores to come outside with me."

Ted remained calm. "Maybe you are right. However, you can't go around hating the world as a result. I want to help you, which is why I brought you here; let's have a calm discussion, and not try to yell over each other the whole time."

His calmness is impressive after Jay's outburst, and while Jay will be scared to actively "hate the world" around this guy, there's no stopping the inevitable. The reason for this stupid dream is a prime example.

Ted was still talking. "The Bible says in Romans 8:28 that everything is part of God's plan, and as your youth pastor I'm supposed to help you see what the Bible says. That verse says that

205

everything happens for a reason. So, maybe it is true that Joey wouldn't have gone to jail if you had gone down to his house, but the point is that you didn't, he did go to jail, and that's how God planned it."

That's a horrible thing to say. That's like saying God gave me a stroke for a reason. This is complete bullcrap. I'm sick of hearing about God. Aren't youth pastors supposed to be cool and chill? Let's keep God out of this discussion.

"But why?" Jay questioned. "Why would God do something like that? Does that mean that God gave me a stroke for a reason?"

Ted was quiet. He took a drink of his cappuccino and then spoke. "God isn't evil. He doesn't do wicked things. God didn't give you your stroke, and He didn't make Joey steal his parent's car. He uses the wicked things that we do to bring about good. That good is usually not clear in the moment, and it may *never* become obvious, but the truth is that God has a plan and we must trust it."

Jay nodded, and I was cussing him out in my mind. *This is the stupidest conversation that I have ever heard.*

Jay vocalized his response. "Why do we have to trust? Why can't we just see everything laid out in a row for us to know clearly?"

"Yeah," I said, despite knowing that no one would hear me. "I say screw all this and move on with life. God's gone; He doesn't care; He hates me. And I hate Him too. He gave me a stroke; He put my best friend in jail. He's not good, and I won't trust Him. If I'm going to trust Him, then I need Him to give me a reason to trust Him."

I must have missed his answer, because Ted was on a different topic. "Do you think Joey's parents will let him live with them when he gets out?"

Jay thought for a second. "It could go either way. Yes, because he is their son. No, because he messed up too badly." He settled with, "No. I don't think they will."

"Why?"

"Well, with all Joey's told me about his family, they hate his guts. Now they have more reason to hate his guts. It's just the excuse they need to kick him out."

Well yeah, he's a smoker. Of course they hate him.

"I disagree," Ted said. "His parents love him. I've talked to them since he got caught. They're planning on letting him come home. Everyone deserves a second chance..."

I zoned out. *Why'd he ask if he already knew the answer? It's so dumb.*

"What would your parents do if you were Joey?" Ted asked.

"My dad would kill me. My mom would cry. They hate it every time I do something wrong. And I can't ever do anything right."

Ted must have opened a can of worms on this one. Since when does Jay not get along with his family? I thought they were close.

Jay was still talking, "I try so hard to make them proud, but it seems like they never notice. All they ever notice is every time I do something wrong. It drives me insane. They yell at me all the time. If I went to jail they would kill me."

Ted's face grew grave. "I know how you feel. My dad wasn't very good either. He was always drunk, and he treated my family like dirt. All you have to remember is that one day you'll be out of there. This is a normal phase: teenagers don't get along with their parents. Just remember that this too will pass, much like Joey's time in juvenile hall, and life will improve."

"My dad's never gotten drunk though. He said he'd kill me if I ever tried alcohol or cigarettes."

I laughed internally at that. *You should be happy you got away with it that first time, then.*

Jay continued, "I just hate all the yelling about everything else and the lack of notice for the good things I do." Jay paused before he finally concluded. "I can't wait to move out. I'll never yell at my kids."

"Famous last words." Ted was smiling.

I'll show him. I don't yell. I hate yelling. It's my biggest pet peeve.

Their conversation continued for another thirty minutes, and then they left.

The next thing I knew, my vision went black, again. *Figures.*

CHAPTER 31

(Day 5, 12 p.m.)

I AWOKE at noon, judging by the position of the sun. I rolled onto my back and sat up from there. I glanced around, trying to figure out what I was supposed to be doing. *Jacob was talking before Kevin came around. What was he saying? I'm pretty sure it was important. What was it?* I stood to my feet and decided to start walking.

I saw dead palm trees as far as I could see, and again—due west—was the mountain that I now knew was a volcano. *I still haven't checked that thing out. I'm going to see what it's like. I hope it's extinct.* From my slowly returning memory of my life I could remember that I had been enthralled with volcanos as a child. I started walking toward it.

The last couple dreams I had had were still resonating in my mind. *Joey went to jail because I played video games instead of talking to him. Then Ted Sweet, my youth pastor, told me it wasn't my fault at all. He's a pastor, so he must have been right. It couldn't have been my fault that Joey went to jail.*

It is your fault. You cared more about a dumb video game than your friend. If anything should have come before him, it was homework, but you chose video games. You're a lousy friend.

Shut up! I didn't do anything wrong. He didn't have self-control, he stole the stupid car, and he ended up in jail. I'm innocent.

I was arguing with myself again, and I hated it. I changed the thought process.

What is wrong with Kevin these days? We used to be close. Now he hates my guts and wants to kill me. I blame this god-forsaken island. Something is clearly wrong with it.

I think so too. How about Jacob constantly bringing up Camille? That's gotta hurt. I think he hates you too.

No. He's just confused; same as me. He forgets we're in danger, that Camille isn't alive, and that I can take care of myself.

You? Take care of yourself? Yeah right. You're a pathetic loser. No one likes you. Camille died. And Jacob has to help you survive by giving you a weapon. How pathetic.

Now my own mind is jamming a rusty knife into my heart. I hate you. I'd get rid of you, but I'd have to cut off my own head to do it. I don't wanna die yet.

My thoughts latched onto the weapon reminder.

He did promise me a weapon. He told me to meet him at noon. I hope I'm not too late. My thoughts paused for a second. *Where is Jacob getting this stuff: food, weapons, cigarettes, magazines, booze? We're both trapped on the same island. Weird.*

Whatever. At least I haven't seen Jared recently. That makes everything slightly better. He wrote part of that note, but otherwise, he's disappeared. It's awesome. I hope I don't see him until after I get my weapon from Jacob.

I also can't believe that Laura thinks I'm the killer. I was almost drowned. I didn't drown myself. So stupid. Some people just aren't as smart as me. The cuts in my leg hurt. I wish I had some ointment.

All I want are answers. I started running toward the volcano.

*   *   *

NO MORE THAN TEN MINUTES LATER I was almost at the base of the volcano. I was surprised I had made as good time as I had in my bare feet.

The landscape at this part of the island was unlike anything else I'd seen yet in my time on the island. Sure, it made

210

sense of why the rest of the island was burnt-out and lava-bomb littered, but as I passed from the palm tree cemetery into a wide clearing at the base of the volcano, volcanic rock made up the ground instead of dirt. The purplish rock extended from within the cemetery all the way up to the peak of the mountain. The sun's reflection from directly above burned my eyes and face, and I had long given up on worrying about sunburns. My feet sizzled from the heat on the rock, which caused me to hop back and forth.

I glanced down and saw my exposed lower legs and arms below my green and black plaid sleeves. If a lobster was looking at me, he would think he needed a tan. I took off my previously-white hat, which somehow had survived the whole experience so far, and used it to fan myself. It was filthy—covered in mud and sand.

I was also alone. *I'm late.* Just then I heard pounding footsteps. *Good. I'm not too late. Jacob is coming to meet me, give me a gun, and then the next time I see Jared or Kevin, I'll be ready.* The footsteps sped up.

They approached from the east, from within the same thick grove of dead trees from which I had just emerged. I saw a figure approaching as I squinted under the hot sun, blinking sweat out of my eyes. However, the closer he got, the more worried I became. He wasn't dressed in baggy, trashy clothes, and his hair wasn't long, brown, and greasy. His hair looked as though it had been neatly trimmed and blonde on arrival, though now was dirt-caked and shaggy, and his shorts were brown. He was shirtless and tan. I cursed repeatedly. *It's Jared.*

"Where's Jacob?" I asked as he entered the clearing I had just stepped into.

"Who's that, Liyfer loser?" he replied. Then he added, "Or should I say, 'loser for life'?"

I let a stream of profanity fly. All of it was directed at Jared. "Jacob's the guy who sent me here, moron."

I was very surprised when he just ignored my profane tirade. "Well, my friend Jason sent me. He told me you were coming. He told me to give you something."

211

Who is Jason? The only person who knew I was coming was Jacob. Jacob has a weapon for me. What does Jason have for me? If he's friends with Jared, it can't be good.

"He said you were expecting a weapon, so he wanted me to give you this," Jared said as he reached into his pocket. He pulled out a BIC pen.

Huh? I thought.

Jared spoke before I had a chance. "Words are weapons. You said it yourself about a year ago." He switched to a high pitched voice mocking me. "I'll take all the beatings you want to give me, as long as you stop calling me names, because names hurt more." He switched back to his voice and finished speaking. "If that's true, here's a pen to write some dangerous words back to me. You just *love* writing anyways; it shouldn't be a problem."

I took the pen from him and answered back, "It's true. I hate being called names. I hate being thrown around. I wanna be treated like a human. Not chewed out. Not beat up. Not made fun of. How would you like it if someone treated you like that?" I wiped the sweat off my face with my arm.

"I'd hate it. You did it to me indirectly by stealing Jaime. What did you do to her before giving her to Red? I swear I'll kill you if you even touched her."

"Never." My thoughts started running wild. *I didn't give her to Red. I never thought of touching her. She's not my type. Besides, I'm a freaking virgin. Plan to be 'til marriage so I don't get a disease.*

Jared kept talking. "In our intimate time this morning, Jaime told me about all you put her through. What happened to Jay, the" he put up partial air quotes, "good, little, Christian boy?" He put them down. "You raping people now?" He paused to regain his breath. "I'm going to kill you if it's the last thing I do."

A smirk crossed my face because of his air quotes. *You can't do them right when you're missing the first two fingers on one hand.*

But then my brain registered his accusations. *What is he talking about? I talked to her for two minutes—unfortunately—the other day and she slapped me and sent me away. I have zero attraction to her. I never touched her. I don't go for anorexic girls. Never have; never will.* I spoke. "What the hell are you talking about? I would never get with an anorexic girl like her. My standards are higher."

"That's easy for you to say, rapist!" Jared shouted. His fist caught me in the stomach.

I crumpled to the ground, coughing. *I'm so confused. Jaime's anything but my type. Yes, she is dirty, but I don't want her. She's been around the block a few times too many. Everytime she speaks I just want to kill myself—maybe an exaggeration— because her voice is that annoying.* I looked up at Jared and spoke. "I'm not a rapist, idiot. In fact, I'm still a helpless virgin. You should enjoy that piece of information. You always have." *I just want him to leave. I'll say whatever gets him to go away.*

"Liar!" Jared spat. "You've abused my girl a lot. Don't deny it. I have proof."

Proof? That's impossible. What kind of crack is he smoking? It's gotta be good, because it's transformed me into the villain in his mind. That's not good for me at all. The words slurred nervously off my tongue as I asked, "What proof do you have that I've been with Jaime?"

Jared reached into his back pocket and pulled out several pieces of paper. He threw them at me and they fell, images facing up, onto the ground. *Photographs.*

The images took my breath away. I felt happy, angry, and ashamed at the same time. *Jaime's naked. I'm with her. It's not true. I only look at this stuff alone. Jared's here.* I couldn't even begin to describe the pictures. They were horrible. And, with Jared standing there, I didn't want to stare at Jaime. "Why'd you PHOTOSHOP my face onto pictures of you and Jaime?" I asked. *That's the only logical explanation.* I was still fanning the sweat off my face with my hat.

"That ain't me, rapist," Jared said. "I've got more abs than that guy. It's clearly you. Stop denying that fact and just tell me

213

why the hell you were sleeping with Jaime." He paused. "Actually, screw it. I'm gonna just kick your ass right now and leave you for dead."

I dropped my hat as I jumped to my feet and ran away. *Where does he find justification to accuse me of sleeping with Jaime? I'm a dang virgin; I've barely even kissed a girl before. I've watched porn—lots of it, yes—but that's not having sex. It only involves me, not someone else. No one gets hurt from it, and no one gets pregnant from it, and no one gets diseases from it. It's purely entertainment—even art in some people's minds.*

Where'd he get those pictures? How'd he get those pictures? There's no way they're real.

I kept running. I looked over my shoulder to see Jared following—gaining ground. I cursed as I tightened my grip on the pen in my hand and kept running. Left foot forward. Right foot forward.

I tripped; fell; landed on my face, scraping my forehead raw on the purplish ground and hearing my shirt tear. I rolled onto my back to see Jared at my feet.

Jared jumped on top of me, pinning me to the ground. His face was twisted in a snarl, and he was screaming. "I hate your guts, Liyfer! I hope you enjoy the pain you're about to feel. It's nothing like the pain you put Jaime through." He pulled a nasty looking knife out of his pants. It was caked in dried blood. He pointed it at my waist.

"Please, Jared," I whined, "I don't know what the hell is going on. Please don't hurt me. I didn't do anything to Jaime. I swear it on my life."

"Well," Jared said, "those pictures don't lie; it looks like your life is done." He used the knife to push my now-tattered shirt up my chest, exposing my boxers and belly.

"Stop!" I screamed. "I don't want to die!"

"Do you think my girl wanted to be raped by you?"

"I didn't rape her. How many times do I have to say that?"

"A million more. As long as you're in eternity you can say it, because it won't change the truth. You raped Jaime. I'll never forgive you for it!"

"Go to hell!" I shouted.

"Aren't we already there?" Jared asked. He pressed the knife-blade to my stomach.

I felt blood start dripping out. I screamed. I couldn't form words. The pain was too much.

Jared kept going. I could feel every turn and twist of the knife. The pain coursed through my whole body. It felt as if he was writing something on my belly. It hurt worse than anything I'd yet experienced on the island. *I wish he'd just kill me.* Then, finally, he stopped.

"Stand up, loser," Jared ordered. He stood to his feet and hoisted me up.

Pain continued shooting through my body. I felt blood drip to the ground. *I'm going to die. No doubt about it.* I fell to the ground in a heap.

"Fine, lie there to die if you want." Jared spat on me as he pocketed the torture instrument.

The last thing I remembered was Jared's partial fist flying toward me.

CHAPTER 32

I CAME TO CONSCIOUSNESS, but held my eyes shut for the time being, since I figured that it was just going to be yet another flashback. *What the hell is wrong with Jared? Why did he carve me up? It had hurt so badly. I had wanted to die, but I knew I couldn't.*

My thoughts might have continued as such, but my eyes opened, and I saw nothing. It was pitch darkness. *Where am I?* I wondered, as I tried to turn my head to observe my surroundings. It wouldn't move. *Why can't I move? I could move fine five minutes ago.*

Just then a bright light shone around me, and a man in white walked into my line of vision. I realized then that I was back in the white room that I had come to refer to as Heaven. A brunette woman dressed in white followed him across my line of sight as well.

The man walked over to my side and smiled. He said, "I see you've come out, Jay."

I wanted to ask what he was talking about, but when I tried to move my mouth, no words came out. Rather I just grunted. *Who is this guy? Where am I? What does he mean by "come out"? What was I in?*

He continued to speak. "The accident was terrible, but I can see that you will make it just fine, though there may be some long-term consequences. Don't fail to rest. You will have to stay here for a while longer, but soon you can rejoin your family."

My family's dead? What accident? The plane crash? I survived that just fine. Jared's brutality? I'm pretty sure I—wait— I'm dead. I'll make it out of this angel-making room into Heaven. How'd my family die? This is all so weird.

The woman whispered something to the man that I couldn't make out. He said something back about one final test the next morning. She looked into my eyes and said, "Be strong. You can make it through this if you want to."

My eyes grew heavy, and I realized the bright lights had turned off. I heard a door close. The last thing I heard before I lost consciousness was a steady BEEP, BEEP, BEEP. *Where am I?*

CHAPTER 33

(October 2008)

HERE IT GOES AGAIN, I thought. *Back to the past.* This time I was back at younger-Jay's high school.

I quickly spotted him, sauntering alone through the quad. *He must be waiting for the bell to ring for first period, based on the long shadows, and it must be cold because he keeps shivering and zipping up his brown sweatshirt.* He was wearing his red backpack and he opened his locker, slammed it, and turned toward me. He was smiling. *Apparently, he's gotten over the whole Joey thing by this point.* He then sat down at an ugly blue picnic table that his school was famous for. He opened up a book, took out some paper, and started writing stuff down, glancing back and forth from book to paper. *Ahh, last minute homework. The best.*

That was when I saw Jared walk up with his wingmen, Johnny and Zac. *They're dead now,* the realization of which quieted my thoughts for a while.

Jared spoke. "Hey Jay! Why is your shirt so pastel today?"

That was when I noticed that Jay was wearing the light blue uniform shirt. He answered quickly, "I felt like mixing it up today. Why is your shirt so black? Is that the color of your heart?"

"Shut up," Jared said. "Black is more manly than light blue."

"I'm more of a man than you'll ever be."

It took me by surprise and kick-started my thoughts. *Did I say that? Man, I'm bolder in real life than I am on the island.*

Jared looked surprised. "Go to hell," he said.

Johnny and Zac were still silent.

Jay spoke. "I might just want to if you won't be there."

What is wrong with him?

Jared felt the same. "Why would you say that?"

Jay went off. "I'm sick and tired of being pushed around by you—'Mr. I'm So Cool'—cuz you get a new girlfriend every two months, and I only wish I could get a girlfriend. They don't like me. So shut your mouth and leave me alone. I'm sick of being teased by you every day, and as long as I don't have to deal with you for eternity, I don't really care if I end up in flames. I just want you to leave me alone." Jay then shoved him onto his rear.

I couldn't believe my eyes. *Did he really say all that? There's no way. I would never have shoved him down in real life, would I?*

Jared's face was in complete shock as Johnny and Zac hoisted him back to his feet.

Uh-oh, I thought. *They're gonna help him beat Jay up now.*

Jared spoke. ""What's going on, man? Are you okay? This isn't like you."

I noticed that Jay's smile was long gone. *There's his typical face,* I thought happily. *That smile looked retarded.*

Jay spoke. "I'm fine. I'm just sick of being treated like crap by you."

Jared looked confused. *He thinks he's innocent, and he can't figure out why Jay could possibly be upset with him.*

Jay was still talking. "My life is annoying enough without your teasing. Words and taunts can break my bones, but stones don't really bug me. So please stop the teasing. It's annoying!"

"So if I punched you right now, you wouldn't care?" Jared asked.

"I wouldn't, but my mom will be super mad if I come home with a black eye. Remember the time Darien socked me?"

I couldn't believe his words. I was starting to question Jay's sanity. *He gave Jared permission to beat him up. Jay's mom was the only thing stopping him before. That's why Jared treats me so*

*horribly on the island. I told him to do it. I'd slap Jay right now if it'd
do any good.*

"I'm not going to punch you, Jay," Jared said after a couple
seconds of silence. His face looked softer than I ever remember
seeing it. "I'm sorry for teasing you so much. I was just trying to
man you up; I didn't know it bothered you." He held out his hand
to Jay. "Truce?"

Shake it. Shake it. End this garbage, man. I didn't want to
get beat any more. *Not that anything will—*

BRIIING went the bell for first period, interrupting my
thoughts.

Jay brushed past Jared, ignoring his outstretched hand. He
opened his locker, slammed it shut, and ran off to class.

Retard, I thought.

*   *   *

LUNCH PERIOD HAD ARRIVED. Fifteen of the thirty kids from
Jay's class piled onto two of the ugly blue picnic tables in the
quad. Jay was with them. So was Jared, on the opposite end of the
table. *What's going to happen this time?* I wondered.

Jared stood up and walked over to Jay. When he was next
to him, he said, "Jay, I know you ignored me this morning, but I
just wanted to say that I'm sorry for teasing you. I didn't know that
you didn't like it. You laughed every time I said anything. It
confused me." He held out his hand to Jay.

What's he going to do?

Jay looked at it and then at Jared's face.

"Truce?" Jared asked.

Everything went black.

220

CHAPTER 34

(Day 5, 4 p.m.)

I WOKE UP, and I wished I was dead. Every part of my body screamed in pain until literal screams erupted from my mouth. I didn't care who heard me. The pain that found its source in my abdomen was excruciating. I tried to sit up, but shards of pain coursing through my body made my head fall down flat against the rock below me. *I'd give anything right now to go back into that dream and be teased daily instead of being turned into a human wood carving.*

I turned my head, and I noticed a piece of paper lying atop a rock or something, six inches from me. I reached for the paper with my right hand—the pain wasn't leaving—grabbed it, and pulled it back to myself. The pain was inescapable.

I screamed. It made the pain worse. *Maybe someone will hear me and help me out. I doubt it though. I'll probably die here, where I'm lying.*

How much blood have I lost anyways? Remembering the feeling of Jared's antics with the knife told me that he had lacerated my stomach horribly. *It burns like hell.* I couldn't bring myself to look at it.

I read the paper instead. It was from Jacob. *Lousy dirtbag,* I accused. *Why couldn't you have been here before Jared played tic-tac-toe on my stomach?*

The note read as follows in a scratchy font:

HEY JAY,

I'M REALLY SORRY ABOUT NOT GETTING HERE WHEN I TOLD YOU I WOULD. I WISH I HAD. BECAUSE YOU GOT THRASHED. WHO DID IT? WHY'D HE DO IT? ANYWAYS, I LEFT YOU A BERETTA M9 UNDER THIS NOTE. AND I'M ASSUMING YOU'VE SEEN IT. PUT IT TO GOOD USE. KILL THE LOSER. WELL, I'LL TALK TO YOU LATER. HOPE YOUR WOUNDS STOP HURTING.

--JACOB

P.S. PLEASE FORGIVE ME FOR USING BLOOD FROM YOUR WOUNDS TO PEN THIS NOTE. I HAD NOTHING ELSE.

I looked back to where the note had been sitting. Sure enough, a sleek, black gun was sitting there. *I don't care what kind it is. It's a weapon. I'm safe now.* I picked it up, letting the note fall to the ground, and felt the gun. Chills went up my spine as I gripped the smooth, cold steel, making me relax more than I'd been able to since coming back to consciousness.

In my newly relaxed frame of mind, I forced myself to sit up, giving full reign to the screams of pain that resulted from my movement. A green palm frond flopped onto my lap. *Jacob must have put it there to slow the bleeding.* "Thank you!" I yelled, instantly feeling more pain shoot through my body.

The sun was sinking in the western sky. *How in the world am I supposed to kill anyone when I can hardly sit up, let alone stand up, or even walk and hunt for anyone? It's going to be dark soon, and then no one will find me. I need to move. I don't want to be alone.*

I tried to stand. The pain sent me back to my rear and came out of my mouth in screams and cries. There were tears in my eyes that I wiped away with my arms, only to then feel more pain shoot through my body. *When I told Jared in eleventh grade that I'd rather get beat up than teased, I never, in my wildest dreams, imagined that Jared would carve me up like a Thanksgiving turkey. Punches are one thing; knife wounds are completely different. I hope he enjoys gunshot wounds.*

I stood up again, trying to completely ignore the pain that was yelling at me like I was crazy. Ignoring the pain was impossible. I've always prided myself on my high pain tolerance, but this was something entirely new. I started to fall immediately, so I angled myself toward the nearest palm tree and leaned against it for support. As I connected with it, it cracked and splintered, and all of it above my hand fell over, away from me. Soot rose as it slapped against the ground, which caused me to sneeze.

I tucked the gun into my back right pocket, and then contemplated my next move. *Where should I go?* The volcano was well behind me. *Jared came from there. That's where I'll go.*

I put my right foot forward. Pain exploded from my stomach. I cursed and swore internally with each step I took. *When your abs get mangled I guess everything hurts.*

I put my left foot forward. "YEOW!" I shouted. *This is never going to work,* I thought. I stopped walking and leaned against another burnt-out palm, breaking it like the previous one.

What am I going to do? I can't just stand around and wait. If I don't move, I'll fall asleep. The pain is unbearable and sleep will decrease it. I want to close my eyes and sleep. I shut my eyes.

Three seconds later, they popped open. *I have to kill Jared,* I reminded myself.

Sleep can wait.

*   *   *

IT TOOK ME AN HOUR to get to where Jared had met me earlier. *Less than two minutes of running with no pain turns into an eternity of slow, painful ambling when your stomach has been lacerated.* I leaned back, slowly and carefully, against the nearest palm tree, as pain shot through my body. It didn't splinter like the others. I stood there, leaning against the tree, and waited.

During my walk I had felt the area where the knife had been used. It had felt rough and sticky, but the blood had clotted well, and while it was clear that something had been carved into my chest, I had comforted myself knowing that the bleeding had

223

stopped. The palm frond had really helped. *I'll have to thank Jacob the next time I see him.*

I breathed in deeply, grateful to be done walking, but it wasn't helpful. Instead of helping me catch my breath, it sent pain coursing through my whole body. I screamed, yelling, "What did I ever do to deserve this?" I made an obscene gesture toward the sky in the same breath.

The next thing I knew, Jared came running out of the forest behind me. *He must have heard me.* It seemed like a replay of earlier.

"SEYDU!" I yelled Jared's last name. Pain shot through my whole torso as the words came out. Jared turned. I spoke weakly, "Where are you running off to?" Every word I spoke made me feel like I was going to die.

"Why are you here, you stupid rapist?" Jared shouted, surprise in his eyes. "Didn't I warn you about coming back?"

"Not that I remember," I said. "Cuz all I can remember is the insane amount of pain I'm in right now, which is going to be nothing compared to what you'll be feeling in a few seconds." I pulled the BERETTA out of my pants and pointed it at him. "Scared yet?"

"No way," Jared spat. He rushed me.

Typical football player. I cocked the gun and fired two quick shots into Jared's chest. His feet flew out behind him and he fell flat on his face, three paces from me.

Jared looked up at me, gritted his teeth, and asked, "You rape my girl and then you kill me? You have serious is—"

I shut him up with a shot through the head. Blood pooled beneath him and his face was unrecognizable.

The sight made me sick. I collapsed at the base of the palm tree. The last thing I remembered was the sound of approaching footsteps.

CHAPTER 35

(November 2008)

THEN I WAS IN THE MIDDLE OF A CROWDED BUILDING, and I felt no pain. *It brought a smile to my face.* I noticed that Jay's hair was longer than the last time I'd seen him. He looked like a sheepdog with brown hair. He was talking to Ray—his group leader from back in junior high—as crowds and crowds of high school kids crowded around everywhere—talking loud, flirting with each other, and making a crazy ruckus—driving at least me crazy. *I hate kids this age. Why do they think they're so cool? Why do they have to flirt right in front of me? Camille's dead. She was my flirt-partner.*

I caught part of Jay's conversation. "Why does life suck? Joey just keeps getting in trouble with the law. My parents are always mad at me. I have no one to hang out with. Supposed friends at school tease me because I don't have a girlfriend. I could go on, but I won't."

Ray replied with a question. "What ever happened to Kevin and Bryce? You guys, along with Joey, were always inseparable."

Jay answered, "I don't know. I've tried calling them, but they never reply. When they were younger and their parents came to church all the time, they came, but now that they can drive themselves, they're never around. I miss them, though I really do miss Joey more, because we've *always* hung out together."

What happened to Kevin and Bryce? I was surprised that they were now distant. Last time I'd seen Kevin—other than on the island—was when Jay had tried cigarettes with him and Joey. *It perfectly matches the situation on the island. Kevin and Bryce were cool, but now they're being jerks. Kevin hates my guts and Bryce thinks he's better than me. That's where Bryce probably is: getting brainwashed somewhere.* I laughed.

Ray replied to Jay's statement about missing them. "I know how you feel. I grew up with many guys who I haven't seen in years. We hung out all the time. I don't know what happened to them. I wish I knew."

"Okay, but why does it happen? And even more importantly, why do the kids at my Christian school make fun of me just because I've never had a girlfriend? I thought they were supposed to be Christians. What does that word even mean?"

"That's a valid point. You just have to remember that no one is perfect. Christians are the people who believe that Jesus died on the cross and rose from the dead for their sins. I'm a Christian; you're a Christian."

See, Bryce? I'm a Christian just like you are.

Jay asked another question. "Why do my parents hate me so much?"

"They don't." Ray's answer was very succinct.

I hope he elaborates.

He did. "You are getting to the age where you want to be independent, but your parents still have to care for you, since you're a minor. They don't hate you. They want to show that they love you, but you—as a near-independent—see it as prevention and hate. You just have to follow the Bible when it says to obey your parents. It's not easy, because if it was it wouldn't be commanded."

Haha. I don't know the specifics, but I guarantee that he doesn't know what he's talking about. My parents hate me, and I want out. I don't have to obey them as an eighteen-year-old adult. Adults don't boss other adults around.

I missed Jay's response in thinking of my own, but I caught his next question. "But what about Joey? I write him letters telling him about Jesus, and to come back to Him, but he always replies saying he misses the good old times we used to have, and then asks me to tell others hello for him. I don't get it. Why can't he just hear what I'm saying?"

"I don't know. I've always worried about that kid, but now that I realize my worries were well founded, it hurts. I pray for him, and that's really all you can do too. Maybe one day he will come around, but until then all we can do is pray."

Not prayer again. I'm so sick of hearing about that. If God wanted to hear prayers, He would answer them. Several of these flashbacks showed Jay praying for his hand to get healed, but none of them were answered. I'm sick of it.

Just then Jay's brother Zeke came over. Ray asked him, "Hey Zeke, how's it going?"

Jay walked away slowly. *Conversation over. Time to be alone again.*

*   *   *

NEXT THING I SAW was all of the guys in a garage sitting in a circle, and not a girl in sight. The whole group was talking about the gospel of John. Chapter 9:1-3. Jay wasn't paying attention though, and I somehow caught everything he was thinking in my own head. *This is weird.*

Jay's thoughts went as follows: "Ray thinks I'm a good Christian kid, but the truth is: I don't want to be seen as a good kid anymore. I want to live life on the edge, risk getting in trouble, and not deal with all the rules that go along with church. I hear the same thing every week: if I pray a prayer, life will be great, and God and Heaven are waiting for me. I prayed that prayer many times, so I'm good, and it really doesn't matter how I live my life. I can't bring this up to Ray because it will ruin his image of me.

"I want a girlfriend. I've liked so many girls in my lifetime, but I've always been too scared to talk to any of them. It's a hopeless cause. So, I settle for internet women. It's so easy. Just search, click, and enjoy. They are there; they are hot; they do it all,

227

and they love it. One day I'll do it for real, and I can't wait, but until then, internet stuff is perfect. I just want a girlfriend."

Wow. Is this really what his mind is like? There's no way I was like this.

Jay's thoughts were interrupted by a question from the group. "What do you think about this passage, Jay?" someone asked.

"Ummm, what passage?"

He doesn't even know what they are talking about. He's thinking about his porn addiction.

"John 9:1-3. I'll ask the next person though since you aren't ready. Lyle, what does it mean to you?"

Jay's thoughts resumed: "I can't believe it. Just because I was distracted, they skipped me. It's so wrong. I hate it. Why doesn't anyone care about me? I'm lonely, bored, depressed. I want a friend, but everyone is too cool for me. Aren't Christians supposed to confront the lonely people? It's what I was taught my whole life. I've never done it, but it's been pushed on me forever. Why can't I just be treated the same way? When I bring it to my parents' attention, they tell me that I should be a friend, instead of waiting to be befriended. I disagree completely; I disagree with everything my parents tell me. Teenage years are freaking retarded. Everyone is this way, so don't judge me."

Preach it, Jay. I think you're kind of crazy, but I totally agree with you on this: Don't judge me. I'm so sick of people judging me.

CHAPTER 36

(Day 5, 5:30 p.m.)

I WAS RUDELY AWAKENED when water struck my face. Salt water, by the taste of it.

I opened my eyes to see Jaime standing over me. She looked terrible. Her normally well-kept, straight brown hair was frazzled and full of sand. Her shirt was tattered and torn and barely covering her skinny frame. In fact, while she'd always been exceedingly thin, she now looked like too little skin stretched over too much skeleton.

My mind started rolling. *Why are you here? You're the person at the top of my "do not see" list. Go away. I'm tired, hungry, and in excruciating pain.* I said nothing though.

But she did. "Where's Jared?" A water bottle—mostly full— was in her left hand.

"I—" I couldn't talk. It hurt too much.

"You what?" Jaime asked, pushing several strands of her auburn hair behind her ears.

"I-I-I'm not—" It hurt way too much. Expletives flew through my mind as I realized, *Jared's corpse is right over there. I'm screwed when she sees it.*

"You're not what?" She paused. "Not sure?" She tipped the bottle toward me, sloshing a few drops onto my stomach.

I'm 100% sure. Jared's dead, because I blew his head off. He accused me of raping this dumb, ugly chick who's currently talking to me. You're so freaking annoying. If I had my way I'd never go within a mile of you. I want to say, "I'm not my classmate's keeper," but it hurts too much to form the words. My diaphragm has to be lacerated from Jared's knife. Breathing hurts. I want to sleep.

"I demand you give me some answers," she shouted. She reached into her back pocket and pulled out some papers. "What does this mean? Don't deny what is clearly visible here."

Crap. She found the pictures Jared had. What should I say? I don't even know where they came from. All I can say is, "PHOTOSHOP is a cool invention, and Jared had fun changing himself into me."

She dropped the pictures onto my stomach and put one hand behind her back again. The other was still holding the water bottle.

I picked up the pictures and was instantly very confused. *Jaime's not here.* The photos showed me killing Jared, apparently photographed earlier today. Two bullet holes were bleeding out of his chest, and I was pointing the gun at his head, about to pull the trigger the third time.

I looked back at Jaime whose face was twisted into rage. I didn't need to speak. *Can't she just see him laying over there? What's the point of these pictures?*

"So you really did blow him away with that gun of yours?" She paused. "Where is it? I should blow your face to smithereens too."

I felt around with both hands. There was no gun anywhere around me. I cursed.

I tried to sit up, and in that motion glanced to where Jared had fallen, but saw nothing—not even a pool of blood—and then the pain forced me to fall onto my back. *What is going on?*

My attention returned to Jaime, as she pulled her hand out from behind her back. What she presented to me at that moment made me scream. Her gaze was focused on me, and she was brandishing a knife.

That's the same knife Jared used on me earlier.

I jumped up and ran. The pain was excruciating, but the thought, *it'll be worse if I stop moving,* kept me going. *Later, I'll regret this, but I have to get away. She's gonna kill me if I don't. I don't want to die. Contrary to Jared's pictures, I'm still a virgin. I'm not ready to die.*

Jaime was following me. "Stop running, murderer," she shouted repeatedly. "If you stop, I'll torture you less. Maybe, I'll just put you out of your misery."

I kept going. *I don't want out of my misery. I want to be healed. Not dead.* Each step I took made the pain increase. *I want to stop, but I don't want Jaime to add to my misery. She's crazy!*

I looked over my shoulder, and she was nowhere to be seen. *I outran her,* I thought to myself. I smiled, as I collapsed face-first to the ground to rest. *Every muscle in my body is screaming bloody murder.*

I screamed when I felt something land on my back.

"Got you, you damn, freaking murderer," Jaime's voice rang out. "Don't even try to escape. There's no possible way you're getting away this time."

I agreed with her, nodding my head to show it. My body was screaming at me for running away. *I'm not gonna try that again.*

"I'm going to put you through more pain than you've ever been through before," she announced.

I felt the knife touch the base of my neck and cut through my shirt—collar to bottom. I shivered.

"You ready?" she asked.

What is this chick smoking? Am I ready to get killed? Who asks that? The knife cut into my left shoulder.

I screamed. I felt it touch the bone and I screamed again.

She slid the knife left, right, up down, forward, backward. I screamed every time it moved, and she just laughed. "Murderer," she whispered under her breath. When the knife reached my right shoulder, she stopped.

I wanted to die. I wanted to take the knife out of her hands and slice my own throat.

The pressure on my back lifted—*Jaime stood up*—but something wet hit my back. *Salt water.* It burned.

"Just kill me!" I shouted. *I'm serious. I'm done. The pain is too much.*

Jaime shook the last few drops out of the water bottle. "I'm not allowed to kill you. Only make you loathe life itself." She paused. "Well, have fun. I'll see you later."

She walked away, and I screamed. I heard her laugh from wherever she was. *My back is killing me. I wish she would have just killed me.*

I heard voices in the distance approaching my location. I didn't know what they were saying. *Uh-oh. I don't want to be in more pain.*

Then I fainted.

CHAPTER 37

(August 12, 2009)

WHEN I CAME TO CONSCIOUSNESS, the first thought that crossed my mind was fear. *How much more of this can I endure? I'm surely going to be dead before too much longer.* I opened my eyes.

I was on a beach. *Is this even a dream?* But then I glanced around and saw cars in a parking lot and houses beyond them. *Definitely a dream. But when?*

The next thing I saw was Jay. It was getting much closer to current time. *It's so weird how all of these dreams are chronological. Is there a point?*

I immediately put that out of my mind. *It's all random. Don't worry about it. In fact, all of life is random. There's no meaning. No explanation for the dreams. No explanations for the torment you've been facing. No explanation for anything. But you already know this. Put everything else out of your mind.*

I heeded that advice and took note of Jay even more closely. He was shirtless, wearing swimming trunks, and he was carrying a surfboard. I was floating behind him.

I didn't know he surfed.

Derek and Zac—wearing his ATLANTA BRAVES hat—ran past Jay, beat him to their group, and announced his arrival. "Jay almost drowned trying to surf. We rescued him just in time."

Oh. I don't surf. I almost died while trying to surf. Haha.

Jay smiled, and said, "That's technically not true. I had been doing just fine. I couldn't get up on the surfboard, and when they saw me, they told me to come into shore before I died. I didn't protest, because I didn't really have to surf anyways, I just wanted to try."

The group laughed. The group was made up of Jay, Ryan, Nicole, Zac, Derek, and four others who I quickly learned were named Jessica, Olivia, Blake, and Max—the same kid who had greeted Jay so well his first day of school. *How many of them are still alive on the island? And if any of them still are, how many will still be by the time we get rescued?*

I watched as Jay sat down on the sand and looked at Ryan. Once again, my thoughts meshed with Jay's as Ryan and Olivia talked. "Ryan makes no sense sometimes. One second he's making fun of Olivia, and the next he's flirting with her. They aren't dating. I would know if they were because Ryan would never let me forget it.

"I want a relationship. I've never had a girlfriend. I've gotten close, but then learned that she was already dating someone. I've had many crushes—some secret, some not—but never a legitimate girlfriend. I recently started FACEBOOKing a girl named Camille and I wonder if it will ever go anywhere. She is super cute, and she actually talks to me on a daily basis over Facebook messages. I haven't gotten her number yet, in fact, I've never even met her in person yet, but I hope it works out. I'm sick of being single."

"Jay," I shouted, though no one would hear me, "She is awesome. It works out. But she dies on a stupid island." I was interrupted when my ears caught Ryan's conversation with Olivia and Jay.

"Are you ready for senior year coming up in a week?"

"Ready enough," Jay replied, forsaking his thoughts about his potential girlfriend. "The senioritis that goes around school has already started showing symptoms. I don't want to do any of the homework that I am soon to be loaded down with. I don't want to have to sit in a room all day listening to someone yap on about random stuff. And I don't want to be constantly teased by Jared every day."

He's dead now, so don't even worry about him, I thought. *But this is the start of senior year? That's awesome. I've almost caught up to the current time. Maybe these stupid dreams will stop soon.*

The girl whose name was Jessica announced that it was time to go to lunch, and the group walked/longboarded to a small fast-seafood place.

*　　*　　*

LUNCH WAS GREAT. The group—Zac, Derek, and Ryan—decided it would be fun to buy some cigars to smoke later, so they had Ryan use his ID to buy the stuff since no one else was eighteen yet. He readily agreed.

My mind read Jay's thoughts again. "I'm excited. It has been a while since I've smoked, and I've never done it in front of people from school. I'm ready to show off what I know. Too bad I have to wait until nightfall though. I want to smoke now. It's been weeks since my last cigarette."

My thoughts took over, *Since when do you like smoking? I thought you were never going to try them again after that time with Joey and Kevin.*

Derek and Zac left the group in order to find some driftwood for the fire later, and put Jay in charge of Zac's keys.

He told Ryan and the girl named Olivia to meet him by Zac's car—a MITSUBISHI LANCER. Jay explained that he wanted to pull a trick on Zac and move his car, but since he didn't have his license yet, he needed someone else to do the moving. Olivia and Ryan looked nervous, so Jay assured them that he'd take all the blame. They both agreed, and Olivia moved Zac's car behind a large RV. "He'll never notice it here," she said as she returned the keys to Jay. He agreed.

You are stupid, I thought. *He's going to kill you.*

*　　*　　*

ZAC AND DEREK RETURNED with stories—highly exaggerated—about girls they met on the way and with the wood for the fire. They piled it in the fire pit and Jessica used her lighter—"purely for candles," she claimed—to get it going. *Yeah right. You're probably a smoker too. Don't lie about it.*

They sat around the fire, sharing memories, smoking, and saying how much they would miss stuff like this after graduation. None of the girls were smoking, and Blake sided with them, saying that he'd recently quit. They commented on the others' smoking antics.

"It's funny that the chaplain is smoking," Zac said. "Don't you think?"

"Yeah it is," Nicole agreed. "Since when do you smoke, Jay?"

He ignored her question, and instead he commented on the chaplain comment. "I'm hardly a chaplain. Honestly, I wouldn't even do that if my parents didn't force me to. I could care less. I don't think of myself as any sort of spiritual leader; I don't even know if I believe the stuff anymore either." He paused.

There you go, I thought. *He's finally at the same place I am.*

Jay took a drag on his cigarette before adding, "This year should help with all that: Senior Bible, Philosophy, and Comparative Religions will all help me establish my thoughts."

If I was a chaplain at school, then it just goes to show that Bryce is full of crap. Of course I'm a Christian. No non-Christian would ever put himself in that role.

Everyone was silent for several seconds. Finally, Jessica spoke up. "Why don't you talk to the pastor who is over the chaplains and get yourself out of it if that's really how you feel? Being a chaplain is an important position. If you don't want to be in it—don't think you *should* be in it—then get out of it. They'll understand."

"It's not that easy. I don't want my parents to know about my thoughts. They think I'm a good kid, Bible-wizard, who knows all the answers."

Our thoughts meshed after that thought. *I don't want to be known as the good kid anymore.*

Nicole repeated her earlier question. "Since when do you smoke?"

"I've smoked for a while with Joey Birjal when we are able to hang out. Do you remember him?"

"Yeah. I remember him. How's he doing?" Nicole smiled.

"He's good. He's in town for the next week or so. Then he's moving to Michigan for a year. I've missed that kid so much, and I'm gonna miss him a lot more this next year. We've known each other since kindergarten."

Joey's moving? Why? What happened?

"Tell him I said hello the next time you see him," Nicole said.

I watched as Jay was about to reply, but then I saw Zac reach into his pocket, turn his head, and yell, "Where are my keys? Where is my car?"

Jay tried extremely hard not to laugh, but a smile was clearly evident on his face.

"Jay, where's my car?" Zac questioned, noticing his grin.

"I don't know. Why would I have it?"

I laughed at his lie.

"I gave you my keys. Where are they?"

Jay cussed before adding, "I must have lost them."

"Don't mess with me," Zac said. "I want my car. Where is it?"

"I honestly don't know, dude."

"You'd better tell me or else I'm gonna kick your butt."

This is entertaining. I laughed.

"It can't be far," Jay said. "Look at the parking lot."

Zac looked away, which gave Jay just enough time to retrieve the keys from the cooler he'd stuffed them inside. He threw them at Zac, hitting him in the back of the head.

"What the—" he shouted, turning around.

"They fell from the sky," Jay said.

"Whatever. Where's my car?"

"Look for yourself. It's hiding behind something."

Zac walked out to the RV and came back smiling. "Dang, dude, you had me good there."

"You're welcome," Jay said.

Everyone laughed, and Jay smiled. "Maybe this school year won't be too bad after all," I heard him think.

What goes wrong?

I watched Jay take a drag on his cigar, watched Ryan turn green in the face from his, and laughed as Derek smoked two at a time. My mind melded with Jay's again. "I wish I'd known my classmates were this cool before the last nine months of knowing them. Either way, life is cool. I can't wait to update Camille on my day."

The name brought a frown to my face. *I miss her. I want her to come back. God, why are you so cruel?*

CHAPTER 38

(Day 5, 9 p.m.)

I OPENED MY EYES to find myself in a palm hut. Joey, Laura, Derek, and a kid with slicked-back black hair were standing around me. *How did I get here?* It was dark outside. *How long was I out? Jaime was torturing me while it was still daylight.* I could make out my surroundings from the light of a torch Derek was holding.

The hut was very simple inside. Burnt-out palm tree trunks laid horizontally made up the walls of the little building, and several more randomly thrown atop the four walls made a makeshift roof that would have been totally worthless in a rainstorm. I realized in that moment that I still had not seen a single cloud in my time on the island.

The pain came back to mind at that point. My back was burning. My stomach was burning. I took a breath; pain shot through my whole body. *God, let me die. Just let me die. I am sick of living. It hurts—physically, emotionally, spiritually. Forget about spiritually,* I decided. *There's no such thing as an afterlife.* I just want to be done with everything.

Joey spoke up first, as he rubbed his hand over his head, "Dude, what da hell happened to ya?"

I didn't know what he meant. *Isn't it clear? I've been tortured within inches of my life.*

Joey was still talking. "Dere's effin' words carved into yo' body..."

Words? What did they carve in me? This is beyond weird.

Joey continued. "It says 'rapist,' by yo' waistband, and on yo' back is carved, 'murderer.' What happened?"

"You're lying!" I shouted. I regretted it immediately as pain shot through my whole body. I kept talking through the pain. "It's not true. I didn't rape or kill anyone. Jared and Jaime are both on crack." The pain was ridiculous. "You've got to believe me!"

Derek spoke next. "What did Jared and Jaime do?"

"I don't want to talk about it. It hurts," I said. "If you can find paper, I'll write it for you though." *I'm sick of talking. I'm sick of being in pain. I'm sick of being stuck on this god-forsaken island in constant danger of being killed.*

"I have a notebook in my bag," Laura stated. "Kyle, can you go grab it? I want to know what happened."

Slicked-back hair left instantly. I adjusted my position in my bunk, and the pain coursed through my body. I let out a squeal, because I didn't want anyone to think I was a baby, but even that hurt. Everything I did caused excruciating pain.

While he was gone I realized that the people in the hut were much better dressed than Jaime had been. Laura's clothes were still relatively clean, well maybe not clean, but definitely not tattered and torn. Joey's white t-shirt and baggy blue jeans were in the worst shape—other than my clothes—but Laura's and Derek's looked clean.

My shirt was no longer on, my shoes were probably still out by the beach, and my jeans were tattered. My whole body hurt: what wasn't throbbing from being carved was burning because of the sun.

The kid whose name was Kyle returned with the notebook, and I noticed that his clothes looked clean too. He handed the yellow notebook to me.

I pulled the pen out of my pocket, and slowly and painfully, I wrote the story down as follows: "I was walking around after talking to Laura, when Jared decided to accuse me of raping Jaime. I told him he was an idiot, and he carved up my belly. Then a little later Jaime accused me of killing Jared, and she carved up my back. Now I'm here and I don't know how I got here." I handed it to Kyle and he read it aloud.

He explained. "Well Derek and I were out looking for you when we heard a scream. We came to the source, and we found you laying carved up in the dirt. We carried you back here, cleaned you up, and put you in this bunk."

I motioned for the paper back, and wrote. "Why didn't you just put me out of my misery?"

Kyle answered. "It's not up to me to give or take life. Don't you remember ethics class when we talked about euthanasia?"

I couldn't say I did. *I didn't pay any attention in that class. In one ear; out the other.*

Kyle continued. "It doesn't matter how much you beg me, I can't put you out of your misery."

I took the paper back again. "Then get me something so I can do it myself. I'm one hundred percent done with living. Please! All my friends hate me, I'm in excruciating pain, and God can't stand anything about me. Please let me end this misery. Or just be nice, and do it yourself!"

Kyle read it aloud and Joey spoke first. "I don' hate ya, homie, and I'm here. Ya don' need to end yo' life. You'll feel better soon. If ya die I gots no one."

Laura spoke, "God loves you, Jay. Don't say He doesn't. Hating God is not a good way to live."

"Shut up," I said. Pain shot through my torso, and I didn't say everything I wanted to say. *Hating God is perfect. Especially since He hated me first.*

Laura ignored me and continued. "John 3:16 says, 'For God so loved the world that he gave his one and only Son, that whoever believes in him shall not perish but have eternal life.' Believe it Jay. This is truth."

I motioned for the piece of paper. I wrote: "That's bull. Not truth. I don't wanna hear it. If God loved me, then He wouldn't have let me get carved up like a freaking pumpkin. Read John

241

15:7. It says, 'ask whatever you wish, and it will be given you.' I've prayed forever for God to heal me. Has He? Nope. The Bible isn't true at all. If it was, He would have healed me." *I had no idea where that specific reference came from in that moment, but it worked.*

Laura read the note, and she had nothing to say.

That's what I thought.

"Kill me, please!" I screamed. "I want to be gone." The pain was hellish.

Kyle spoke. "No one else needs to die. We lost two more earlier today—Richard and Ryan—so we need to save as many as possible."

I disagreed, and let him know it. "What's one more? I'm useless."

"Not going to happen," all four said simultaneously.

I flipped them off and cussed them out. The pain was too much to bear, and I passed out.

CHAPTER 39

(August 17, 2009)

I WAS FOLLOWING JAY again, as he walked up the driveway to Joey's house with a pillow slung over his shoulder. *I guess it's a sleepover, and as far as the last dream goes, I guess Joey hasn't left yet.* The sky was not quite dark, but the sun was definitely traveling toward the horizon.

Jay knocked on Joey's door, and Joey answered. "Hey, homie," he said, high-fiving and bro-hugging Jay as he let him in.

Jay spoke. "I'm so excited for tonight, bro. Ima miss you this year, so we gotta make tonight a night to remember."

Joey must be leaving like tomorrow or something.

"For sure, Jay. I don' know what I'm gone do in Michigan when we can't kick it."

"I know what you mean, bro. I still can't believe that you leave tomorrow afternoon. After twelve years of constantly hanging out, it's crazy that you're leaving."

"Yeah. It's been real." They walked up to Joey's room and he lowered his voice. "Ima hit up da homegirls, and see if dey can stop by later."

"Sweet." A sly smile crossed Jay's face.

He's excited, because his brain is scanning through all the possible scenarios that could happen, though none of them probably will. He doesn't do that kind of stuff, regardless of pictures that Jared pulls out of his butt.

Jay pulled out his phone—*It must have vibrated*—to see a text message. I saw that it was from Camille, and it read: That would be great hun :)

So after a week, he now has her number? Awesome. The realization reminded me that she was gone. *Enjoy it while you can. She's gonna be dead in about nine months.*

Jay texted back: Sweet. i'll see what i can do.

Joey asked who Jay was talking to. Jay explained that it was Camille Queensley, his soon-to-be-girlfriend. He told him that she was good enough to pass his parents' tests, but she also had a bad side that would allow them to do anything. *Do we really? If so, Jared's claim during our very first interaction on the island was completely unfounded. Maybe I'm not a virgin?*

Joey asked what she wanted, and Jay explained that Camille wanted to go chill at the mall the next day. Jay said that he hoped he could, but he wasn't going to get his hopes too high. He told Joey how much he loved the fact that she called him "hun," even though they weren't actually together yet. I watched a huge smile form on his face.

Joey asked how old she was. Jay explained that she was six months younger than him—emphasized that it wouldn't be a problem for the next five and a half months—and then stated, "I'm so lucky, bro. She's awesome. I really hope it works out."

"What does she look like?" Joey asked.

"She's beautiful—" Jay began.

"Do ya have a pic?"

"Not yet bro, but I'll get right on that."

Jay punched in another text to Camille. Can you send me a pic? I'll send you one too :)

"Give it five minutes," Jay told Joey.

His phone vibrated. What kind? ;P

That wasn't even close to five minutes. Wait, did she really say that? You'd better not show Joey one of those.

He texted back: Just one of your beautiful face.

Yeah, you can get something else later.

Joey broke the flow by asking, "Can I borrow yo' phone to hit up Sharon?"

"Sure, bro." He handed it over.

Who's Sharon?

Joey punched in a number, typed up a message and handed it back to Jay.

It buzzed twenty seconds later. Camille. The image brought my memories back. *I miss her so much.* Her picture showed her dirty blonde hair accenting her blue eyes and her pink lips. Her nose displayed a small diamond stud as well, highlighting her short, pointed nose. My mind read Jay's thoughts at that moment, "I hope one day soon I'll be able to kiss them. The only question is: when?"

My mind alone thought, *Yeah, Jay's haven't kissed a girl before, and he's looking forward to his first time. Camille will be his first.*

He handed his phone to Joey so that Joey could see what Camille looked like.

"Nice, homie," He high-fived Jay. "How'd ya manage dat?"

"My dashing good looks." They both laughed, and I laughed too. Jay spoke, "Naw, bro, I just have a way with women." He laughed again.

"Ya just dang lucky, homie."

Sharon texted back. Joey typed a reply before handing the phone back to Jay.

Joey spoke. "Sharon's gone come over around ten. I told her we'd meet her at da cul-de-sac between yo' house and mine." Joey's face lit up at his next words. "She's going to a party and she said she'll have some alcohol wit' her."

*　　　*　　　*

SHARON SHOWED UP—along with two other female friends, neither of whom I considered cute—and immediately started conversation with Joey. Jay ignored it. He motioned to Joey for a cigarette, and Joey gave him one. Jay lit it and started smoking. *What a rebel.*

The sky was dark and moonless, and the only sound was the occasional car passing by on the street adjacent to the cul-de-sac they were standing in. Crickets chirped in the background as well.

My mind melded with Jay's again. "I am going to miss Joey so much this next year—it is driving me crazy. And now Sharon is stealing him from me."

My thoughts resumed, *Why does that happen sometimes? I can be thinking my own thoughts, but then my thoughts aren't mine at all. It's rare, and it's weird. I don't get it.*

Sharon pulled out a bottle of rum and Joey's face lit up like a neon sign. "I love dis stuff," he said.

She only let him take a small drink, because she needed it for the party that she and her friends were going to. She offered Jay a drink too. *I hate alcohol. There's no way he accepts this stuff right now.* I was wrong; he eagerly accepted.

Jay took a sip, and I could tell by his face that he wished he could have drank the whole bottle. *Did this really happen? I need some rum. Maybe it'll help me get through the pain I'm in on the island. I'll ask Jacob the next time I see him.*

Sharon took my thoughts back to earth. "What happened to good-kid-Jay who knew all the answers at church? Now he's smoking and drinking? Typical."

Jay stayed quiet, but I knew the answer. *Jay is destroying good-kid-Jay on purpose, because that guy has no life. That guy is a loser. Jay wants to fit in, and good-kid-Jay doesn't.*

With that, my eyes went dark. *Back to the island,* I feared.

CHAPTER 40

(Day 6, 9 a.m.)

I SAW BRYCE when I woke up, and the unexpectedness of seeing him made me flinch, which shot pain throughout my shoulders, and caused me to curse in pain. *He is Kevin's friend now. And Kevin hates me, so Bryce hates me too—right? What is he doing by my bunk?*

I wonder what time it is. It was dark when I fell asleep. It looks as bright as day outside now.

Bryce spoke. "Good morning, bro."

I'm glad he didn't preach a sermon to me about cussing when I saw him. "What's good about it?" I asked, wincing at the pain brought on with each word. *I'm not enjoying life at all. This pain is driving me crazy. I want to die.* "The best thing you can do for me is put me out of my misery."

"No. That would be the worst thing I can do. You aren't ready to die, Jay. You need Christ first. You—"

"Seriously?" I groaned under the pain. "I already told you I'm good. God saved me when I was seven. The first time I prayed the prayer. You can ask my mom and dad. They were there too. They heard me." *I need to stop talking. I wish this loser would just shut up. Go be Kevin's friend. Bring Joey here; he's the only friend I need.*

"Can you let me talk for five minutes, bro? Please? I just want to say one thing to you, and then I'll stop bringing this up."

"You've got five minutes. It's not like you'll change my mind though." *I'm going to enjoy sitting still, not talking. It will help me feel better.*

Bryce began his monologue. "In Luke eight, Jesus tells the story of a sower who planted seeds. The seeds fell in four different soils—all growing at first—but many of the plants died. He explains the story later. He says that the sower is a preacher. Everyone he preached to reacted and showed signs of being saved. However, only a quarter of those who showed growth actually produced fruit. One group, Jesus specifies, are stolen away by the devil because the Word of God doesn't abide in their hearts.

"No need to speak, but when was the last time you read your Bible? In 1 Peter 5, Peter explains to his church that the devil is looking for someone to destroy. He says the way to resist is to stand firm in the faith. Hiding the word of God in your heart by reading it constantly is a very key way to stay grounded in your faith. If you don't read it, you will never know if you are saved or not."

I can't believe my ears. Bryce is accusing me of being chased by Satan? There is no way Satan is after me. The only person after me is Bryce—to get me to feel like a bad Christian—and Red—who is trying to kill me. How does Bryce know that my Bible has never been read? It makes no sense. I decided to risk the pain and speak. "The only demon after me is that psychotic Red killer dude." I paused, taking a deep breath in an attempt to swallow down the pain. "And how do you know my Bible has never been opened?"

"I found it, wrote you a note, and sent it to you in Ryan's hands. Didn't you get it?"

"No. It got sniped out of his hands by someone. Probably Red. I mean either way, it's not like I would have read it. That thing is full of lies. I can't stand reading it. I hate every word in it. And I wish you'd leave me alone. I'll be in Heaven when I die, just like everyone else on Earth. Don't even worry about it.

"And why in the world are you even here? You're friends with Kevin. Not me and Joey." I pounded my fist on my bunk, cursing under my breath, trying to assuage the pain that was persistent and powerful. *I want to lie here still, without moving and without talking.*

"Joey came and told us about what happened. You got messed up bro. I wish I could help—"

"Kill me. That's the most help you can give me." *At least then I don't have to move or speak.*

"You don't mean that, bro."

"I do so. Every time I move and talk, pain shoots through my whole body. I just want to die."

"You'll survive, bro. I've been studying paramedic stuff recently, and I can promise you that this is not life threatening." He paused and reworded his statement. "Well, maybe life-threatening, but you can recover."

"I don't want to, bro. I want to die!"

"Everyone's dying already, man. Your classmates. Justin. Joey—"

"Joey's dead?" I sat up straight and tense, ignoring the pain that shot through every nerve in my body. *The kid I've gotten into trouble with my whole life is dead? How? When?* My thoughts instantly flew back to the last dream, hanging out with Joey. I couldn't believe it was now all over forever.

"Yeah. Kevin strangled him to death last night when he came to tell us about your knife-inflicted misfortune. He tried—"

I interrupted him. "Kevin is a murderer too?" I paused. "I bet you he's Red. I bet he killed Justin just so he could pin it on me and try to kill me."

"It's possible, bro. But yes, he killed Joey."

"I'm gonna kill him!"

"That's not a good idea, Jay. You are not supposed to fight murder with murder. You—"

"The Bible tell you that too?" I then made up an acronym to describe my thoughts on the B-I-B-L-E, and I ordered Bryce, "Don't give me any lies from that. I don't believe it."

Joshua Wingerd

Bryce had a stunned look on his face, so I continued. "Ima kill that a-hole. Don't try to freaking stop me."

"You're in no position to go anywhere, Jay. Don't be stupid. The pain is too much for you."

I couldn't feel the pain anymore. I was suppressing it because rage had taken its place.

I stood up and ran out of the hut—shirtless and scarred—and headed toward the volcano. I ran past several huts and several stunned classmates—who just stared at me, dumbly—until I was out of the village. Soon I was amongst a forest of burned trees. Still running. *Cross country never made sense to me, but now I appreciate the fact that I have done it for three years. Running across this island is no problem.* In all honesty though, it had been much easier to run before Jared had filleted me like a dead fish.

Where in the world is Kevin? He's probably at the camp by the lake. I changed my course away from the volcano and went toward my old campsite. I was cursing Kevin the whole way there.

When I reached the pool, I stopped running and realized that Kevin was not in camp. Pain shot through my body as soon as I stopped moving, and I fell to the ground in a heap—unconscious.

CHAPTER 41

(December 4, 2009)

I'M SICK OF OPENING MY EYES. Every time I open them it turns out that I'm either on the island being hunted and fileted by psychopaths, or I'm watching myself grow up. I don't see the point. What does this have to do with anything? Why can't I just stay on the god-forsaken island and get killed and go to Heaven already? Oh wait, I remembered, *according to some of the psychos here, I won't even get* there. *Screw you, Bryce.*

But, I opened my eyes anyway. The sight that came to my eyes completely surprised me. I wasn't watching high-school-Jay. Rather, I was staring at fifth-grade-Jay. *This is weird. Why am I back in time all of a sudden?* A girl was running toward him, and when he realized she was coming, he booked it, and I floated behind him.

I turned to see that she was following him. *Who is this girl? Why is he scared of her?* Her hair was dark brown and curly, and she was about Jay's age—the age of fifth-grade-Jay. *This is all so confusing.* She had a smile that spread from ear to ear.

"Jay, stop running away. I just want to tell you one thing. Then I'll leave you alone." *This is so weird.* I couldn't get past the fact that I had gone back in time. *It was bad enough the first time. I thought I was about to finally get some answers. Why am I back here?*

Jay yelled over his shoulder in reply to the girl who was chasing him. "No, Angela. I'm tired of this. I don't like being chased." He stopped running, breathing heavily.

Cross country will help you out significantly one day, I thought, remembering my running experience from just a few minutes prior.

Angela caught up to him and announced, "I go back home tomorrow. So I might not ever see you again. I just wanted to say bye."

Jay thought for half a second before he replied, "Good."

Scared of girls? Boy, you got so much to learn. I noticed her face droop and she slowly turned and wandered away.

*   *   *

MUCH-YOUNGER-JAY WAS SITTING in the car, being driven home. His dad was driving, and he broke the silence with a question. "What did you say to Angela earlier this evening?"

"Nothing," Jay said, but then added, "Nothing but good."

"That's not what she told us," his mom spoke up from the passenger seat. "She told us—"

His dad interrupted. "She came up to us crying. You didn't say anything good to her. What did you say?"

Really? Crying? What a girl. I smirked.

"All I said was good."

"That's not what she said," his dad said.

"But it's true. All I said was, 'Good'. She told me she was going home tomorrow, and I'm so sick of her chasing me around like, like—I don't even know what it's like—so I told her, 'Good.' I'm happy she's going home. I won't have to ever see her again."

"You really hurt her feelings, "his mom said.

Well she should grow up. This is one guy who isn't going to be tied down. I laughed.

"And you're going to apologize as soon as possible," his dad added.

"But I don't want to."

"It doesn't matter. You need to. When you get home, you're going to call her aunt's house and ask to speak to her."

Jay groaned and looked out the window. *This is awkward.* He spoke. "That's crazy. She'll think—"

I didn't even let him finish before my thoughts filled it in. *She'll think that he likes her back. It's blatantly obvious that she's interested in him.*

They pulled into the driveway, and all three got out of the car.

Jay's dad concluded the conversation. "Elizabeth, get Jay the phone number. He isn't going to bed until he makes that call."

This is pure torture. Just put the kid out of his misery. That was when it struck me. *During these dreams I have no pain. The torture I've been receiving is nonexistent here.* I smiled. *Maybe I can get used to this.*

I watched as Jay picked up the landline phone. "What's the number, mom?" She gave it to him, and he punched it in and held the phone to his ear. A few seconds passed before he spoke. "Hey, this is Jay Liyfer. Is Angela Johnson there?" A pause. "Oh, okay. Thank you." He paused again. "Oh ok. Well, thank you. Have a good night. Bye." He ended the call and replaced the phone on its cradle.

His mom was next to him. "What happened? Why didn't you apologize?"

"She's already in bed. They have to wake up super early tomorrow to get to the airport, so that they can take the super long flight back to Tennessee." He paused before adding, "I guess I got lucky."

I laughed to myself at the greatness of that comment.

"We'll see about that," his mom replied.

"Please don't make me get up early to apologize in person in the morning."

His dad walked into the room. "What's going on?"

"Jay called, but she was already in bed," his mom answered.

Joshua Wingerd

"That's easy. Elizabeth, call her aunt tomorrow and get Angela's address back home. Jay's going to write an apology letter tomorrow. In fact, he's not going to play any video games until he has finished it."

I followed Jay out of the kitchen, into his living room—this was his old house—and as he passed through the threshold that separated the two rooms, the whole scene began to change. *What in the world?* The walls changed color, and the room greatly expanded. The blue carpet was traded for red-and-black-flecked grey carpet. *Where am I?* Then I noticed Jay; he was taller—he looked like the Jay I'd come to recognize as basically the same age as myself. He pushed open a pair of double doors into a large gymnasium filled with chairs and tables. *This is so weird.*

I heard him mutter something to himself. "I hate this. Why'd I have to come to this stupid thing? I was supposed to hang out with Camille tonight. This is so boring. And Angela will be here; I wish I'd never been forced to write that apology letter."

What? Why am I back in the future again? This was all so clear right up until I went way back in time. It was steadily moving forward. Why can't it just keep moving forward? Why'd it have to get stupid? I comforted myself knowing that we were now almost back to the present time, so I decided to watch what would happen and enjoy not being in agonizing pain while I could.

A girl approached Jay, and I was surprised. She had a slender, athletic build, and her dark brown hair hung just below her shoulders. It was very curly, and she had a smile that spread from ear to ear. *It's Angela.* She was older for sure, but it was her. "Jay," she called.

My mind meshed with Jay's. "Dang it. It's Angela. Ugh, I don't want to deal with her. Ever since my mom told me she'd be here tonight I *really* didn't want to be here. Why do they love her so much. She's so annoying." He pulled out his phone to appear busy, and he started sauntering toward the stage at the front of the room, away from her.

254

She walked all the way up to him. "Did you not hear me?" she asked, tapping his shoulder.

"Wait, what?" asked Jay, as he stopped walking. He continued, "Oh, I'm sorry. My mind was busy. There was too much going on."

"Boys," she said, smirking. "They can't think about more than one thing at a time."

Did she just say that? I was surprised. *Sexist, much?*

He cut her off before she could continue. "So?"

"It's just weird." She laughed as she changed the subject, "So how's life?"

"It's been better," he said. He started walking again.

Yeah, right before she showed up. What's the point of this?

She was following him, so Jay asked her how her life was going in return. After asking, he glanced down at his phone again. His face told me that he was thinking, "Why hasn't Camille texted me back yet? This isn't normal. She could totally save me from this stalker."

"Life's great," Angela answered, smiling. "Six months 'til summer. Exactly five months 'til my birthday. I can't wait. Oh, and I start softball again in like three weeks—"

Jay cut her off, looking at her as they kept walking. "You like softball? I mean baseball. I mean, uh, never mind."

"Yeah. I like both. The ANGELS are my favorite team."

"You're joking." Jay looked surprised. "How long have you liked the ANGELS?"

"Like five years," she answered. "You?"

"Like sixteen or so," he answered. "They've been my team as long as I can remember. Though, they haven't been very good lately—like since they won the World Series seven years ago."

"Don't bash my team," she gave him a death glare.

He just laughed. "I can bash *my* team all I want."

"Whatever," she answered.

"Want a cookie?" asked Jay, changing the subject. They had taken a seat at a table for designing sugar cookies, and he had just created a simple one with green frosting topped with a pile of sprinkles. He stuffed it in his mouth.

"Sure," she answered.

"Okay," he said. He grabbed a bell shaped cookie, spread some red frosting on half of it and green frosting on the other half. He then sprinkled a few sprinkles over it. "Here you go," he said, passing it to her.

I vocally spoke, even though I knew it wouldn't be heard. "Jay, why are you flirting with her? You have a girlfriend!" If I could have smacked him, I would have.

She smiled as she thanked him, took the cookie, and ate it faster than Jay had eaten his.

Jay nodded his response, smiled, and suppressed a laugh.

"What?" asked Angela.

"Nothing," he replied. "Did I say anything?"

No. But she sure stuffed that cookie down her throat. That was not a polite way to eat a cookie.

She dropped the issue, not caring about it enough, and asked, "Do you have a girlfriend?"

"I do," he smiled. "But don't tell my parents. They don't like her at all."

They don't like her? I thought she was good in their opinions. That's weird.

"Oh, well I won't tell," she promised. "I know what you mean. What's her name?"

"Camille." As he said it, the corners of his mouth turned up into a grin.

The name and his obvious happiness brought chills to my spine. *I just want her to come back. I miss her so much.*

"That's a cool name." Angela smiled. "Good luck to both of you."

Sucks that we have no luck. She's freaking dead and I'm alone, trapped on some god-forsaken island. I want Camille back.

"Thanks," said Jay. He was beaming.

See, Camille was everything. I need her to come back. I can't live without her.

Jay asked yet another question: "You have a boyfriend?"

"Nope," she replied. "Don't plan to have one for several years either. They just cause me to not focus on what's truly important."

"Oh, okay," said Jay. "Have fun with that."

Come on, what's truly important to you, Angela? Love is the most important thing in this world, and relationships are where it's found. What's more important than that? This chick is crazy.

*　　　*　　　*

TWENTY MINUTES LATER, based on the clock on the back wall, they were still talking. Angela had the stage at the moment. *She'd have the stage her whole life if it was up to her. I hate this dream. There was a reason young Jay said it was good that she had left. Why's she even back?*

"...that letter was like the nicest thing anyone has ever done for me. I seriously had thought you were a little punk kid, but after you sent the letter to me I realized differently. So thanks."

Jay was silent.

I don't know all of what she's talking about, but I'm sure that it isn't good.

He finally spoke. "You're welcome," he hesitated. "I still remember the flower you drew on the top of your reply."

She was about to speak when Jay's dad walked over. "It's time to go, Jay." He turned to Angela and said, "Nice to see you, Angela."

"Nice to see you too, Mr. Liyfer," she replied with a smile.

Jay walked away, and I followed behind him. "I'll see you later," he said.

"Don't be such a stranger," she called out as he got farther away.

Camille. Camille. "Camille!" I yelled at him. He didn't even flinch though. "Stop worrying about this dumb Angela chick. Enjoy

257

Camille for the next six months until she dies. Eat, drink, and be merry!"

Jay's dad spoke as they walked out to the car where the remainder of his family was waiting. "You should marry her. She'd be a great wife."

"Dad," Jay began, "I wasn't on a date tonight. That was small talk. If there's one girl I would never even consider dating, it's her."

Don't forget: Camille! Are you really that stupid?

CHAPTER 42

(Day 6, 12 p.m.)

I AWOKE, wondering what in the world that dream had to do with anything, and I opened my eyes to see Jacob sitting next to me. He was holding something in his hands. I couldn't tell what it was. *Maybe he will put me out of my misery with a knife or something. I hope so.*

The sun was beating down on me from directly above, and I wanted to roll five paces to my left and rest in the trickling pool. My friends' duffel bags were all lying sprawled open around me, and the smell of melted chocolate bits in the littered plastic wrappers reminded me that I hadn't eaten in a very long time.

"You got messed up, Jay. What happened?" Jacob asked, replacing the chocolate smell with his scent: stale cigarettes and cheap beer.

I realized, *Jacob hasn't ever been told what had happened. But isn't it clear? I was brutalized by my peers. Instead of getting a gun, I got a beating.* It reminded me, *I really don't want to see Jacob right now.* The memory of Jaime's attack returned; someone had taken my weapon away just prior. *Why in the world would you take my gun back? I do not want to see Jacob.*

I finally spoke, deciding I was angry enough at Jacob to ignore the pain that would surely result. "Why do you care? It's your fault this happened to me anyways. If you had just given me the gun at noon like you said you would, then I would have killed Jared before he could slice me up like a carrot. And then, if the gun hadn't disappeared, I could have killed Jaime before she did the same. So, you know what?" I paused before continuing my rant. "Screw you. I think you're a joke. A lying a-hole who doesn't give a damn about my life. I wish you'd leave me alone. Every time you're around you ask me about Camille and I-I-I." I was choking up. I wiped my eyes and swallowed my sadness. "I just want to get off this stupid island. I want to be healed. I want to be loved. Why does no one love me?" The pain that resulted from this tirade was much less than I was expecting. It encouraged me to be more open to making my anger and frustration openly known.

I moved into a sitting position, and Jacob scooted closer, unfazed by my tirade. It was like it happened all the time and he was used to it. He spoke. "What about your friends? Don't they love you?"

"I wish. Kevin wants to kill me. Bryce wants to convert me, even though I'm already a Christian. Joey's dead; Kevin killed him. And Joey was the one I'd always been closest to. I was closer to him than C-C-Cam-Camille." I started crying.

Jacob put his arm around me and spoke soothingly. "It'll be fine, Jay. I love you. Don't worry about a thing."

I shoved his arm away. "I'm not gay, man. Don't say you love me."

"I'm not either," Jacob said. "I care about you."

"Oh," I said. I replaced his arm around my shoulder. "What is that you're holding?" I finally asked.

Jacob picked it up with his free hand and handed it to me. "It's a gift. Recognize it?"

It was the BERETTA. "Why'd you take it back? Jaime could have killed me!"

"Well look, Jay," Jacob said. "She didn't. You're still alive. As far as I'm concerned—"

"If you truly loved me," I interrupted, "you'd put me out of my misery with that gun." *I haven't gotten drunk, high, or laid yet, but at this point I don't care.*

"I can't do that," Jacob said. "It's not your time yet. You can attempt it yourself, but I doubt it will work. So don't try it. This is for self-defense—nothing else—so don't use it for anything else."

"If I want to kill myself, I can," I said.

Jacob didn't speak immediately, but soon said, "You can. You have the power to do it—one hundred percent. But the thing is: do you really want to? You're still a virgin. Remember? You wanted to get laid before you died. If you kill yourself now, that won't ever happen."

"How do you know that?" I asked. *I'm surprised that Jacob knows. I don't remember ever sharing that with him. I told it to Joey and Kevin enough over the years, but never to Jacob the past six days. It's weird.*

"You told me, like twenty seconds ago. At least I thought you did." He fingered a hole in his jeans.

"No." Now I was creeped out. "I never told you that. Especially not in this conversation. I'd remember."

Jacob was flustered now. "I thought—never mind. Maybe it was a few days ago. This island does weird stuff to people, Jay. You know that." His eyes darted about in every direction.

"Yeah. I do. It's turned my best friends into murderers and preachers. It's turned classmates into torturers. It just goes on and on. This island is stupid as hell."

"You can say that again," Jacob said. He paused before adding, "I gotta run, Jay. I'll talk to you later."

"Okay, man," I said. *He always runs off at the weirdest times.* "See you later."

I was holding the gun. I flipped it over in my hand as I sat there, resting. Despite the surprise of Jacob's comment, he did have a point. *I don't want to die yet. I want to have sex before I die. I'm currently a virgin and I'm not going to leave earth this way. It's plain.* I stuffed the gun into my back pocket as I stood up.

The pain was disappearing. It was still there, but moving was not as big a deal as it had been. I had full mobility in my joints. *I expected the pain to last longer, but maybe I was wrong.*

261

Joshua Wingerd

Footsteps were pounding toward my location. *Who is this?* They were moving considerably closer. Finally I could make out the person's shirtless form. It was Kevin.

He stopped six inches from my face and shouted, "Ya sad, little screw-up. I hate ya. I'm gonna make yo' life a living hell." He pulled a knife out of his pocket. It was the same knife Jaime and Jared had tortured me with.

I cursed in my mind when I saw it. "Why do you hate me? What did I ever do to you?"

"Ya told me my best friend—my cousin actually—is in Hell because God hates him. It's a lie! You're a damn liar. I wish I could kill yo' ass, but I can't. I'm only supposed to make ya wish ya were dead. I—"

"I already wish I was dead, man. Don't touch me! Justin died first because God hated him more. It's why I'm dying now, not first. Please, don't hurt me. I don't want to die."

"Shut up."

I pulled the gun out of my back pocket.

Kevin laughed. "What? Ya gone kill me now after lying to me my whole life?" He started making fun of my voice. "I'm a Christian, but I think God is a piece of dirt who hates everybody and is looking forward to sending them to Hell." He went back to his voice. "I don't know what to believe anymore, Jay. I think you're a piece of dog crap. I think ya deserve to die. I think you're a freaking liar. So ima carve the word 'liar' into yo' ugly forehead. That way, everyone knows that they can't trust a damn word ya say."

I cocked the gun. "You killed Joey. You deserve to die."

"Screw it," Kevin said, rage flooding out of his eyes and nose and cheeks. "That guy that told me not to kill ya can get over himself. Ima kill ya like I killed Joey, except there will be blood flowing this time."

His face was twisted in a snarl as he dove at me. I didn't have time to react, so I screamed and pulled the trigger. The bullet flew, without being aimed, straight into Kevin's face, and out the back of his head. The blood pooled around where he fell and stained the ground red. I couldn't look at the mess.

I limped away five steps, and fainted when the smell of blood hit my nose. The last thought that I remember thinking before total unconsciousness hit was, *What guy was he talking about?*

CHAPTER 43

(February 13, 2010)

I OPENED MY EYES to find myself in Jay's room. The decorations had greatly changed since the last time I had seen it. His door was shut, and he was laying on his bed staring at the same decorations that I was surprised by. *There's no way his parents are cool with this.* There were a bunch of posters of rap artists all over his walls that showed scantily clad women stealing glory from nice sportscars. EMINEM covered a whole wall, and it was a wall of no women. *That's probably the only wall my parents can stand to look at when they come in.* Two other posters that had no women on them were a KJ-52 poster and a MANAFEST poster. Seeing the posters brought another memory to mind. *My parents hate this kind of music. Do they ever come into Jay's room?*

My attention returned to Jay; he turned his eyes to his phone, and rolled over, away from his window, as he checked a text from Camille.

I could see the message. *The perks of him turning away from me.* She had texted: Hey babe, let's go catch a movie.

He punched back: Where?

A few minutes later, a text came in: At the mall.

He quickly replied: Okay. I'll be @ your house in thirty minutes. :)

Jay climbed down from his bed, and I followed him as he walked downstairs. *That's what these dreams feel like. I feel like a dog being walked around.* I wasn't thrilled with the realization. *I hate these stupid dreams.* Jay entered his dad's office room. "Dad, Ryan was wondering if I could go over to his house for a few hours."

No he wasn't. It's Camille who wants—I interrupted my own thoughts. *Ohhh. They hate her. That's why he can't say he's hanging out with her. That makes sense.* Then a different thought hit my mind. *I want to wake up. I don't want to see her again. It will bring the pain back.*

His dad looked up from his computer. "What?" He was engrossed in work.

Oh yeah. Jay's dad is always working. He's never able to do anything with him.

"Can I borrow the car and go to Ryan's house?" Jay repeated.

"When will you be home?"

"No later than nine." Jay looked at his phone. An unread text waited, and the time read 3:30.

"What did your mom say?"

"I don't know yet," he answered.

"If she says it's okay, then go for it," his dad answered.

"Okay thanks." He walked out and climbed back up the stairs to his mom's room.

She sat on her bed reading a book. When she saw him, she asked, "Yes, Jay?"

"Can I go to Ryan's house?"

"When will you be home?"

"Nine. I'll eat with him."

I noticed that Jay kept his fingers crossed as he asked it. *Superstitious liar.*

"What did your father say?"

Typical. Neither want to say yes, but neither wants to say no. Why is that? Is it some stupid parenting strategy?

"He told me to ask you. Otherwise it's fine."

"Okay." She smiled. "Have fun."

265

Joshua Wingerd

"Thanks." Jay ran over to his room and grabbed a CD. He ran downstairs and grabbed the keys. He ran out to the car and grabbed the handle, opening the door. I followed behind him the whole way; *it's not like I can do anything else.*

He hopped into the car, inserting his CD into the disk player. The first song started thumping. I jammed to the rap music as I watched what followed, trying to forget that the most beautiful—now dead—girl in the world was about to be in his car.

Jay pulled out his phone and finally read the text from Camille: I love you <3

Jay punched back: I love you more <3

He threw his phone into the cup holder and backed out of the driveway. The verses of the song played loud, and Jay rolled the windows down and cranked the bass to the max. *This is how I always roll when I drive,* I remembered.

*　　*　　*

THE NEXT THING I KNEW, Camille was with him, and they were driving toward the theatre. She looked amazing. She had specially curled her dirty-blonde hair just for Jay, and her blue shirt brought out her eyes extremely well. She wore a denim mini-skirt that made my imagination run wild with sadness.

"You're gorgeous, babe," he said.

"Thanks," she replied. "You're not too bad looking yourself." She winked.

Why? Why? Why do I have to be with her right now? Why can't she be sleeping beside me in real life right now? Instead, she's dead. I'm never going to see her again.

When they reached the theatre, they purchased tickets for the latest romantic comedy and went inside. Inside, they found seats and sat down. Down, Camille looked straight into Jay's eyes and fluttered her eyelashes. He couldn't resist. He put his arms around her head, and he pulled her lips to his.

Really? This is awkward. I was seated in the row right behind them. I didn't want to watch this. I tried to stand up. I couldn't move. *What was I thinking? I can't ever move freely during these dreams. I'm always stuck a short distance behind him, floating along like a stupid dog.*

Jay's hands were rubbing her back as their lips were still pressed together. They separated for air, and she spoke, "You're a good kisser. Get back here." She pulled his head back to hers, and they continued.

Just get a room and do it all. Jared really thinks I'm still a virgin? With all this hanky-panky, I doubt that's true. "Jay, you're in the middle of a crowded theatre," I screamed, "what are you doing?" Again, my speaking went unheard. *If I'm not really here, why do I have to watch them?* I tried to turn my eyes to watch the movie, but they were immediately forced back to staring at Jay making out with the most beautiful girl in the world. *You'd think I'd be happy, but she's gone; I'm not really here; that guy isn't me. He might have been. But everything has changed since then.*

Another internal voice said, *Everything's changed?*

I ignored it. *I haven't had an internal conversation with myself in a while, and I'm not going back to it right now.*

*   *   *

THEN THE MOVIE WAS OVER. They were walking out to his car—a '99 TOYOTA CAMRY. Jay's arm was wrapped around her waist. I forced myself to not stare at her as I followed behind them; *I don't want to think about how sexy she is. It's going to bring everything back: memories, tears, loneliness.*

"Let's go get dinner," suggested Jay as they headed to his car.

"Sounds good," she replied.

"What would you like?"

"RED ROBIN."

The picture of us that she had in her purse was taken at RED ROBIN. If these dreams had sucked before, then this one tops them all. I miss her so much. No one loves me.

They got to his car, and Jay opened Camille's door for her before getting in the driver's seat himself. He started the car and drove five minutes down the street to Red Robin. When they got there, Camille asked a group leaving if they could take a picture of her and Jay. A woman answered in the affirmative, and Jay and Camille stood next to each other with their arms holding each other. Their lips pressed together.

The camera flashed.

My world went black.

CHAPTER 44

(Day 6, 4 p.m.)

I OPENED MY EYES and wondered, *Are my eyes even open? I can't see a thing. It's darker than night. I wonder how that happened. It was only just after noon the last time I blacked out, and now it's night. What the hell is going on?*

That dream though. Out of all of them, that's got to be the freaking most annoyingest one. I don't care that my grammar is all stupid with that thought. I want her back, but she's dead. I miss her so much, it's breaking my heart, and my new last memory of her is too good. That night had been excellent, and I had to watch it. Why couldn't I have relived it myself? I need her back. I want to die.

I heard a scratching sound somewhere in the dark, and vocalized, "Who goes there?"

"It's Jacob, Jay. Where are we?"

Hearing the familiar voice brought me comfort in the syrupy darkness. "I don't know. It's dark, and I can't see anything. How'd we get here?"

"I don't know. You blacked out after shooting that one person as I was walking away. I don't know what happened."

"Who'd I shoot?"

Jacob's voice changed pitch to a somber tone. "I think his name was Kevin." He paused. "I never thought you'd kill someone. That was crazy—"

"But you gave me the gun. You told me to kill people."

"I did?" Jacob paused. "I don't remember that."

Joshua Wingerd

"It was in the letter you wrote me."

"It's cold in here."

It's true. I hadn't noticed it before. *It's excruciatingly chilly in here. I wish Camille was with me. She'd surely keep me warm. Why'd she have to die?*

"Don't you wish Camille was still around?" Jacob asked.

"Seriously? I told you not to bring her up again. You promised. You swore on Heaven! Now you're going to Hell. I can't believe you would do something like that. If I could see you right now, I'd punch you in the nose."

Just then the room glowed red, like the light of a flame reflecting off the walls. A man, dressed in a grey hooded sweatshirt and black pants shredded off at the knees, was sitting where Jacob's voice had been coming from.

It took me totally by surprise. "What the hell is going on? Who are you? I-I-I di-di-didn't mean anything by that comment."

"You're such a little pansy, Jay." Jacob's voice was deep and scratchy as opposed to the average voice I had grown used to. "You don't stick to anything you say. Do you?" He paused before adding, "Besides, I'm going to Hell anyways, so my oath didn't mean anything in the first place."

"Who are you?" I asked, as I felt my whole body start shaking. The incisions in my shoulders and belly were burning again. "You aren't the homeless guy who dreamed of playing baseball your whole life only to have it blow up in your face." *I want explanations.*

"No, Jay, I'm not. Just like you're not Mr. Christian like you think you are." He took off his hood to reveal long hair pulled back behind his head, disappearing inside his sweatshirt.

Jacob too? Why is everyone convinced on telling me that I am not a Christian? "Why do you say that?"

"Let me show you."

The next thing I knew, I was watching myself again.

*　　*　　*

270

STRANDED

JAY WAS DRIVING HOME from school with a very angered look covering his face. His radio was off. I was sitting in the back seat watching it all unfold before my eyes. *So this will prove that I'm not a Christian? Yeah right. Jacob is such an idiot.*

The deep, scratchy voice of Jacob totally surprised me. I turned to my right to see his hooded shape sitting in the backseat of the car with me. "Jay, this kid driving is you. As you may have realized by now, these are your memories. In fact, right now you are extremely angry at one of your teachers." He paused. "And, you might want to keep all your negative comments and thoughts to yourself. I'm no idiot. I know much more than you. Much more.

"You see, you've been completely fed up since Mrs. Peterson started mandatory, Friday morning devotionals at school. You've grown to loathe anything Biblical. Her comments drive you crazy." He started imitating a woman's voice, "She repeatedly says, 'I drive to work with my radio off so I can hear God speak to me.' 'Yesterday on the way to work I heard God speak to me.' Or, 'Have you ever had God speak to you?'

"That question did it for you. You ran out of that room so quickly, as soon as you were technically allowed to, because there's no need to ruin your," he held up air quotes, "good kid," he put them down, "mantra.

"Jay Liyfer: a good kid? Yeah right. You've been bad your whole life." Jacob cackled.

"You've heard your whole life that God is up in Heaven and that He loves you. You've heard at this point in your life that He speaks to people. Why would this God, who is up in Heaven and supposedly all powerful and all good, not hear you, let alone not heal you? A complete healing, at least according to the Bible, shouldn't be hard at all. Just a snap of His fingers, if the Bible is even true."

Jay—the one driving—spoke. "Is it true? I've always wanted to trust it, but the longer I've been alive the more I feel that there is no possible way it could be. If God is all-powerful, like the Bible claims, then why am I still dealing with stroke symptoms? And if

271

He is all-good, as the Bible claims, why hasn't God been good to me and healed me? It seems like everything I know is contradicting everything else that I know."

Is Jacob conversing with him? Maybe I can try. "Jay, can you hear me?"

Nothing.

Jacob spoke again instead. "Philosophy class isn't changing your mind about God either. While it does show the stupidity of other religions, it doesn't offer anything positive for Christianity. You know you have to choose Christianity if you will choose one, but we both know you prefer self-worship. At least until God proves Himself to be real."

"God," Jay called out as he drove, "if You're real, heal my hand before I get home. If You do, I'll believe in You for the rest of my life. If not, then You're not real, and I'm done with Christianity because it's stupid." Jay—the driver—looked over at his left hand, resting on the windowsill of the car.

My mind matched his thoughts. "A spasm? Is it working? My thoughts took over. No, it's not. God is stupid and incapable. Don't think anything less."

Jay lifted his arm off the windowsill and tried to make a gun with his fingers. *It's how he always tests these prayers.* His pointer finger went out, almost straight. His middle, ring, and pinky fingers were trying to touch his palm, but stopping three centimeters away. And his thumb felt like it was glued to the side of his hand. It wasn't the first time this had happened to him. False alarms were a common occurrence. "Nope, not healed yet," Jay decided in his mind, as I thought his thoughts. "Ten more minutes, God," he reminded silently.

*   *   *

BY THE TIME Jay pulled into his driveway, nothing had changed.

Jacob spoke. "What did you expect, idiot? Of course God's not real. If He was, and if He truly loved you like it says in John 3:16, then He would have bent over backwards to heal you. Don't deny it." He cackled. "Tell God exactly how you feel. Scream it to Him. If He can even hear you, that is."

Jay opened the car door and swung his left leg out. Before moving any farther, he said, "God,"—yelling at the windshield—"since you hate me so much, and since the Bible says that You are love, I refuse to believe in You. You must be fake. So go bug someone else. I'm done. My belief is that You are fake. Or, at least, that if You were once real, You are dead now. So don't bother me anymore!"

Jay slammed the door of the car and walked up to the front door of his house.

His mom met him at the front door. "How was your day at school?" she asked when Jay opened the door.

Jay ignored her and ran upstairs.

"Did you hear me?" she repeated.

"Stop yelling at me!" Jay snapped. He continued to his room as his mother walked away with a hurt expression on her face. Jay didn't even notice.

When he got into his room he sat down in his desk chair. Jacob was right with me, as we followed him around.

Jay's dad burst through the door. "Why is your mother crying?" he questioned.

"I don't know."

"Don't give me that. What did you say?"

"All I said was to stop yelling," Jay responded.

"I didn't hear any yelling from her," his dad's voice was getting louder. "I just heard it from you."

"Well, whatever," Jay said. "It's not like I can take it back now."

"You go apologize!" his dad ordered.

"Why?"

"Because your mother deserves one."

"Well, it's not like I was trying to make her cry," Jay protested.

"No, of course you wouldn't," his dad said. The sarcasm was obvious. Then he ordered, seriously, "Go apologize!"

"No."

"Isn't one of the Ten Commandments to honor your parents?" his dad preached.

Jacob spoke up here, "Don't forget that you don't believe in the Bible."

"Only if you believe in the Bible," Jay spat back.

What the hell? I couldn't believe what was happening. Jacob was putting words in Jay's mouth.

"What are you talking about?" Jay's dad was irate.

"I don't believe any of that crap anymore."

"Shut up."

Jay kept going. "If any of it was real, God would have healed me by now. Where is it—"

"Shut up."

"Oh yeah, John 15:7. Ask whatever you want and God will do it. Well obviously it's not true or God would have done it."

"That's not what that verse says and you know it."

"Well that's what it means." Jay continued, "I don't believe in God anymore. So please, stop preaching to me. It won't do any good."

"I—" his dad cut himself off and left the room.

"It's about time," I thought with Jay.

Just then his cell phone buzzed. It was Kevin. Hey bro, wanna come kick it tonight?

Jay: I can't.

Kevin: Why?

Jay: Because my parents won't let me

Kevin: Oh.

Jay: Yep. Hey, r u going to church this week?

Kevin: Naw, there's too much drama. I don't go anymore.

Jacob spoke. "You are going to tell Kevin how much you hate church now. This is great. I think this is my all-time favorite part."

I really didn't know what to say, but I felt like it was necessary to say something. "The only thing worse than these stupid dreams is you. You know that?" *All of my friends have turned on me in the last few days. Why?*

Jay texted: I wish I could stop going.

Kevin: Why?

Jay: Cuz I don't believe any of it anymore.

Kevin: Why would you say that

Jay: Cuz the Bible isn't true.

Kevin: How can you say that bro? I always saw you as my role model. Like the dude who was so into God. Why would you change your mind?

Jay: If God was real he'd have answered my prayers by now. It says so in the Bible.

Kevin: Oh. I see. Well I hope you change your mind. I'll ttyl.

Jay: It's not likely. God's had his chance to prove himself. He failed.

My vision went dark, and I was grateful. *Stupid dream is finally over.*

*　　　*　　　*

THE ISLAND RETURNED, though I had no proof I was actually on the island. I was back in the room where the eerie red light was flickering off the walls, and Jacob started speaking again. "You're mine. I only have control over non-Christians, and you, my friend, are no Christian. You think you are, because you prayed that stupid little prayer every year since you did it when you were seven, but that doesn't mean anything. More people in this god-forsaken world—who prayed that prayer—are under my control than you would ever know. You were baptized at age twelve—big deal. You're not safe from me, Jay.

"That gunshot that went off right next to your ear, was shot by me, from the top of this volcano, and it told me exactly who I have control over. I've killed many of them. Peter, Slater, Ryan. I've used people to kill each other off. Jared, Joey, and Kevin.

275

Joshua Wingerd

"But you, Jay, are the one I wanted all along. It's all been building to this point. I sent Jared down with a weapon for you. I gave him your secret photos. I told you to kill him. I told Jaime what you did. She had already half drowned you, and she wanted to hurt you more for killing Jared. I sent Kevin to carve "liar" into your ugly forehead, but had told you earlier to blow him away before he could hurt you. Now you're completely under my control, and there's not one thing that you can do about it. I own you. Don't try to get away."

I can't believe my ears. What is this psycho-freak talking about? Who is he? He's no homeless loser on the streets. He's a psychotic killer. I'm freaking out. I don't want to die.

"You're completely confused," Jacob went on. "I'm not just a psychotic killer. I'm *the* psychotic killer. Ever since I got kicked out of Heaven six thousand years ago, I've been helping people just like you keep their souls hardened before God. I help them understand that God is not worth worship. I help them understand that life is about having fun. I help them understand that good works are the way to go. I help—" He interrupted himself. "And if none of that works, I show them how unworthy they are. God requires perfection—though with that detail, I'm not sure why I got kicked out. But you, Jay, are anything but perfect. Look at you. You're a rapist. A murderer..."

I want to object, but I couldn't bring myself to open my mouth. *Whoever this guy is, he has done a lot of acid over the course of his life, and he has gone completely insane. What the hell is he talking about?*

"...You hate your parents. Let me prove it to you."
The next thing I knew, I was watching myself again.

*　　*　　*

I WAS BACK in my house, watching Jay yell at his parents. He was standing by the front door, frozen, with his hand on the latch about to fling it open. *That's peculiar,* I thought to myself. *Freeze frames haven't ever been a part of these before.*

276

That's when Jacob spoke again. "You're right, Jay. Your dreams haven't been freeze framed before, but now they are. I need to catch you up to speed before you watch yourself make a complete fool of yourself in front of your family." Jacob paused before saying, "Wait. All you ever do is make a fool of yourself in front of your family.

"You see, until this point, you've never been truly angry at your parents. You're about to run out the door. It started when you hesitated giving your phone to your dad because you had pictures and messages you needed to delete. He suspected something, but you denied it, and he grabbed up your phone before you had a chance to know for sure if they were gone. The conversation turned into a talk about grades. Grades turned into responsibility. Responsibility turned into chores. Chores turned into waking up. And waking up is what you hate the most. I mean, honestly, it's hard to wake-up after a long day of school, chores, and homework, and in your specific case, your parents demand too much of you. They demand that you wake up three hours before school starts to get ready for the day. You don't need that much time. You're a dude. And then, you called your dad's bluff: 'if you want to live in this house, you need to follow our rules'."

I couldn't take my eyes off Jacob. There was too much input coming into my brain.

Jacob was still talking. "And that's where we find ourselves now. Let's see what happens next."

"You'd better sit your tail back in that couch, young man," Jay's dad said.

"I will not," Jay stated pointedly. He gripped the front door handle even tighter.

My thoughts melded with his yet again. "Do I really want to leave? I mean, there is food here and other stuff. What will I do out there all alone?"

Jacob was standing right next to Jay. He set his left hand on Jay's shoulder, and Jay glanced at it, but saw nothing.

That's weird. How'd he feel that?

Jacob spoke. "I can't stand it here. Your rules suck. Your standards suck. And I'm leaving."

Jay repeated his words verbatim, and a cold shiver went up my spine. "There's no way!" I shouted.

Jacob put his hand on Jay's hand and together they opened the front door.

I looked back to Jay's dad. "You walk out that door, and I don't want to see you again until after school tomorrow." His face looked like he could wring Jay's neck.

"Fine," yelled Jay. He slammed the door behind him and walked toward the street.

*　　　*　　　*

NEXT THING I KNEW, I was outside following Jay. I noticed his outfit. *He isn't prepared for this weather.* He was in jean shorts and a random tee.

"Yeah, and it's the middle of March," Jacob said. He was walking right next to me.

My thoughts melded with Jay's. "Well, I'd better get walking if I'm going to find somewhere to sleep tonight."

He set off east, toward the end of his cul-de-sac, which had a walkway at the end of it.

"You're way too mad to stay in this area right now." I didn't know if Jacob was explaining that to me or Jay.

Why is he controlling him? That's so weird.

"You know that they'll feel bad for you, and you have to prove a point to them." Jacob laughed.

And Jay kept walking. Across the street; up another one; through a desert. He vocalized his internal thoughts. "Dad changes his mind about my punishments all the time. He'll be out looking for me soon. I got to get as far from here as possible.

"I hope those things got deleted. I can't stand to hear about how much they hate Camille. She is amazing. If they find those texts or pictures, then I will never hear the end of it. As long as I don't hear about that, I'll be fine.

"If I would have just kept my grades up, my electronics wouldn't have gotten taken away. Dammit. If I had my phone I could call someone to pick me up. Maybe even Camille." The thought made him smile, "but since I don't, I'd better get going.

"Brrr." Jay shivered as he got to a big intersection complete with a traffic signal. A McDONALD'S was on one side of the street, and a gas station was caddy-corner to the south west, and another gas station was caddy-corner to the south. "It's cold out here."

Jacob spoke up again as Jay crossed the street. "For mid-March, it is a lot colder than it normally is. It had started with fourteen inches of snow right before Christmas, and the cold weather doesn't want to go away. It's very strange for where you live—rarely ever dropping below forty degrees Fahrenheit during the day."

I couldn't tell why he cut himself off right there, but Jay spoke up so it didn't matter. "I hope it warms up soon. My choice of dress is not going to cut it tonight."

HOOOONK! HOOOONK! A car decided to be funny as Jay walked along the street.

Jay hurled a river of expletives at the car as it drove farther and farther and farther away from him. I remembered that I've always hated people who honk at runners, and apparently even walkers. *This isn't the day to mess with Jay.*

By this point, Jay was halfway to the local mall. He walked the remaining two and a half miles, and within an hour and twenty minutes he was there.

Jacob spoke as Jay wandered through the parking lot. "You're about to run into Bryce Beyra, your friend who you haven't seen in a while. He doesn't go to DVC anymore because he prefers smoking and drinking and partying to going to learn about Jesus. This is the way it should be. You'd be there with him, but you're scared of your parents."

What a psycho.

As Jay made his way through the parking lot, a green Toyota Tacoma pulled up next to him and rolled down the driver's window. Jay's first thoughts were fear, but then he laughed. It was Bryce Beyra.

"No freaking way," my mind matched Jay's. "I haven't seen Bryce in forever. Maybe he can help me out."

"What's up, Jay?" came Bryce's first question.

"Not much. Just looking for somewhere to sleep tonight. I got kicked out."

Jacob spoke up. "That's a lie. You didn't get kicked out. You chose to leave."

"You got kicked out?" Bryce exclaimed. "What happened?"

"My parents pissed me off. I was yelling too. And here I am."

"Wow," said Bryce—stunned. "You need somewhere to stay?"

"Yeah," said Jay. "But I can't get you caught up in this too, bro, so I'll figure something out. My parents are pissed, and they can't know that I talked to you. If they call to see if you've heard from me, tell them no. Please."

"Okay, man," said Bryce.

"What a great friend you are, Jay." Jacob snickered.

"Shut up," I told him.

"I won't shut up. You have no authority over me. Besides, this memory isn't over yet."

I ignored Jacob the best I could, madder than a bull at the fact that he was making me feel horrible. *I want to be out of this dream. But if I get out, then I'm talking face-to-face with this psycho. He thinks he got kicked out of Heaven six thousand years ago? Who the hell is he?* I turned my attention back to Jay, trying to forget all about Jacob.

"Can I borrow your phone really quickly though?" Jay asked.

"Sure," said Bryce as he quickly rummaged through his pockets and handed Jay his phone—through the driver's window. "Let me park real quick."

"For sure," Jay replied, as he began trying to figure out the smartphone he'd been handed. When Bryce returned, after parking the truck thirty feet away, Jay asked, "Where were you headed?"

"I was just heading home," Bryce answered. "Why?"

"Wanna walk the mall for a little?"

"Sure."

Jay had finally figured out the phone, so he quickly typed a message to Camille. Hey babe, this is Jay. Just wanted to let you know I got kicked out of my house. I'm at the mall for now. I love you. ttyl.

As they entered the mall, Bryce's phone buzzed. Jay looked at the sender's number, and sure enough, it was Camille. He opened the message to read: that sucks hun. I wish I could see you but im stuck at home. I hope everything works out.

Jay replied: Thanks. I wish I could come over ;) unfortunately I cant.

Jay and Bryce walked the mall for another twenty minutes. So many happy people cruising around with their girlfriend on their arms. Making out. Holding hands. Laughing. Smiling.

Screw relationships, I thought. *I'm so sick of all these people. I miss Camille. Even young-Jay misses Camille right now. I hate my life.*

Bryce's phone buzzed again, and it was Camille. That would be nice ;P *kiss*.

Jay quickly replied: *kiss*

As soon as he had replied, a call came through for Bryce. Jay handed him the phone.

Bryce answered, talked for a few seconds, and hung up.

"Who was that?" Jay asked.

"It was my mom. I gotta go home." He pocketed the phone.

"Oh, okay. Well I'll talk to you later."

"Definitely," said Bryce as Jay turned to walk away. "Wait, man," he called out.

"What is it?" Jay stopped.

"I've got something for you in my truck."

"What?" Jay asked.

"In the past few months, I've found a new church to go to. I want to give you something from there. A sermon on CD. It's really good. You should come check out the church sometime."

Jacob couldn't resist. "Don't listen to him. He doesn't go nowhere. He parties all the time."

What's wrong with DVC? Why can't Jay keep going there? Why should he go to a new church?

"Okay man, I'll walk you to your car," Jay replied.

"Okay. The CD is in my glove box."

"Are there any cute girls at your church?" Jay asked.

Jacob spoke again. "All church is for is the girls. DVC has no good looking ones, unless they're extra young, freshman types." Jacob laughed. "Go for one of 'em. No one said you had to be committed to only one girl."

"But—"

Jacob interrupted me. "You don't believe the Bible, remember? You can't follow something that you don't believe in. Get all the girls you want. Just don't let Camille find out. Believe me, it's fun."

I ignored him, and I instead focused on Jay and Bryce's conversation. "There are a couple," said Bryce, "but that's not the reason to go."

"Tell him that's not true," Jacob said. "You know that's the only reason to go to church."

Jay held his tongue. "True," was all he said. As he walked to the truck, he asked, "Can I borrow your phone one last time?"

"Here you go," said Bryce, quickly handing over the piece of electronics.

"Thanks." Jay quickly punched in Ryan's number, and texted the following: Hey Ryan, it's Jay. Just thot u should know i got kicked out today. I have no uniform shirt for skool tomorrow. If u could bring me an xtra one that would b awesome. Thanx. Also, don't tell my parents you heard from me.

There was a message from Camille there as well. I love you, Jay. Be safe. ;)

He replied: I love you more =) unfortunately, I have no phone after sending this. ill tty when I do. *kiss*

Ryan's reply came through: I will do that bud. Be safe. See you tomorrow.

Jay sent one final message: Thanks

I gotta admit, Jay's got his hook-ups. He ain't gonna hurt himself.

Jay handed the phone back to Bryce as they reached his truck. It was pitch black dark outside by this point, and if it wasn't for the parking lot lights, Jay would have been blind.

Bryce unlocked the passenger door and handed Jay the disk. In the light of the parking lot lights, I saw that it read, "GRACE VALLEY CHURCH; 'Death in Adam, Life in Christ'; Romans 5:18-19".

"Thanks man," said Jay. "I'll listen to it one of these days."

"No you won't," Jacob explained.

"Sweet, bro. You should check out our Wednesday night youth group one of these days." Bryce climbed into his truck.

"For sure, man. I'll hit you up when I'm free. I have youth group Wednesday nights already, but if I'm ever free, I'll let you know."

"You are free, but you won't go. You hate your youth group. Why add another one?" Jacob was not letting Jay act like a good kid.

"Cool. Good luck tonight. I'll be praying for you." Bryce started up his truck.

"That's a lie. He won't pray for you. Who would pray for you? You're a piece of dirt who completely hates his family. You need nothing but professional help." Jacob had a sinister look on his face.

"Thanks," said Jay about Bryce's prayer promise. Then he asked, "Do you have any smokes?"

"Actually," began Bryce, "I have one. I'm quitting once this pack is gone. You can take it. I need to stop anyways." He opened the glove box again and pulled out a pack of MARLBOROS.

"Thanks," said Jay, accepting the treasure.

"Here's a lighter," Bryce added, handing it to Jay. "It's almost dead, so keep it. I gotta go though, man."

"See you later," said Jay.

Bryce waved as he drove off, leaving Jay alone in the cold night—outside the mall—with only a CD and a cigarette to keep him company.

Jacob had to have the last word. "What a great friend he is. He wouldn't even help you find a place to stay."

"Shut up," I said, as Jay walked away.

The scene went dark. It seemed like the parking lot lights faded to black.

*   *   *

THE RED-SHADOWED ROOM RETURNED. It was no longer chilly, but quickly growing warm. I was sweating. I couldn't decide if it was fear or the actual temperature that was causing my pores to pour.

What I had decided, though, was that I wanted Jacob to shut up. *He has no clue what he's talking about. Those memories— or made up stories—are so out of context.*

"That's what you think," Jacob said. "The truth is, these stories, every single one from the day you showed up on this island, have been exposing different parts of your heart. You had faith—but you lost it. You liked your parents—you lost it. You liked church—you lost it. You are a pathetic Christian. In fact, you're not one. Remember? If you were one, I couldn't touch you. Let's see if I can touch you now."

Jacob pulled out a really big knife and walked toward me, with a snarl on his face. In fact, it looked like the same knife that Kevin, Jared, and Jaime had possessed. I let out a scream. *I don't want to be filleted again.* Jacob came closer and closer.

"Stop, you crazy maniac!" I screamed. *I don't want to die.*

"I'm not going to kill you, Jay," Jacob said. "I'm going to torture you within inches of life. You'll be begging for death, and then, when I offer it, you'll cry out for life, and you won't find it. Ima expose more of your insides."

I screamed. *My insides? That doesn't sound pleasant at all. I'm not ready to be carved into lunch meat.*

Jacob was on top of me, holding me to the ground. "You'll be lunch meat by the time this is done," he said.

I screamed again. "Don't butcher me, Jacob!"

"I'm not going to. Yet." The last word rolled off his tongue slowly. He looked deep into my eyes. "First of all, my name isn't Jacob." He paused before explaining, "It's Red, or Liyon, or Ophis, or Hunter, or Diablo, or A-O-L." He cackled. "Take your pick, Liyfer. I have many names. Jacob ain't one of them though, so please stop using it."

"What's A-O-L?" I managed to squeak.

"Angel of Light. If you read your Bible, you'd know some of this stuff." He carved the knife into my flesh—between my nipples—and I passed out.

CHAPTER 45

(May 21, 2010)

WHEN I OPENED my eyes, I found myself in a classroom at my high school. I quickly looked around to see if Jacob was around this time. *I mean Red; I mean Hunter; I mean Jacob; uh,* I didn't know his name. I threw up my middle finger to the sky. *I don't know where you are or what your real name is, but you certainly aren't a friend of mine.* I brought my hand back down. *That sob story he told me when we first met was a mirror image of mine—other than getting injured in college and not having a stroke at age two.*

I turned my attention to what was going on in the classroom. A bald teacher was lecturing the class. "Benjamin was a student at this school some years back. He even graduated from here. He showed all the signs of being a true Christian. Then he went to college, and that was when things began to change. A professor took him under his wing and convinced him that the Bible was garbage. Since then he has been an atheist. However, due to his past acts as a Christian, if he died today I believe he would still be saved—"

An adult agrees with my stance. I'm not in danger of Hell. This is awesome. I'll live how I want and do what I want for the rest of my life. I prayed that prayer. I memorized all the verses. God can't refuse me one day. Anyone who says otherwise is stupid.

Some girl cut the teacher off almost rudely, "How is that possible? How can a Christian just change their mind about their Savior? How can a denouncer hope to be saved at the end?"

"Once saved, always saved," the teacher replied.

"But wait," cut in another girl. "Doesn't the Bible say that anyone who denies the Son will be denied by the Father also?"

The teacher calmly replied, "Didn't Peter deny him three times?" His students nodded. "Yet he also founded the Catholic Church. I'd say it does not matter."

The first girl spoke up again, "Well yeah, but—"

Stop arguing with the teacher. He's been to school. He knows what he's talking about.

BRIIING went the bell.

Why does the bell always have to ring? That was great. I wanted to know how that was going to end.

"Have a good weekend," the teacher said. "Don't forget to bring in your completed worksheets on atheists on Monday."

Everyone rushed out of the room, and I noticed Jay in their midst. *That would explain why I'm watching this.* He looked really confused. Our thoughts meshed: "I have always been taught that if you pray that little prayer you will be safe for eternity, however just yesterday a guy talked to us who cared nothing for God, even though he had prayed the prayer when he was a young man.

"I feel like that guy. I know I prayed the prayer in kindergarten, in sixth grade, and in eighth grade, but I also told God that I couldn't care less if He existed or not just two months ago, because after thirteen years of praying for God to heal my stroke symptoms, nothing ever happened. It bugs me. God can't be real if He can't heal my condition. And if this pastor is right, then it doesn't matter what I believe now; I'm still sealed for eternity, and I can live life my way from now on.

"That thought lifts a huge weight from my shoulders. All of the kids in my class who say one thing but do another must have learned this truth a long time ago, because they all act on it daily. In Bible class they know the right answers. In chapel they pay attention and sing the songs loudly with their hands raised. In church they are the popular kids with the helpful tips to the not so popular people. But, on Friday nights, they are the ones throwing the parties with the drugs and alcohol. They are the ones bragging about all the chicks they'd gotten with. They are the ones who cuss up a storm during lunch break. It all makes perfect sense. All you have to do is pray a prayer to be saved. That's why Jared can't fathom how I'm still a virgin, and it is why he makes fun of me all the time. He did say that he was just trying to help me. Maybe this was how he was trying to do that; he just didn't know how to put it into words."

I noticed Kyle—complete with his slicked-back haircut—walk up to Jay, as my thoughts separated from Jay's. When Kyle reached him, he asked, "Hey man, what's up?"

Jay's face showed surprise. *Does no one usually ask him that?*

"Not much," Jay replied. "Just confused a little."

"About what our teacher said?" Kevin asked.

"Yeah. Does it mean that Christianity is just a prayer and you are good to go?" asked Jay.

"Definitely not," said Kyle. It's a whole lot—"

BRIIING went the bell.

"We're late to class." Kyle said. "Find me later, and I'll answer your question."

"For sure, dude," said Jay. He then opened the door, and the two of them entered class.

My thoughts didn't mesh with Jay's throughout the time in class except for me to remember that everyone in my class thought that our junior year English teacher had been fired before senior year had started. Why? No one knew. The point was that the new teacher was not qualified to teach English. I watched as she sat at her desk, doing nothing, as the whole class sat around chatting and working on their assignment: draw a picture that describes your life. *Really? This is senior level English? I want to know how this helps me in life. Oh, wait. It's high school. It doesn't mean a thing. This is like kindergarten all over again.*

Finally the bell went BRIIING, and I saw Jay heave a sigh of relief. It was lunch for the next half hour. Kyle rushed out of class first, and by the time Jay got out the door, Kyle was halfway to his JEEP. Jay waited for him. *He really wants Kyle to answer his question, so he's waiting for him to pull around.*

When his green JEEP turned the corner, Jay waved him down. "Hey man, what were you going to say when the bell rang?"

"Just read First John and you will see," said Kyle. "I really need to get going."

"Oh ok. Later."

Yeah right he's going to look up some Bible verse. He doesn't have time to read a bunch of nothing in a stupid, ancient book. Plus, what kind of Christian says that he'll answer a question, but then turns around and runs off as soon as possible without answering it?

My vision went black.

CHAPTER 46

(Day 6, 8 p.m.)

I WOKE UP and found myself on the outside of the volcano, on the edge of a level cliff on the otherwise perfectly conical slope. I was looking out over the island. It was almost totally dark outside. The full moon was low in the sky, and it reflected grandly off the ocean in the distance. Most of the light at the moment was coming from the moon, but a reddish-glow was also emitting from somewhere ahead of me, casting eerie shadows around the ledge I was laying on. The air was chilly, and in the moonlight I could see the huts in the distance where my surviving classmates were staying. *Will they hear me if I scream?*

I felt a burning, stinging sensation in two new places. My forehead and my chest ached, and both felt wet as I lay on the ground. I glanced down and saw fresh cut marks in my chest, though I couldn't make out if it was anything more than just a long gash. I reached my hand to my face and sure enough, blood came off onto my palm. *What did I ever do to deserve this?*

Jacob—actually Red Savage, as he had called himself in his notes—was standing over me, staring away from me. His facial features, now hoodless, were plain in the moonlight and the eerie red glow. His eyes were tiny yellow circles, pupil-free. He had a sharply curved nose that appeared like a quarter circle when viewing his profile. He spoke in his deep, gravelly voice, as he turned his head to glare down at me, "You pathetic piece of crap.

How can anyone love you?" His mouth was toothy, and if I wasn't mistaken his incisors protruded from his mouth, over his pale lips.

"Why do you hate me so much?" I moved slowly and painfully into a seated position.

"I don't, Jay. I love you. I want to spend the rest of eternity with you. And I'm going to, because I'm going to kill you. And since you aren't a Christian—since you don't believe in God—I have you for eternity. We're going to have a wonderful time together in Hell, aren't we?"

God, please get me out of here. Rescue me. I'll trust You forever if you don't let me die. Please!

"God can't hear you, Jay." Red was smirking. His tongue passed between his teeth, over his lips, and it brought images of snakes to my mind. He kept talking, "You created this island yourself. You're scared to death of Hell, and that's why I'm here. You said God's not real, so that's why He isn't going to hear you. You've committed the most heinous crimes—thievery, lying, disobeying authorities, raping women, and murdering people—so the proof has all been tattooed across your body, so you never forget, for all eternity, how much God hates you and how much you fit in perfectly with me..."

Red was still talking but I was completely lost. *When had I ever stolen anything? When had a lie been a big deal? When did I disobey the law? When had I raped anyone? When had I murdered someone? Since when does God hate anyone? Church has always told me that God loves everybody. This lunatic is smoking something strong. There's no other explanation.*

"Would you like photographic proof of all these crimes? I have them. In fact, I have more than you can imagine. The Titanic couldn't hold them all—especially the rape, murder, and thievery ones. They're stacked a mile high."

Five huge piles of what I assumed to be photographs appeared out of nowhere on the ledge we were situated on. *Huh?*

"These are why you are going to be with me in Hell. It's simple, really." Red grabbed a few random photographs from one of the piles. He handed them to me.

The first showed me talking to Kevin—on the island—about why Justin was killed. The next was when I was talking to my principal after the fight with Darien. The next was me talking to my parents about taking the car to hang out with Camille.

Red explained. "You're a dirty liar, Jay. You always resort to lying, because it's easier than the truth. Sure, there's some truth in it. There always is. But it's still a lie. I'm the father of this, so take it from me. You and I are cut from the same cloth. You're never going to be able to escape me. Here's more proof." He reached into another pile and handed me a picture.

I looked, and there I was—shooting my little brother. Red handed another from the same pile. I was shooting my sister. Red handed another, and in it, I was drowning my dad. Red handed yet another, and I was killing Kyle—Laura's friend. The shock was too much to allow me to speak.

Where did he get these?

"These are straight off your heart, Jay. You're a bloodthirsty murderer. You've killed your whole family multiple times. You've killed various classmates as well—Ryan, Kyle, Jared, Jaime. Don't you see it, Jay? You deserve Hell, just like me. And you're so horrible that you can't get away from it. No good deeds will ever get you into Heaven." Red reached into another pile and started handing pictures to me.

I was telling my parents one thing when I actually did another. I was listening to rap music. I was eating before praying. I was yelling—as my parents told me to be quiet.

"I understand this one," I said. *I still don't think it's that big of a deal. Didn't my youth pastor say that every guy disagrees with his parents?*

He handed me another stack from the same pile. I was smoking cigarettes with Joey and Kevin on the way to Bible study. I was drinking rum while Joey and Sharon looked on.

I don't understand what these have to do with the others.

Red explained. "It's a thin line between disobeying your parents and disobeying the law. Admit the truth: you despise the authorities placed over you. The law says no smoking 'til age eighteen—you weren't eighteen at this point. The law says no drinking 'til age twenty-one. You're still not there yet."

Before I could reply, Red reached into another pile and pulled out a handful of pictures. "You're a dirty little thief, Jay. Thieves can't enter Heaven."

I took the pictures and flipped through them. I was at a recording studio, sitting down, copying all the song files off a computer. Another one: I was outside the playboy mansion, running off with a handful of DVDs. Another: I was pocketing a package of CHEEZ-ITS from Joey's duffel bag.

"Really?" I said. "I never did either of the first two. And was it really stealing to take the crackers?"

Red ignored my question about the crackers. "You've downloaded plenty of music and videos for free, Jay." Red paused. "It's no different. Stealing is stealing, and people that steal are called thieves. There's no possible way you can get into Heaven. Give stuff to people for free, but it won't cover this up. You're mine—forever—but just to enhance the point..." he trailed off. Red grabbed a stack of photos from the last pile. The pile that was significantly taller than the rest of them combined.

I took the ones he handed me and grimaced. *The photo Jared had showed of me and Jaime.* I felt sick. I threw it to the ground and saw more—of other girls—every girl in my class, Camille, girls from church whose names I didn't even know, porn stars from the computer, girls I'd seen at amusement parks. I threw the remaining photos on the ground—not wanting to look at them.

"I never did any of that!" I protested loudly. My shout shot pain throughout my whole body.

Red's tongue flicked out between his teeth. "The pictures don't lie, Jay. Just imagine how much pain you'd be in if every one

293

of those girls' significant others were here, and they could carve the word 'rapist' in you.

"You do realize that's why Jared carved you up, right? I sent him to you, decided to be late with your weapon, and let him carve the truth in you. You're an evil, freaking rapist. How can you ever expect God to love you?" Red laughed a deep, guttural laugh, stared me straight in the eyes, and said, "You, my friend, are no virgin. Don't deceive yourself!"

I slowly stood to my feet as Red walked back a few paces to the cave entrance in the side of the volcano. He shouted, "Camille, girly, come on out. I need you for something."

What? I was too surprised to speak. *She's been dead as long as I've been on the island. I saw her body myself. And this lying bastard has been asking me about how I've been feeling every god-forsaken day since then.*

Still too stunned to speak, Red spoke instead. "You got the lying part right. I have been known as the Father of Lies for at least two thousand years now. And of course I've been bugging you about it. I've been preparing you for this moment."

But she was dead.

"Didn't it strike you as odd that out of everyone on the plane, the only one who died in the crash was the one you cared the most about?" He paused, and cackled loudly. "Remember when we first met? It was on the airplane when you were learning about your," he put up air quotes, "loss." He put them down as he continued, "That set-up couldn't have gone better. I waited there for you—remember that this whole time has been about you? The other deaths were collateral damage on account of you." He paused as a shadow passed behind him. "Feel even more guilty." He enunciated every word of his next sentence. "People, died, be-cause, of, you." He flicked out his tongue again. "And I blew up the plane to remind you that there hadn't been any real closure." He cackled. "I've been running all of this the whole time, and you've played right into my hands at every point."

I wasn't registering everything he was saying as he said it, especially after the shadow passed behind him. All of my focus was drawn to it. He stopped talking when she came into view, and I almost fainted at the sight. It took every ounce of my remaining strength to remain standing.

It was Camille. A much skinnier—competition with Jaime now skinny—Camille, but Camille nonetheless. Her dirty-blonde hair was knotted and frazzled. Her green t-shirt was by this point all but shredded completely away, and her skirt was full of holes.

What should I say to her? The last time I had truly interacted with her was in a much more preferable situation, and I'd all but forgotten my whole life since then.

"Tell her you want her," Red said. "Tell her you'll make me go away. Tell her you'll rescue her from me. Lie to her like you've lied to everyone your whole life."

She spoke, in a hollow, hoarse voice, "Jay, is that you? What's going on? This creep told me you were dead. I've screamed and cried and cried and screamed ever since then." She choked up. "This was supposed to be a fun trip. It's turned into a nightmare." Despite the fear in her voice, I thought it was the most beautiful sound I'd heard in a week.

Red interjected before I had a chance to say anything. "Enjoy a conjugal visit before I kill you, Jay. This is what you've been looking forward to, right?" He paused. "Come on over here. She's ready for you." His face twisted into a sly smile.

I couldn't argue with that. However, as I got closer to Camille, she spoke, and the words hurt.

"What's written all over you, Jay?"

"Nothing, babe," I said. "Just ignore it."

"But it says, 'Thief,' across your chest, and it says, 'Rapist,' below your belly button." She paused before adding, "And it looks like it says, 'Liar,' on your forehead." She looked confused, and as my hand reached out to touch her face, she flinched back. "Why would those words be written on you?" All of her words came out slowly.

295

"Cami, babe." I paused, hoping that phraseology wouldn't offend her. It didn't change anything about her blank facial expression, so I continued, "This psychopath behind you carved all these words in me. He's trying to convince me that I'm some sort of terrible person. Apparently, he's also convincing others of it too. Bryce thinks all this is true of me; he hates my guts. Now you think this is true of me too." I paused again, on the verge of tears. *My girlfriend is alive. I'm about to die. She thinks I'm a bad person. Why is this happening to me?* I spoke again, "Please let me comfort you, babe. Your time here's probably been worse than mine. Please let me help you feel better." I leaned in for a kiss.

My appeal worked; she didn't think I was a bad person. She didn't believe what Red had written on me. She reached her hands up behind my head and pulled my head down to hers. Our lips met.

She gasped, jerked her hand away from my head, and clutched her chest instead. Our lips separated.

Red's terrible voice spoke again. "It's so sweet, I know, but how weak would I be if I actually let you get what you've wanted this whole time?"

I glanced at where Camille's hands had moved and saw a jagged blade sticking out the base of her neck. Blood was flowing, spurting onto my chest, and her breathing was coming in short gasps. The blade slid out, and I had to turn away. I couldn't watch it.

Instead the tears started flowing. I heard her body slump to the ground, and I yelled, "You're heartless!"

"If you really were a Christian, you'd know that I'm the king of promising more than I deliver," Red laughed sinisterly. Without missing a beat, he asked, "What about door number two?"

Huh?

"Would you like Jaime to fill in for Camille? She's pretty desperate too. In fact, she was infinitely more desperate than Camille until about thirty seconds ago."

I screamed. *So that's what he's saying? What kind of heartless freak kills a guy's girlfriend in front of his eyes and then offers him a backup woman less than thirty seconds later?* (However, being the stupid young man that I was, I debated his offer in my mind.)

I want sex for sure, but not with her for the first time. Yes, the pictures showed that it would not be my first time, but in truth, the pictures were fakes. I'm still a virgin. I'd kept my pants on around girls my whole life. I am not sexually active. What those pictures mean, I don't know, but they disgust me. I've never had sex with any of those girls. It is crazy. If only—but no, it's never happened. And besides that, I am in too much pain to even want to do anything.

"You're such a pansy," Red taunted, before I could ever officially answer him. He started mocking me. "I'm such a good boy. I'd never have sex with anyone I wasn't married to, but I'll have sex with as many girls as I want in my head without their permission." He went back to his voice. "You're a serial rapist, Jay. You are a dirty piece of dog crap that deserves to be scooped up and thrown away. You don't deserve to be loved by God. You don't deserve to be loved by your parents. You don't deserve to be loved by a single girl on the face of this planet. You got lucky with Camille, because she was a whore. She'd get with you or the next guy any day—which makes me wonder about your manhood, cuz you never actually did anything with her. What a pathetic loser!"

I lunged at him, but fell to the ground without touching him. He added another thought, "Even if you wanted Jaime, she's been dead since just after the last time you interacted with her." Red laughed hysterically and said, "Enjoy this flashback, you heathen."

The next thing I knew, I was watching myself. Again.

*   *   *

HOW MUCH LONGER is this nightmare going to last? I'm sick of being reminded of all this stuff. It's past. God will forgive me. I prayed the prayer.

"I've told you that's not true," came Red's voice from behind me. "You're going to Hell. Remember all the pictures? If there's any evidence needed on Judgment Day, I've got all of it on you. You're done for."

"Shut up." *Why does he have to be here again? Why wasn't he here last time?*

"That's easy. I'm not there when you're unconscious. Right now you're fully conscious." He walked up next to me.

It was then that I noticed that I was staring at another freeze frame. Jay was in his bald teacher's class again. His red backpack was on top of the table, and he was holding his phone right behind it.

Red filled me in. "You're sitting in class. You've sat in this class every day for eight weeks. Tomorrow's your last day. Today is a half day. This is your last class of the day and the bell is about to ring.

"Regardless of whether or not the bell's rung, just look at what you're doing. You're texting that stupid Camille. You know class isn't dismissed, but you're still texting. Great Christian values." Red coughed and laughed. "She's dead now. Proves how worthless relationships are, right?"

He kept going, "All you've heard the last eight weeks is a bunch of biased junk about how stupid every religion is except for Christianity. The thoughts and opinions of them all are mixing and melding in your brain. You don't even know what you believe anymore. You admitted as much as you sat there in class. Mormonism, Islam, Buddhism, Jehovah's Witness, Catholicism, and Christianity are all mashing together in your mind.

"Let's look at just how bad it is. This flashback is awesome."

I waited a split second to see if he was going to keep going. He didn't. *Thank God.*

The action resumed.

BRIIING went the bell.

"Don't forget to prepare for tomorrow's final," the teacher announced as Jay's class ran outside.

Amid shouts of, "Two more days of school!" and "I'm so ready to graduate and leave this school," Jay walked out to his car to go home.

Red spoke again, "Aren't you excited that you have nothing the rest of the day. Forget about your final tomorrow; you don't need to study. Wednesday night study ended last week so there's no Bible study tonight. You hated those anyways. You should see if Camille is available tonight. You know how eager you both are to get together. Send her a text."

Jay reached into his pocket and grabbed his phone. He instantly began typing. Hey babe. R U free 2nite? :)

What? How did Red get him to do that?

Jay climbed into the front seat, threw his phone in the cup holder, and I instantly found myself in the back seat, right next to Red. Jay turned the key, and the engine turned over and started purring. Then the rap music started blaring, and he rolled down the windows. He pulled forward, turned left, passed a group of his classmates chit-chatting back and forth on the picnic tables, turned right, and drove out of the parking lot.

When he reached a red light, he picked up his phone again. He had a message. It was from Camille. sorry love. I can't. my parents and I aren't getting along right now.

Jay replied. I'm sorry, babe. I'll FACEBOOK you when I get home.

Red spoke up. "You think you're so good? Look at that. Texting and driving. That's breaking the law. Isn't that a sin too?"

"You don't know anything," I shouted. "All you want to do is accuse me. I thought you loved me."

"I do. I'm just pointing out how much we have in common."

     *   *   *

JAY'S MOTHER MET HIM when he came inside. "Jay, don't forget to pack for your trip. You leave in two days."

"Your mom always harps on you when you have stuff to do. Ignore her."

I wish I could ignore Red. How do I get back to the island?

Jay gave her half a nod and ran up to his room without saying anything to her. He muttered under his breath, "I don't plan on packing today—I have all afternoon and evening tomorrow. Packing only takes fifteen minutes anyways, once I have a duffel bag. Why do my parents think stuff takes so much longer than it really does?"

As soon as he reached his room, he turned on his stereo and shut his door. Shuffling through his CD's he landed on EMINEM. *Typical,* I thought. He kept the volume low. *He doesn't want to upset "Christian-music-only" people with his blatantly secular music.*

"Why should I listen to Christian music when I don't believe any of that stuff anyways?" he cried out over the music as he flopped into his easy chair and thumbed through his IPOD touch until he found FACEBOOK. From there he sent an instant message to Camille. Hey sexy.

Not fifteen seconds later: Hey

Jay: are you okay? there's no smiley :/

Camille: I'm fine. It's just my parents are still being annoying like usual.

Jay: I'm sorry babe. I wish I could help, but I'm actually going out of town in two days so I can't really go anywhere until then.

Camille: Oh, okay :'(

Jay: I'm really sorry. *kiss*

Camille: *kiss* where are you going?

Jay: Florida, for my senior trip. Our flight leaves at seven AM on Friday.

"Isn't it great?" Red laughed. "Your physical relationship is totally cyber, and nonexistent."

"She's dead now. I hate these flashbacks. Shut your damn mouth." I was fed up with hearing about how much we didn't do anything sexual. *At this point I'd give anything to just sit next to her and talk to her again. I don't even need to kiss her.*

"That's what you say now," Red said. "You know that's not true though."

My thoughts were drawn back to the instant message conversation when I heard the DING of a new message.

Camille: Is that seriously when your flight leaves?

Jay: Yeah. 7AM Friday. why?

Camille: =) my day has just infinitely improved. What airline are you taking?

Jay: DELTA

Camille: =) my parents are my favorite ppl now.

Jay: huh? I'm confused.

Camille: they decided to send me to Florida to visit my cousins. I'm leaving on Friday at 7 AM and flying DELTA.

Jay: I'm totally sitting with you. this might actually work out well.

Camille: I hope so. We can chill the whole time ;)

Jay: I hope so. ;) *hug* and *kiss*

Camille: *kiss* and *cuddle*

Stop it, I cried inside. *Stop flirting. Do her parents realize that they are sending her to her death?*

"That's not even the important part," Red explained. "The messages continue to go back and forth between you two. You discuss everything you planned on doing together while in Florida. You already saw the pictures. Use your imagination." He laughed.

Jay moved from his chair to his desk. He opened up a word processor and typed the following two sentences: "Jay Liyfer had mixed feelings about the week to come as he drove home from school. Part of him was excruciatingly excited for his senior trip, but another part was dreading it with all his being."

Jay muttered an explanation. "It's the truth. I'm excited to get out of my house, and to be able to hang out with Camille for a week, but I have zero desire to be anywhere near my classmates—

especially Jared Seydu. That kid drives me crazy, and I would give anything to be able to kill him."

Jay minimized the document he had started, and instead opened up INTERNET EXPLORER. While there, he went to FACEBOOK to check on anything new from Camille. Nothing. Then a message from Bryce Beyra popped up. Hey Jay, are you free tonight? I was wondering if you'd like to go to Bible study with me. I can pick you up at your house at 6 o clock, and drop you off after. Hit me back.

Jay quickly wrote back: I would, but I don't know if I can. I'll check though and get back to you.

Bryce: Cool.

"This is where it gets good," Red explained. "You all of a sudden decide that you want to go to Bible Study, but it's not at all what you expect."

Huh?

Jay left his room and ran downstairs to his mom, and he quickly came back and replied to Bryce. I'll be ready at 5:50. Pick me up whenever.

Jay spent the next three hours cleaning his room and doing laundry.

"What a suck up," Red criticized. "You hate cleaning and you hate laundry, but you want to give your mom a reason to like you. That's the only reason you even acted interested in Bryce's study. If you truly wanted to be a good son, you'd pack like you were told, but you aren't, so you won't."

"Go to hell," I commanded. *I can't listen to his crap anymore.*

*   *   *

BRYCE SHOWED UP at 6:08 in his Toyota Tacoma. Jay walked out of his house when he saw the truck out his front window.

"How was your day?" Bryce asked as he pulled away from the curb toward the stop sign at the end of the street.

"It's going well," Jay answered. "Nothing exciting. Just talking to my girlfriend all afternoon and getting ready for my senior trip."

"Cool, cool," Bryce replied. "Where's the trip at?"

"Florida. For a week."

"That should be fun."

"Hopefully," Jay replied.

"I've always wanted to check out Florida. I'd say I want to come along, but I have school next week."

"Well, maybe someday we'll go. Road trip." Jay laughed.

The small talk continued for the next twenty minutes. I recognized the route as the route to Camille's house. "If only I could swing by tonight," Jay's thought entered my brain.

Finally, they reached a little gated community on a hill overlooking Camille's neighborhood. Bryce punched in the gate code, and within two minutes the car was parked.

"Do I know anyone here?" Jay asked, looking up at the house.

Bryce gave a couple of names as they started walking up to the door, but I recognized none of them. Jay said he remembered one or two of them.

When they reached the door, Bryce knocked loudly, and an energy-filled, blonde woman answered. "Hey, Bryce!" she exclaimed. "How are you?"

"I'm great. How are you?"

"I'm awesome. Unfortunately, Thomas is at work right now. He won't be here until about eight thirty tonight. Pamela is leading the discussion."

I noticed that Jay hadn't been noticed yet. *Is he really invisible?*

Then Bryce announced, "This is my friend Jay. I've known him since kindergarten."

"Hi, Jay," the blonde woman replied. "I'm Sally." She extended her hand for a handshake.

"Nice to meet you," Jay replied, accepting the hand shake.

"Come on in," she urged. "No need to stand outside."

Bryce eagerly accepted the offer, and Jay followed him inside. Directly ahead was a set of couches facing an entertainment center. To the left stood a dining room table, which was followed by a good sized kitchen. Several people were stationed in the kitchen—a bald guy holding a guitar who was introduced as Mike, a black woman who was introduced as Pamela, and several kids whose names I did not catch.

I haven't heard Red in a while.

"Don't speak too soon," he reiterated the fact that he was still around. "Look at everyone talking to each other. They look so happy. Even Bryce is chatting with other people. What a great friend. They're not talking to you." He laughed. "Oh, and they all have their Bibles. Where's yours? What a great Christian you are," he accused. "You should be ashamed of yourself."

After forty minutes of chit-chat, everyone was called to the couches where Mike was now waiting with his guitar. Everyone squeezed onto the sofas, and Mike led the group in three worship songs—none of which I recognized. Then he introduced Pamela and the topic for the night—Jehovah's Witnesses.

Pamela led the group of about ten people through the reasons why Jehovah's Witnesses were not real Christians, including the most obvious reason: their modification of John 1:1. She explained, "In the New World Translation, their false translation of the Bible, they make it read, 'In the beginning the Word was, and the Word was with God, and the Word was a god.' In reality it reads, 'In the beginning was the Word, and the Word was with God, and the Word was God.' The Jehovah's Witnesses think that they can translate it as 'a God' instead of 'God' because the Greek word for God doesn't have a definite article. However, with the use of the 'to be' verb, the function of this sentence is the same as saying, 'The boy is tall.' The word after the verb is a predicate adjective that describes the subject. In the Greek, John is explaining that Jesus is God, but in light of the Trinity, He is distinguished from the Father. If they were completely one and the same, and the Trinity didn't exist, then God would have had a definite article as well, but John wants to keep them distinct."

Red spoke up. "You don't care about all that technical jargon. It's for the nerds who don't have lives."

I didn't disagree with him.

Pamela then shared her story which focused on being married to a Jehovah's Witness, while she was also one, and how—ever since her conversion to Christianity—she prayed hard every day for his conversion. In closing, she asked for prayer concerning that situation.

Then everyone shared prayer requests, and when it reached him, Jay said that he was good, and didn't need any. Pamela closed in prayer, and everyone was dismissed.

It was eight forty when the study was finished, and the front door opened to reveal a tall, husky man dressed in fireman garb.

He greeted everyone at once, "Whatsup yos?" Then he noticed Jay, and he moved over to Bryce, shook Bryce's hand, and asked him, "How are you doing, man?"

"I'm good, Thomas. This is my friend Jay."

Thomas offered his hand to Jay and said, "Nice to meet you, Jay. What did you think of the study?"

"It was cool," Jay replied, "though this is the exact stuff I've been doing at school recently."

"Where do you go to school?" Thomas asked.

"Oasis Christian."

"That's cool. How do you like it over there?"

"I don't. Not gonna lie," Jay answered.

"Oh, okay. You coming back next week?" Thomas inquired.

"I can't. I'll be out of town."

"That's too bad," Thomas said. "I'll be leading the discussion on Mormons next week. You're welcome to come back whenever."

"Thanks," Jay acknowledged.

"Well, if you'll excuse me," Thomas said, "I gotta get changed."

"No problem," Bryce said. "But I think we're gonna get going. See you next week."

"Later," Thomas said, before adding, "It was nice to meet you, Jay. Hope to see you again."

"Nice to meet you too," Jay replied politely.

Red spoke again. "You're such a stupid, little suck up. That was exactly what you were discussing in school. You hate the subject. You want to live your life your way. Don't say it was nice to meet them."

I kept my mouth shut. He seemed to talk less when I ignored him.

Bryce led the way to the front door, saying bye to everyone on the way out. Sally walked them out and called, "Have a good week!" as they walked down to Bryce's truck.

"You too!" shouted Bryce as they climbed inside and pulled on their seatbelts.

*   *   *

WHEN THEY WERE HALFWAY HOME, Bryce asked, "So what did you think? You gonna come back when you can?"

"I don't know," Jay answered. "It wasn't really my thing. I've just gotten through all the religion stuff in school, and it's annoying. Sure, everyone was nice, but it still doesn't mean I like it. I'm not big on giving out prayer requests to total strangers. They will judge me."

"These people won't," Bryce assured him.

"How do you know?" Jay questioned.

"Believe me," Bryce answered.

"I don't know what to believe anymore, Bryce," Jay replied. "But I'll be sure to hit you up in the future if I'm interested." He thought for a few seconds.

Red spoke. "Tell him you won't be interested. The Bible is stupid. Why study it?"

Jay concluded his statement as the setting began to change back to the volcano. "Though I doubt I will be interested in coming back."

*   *   *

RED STARTED TALKING AGAIN, as the ledge of the volcano came back into focus. "See, Jay? You hate anything having to do with Christianity. It shows itself in your attitudes and your actions. Attitudes of," he started mocking my voice, "I doubt I will be interested," he reverted to his voice, "and actions of murder, rape, theft, lies, etcetera.

"Jay, the truth is, you're mine and there is absolutely nothing you can do about it. You be—"

Bryce's voice was heard at that moment, interrupting Red's rant. "Jay, are you up here?"

Red's yellow eyes glared at me, ordering me to keep my mouth shut.

I hope Bryce finds me. I don't want to die. I am in so much pain. I am so confused. Bryce is the only friend I have left. I want to call Bryce.

Red will kill you though. An internal argument again. *This is not a good time.*

Bryce is right over the edge of the volcano

Red is two paces away.

I want freedom. "Bryce, I'm up here! Some psychotic killer is about to kill me. Hur—"

A blow to the side of my face knocked me out.

CHAPTER 47

(May 27, 2010, 12:00 p.m.)

I KNEW IF I OPENED MY EYES that it would be yet another flashback to my past. So I refused to open them at first. However, even with my eyes closed I could still hear what was going on. It sounded like I was in the car, as Jay was driving with the music blaring—like usual. I didn't care to figure out who he was listening to; the repetitive thumping of the rap music told me all I needed to know. *I hate these dreams. They started out boring. They reached a peak. Now they're boring again. And all of Red's stupid comments don't help. I hope he's not here this time.*

I opened my eyes worried about what I would find. Nothing but Jay driving himself home. I looked left, out the rear left window: nothing but desert being passed at 55 miles per hour. I looked right: an empty seat. *Awesome. No Red. I can try to enjoy myself this time.*

You can try *to enjoy yourself,* my mind retorted. *Remember that you just said these dreams are boring.*

Shut up. This hasn't happened in a while. I hate internal conversations with myself.

You hate conversations with everyone.

That's not true. I enjoy talking to Camille. I paused, as my eyes grew moist. *I mean, I used to enjoy talking to her.*

But apart from her, there's no one else. You hate your parents. Joey's dead. Bryce is crazy. Kevin's dead. Your classmates are idiots. You've got no one.

*　　*　　*

THE INTERNAL ARGUMENT LASTED until Jay got home. As he sat in the driveway, he checked his phone. A text from Camille. Hey babe. I'm sooo excited for tomorrow :) <3

Jay smiled, and he muttered under his breath, "Oh yeah. We're going to be on the same flight. That should solve all my problems: Jared won't be a problem; parents won't be a problem. I'll be golden." He texted her back. Me too. You have to sneak me to your cousins' house. I don't wanna be on my trip at all.

Don't go on the trip. She's going to die as a result. You don't want that. I decided Jay needed to know the truth. I reached out to smack him to get his attention, but as I did, my hand passed right through his head. *Weird. How come Red can interact with these people?* "Jay," I yelled, "don't let her go. She is going to die." I pronounced that last sentence slowly and deliberately but to no avail. He was not going to hear me.

Camille texted back: I think I can do that ;)

Jay: Thanks.

He got out of his car, and he walked up to the front door, lugging his backpack with him. I followed behind him. *As if I really have a choice.*

Jay's thoughts meshed with mine. "I love Camille. She is so awesome. I was looking for a girl like her all through high school and I finally found her—six months before graduating. Sure, my parents don't approve, so I keep it behind their backs, but at least I am happy. Camille loves me, and she is nice to me; she isn't someone who hates my guts and only 'loves' me because she has to. Camille and I will be together forever. I am sure of it."

It was too much for me. *I don't get all of his thoughts, so why would I need to get that one?* I started crying. *I miss Camille so much. I want her to come back. I want to hold her, and love her, and keep her from going on that stupid plane. She was the best thing that ever happened to me, and now she's dead. God, if You're in*

309

control of dreams, I hate You. I'm sick of these stupid things. I want her back.

Jay turned the doorknob, pushed the door open, and his mom was waiting for him when he walked through the door. "Why are you home already?"

"Don't yell," he answered back. "I'm home because I have to pack for my trip. We are leaving tomorrow morning."

"Don't tell me not to yell. You were supposed to wait at school until 2:40 to bring your brother home."

"I know, but today is a special day. I have to go pack."

"I thought I told you to pack yesterday before you went to Bible study with Bryce?" she questioned.

"I don't remember that."

You clearly remember it. You put it off on purpose. Maybe this kid really is a liar.

"I said it when you were standing right there."

"Whatever. I'll go back and get Zeke at two o' clock."

"Okay, but don't forget," his mom said.

"I won't." With that he went up to his room.

Memories returned. *Jay used to think that all his troubles with getting talked to by his parents would stop when he turned eighteen, but in reality they only got worse. This right here is perfect proof. Now that Jay finally has his driver's license, they always get on his case about where he is going, who he is with, and when he's going to be back. And, on top of that, he is his siblings' free chauffeur. So annoying. Can't a guy get some freedom?*

Jay threw open the door to his room, exposing all of the posters that he had plastered across his walls. Seeing EMINEM on the wall must have reminded him of playing some music, so he thumbed through his IPOD until he found a good song, placed his ear buds in his ears, and cranked the volume to just below the max.

While the music was in his ears he decided to pack for the trip. He packed up a bunch of clothes—mainly short-sleeved t-shirts, dickie shorts, and jean shorts. He also threw in a button down shirt in case he needed something a bit dressier. Finally he threw his Bible in his suitcase, along with a pen and a notebook.

My thoughts meshed with his again. "I don't plan on using any of the last three items; I'm only packing them because I have to. In fact, I haven't opened my Bible willingly in six months. Why? I don't know; I just haven't. It could be any number of reasons: not having enough time, not feeling it is necessary, or the fact that it does no good for me anyways. I don't know, and I don't care which one it is. Church has been shoved on me my whole life, and when I graduate, I can't wait to escape it. The only reason I even go to church on Saturday nights is to possibly get to see my friends— who rarely go anyways. Joey is in Michigan—where his parents sent him to try to straighten him out. Kevin thinks church is just a bunch of drama—in the youth group—so he is almost never there. And Bryce is going to a new church these days. Even Camille goes to a different church on Sundays. In fact, I've never seen her at DVC. Not even once."

My thoughts took over. *Church is bull. Some band having a concert for twenty minutes. Then some guy yapping his mouth about nothing for the next fifty; it's retarded. I hate it. I wish my friends were still around. Too bad they'll all be dead within three days of this stupid flashback.*

Jay shoved the duffel bag off his bed, onto the ground, and climbed up to his bed. He was tired; his eyes weren't staying open on their own. *Too much school and choices to be made.* I watched as he fell asleep very quickly, and in that instant, so did I.

CHAPTER 48

(Day 6, 10 p.m.)

I WOKE UP, and it took a second for my eyes to adjust. The only sources of light were the full moon, which was now much higher in the sky, and Red's glow. *Why is he glowing? The glow wasn't coming from him before, was it?*

It's the fires of Hell, you moron, my psyche reminded me. *Pay attention to what actually matters.* Sharp pain running down the length of my back made me scream. I tried to move, but I felt stuck to the ground.

Bryce was now in my vision. *Has he come to rescue me?*

"Don't get your hopes too high," Red sneered. "Bryce isn't really here. You've been imagining him the whole time."

That's a lie! I know for a fact that Bryce really is there. I saw him. I see him right now. It can't be a dream.

"But it is," Red said. "Watch."

Another flashback. I was watching myself again.

*   *   *

AS I OPENED MY EYES, Red set the tone. "Jay," he began.

Aww, dammit. Red's here this time. I noticed that Jay was sitting on his bed listening to music.

Red kept speaking, "This is a dream. In reality, you are asleep on that bed." The scene quickly flashed to what I had seen before awakening in front of Red a few seconds prior, and then returned to what I was now seeing.

312

STRANDED

"That's not possible, though," I said. "I'm sitting right there, wide awake."

"Watch and listen very carefully to this phone call that you're about to have."

Jay's phone rang, and I watched as he quickly picked it up and answered it. Somehow I was able to hear the voice on the other end.

I was surprised to hear the voice of Joey. "What up, homie," he asked excitedly. "Hey, I was wonderin' if ya have any plans next week."

"Unfortunately, I do," Jay replied sullenly. There was a second of silence before he asked, "Why were you wondering?"

"Bryce, Kevin, Mike, and I decided to go on a fun trip to Florida for a week before I go back to Michigan, and we have an extra plane ticket. We thought ya might wanna go."

"That would be pretty sick, but I have to go on a Florida trip with my senior class from school," said Jay. "It's gonna be really lame. We have a set schedule of stuff we have to do, and we cannot veer off it at all.

"I didn't even want to go, but my parents forced me. I didn't feel like arguing, because that always gets me in trouble, so I'm acting like I actually want to go so that they don't get mad. You know what I mean?"

"Yeah I do. Dat sucks, homie," Joey said. "It woulda been so awesome if ya coulda gone with us. We haven' chilled much since I got out."

"Yeah, I know. I'd love to kick it with you guys for a week. The last time we chilled was right before I started senior year, a day or so before you left for Michigan," Jay said.

I instantly remembered that flashback as he spoke of it. *Sharon and the rum.*

"Fo sho. We had some good times dat day."

"Tell me about it. That was so fun. I wish we could hang out again."

313

"Me too, homie," Joey replied. "I've thought about all our memories every day since I got outta jail, and looking back on it, I realize dat I was really stupid, and shouldn've gone in da first place."

"I know, man. That was a sucky year and a half," Jay answered. "I'm just glad you finally snapped out of it."

"I am too, homie, and I'm thankful fo' all yo' help," Joey said solemnly before changing the subject. "Back to why I called: since ya can't go, den who should I give dis extra ticket to?"

"I don't know," Jay answered, and, after a few seconds of thinking, changed his mind. "You could always see if Justin, Kevin's cousin, could go."

"Dat's a good idea. I'm gone do it," Joey exclaimed.

"Well, I'll talk to you later then," responded Jay. "Sorry I couldn't go."

"No problem. I'll talk to you later. Peace!" With that Joey hung up.

*　　*　　*

"SEE, JAY?" RED CONTINUED. "Bryce isn't really here." His tongue flicked out between his teeth.

As Bryce took another step toward me, Red pulled my BERETTA out from behind himself and fired five quick shots straight at Bryce. However, before he got the third one off, Bryce vanished. It was the craziest thing I'd ever seen. One second he was there; the next he was gone.

"Come back!" I pleaded, as I hopped to my feet, ignoring all the pain receptors screaming at me to stop. "I'm not ready to die. Please! I don't understand."

"You fell asleep. That phone call was a dream. Just think. In the previous flashback your thoughts meshed with Jay's and you realized that Joey was still in Michigan. There's no way he could have called you to give you a plane ticket. Where would he have gotten the money? Also, you know as well as me that he hasn't changed at all; at least not while he's been here. He's still the same drug-addicted, sailor-mouthed, girl-chasing loser he always was." Red paused. "That phone call was a dream. But, we both already know that you only believe what you want to believe. You need serious help.

"But you are ready to die. In fact, you deserve nothing but death. Just look at all these other people who deserved death as well. They got it. Now it's your turn.

"And since when do you care about Bryce being here? Just a little bit ago you were talking like you hated his guts since he was always preaching at you. Why the change?"

A rumble shook the ground, and the volcano started erupting, keeping me from being able to answer. Lava started to flow down toward the area, shedding more light on my surroundings.

I looked around and saw numerous bodies scattered across the ground. With most of them, I couldn't make out their original identities anymore, because large chunks of flesh were missing from their skeletons. However, a few I recognized clearly: Joey, Kevin, Jared, Jaime, and there—in the corner—was Camille. How I recognized any of them, I had no idea. Their bodies were so mangled by torture that it was disgusting. I wanted to run and hold Camille's body—the one that was in the best condition of them all—but the pain wouldn't let me move.

"In case you're wondering why they look so mangled," Red began. "I often get hungry. And, I'm a carnivore, like a lion, so I need meat. On this god-forsaken island the only meat I can find is people like these. So, I hope you're ready to join them."

The heat from the volcano is making me go crazy. Did Red really just say what I think he said?

The volcano continued to erupt, blasting burning bombs in all directions. For the previous six days I'd been trapped on this god-forsaken island, I had assumed that the volcano was extinct— or at least dormant. *It's a portal to Hell probably.* I slapped myself for thinking it. *That's crazy talk. Hell isn't real. The Christian school is wearing off on me. Hell, Hell, Hell. The place where all the evil*

315

people go. I am sick of it. Why is the volcano reminding me of spiritual matters? I just want to be free of all that garbage.

A bomb landed just behind me. Another crashed next to my feet. And another. And another.

"I'm going to devour you like a lion eating a gazelle in the safari."

"Holy—" I shouted. *Am I hallucinating, or did Red really just say that? Is he going to eat me alive?*

"Not quite. I'm going to kill you and then eat you." Red was talking like a crazy man.

"You sicko!" I took off running. I ignored the pain. I had to escape. I'd been imagining my best friend being on the island—the one person who could save me—and now he was gone.

I ran straight off the ledge, away from Red, and fell several feet. Miraculously, I landed on my feet, and I was able to keep running, despite the steep decline of the mountain. Lava bombs fell all around me, and then I crashed into a granite wall that came out of nowhere.

"Where do you think you're going?" Red asked, who was now standing over me. "You're mine. And you're trapped!"

"I'm. Not. Yours." I stammered out the words slowly. I couldn't talk.

"Yes you are, Jay. You are dead and en route to Hell." He paused. "Remember this last flashback?"

Again, I was watching myself.

*　　*　　*

I OPENED MY EYES to see Jay sleeping in his bed.

Red spoke up. "See, I told you that last one was a dream. You're still sleeping."

"That doesn't prove anything. Sure he's wearing the same clothes, but I often wear the same outfit different days." I wanted to prove the psycho wrong.

"Well, let's see what happens next," Red said.

I heard footsteps come up toward where Jay was sleeping, and then I turned my head as the bedroom door opened and Zeke ran into the room. He climbed up to Jay, picked up a pillow, and smacked him awake. "Hey lazy, guess what you forgot to do today?" Zeke taunted.

Jay cussed as he instantly became wide awake. "Mom's mad, isn't she?"

"Yep. The whole way home I got the brunt of her anger. Plus, I had to wait at school until 3:30. I waited and waited for you, but gave up at three and called mom. That's when she left, and when she finally got there, I had to listen to her the whole way home." Zeke walked out of the room.

Wait, I thought. *The one flashback I was supposed to pick Zeke up, but I fell asleep instead. Here I forgot to pick Zeke up. It is the same day. That last one was a flashback of a dream.*

"And a very important dream at that," Red explained. "It sets the stage for this whole island experience. Let's keep watching so you can figure it out."

"Jay Matthew Liyfer," yelled his mom from downstairs. She then continued loudly, "Come down here right now. I need to talk to you."

"More like yell at me," muttered Jay under his breath. Then he answered, "I'm coming." He slowly ambled out of his room, to the stairs, and down to the kitchen where his mom was preparing dinner.

When Jay reached her, her face told me everything. She was upset. "You told me you wouldn't forget to get your brother later. You said you wouldn't, but what did you do? You did the exact opposite, and you forgot to get him. I had to waste time out of my day to get him," She exclaimed loudly.

Red filled in some commentary. "Apologize like the good kid you're supposed to be, but obviously don't mean it. Teenage rebels like you don't need their parents."

"I'm so sorry," said Jay, trying to sound sincere when it was obvious to me—even apart from Red's advice—that he really was not. "It won't happen again."

"It better not," his mom said. "You always tell me that you are sorry when this kind of thing happens, but every time, it just happens again. It's getting old."

"I know," answered Jay flippantly, "It is." His thoughts entered my brain. "I wish she would just shut up. Her criticizing is what is getting old."

"Don't talk to me like that," yelled his mom. "I'm your mother. I deserve your respect."

"You're right. I'm sorry." Again, it was obvious that Jay did not mean it.

"Thank you," his mom said. "Just don't forget your brother again, and we should have peace in this home."

Is she oblivious to his insincerity, or is she just ignoring it? I wondered.

Red answered my question for me. "Keep watching."

"Okay. Are you done?" Jay asked his mom.

"Yes, you can go now." She sighed as Jay turned to leave the kitchen, and I noticed her lift her head toward the ceiling.

Is she praying?

"Does it matter?" Red asked. "We both know that prayer is useless."

I followed behind Jay as he ran back up to his room, turned on his IPOD and put it in his ears. He cranked up his rap music as loud as possible and climbed back into his bed.

Just then he looked at a text message he'd gotten from Camille; according to the time received, he had gotten it before he even fell asleep: How's your afternoon going? I love you. <3.

He replied: I can't wait 2 move out of my house... :(

A few minutes later she answered back: What's wrong? What happened?

Jay punched in: My mom is mad at me 4 stupid stuff...

She replied: I'm sorry. :(I hope you work it out.

Jay responded: Thanks. how was ur day?

She answered: It was good. Can't wait until tomorrow.

Jay asked: Me too. ;)

Camille replied: ;) It'll be a week we never forget. I so can't wait. Probably won't be able to sleep tonite. Too excited. =)

Jay texted back: Same here, but you've gotta get me away from my class. If I get stuck with them, we can't see each other at all... :(

Camille: I'll see what I can do ;) I wanna be with you all week ;)

Jay: Sounds beautiful... kinda like you, sweetie =)

Camille: You're too sweet, Jay. I love you. *kiss*

Jay: I try. Lol *kiss*

Camille: I want you here with me right now.

Jay: I want to be with you

Camille: *kiss* *kiss* *kiss*

Jay: On the plane tomorrow ;) well I gotta get 2 work, so I'll ttyl. I luv u... <3

Camille: No problem. Call me later. I love you too. <3

Red spoke again. "You don't mean literal work, as in going to a job, because you don't have a job. You actually mean chores and packing, because you consider work to be anything you can't stand doing. What a lazy failure. How do you expect to be successful in the long run?"

*   *   *

JAY TALKED TO CAMILLE for an hour after he finished packing. Hearing the conversation and her beautiful voice brought tears to my eyes. *I miss her. Why'd she have to die?*

"What a baby," Red had criticized. "She's just a girl. There's plenty more of them in this world." He laughed.

That's when I heard Jay's dad yell for Jay from downstairs.

Jay was still on the phone. "I gotta go, hun," Jay complained to Camille. "My dad's yelling at me now."

"Okay, babe." She sounded calm. "Call me when you have a chance."

"I will. Bye." He hung up the phone.

"JAY!" his dad yelled again. "Come downstairs right now!"

"I'm coming," Jay yelled back.

"Hurry up!" came the angry response.

"I'm moving as fast as I can," Jay muttered as he trudged out of his room and down the stairs. Our thoughts meshed. "I am so completely sick and tired of being yelled at and treated like dirt. Every day is like this these days. Anger. Yelling. Fights. It is so annoying."

"Only two more weeks and I'll be out of here," he muttered.

Red commented, "Once graduated, you figure you can move out and your problems will be solved." He cackled uncontrollably.

Jay was only halfway down the stairs when his dad walked around the corner and began yelling. "You are so irresponsible. Why don't you ever live up to your word? You told your mother you'd pick up your brother, but you decided to take a nap instead. You're so lazy! I raised you better than this." His tone grew louder. "You seriously need to grow up! If you ever want to get along on your own and hold a job, then you're going to have to learn how to do what you're told. If you worked for me, and you pulled the stunt that you pulled today, I'd fire you!"

Jay cut him off before he could add more. "Well it's nice to know I'm loved."

"You know what," his dad began. "It's very hard to like you when you act like this." He paused for a split second before adding, "You know how many times the Bible says that lazy men are fools?"

"Do you?" Jay questioned.

"A lot."

"Exactly my point." Jay continued, "You don't even know the answer. Besides, why should I care about the Bible? It's a bunch of stupid, false stuff anyways."

"You tell him," Red urged.

"Shut your mouth!" his dad said.

Red clapped. "Default lost argument comeback. Oh, it's the best." He copied Jay's dad's words and tone in a mocking fashion. "Shut your mouth." Red laughed hysterically.

"I won't shut up! Doesn't the Bible say to pray for whatever you want, and you will get it? I think so! But it doesn't work. Therefore, it's false! I've prayed every freaking day for the past ten years for God to heal my hand. Has He ever? Nope! Why should I believe that book of fairy tales?"

Jay's dad was irate. "The Bible also says that the fool is the person who doesn't respect his father. You're being a fool every time you run your mouth."

"Shut up!"

I thought back to Red's last words. *There's the losing—*

Red interrupted me. "You tell him Jay. You know he doesn't know what he's talking about. Tell him to shut up. Good job."

But—

"No, you shut up." Jay's dad continued, interrupting my thoughts. "You're headed down the wrong path right now. You need to pray to God, set your life straight, and get back on track. Learn how to respect me and your mom. Learn how to be responsible. And learn how to act like an adult. You're eighteen years old, but nowhere close to being an adult! I'm sick and tired of your 'poor me' attitude. Man up. Very very soon!" He was still yelling.

So Jay continued yelling too. "I'm eighteen. I'm an adult. I can buy cigarettes. Get laid. Do anything I want, except drink! Treat me like an adult."

"And you can also go to jail for statutory rape! So don't give me that!" He continued, "I'll treat you like an adult when you act like one. Not when the government says you are one."

Red urged yet another response from Jay. "Pull the 'false-love' card again. I love that one."

"Why do you hate me so much?" Jay asked.

He listens to Red an awful lot. I don't understand.

321

His dad slapped him across the face. "Stop it with the 'poor me' attitude!"

"I hate you!"

"At least the truth finally comes out," his dad said.

"You think I'm joking?" Jay yelled.

"No, I totally believe it." His dad continued, "You hate my rules, so logically you hate me as well."

"No. I hate your rules, and your attitude, and your whole self! Life will be great when I'm out on my own—away from Christianity, rules, and parents."

Red put my thoughts into words. "Those are the three biggest problems in this world."

Jay's dad replied. "I think your biggest problem is God. The God who gave you breath is your biggest enemy just because He won't heal your hand! I think it's pretty pathetic. Romans 8:28 says that God works everything together for good."

"That's easy for you to say," Jay began, "because you never had anything bad ever happen to you. Life's been great for you, but hell for me. You wouldn't understand, but yes, I hate God! For all I care He can explode into one cosmic ball of fire!" Jay ran to the front door.

"Shut your dang mouth," Jay's dad yelled. "I'm sick of this 'poor me' attitude. God's got a plan for your life, and all you want to do is throw it away!"

Red's hand was on the doorknob as Jay opened the door and walked out, leaving it wide open.

I couldn't believe my eyes. Red interacted with the world again. *How come I can't do anything that affects anything? That time was just like the last time Jay ran away.*

Jay yelled as he ran toward the street. "It's my life, not yours. Let me throw it away if I want. Stop worrying about my freaking life! It's mine to do with what I want!"

Red gave more commentary. "Your dad always pulls the same exact argument. 'You're not an adult until you act like one.

You're lazy. You're acting like you're the only one who has anything going wrong in his life.'

"Your dad has no clue. You try to act like an adult but he never notices any of it. Only the bad gets noticed. You do amazingly in school. Good grades and all. And besides, you are teased at school in addition to your prayers for healing that never come true. Life is no good.

"Why can't life be easy? The Bible promised it. At least, that's what you were told your whole life. It is *so* annoying. Why can't it be true? If it was easy, you'd believe the Bible. Didn't Jesus say that His burden was easy? Didn't Jesus say that you could ask for anything, and you'd get it? Didn't Jesus say that if your faith was small you could move mountains? It is all there, but in reality, none of them are true. It drives you crazy. You hate God."

A white pick-up truck roaring down the street took my mind off Red's words, and I noticed Jay glance in its direction as well. But neither of us thought anything of it, as Jay kept walking across his lawn toward the street.

Red was still talking. He stood right next to Jay, as Jay stood on the sidewalk. "God can die for all you care. He is a liar. If the Bible is His Word and everything in it is false, why should you believe any of it? You know it drives you crazy." His tongue motions resumed, and watching it made me nauseous, so I turned my attention to the street.

The truck was flying toward Jay's spot on the street, and Red had his hand on Jay. I yelled as I saw Red pull his hand back and bring it forward, shoving Jay directly into the path of the truck. I heard screeching brakes, and then I saw Jay's body fly down the road.

*   *   *

RED WAS IN MY FACE, and I was on the ground, as volcanic bombs continued to fall around us. He had the knife angled toward my throat. "Do you understand now? Those flashbacks were your life flashing before your eyes. In fact, it was extremely annoying hearing you refer to yourself as 'Jay' the whole time. Man up and say 'me' next time. This island is the state of your soul. You're doomed." His tongue flicked out, and I felt saliva land on my face.

I screamed. "You killed me. I thought you said you loved me."

"I do," Red said, yellow eyes boring into mine. "As soon as I cut your god-forsaken throat you'll be in Hell, and I'll be waiting for you. We'll get to spend eternity together. You loved Camille, and you wanted to spend eternity with her. I love you, and I wanted to begin eternity with you as soon as possible, so I pushed you in front of that truck. God failed to stop it, so I win. God really doesn't love you, but I do."

It can't be true. Or could it? I have no idea what to believe. I want to escape.

When the knife touched my throat I knew escape would be useless. The last thing I remembered was warm blood pooling down over my neck—running onto the ground below.

CHAPTER 49

I OPENED MY EYES in a cold sweat. *He slit my throat. I'm dead.*

I opened my eyes, but to no avail. They were already open. *Why can't I see anything? It's dark. What is going on? Was Red telling the truth? Am I in Hell?*

Just then I started feeling warm. It felt like the heat was suffocating me. I tried to move my hands but they wouldn't move. I tried to scream, but I couldn't let out a sound, except a muffled grunt. I tried to listen to my surroundings, but all I could hear was a steady HUMMM. *That's odd. Is that the fires of Hell warming up for me?* The heat was growing unbearable. I'm slightly claustrophobic, so this cramped in, warming feeling was causing me some serious problems. *Why can't I see the flames?*

The thought struck me, *I need God. Maybe He will hear me.*

A counter thought spoke up. *You're in Hell. You don't get God anymore. You had your chance, and you lost it. Sucks for you.*

It couldn't be true. I mean, I admit, my life was not pretty, but it didn't by any means deserve Hell, did it? *I want to live; I can't die. What is going on?*

Just then I was enveloped by bright light, and I had to close my eyes. I couldn't see a thing. Everything was white. It was still hot though. *I don't understand what is going on.*

The angel I had seen previously came into my line of vision and said, "We're awaiting the test results, but there's some people who want to see you."

CHAPTER 50

THE ANGEL WAS still speaking. "Can you hear me, Jay?"

"Am I in Heaven?" I asked. "The killer told me I was going to Hell."

"What are you talking about?" the angel asked incredulously. "You are at Desert Valley Hospital. You had a terrible accident. It appears that you are going to be okay, but you've definitely had us scared for the past few days. No motion, except some recent eye movement, no speech, no signs of any hearing. You're lucky. You are very lucky."

I noticed that his white garment had a tag clipped on it. It read, "Dr. Gustavo Jerhandez." I almost screamed with joy that I was alive, that Red had been wrong.

Just then another doctor walked in. This one was blonde. Gustavo turned to him and asked, "What are the results, Michael?"

"Miraculously, everything came back normal. Jay Liyfer is the luckiest kid I've treated in a long time." With that Michael walked out of the room.

As I was wheeled back to my primary hospital room, Gustavo explained to me that I had been in an MRI when I'd awoken from a coma just a few minutes prior.

*   *   *

SEVERAL PEOPLE WERE WAITING to see me when my bed was wheeled in. Angela Johnson was there, Bryce Beyra was there, my parents were there, and some random stranger who looked like he was holding a Bible.

The first to speak was Angela. "Jay, I'm so sorry you got hurt. I've been here ever since I found out. You've been in a coma for the past five days. Miraculously, nothing else was wrong with you. Thank God."

I just heard all this from the doctor. I wonder why she's even here. Where's Camille?

"Yes, thank God," the man with the Bible spoke. He walked over, put his arm on my shoulder, and started speaking, "Jay, I know that you don't know me, but my name is Paul, and I really just have one thing to say to you. You may have done some horrible stuff in your life: lie, steal, cheat, lust, hate, or any number of other things that God calls 'sin,' but you do not have to go to Hell. While Satan wants to convince you that you have to have never sinned to get to Heaven, or that you need to do more good than bad to get to Heaven, don't listen to him. The truth is, God loved you enough to send Jesus Christ to Earth two thousand years ago. He lived a perfect life of no sin, and then He died on the cross for the sins of anyone who believes in Him. Specifically, *anyone* who *believes* in Him. If you don't believe, you can't possibly hope to ever get to Heaven. It's kind of like if you wanted to play baseball for the ANGELS, but you decided you could play on the field without the jersey. Not going to happen. In the same way, God can't let you into Heaven if you don't put on Jesus Christ." He looked very serious. "Jay, I hope and pray that you give your life to Christ, and then seek to live for Him and Him alone every day."

Paul walked away, and something clicked in my head. *That's what I've been missing all along. Wow. I wish someone had explained that to me sooner. Thank you, God, for sending Paul to this hospital to tell me that.*

Jay's parents started talking. "Jay, we were so worried about you. How are you feeling?"

At the reminder of potential pain, I lifted my hospital gown and was stunned to see no markings on my body. A few strange stares followed. "I've never been better," I answered. *My soul feels free. My body isn't scarred and burning. I'm free.* "When can I go home?"

"You'll be here to rest for the next twenty-four hours, but then you can return home," Gustavo said.

"Hey, Jay," Bryce said.

"What's up, Bryce?" I replied. "I had the craziest dream about you, me, Joey, and Kevin while I was out."

"What happened?"

"It's a long story. I'll explain it some other time."

"Cool, bro. I'm so glad you pulled through. I've been praying for you since I got the call."

"That's my best friend," I said. "Praying for a guy who needs prayer. Thank you very much." I turned to my mom, "Can I have my phone?"

She handed it over, and I typed up a text to Camille. Hey hun, what's up? <3

*   *   *

TWO HOURS LATER, after everyone had left, I texted my parents. I'm so sorry for how I've treated you for the past while. I'm really sorry. Can you forgive me?

My mom replied: Your dad and I both love you, and we are so happy you are still alive. Of course we forgive you. Can't wait until you come home again. Romans 8:28

I was too tired to look that verse up at the moment, but I decided I would as soon as possible.

I closed my eyes, and just then my phone buzzed. Camille. Hey Jay, not to be rude, but we're through. You didn't show up at the airport and I met someone in Florida. Sorry. Have a good life.

Jay: I will. I met Jesus today :) Do you know Him?

She didn't reply.

EPILOGUE

(Day 7)

THAT NIGHT, after I had returned home from the hospital, I closed my eyes to sleep, and it happened again. I dreamed.

I opened my eyes to see my dead, heavily thrashed body being carried on a stretcher off the volcano. Carrying the stretcher were tall, white figures with blonde hair, and green crowns made from leaves. They were dressed in green and silver tunics and their pants were brown tights.

The whole landscape was dead, and the new lava deposits could clearly be seen. The volcano had made quick work of any new life that had been springing up on the island. Any fresh shoots of plants that had existed were now long gone. *I guess that explains why the place was so dead.*

I glanced at my body. *This is the first time I've had an out of body experience here, but I guess that's because this was all a dream. The other dreams were my real life.* The damage was obvious. There was a red slit across my corpses' neck stretching from east to west, his lifeless head was facing right, and his eyes and mouth were wide open. It was a ghastly sight. Then there was the writing all over his body. *Red really went to work after I killed Kevin.* I remembered that Jaime had carved "murderer" on my back, and, since my corpse was lying on its back, I couldn't see it. But I did see "rapist" carved into the flesh right at its underwear line, which was Jared's handiwork; I saw "liar" carved into its forehead; and I saw "thief" carved across its chest.

329

I floated—basically flew—five feet above my corpse as my pall-bearers carried my corpse across the wasteland of the island. They walked north, heading straight toward the inlet with the skeletons in it. *Well, that explains it. They're going to dump my corpse there to be with the rest of them.*

When they reached that spot, a few minutes later, I saw a boat anchored in the water. The tide was up, hiding the skeletons from view. The boat was an old looking vessel. It had a white sail with a red cross in the middle of it, and it was medium-sized. The whole thing was made of wooden planks. My pall-bearers carried my corpse onto the boat, and then they set sail.

As soon as the boat was sailing away from the island, the pall-bearers started playing doctor with my corpse. I was content to simply watch. One took out several vials that were filled, some with a red liquid and others with what looked like water. Another presented a portion of a bush, and I heard him refer to it as hyssop. *I wonder what that is, and why he has it.* I kept watching, gaze unhindered, from my perch now above the top of the sail. The pall-bearer doctors then dumped two vials of the red liquid on my chest and belly. They used the hyssop branch to rub the liquid around—over all of the carvings present in the corpse. When the liquid entered a carving, steam would issue forth from the wound, and the area would turn perfectly white. They dumped half of a vial on my forehead and the steaming resulted yet again, followed by whiteness.

When the front of my corpse was complete, they flipped it over, and I noticed that not only was "murderer" carved into its shoulder blade area, but "authority-despiser" was carved into my corpse's back diagonally from under its left shoulder blade to the top of its right hip. The sight reminded me of the suffragist women from the 1920's with their little sashes, except this one was nothing to be proud of. *I hate the fact that I was such a big jerk to my parents.* Carved above its pants, in the small of the back, was the word, "blasphemer."

While they repeated the process with the red liquid and the hyssop on my corpse's back this time, I glanced up to see where we were headed in the boat. The whole time I had been on the island I had seen no boats or ships anywhere at all; there had been nothing but water for miles in all directions. The remembrance of that fact was what shocked me so much about what I saw when I glanced up. The boat was about to enter a port. I looked back and the island was only a half mile away at the most. *That's odd. Why couldn't I see this before?*

I glanced back to my corpse in time to see that the whiteness had set in. I could still read whatever had been carved there before, but instead of red gashes, they were now white clean words. *Talk about disinfectant,* I thought to myself. The pall-bearer doctors then opened up the vials of water and poured them on every spot that had the white words. As soon as the water touched it, the words washed away, and my skin was left untouched. *It's a miracle,* I realized.

The boat was pulling into port. I could see a crowd of people dressed like the pall-bearers waiting for the ship to dock. As the boat pulled closer, I noticed the crowd split to make way for a woman, who was dressed in absolutely brilliant clothes, walking down to the ship. Next to her, holding her hand, was a grey-haired man dressed in regal robes who had a crown on his head. *He's a king. Where am I? Who is that beautiful woman holding his hand?*

The boat stopped. The gangplank was extended, and the king and the lady stepped on board.

He spoke in a clear, crisp voice that was several octaves lower than I would have expected. "Jay Matthew Liyfer, born February 2, 1992, has on this first day of June, 2010, been convinced of his dead state. Red Savage killed him on the Isle de Pravity to prove it to him, but my servants have been hard at work to prepare him for resurrection. He's been washed in the blood of my son, prince Yeshua, and sprinkled with clean water to prepare him for his return. Upon the intake of this living water that I hold in my hand," the king reached into his robe and pulled out another vial, "Jay Liyfer Theoson will be resurrected to life at this Port of Salvation. He isn't the first for this to happen to, and he will by no means be the last."

He handed the vial to the woman, who popped the stopper out of it as she walked to my corpse. Her hair was golden blonde. She wore a dress that looked like a bridal gown. Her eyes were blue, and her teeth shone brightly. I could have sworn that she was one hundred percent perfectly flawless in every way. When she reached my corpse, she positioned the opening of the vial in its mouth, and dumped it down its throat.

*   *   *

THE NEXT THING I KNEW, I was in my own body, and I wasn't supposed to be watching anyone else. It felt good to be back. I looked down to see what I was wearing, and I noticed that I was dressed in a pure, white robe. I wondered where it came from, but then glanced to my left to see that the woman was walking beside me. I glanced to my right to find the King next to me. The blonde-haired, wreath-crowned servants of the king were cheering as we walked down the gangplank and through their midst.

I turned my head to the woman and asked, "Where am I?"

She smiled as she replied, "You are in the city of Berith in Lev-Erets."

What language is that? I wondered. I asked her what those words meant.

She answered kindly. "This is the city of Covenant in Heartland."

"Who are you?" I asked next. I truly hoped that I didn't come across demanding.

"I am Jewel Betterdan. I am the first created being in Heartland. My father, King Adonai-Kurios, created me before the creation of this world. And, in case you wondered—and I'll admit that it's confusing—Prince Yeshua has been around as long as his father. He was not created like I was, but he still refers to the King as father, and the King refers to him as son." She paused. "We are heading to the great hall to celebrate your coming to this kingdom. Red Savage has many captive on the Isle de Pravity, but today we celebrate your freedom and resurrection."

I was stunned. First and foremost by her statement about Prince Yeshua. *How is that possible?* But second, I was stunned by the fact that they were going to celebrate me. *Why celebrate me?* I wondered. *We should celebrate the King who gave me breath again. I don't deserve this.*

AFTERWORD

IN JOHN'S GOSPEL, chapter 15 verse 6, Jesus says, "If anyone does not abide in Me, he is thrown away as a branch and dries up; and they gather them, and cast them into the fire and they are burned."

As I look at that verse now, in November of 2017, after reading through this manuscript for the sixth full time, I am surprised by the number of parallels between the Isle de Pravity and what Jesus says in John 15:6. I will spare you my pointing them out, because I hope it is clear at this point, but what I would like to point out is that while this is a book of fiction, the message inside is not fake at all.

We were all trapped in our sin—dead in it according to Ephesians 2—and we had no way to escape from it. That alone is what makes the gospel of Jesus Christ so amazing. However, what makes it more amazing, and what I hope was clarified more than anything else through this novel, is getting a firm grasp on just what the bad news is that makes the gospel Good News.

As I pointed out in the introduction, Jay represents me and my testimony of salvation, so I told the story exclusively in the first person partly so that the reader would constantly read, "I did" this, "I said" such and such, "I think" one way or another. As such, if I did my job well, it will have accomplished at least one of two things. Either, primarily, it will have made you uncomfortable (at which point I commend you for reaching the end) and you will have said, "I'm not like this," for which I praise God and pray it is by His grace alone; or you will have said, uncomfortably, "This is me to a t," for which I pray that God would use this to help convict you of sin and steer you to get on the straight and narrow path that He offers through Christ. Or, secondarily, it will have made you comfortable because you recognize that this is where you were before Christ, and it causes you to praise God because it is only by His grace that you don't look like Jay Liyfer any longer.

But with that said, I would like to clarify one major thing. As I pointed out above, this is primarily fiction. As such many facts were changed, including the hospital scene at the end of the book, and all of the "real life" events directly leading up to it. I have never been hit by a vehicle, but I did hear a pastor once say something along the lines of, "If you say you got hit by a locomotive, but we couldn't see anything different about your appearance, we'd know you were a liar. God is much bigger than a locomotive, and when He crosses your life there should be a difference."

In reality, I was saved exactly a month after the occurrences of this story. In reality, I never even planned to go on my senior trip—the ones who went didn't go to Florida. In reality, I was saved at a summer camp on July 1, 2010.

It was a summer camp I didn't want to be at. It had a heavier emphasis on Scripture than I was used to when it came to summer camps, and it was a much smaller group of people than the normal camp, so I couldn't blend in as easily. The theme for the week was Talmidim (pronounced tal-mē-deem) which was explained as literally meaning "covered in the dust of your rabbi." The theme therefore was centered on discipleship and on being a true disciple of Christ. One phrase that stuck out to me clearly that week was, "Are you following Jesus so closely that you are covered in Him?" It was there that I first discovered my love for Scripture, and John 15:6—one of the first verses to shatter my false thinking—was part of the memory passage for the week.

My biggest fear has always been getting burned to death, so when I read a verse about getting burned, and I realized it was describing me at that moment because of things I'd said to God in the previous six months, it totally rocked my entire philosophy. I hope that this novel has either caused you to question the philosophy that you hold, or given you an artistic way of defending the one that you already hold.

But before I ramble on too long, I realize that Jay raises a ton of theodicy questions, and I did not give him answers in the story. There is a reason for that. People need the gospel more than they need the answer to the question, "Why does God allow bad things to happen?" In fact, the gospel itself is an answer to that question. As the story showed, Jay was evil. If God stopped bad things from happening, He'd have to stop the lives of every human being on this planet, because we are all just as guilty as Jay in God's eyes. However, He didn't. Instead, He sent Jesus to suffer the greatest injustice in the history of injustices so that we could be made right in God's eyes. If anyone had a right to say, "Why do bad things happen to good people?" it was Jesus, but instead He simply said, "Father, forgive them; for they do not know what they are doing" (Luke 23:34).

I pray that you would take His forgiveness today. Enter into covenant with God today and escape the Isle de Pravity. Repent of your sin and believe the gospel!

Soli Deo Gloria.

www.ingramcontent.com/pod-product-compliance
Lightning Source LLC
Chambersburg PA
CBHW060942030726
47503CB00003B/690